THE
WAITING
KING

The Queen's Quests Trilogy

The Wizard's Ward
The Waiting King
The Destined Queen

THE
WAITING KING

DEBORAH HALE

THE WAITING KING

ISBN-13: 978-1-7751702-9-7

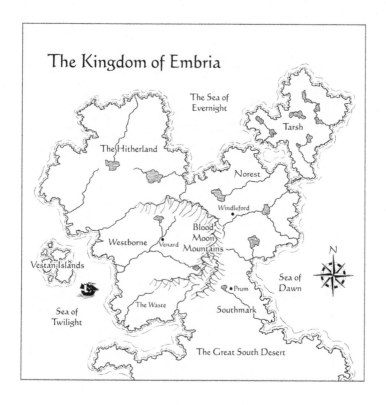

Acknowledgements

I would never have been able to make the jump from historical romance to high fantasy writing without the invaluable assistance of my fantasy consultants: Ian and Patricia Galbraith, Robyn Hale, and Ivy and Mike Moore. Thanks for all your help, guys!

Chapter One

"I AM GOING with you," said Rath, "and that is final, so do not waste your breath arguing."

He had been sitting there for what felt like hours, wrestling with his decision. By the time Maura gave the slightest hint of waking, he could not wait another moment to tell her. Once he had said it aloud, there could be no turning back.

"Hmm?" A yawn stretched Maura's pretty mouth wide. Then she rubbed her eyes with sooty fists, leaving dark shadows around them. "Go where? What are you talking about, Rath?"

"Go here." He held up one half of the ivory "egg." He had been staring at the tiny map etched on it for so long his eyes felt as though they'd been burnt by pain spikes. "To Everwood. According to this, it is where you will find the Secret Glade. This half shows all of Embria. The other half is a map of the wood itself."

"Everwood?" Maura stretched her arms high, then peered toward the fine etching. "How can you tell?"

"See that crescent in the middle?" Rath pointed. "Those have to be the mountains."

His fingertip was not much smaller than the map itself. It made him wonder what sort of deft fingers had wrought such delicate work. Or had the markings been put there by magic?

"The mountains." Maura yawned again. "I guessed that much."

"Those two spots above the upper tip of the crescent must be the North Lakes," Rath continued. "So that mark just south of Great Forest Lake has to be Everwood. I grew up not far from there. It is wild country and few folk venture far into the forest. There's a daft old tale that ..."

"That what?"

A memory made the back of Rath's neck prickle. "Nothing. Just a yarn the oldlings would tell to keep foolhardy lads from wandering into the forest and getting lost."

"What sort of yarn?" Maura pulled a slender jug from the nearest shelf and removed the stopper.

"Foolishness," Rath insisted. "I hardly recollect it."

"Try." Maura took a long drink followed by a sigh of enjoyment. "After last night, I could use a laugh."

"Oh, very well. Ganny and some of the other old folk used to say there were parts of the wood where time stopped. They claimed there was once a lad from the village who strayed too far into the forest. Everyone gave him up for dead until he strolled back home twenty years later, not aged a day. He thought he'd only been gone an hour."

"Oh, my," whispered Maura. She took another drink. "That would explain a great deal."

"If it was true."

She turned to stare at him. "After all that has happened, can you still doubt?"

"I doubt everything." Rath tossed one half of the egg-map up in the air, then caught it in his hand. "It is my nature."

"Then why do you insist on going with me?"

He had asked himself that same question many times during the past several hours. And he had not been very satisfied with the possible answers.

"Perhaps because I have a taste for adventure." That was true enough. "Perhaps because anything that sets the Han in such a stew is worth doing."

Maura made her own guess. "Perhaps because you think I cannot manage without your help."

"No." Rath dropped the two halves of the map onto the lap of her apron, then reached for her hand. "I may not be certain what my reasons are, but I know what they are *not*. Any woman who can do what you did to three Hanish soldiers and a death-mage does not need some ill-bred outlaw to take her where she wants to go."

With her free hand, Maura patted her sash. "The credit belongs here, not with me. Only the Giver knows what will become of me once I have emptied its pockets. I used up all my spider silk last night, but I do have a fresh supply of quickfoil and dreamweed from Exilda's garden."

"Then you should make an effort to restock your supply whenever you get the chance." Rath pointed toward the ceiling of the cold hatch. "There's a nice bit of cobweb, for a start."

Maura picked up the map of Embria. "Is it a very long way to this Everwood place? What is the quickest route to get there?"

"That depends," said Rath. "If we were a pair of sunhawks, we could fly over the mountains, then head north. Have you a spell that can make us fly?"

Maura chuckled at the notion.

"A shame we had to come all this way to find the map," said Rath. "If we had headed west from Windleford instead of south, we might already be there by now."

He pointed to Windleford, then traced their route to Prum.

"And Everwood is way up there?" Maura asked, a plaintive note in her voice.

Rath gave a rueful nod. "I am sorry to bear ill news."

"So we must go back the way we came, then travel that much farther again to the west?"

She had said *we*, not *I*. That pleasant surprise distracted Rath from the rest of her words for a moment.

Then they sank in. "We cannot go the way we came. It is too dangerous with the Han on alert in the Long Vale. And I would not fancy meeting up with Vang or any of his crowd."

Maura shuddered, "Neither would I. But what other choice

do we have? Surely you cannot mean to …"

"Go through Westborne?" Rath completed her question. "That is just what I mean. It is a straighter route and, say what you will about the Han, they keep up roads well."

"But there will be twice as many Han in Westborne as in the Long Vale … five times … perhaps ten!"

"True, but they will not be expecting us to march right under their noses."

"With good reason — it is folly!"

Part of him agreed with her. Long ago, Rath had sworn that he would never again set foot west of the Blood Moon Mountains. It *was* the quickest way to Everwood from Prum, but what did haste matter if he did not believe in Maura's Waiting King?

"I will not let any harm come to you," he promised.

A country-bred lass like her, with scant knowledge of Comtung or Westborne ways, she would need to rely on him. Was that what compelled him to insist on travelling through the heart of Embria, where Hanish control was strongest?

Or was it something else that made even less sense?

"I cannot believe I let you talk me into this," said Maura, two days later, as she and Rath rode up into the foothills of the Blood Moon Mountains.

"Into what?" Rath glanced back over his shoulder. "Taking this route to Everwood, or letting me come with you?"

"Both." She gave a chuckle to show she did not mean it … at least not entirely.

True, she quailed at the thought of passing through Westborne. But it seemed there was no *easy* or *safe* way to get where she needed to go. At least this route offered them a little respite from danger while they travelled through the barren lands of the Waste.

As for letting Rath come with her, she was grateful he had insisted. Too grateful, perhaps. She sensed his presence posed a different kind of danger to her quest. A potent danger to her heart.

"Is it safe to stop yet?" she asked. "My backside is aching something fierce from this long ride."

They had stolen out of Exilda's cold hatch just after sunset two days ago. Then they had sneaked back through town to the inn, where they retrieved their horse and a few supplies. Twice they'd had close brushes with Hanish patrols, but Rath had managed to avoid them both. Once out of town, they had gone as quickly as they dared in the darkness. At times, Rath had dismounted and led the horse with Maura on its back.

When the sun had risen again, they'd hidden and slept until dusk, then struck off toward the high country. They had been riding ever since, with only brief pauses to snatch a little food and drink.

"Just a bit farther." Rath shifted in his saddle. Perhaps he had a sore backside, too. "I know a place where we should be safe to stop for the night. A great many plants grow around there. I thought you might want to replenish your stocks."

Maura nodded. The emptier the pockets of her sash grew, the more vulnerable she felt. "Would there be any water around this place, by chance? After grubbing through all that soot at Exilda's cottage, I am so dirty I can scarcely stand myself."

"And I." Rath gave a growl of wry laughter. "A few weeks ago, a little soot would not have bothered me. I am going soft, I tell you, and you are to blame for it."

"There is nothing *soft* about you, Rath Talward." Maura batted at his hair, on the pretense of knocking some of the soot out of it.

"There had better not be, if I am to get us through Westborne safely." Rath ducked his head to dodge her touch.

"And to answer your question, there is plenty of water where we are headed. A warm spring pool, as it happens."

"Warm spring? What is that?"

"Just what it sounds — a spring of water that comes out of the ground warm. I do not know why, but there are several of them here in the foothills."

"Warm water?" Maura tried to imagine it. "Without hauling it from the well and heating it on the hob. I fear I shall never want to leave."

She feared it even more once she saw the place.

Nestled in the hills, surrounded by great swaths of green fern and sheltering trees, it was a tiny paradise.

"I cannot decide what to do first." Inhaling a deep breath of the faintly pungent air that rose from the surface of the pool, Maura dipped her hand in to confirm that the water was warm. "Should I do some gathering, wash my clothes or bathe?"

"I know what I *want* to do first." Rath said as he heaved the saddle off the horse and tethered the beast to graze. "But perhaps we should look for plants while we still have light to find them."

"Duty before pleasure?" Maura directed a teasing grin his way. "That does not sound like the outlaw code."

"*Necessity* before pleasure," Rath corrected her. "If my blades needed sharpening, I would do that before I sat to eat. Our lives might depend on these plants of yours. Besides, I would just as soon bathe after dark."

"Indeed? And why is that." She had to admit, the notion of soaking in a warm pool under the stars appealed to her.

"Because I think it unwise to tempt myself with more than a glimpse of what I cannot have." As he spoke, desire shimmered in his eyes.

How could he possibly find her the least bit appealing, all sooty and sweaty? It sent a delicious yet frightening tingle through Maura's flesh. She tried to suppress it, and when that did not work, she tried to ignore it.

That was no great success, either.

"Your pardon, Rath. You know I cannot. And you know why."

"Aye to both." He made a visible effort to subdue his desire. "Let us get to work, then. What should I look for?"

"I can always use more queensbalm." Maura forced her mind to their task. "I have plenty of dreamweed and quickfoil from Exilda's garden. I could use more madfern, though."

She described what it looked like. "You will probably find it near the pool."

"Madfern?" Rath seemed to savor the word. "I know what it looks like. What does it do?"

Maura had spotted a tiny patch of summerslip. She stooped to pick some of the pale blue flowerets. "Remember the day I turned you invisible in Betchwood?"

"It is not one I am likely to forget." Rath moved off to search around the pool. "Why?"

"I used powdered madfern to confuse the Han. It made them think they saw you still running ahead of them after you had disappeared."

"Aha!" Rath held up a delicate frond. "It sounds like handy stuff."

Maura nodded her approval. "It is, though you have to be careful with it. You cannot always predict what way the confusion will work on a person's mind."

They continued gathering in silence for a while, then Rath brought Maura several madfern fronds.

"Does it ever feel strange to you, using magic?" He glanced from the lacy green fern to her face and back again. "I mean, my blade has a sharp edge. I swing it and what it hits, it cuts. The larger the blade, the harder the swing, the better the aim, the worse damage I inflict on my foe."

His description made Maura's stomach clench. "What has

that to do with vitcraft?"

Rath shrugged, as if he found it difficult to put into words. "You sprinkle a little pinch of fern or feather or web and people disappear, or fall asleep against their will, or cannot move. Is it never hard for you to believe such small things could have so much power?"

"Langbard taught me that everything has power, however small. It is all a matter of finding out what form that power takes and how best to release it."

Rath nodded, but his brow furrowed as though he still did not grasp her meaning.

When the light had become too dim for Maura to tell candleflax from moonmallow, she and Rath agreed that they had earned a rest and a good long soak in the pool.

Pulling off her stout boots and thick stockings, Maura eased her hot, itchy feet into the warm water with a sigh. "Oh, my! Every home in Embria should have its own warm spring."

Rath ungirded his blade belt and let it drop onto the grass with a muted clatter. Then he pulled off his padded leather vest. The light had grown too dim for Maura to see more than a vague shadow. But even that unsettled her. Rath had been right about the wisdom of waiting until dark to bathe.

Over his shoulder he tossed a jaunty quip. "Is that a royal decree, Your Grace? A warm spring in every home? It would make you a most popular queen."

Maura shrugged out of her tunic. "You may not believe in what I am doing, but you need not make fun of me."

Beneath a layer of soot, her cheeks stung. It did sound ridiculous — her, a queen.

She had only the faintest rustle of the grass to warn her of Rath's approach. Suddenly he was there before her, on his knees reaching for her hand. "Your pardon, Maura. I mock many things, myself included. I swear, I never meant to mock you."

He had shed his shirt. The stars twinkling in the clear, dark sky overhead cast enough light to show Maura that. The force of his masculinity seemed to give off an aura of its own — one that drew her with all the power of a spell. How easy it would be, and how pleasant, to surrender to the pull of her desire for this man.

But how wrong, for both of them.

"The Waiting King is real." She wanted to speak the words in Old Embrian, as if they were a counterspell to protect her from the potent enchantment of Rath's nearness and her own yearnings. "You will see."

"Perhaps." Rath tilted his face to press his cheek against the back of her hand. "But tell me, if you were to discover he is not, and that you are free from this great destiny, would you …?"

She waited for him to finish, torn already as to how she would answer.

Did she dare confess how urgently she wanted to be in his arms? Learning the most powerful kind of life-magic that needed no ingredients but a man and a woman. No incantation but the endearments of lovers and the wordless enchantment of kiss and touch.

He was a strong, masterful man. If he knew the true extent of her weakness for him, might he exploit that frailty, as he did in battle, to force her surrender?

Yet, how could she deny the truest feelings of her heart?

"Would I … what?" she asked at last, willing her voice not to quaver.

She could feel the tightness in the muscles of his hand and face. And something more. A strange energy beyond her physical senses perceived his heart and will pulled taut as a rope in the hands of two intense conflicting forces.

Then the cord snapped. Maura felt it so surely, she could almost hear the soundless rending.

"Nothing." That word crackled with the release of pent-up pressure as Rath let go of her hand. "Forget I ever started to ask such a daft question."

He leapt to his feet and disappeared into the shadows. A moment later Maura heard a splash from the pool as he plunged into the water. The breath she had been holding hissed out of her and her body felt limp and spent.

The soft trickle of water into the pool could not begin to fill the awkward gulf of silence between them. Even the haunting call of a nightbird and the occasional sighing nicker from the horse did little to help.

After a moment, Maura dropped to her knees and began to wash her tunic, with loud splashing and vigorous slaps against a large, smooth rock that helped to vent her frustration. When she had finally pummeled the poor garment as hard as she dared, she hung it over a tree branch to dry.

Then she wriggled out of her undergown and shift. Though she knew Rath could see no more than a faint shadow wrapped in shadows, she found herself bashful of the subtle sounds made by her clothes parting from her body.

The memory of his words — *I think it is unwise to tempt myself with more than a glimpse of what I cannot have* — whispered through her thoughts, heated her flesh in a way the mild night air could not cool.

She eased herself into the wet, concealing embrace of the pool. Slowly the warmth of the water and quiet of the night seeped into her, untying some of the knots in her flesh, soaking her clean … in body at least.

Untying the bit of ribbon that bound her hair, she unplaited it then tilted her head back to wash it. The majestic beauty of the night sky caught and held her gaze, as though she was seeing it for the first time.

"The stars are brilliant tonight," she whispered to herself, almost forgetting Rath's presence. "How the eye of the Steed sparkles! I can almost believe he will put on a great spurt of speed to bear his master after the Black Beast of Ursind."

Ahead of the Steed with its swirling mane of tiny stars lurked a dark, starless void that reminded Maura of an open mouth, ravenous to consume every spark of light from the sky.

"I know the names of the stars." Rath's voice reached out of the shadows from the other side of the pool. "And how they move through the sky as the year passes. But you make it sound as if they tell stories."

"So they do." As Maura's gaze wandered the night sky, all the star tales Langbard had told her rekindled in her memory, and with them a bittersweet sense of closeness to him. "The Steed bears Lord Velorken, who holds the Sword aloft."

She pointed toward the long straight shaft of bright stars that pointed the way north.

"And I suppose," said Rath, "The Hound runs at his heels while the Hawk wheels above, ready to stoop and strike?"

"Just so."

"And who is this Lord Velorken?" Rath's voice took on warmer, more relaxed tone, for which Maura was grateful.

This unsettling attraction would always be there between them, like a stew simmering on a low fire, giving off a mouthwatering aroma. It needed only a breath of wind to stir the flames and make it bubble away, threatening to boil over.

"When the world was new," Maura savored the words that began so many of the old stories, "and the Children of the North and the Children of the South were all one kin, the Black Beast of Ursind tunneled beneath the earth, throwing up these mountains. It shook the ground in its rage, spewing out fire and death. The ancient writings say it was the Beast who poisoned metals and gems with death magic.

"Velorken was Lord of the Greatkin. He climbed the Mountain of Snows and there beseeched the Giver to destroy the Beast and deliver the world from its evil. When he woke the next morning, Velorken found a magical horse, twice the normal size, that could outrun the wind and leap so high it seemed to fly without wings.

"Beside the magical steed, Velorken also found a blade of such sharpness and power it could cleave rocks with the lightest stroke. A hawk with eyes so keen, it could see all the way from the shores of Westborne to the Vestan Islands. And a hound with a nose so sharp it could track a fish down a stream."

"A good thing the hounds that tracked us in Betchwood that day were not blessed with such noses!" Rath gave an exaggerated shudder.

Maura reached for her cloak and used the hem of it to rub her hair dry. "Armed with his magical gifts, Velorken harried the Black Beast out from under the mountains, then pursued it from Tarsh to the Waste and back again. As you can imagine, they left havoc in their wake. At last, Lord Velorken entreated the Giver to have mercy on his people. He said he would chase the Beast as long and as far as need be, if only he could be given a hunting place where they would do no one any harm."

"So the Giver put them in the night sky?" Rath's voice rumbled with amused disbelief.

"Is it so very hard for you to accept?" Perhaps it was, given the kind of life he had led. "I sprinkled a few feather cuttings and said some words, then no one could see you — not even yourself. What little power I have is lent me by the Giver. Even if a feather did nothing more than help to keep a bird aloft and make it invisible to predators, would that not still be a marvel?"

Rath's only reply was a vague grumble of agreement.

"Langbard taught me the world is full of wonders." Like *warm* water welling up out of the ground. "But people take them for granted because they are familiar and commonplace."

"What else did Langbard say?"

Maura thought for a moment. Then she remembered something Langbard had told her about the story of Velorken. Something that might make sense to a man like Rath.

"He said the star tales might only be that. Tales — fancies

of things that never happened."

"Aha!"

"Save your *aha*, Rath Talward. He also said that the most unlikely tale may still contain a great truth."

"That sounds a proper riddle."

"But it is not, really. Think about the story of Velorken. He asked the Giver to do something for him, but instead the Giver provided him with the tools to do it for himself."

Had the Giver provided her with the tools to fulfil her quest? Was Rath Talward one of those? Might his doubt be a whetstone on which she was meant to sharpen her faith? Her desire for him a test of her fidelity and worthiness?

"And when he was willing to sacrifice himself for his people, the Giver made that possible." As she spoke those words, Maura's voice grew quiet and anxious.

Would she be called to give her life or something she valued almost as much in order to deliver Embria from the Han? And if she were, would she find the courage to do it?

Chapter Two

WHEN THEY SET out early the next morning, Rath sensed Maura's reluctance to leave behind the small haven of safety and comfort they had found.

He could hardly blame her. Since leaving Windleford their journey had been little different from his accustomed life of hardship and danger. He tried to imagine how much of a shock it must have come to Maura, after her sheltered years as ward of a powerful wizard. And the worst might be yet to come.

"We can stay another day, if you care to," he offered. "It would not hurt either of us to rest a bit before we go on. You might find more supplies for your sash."

He would not mind lingering here, tasting a sense of peace that was sweet, yet piquant. His outlaw wariness warned him to distrust the ease and contentment he found here. But the convictions by which he had lived for so long were beginning to chafe, like the outgrown clothes he had worn as a child.

Maura looked around the spot, so peaceful and green. "Remember what you said last night, about thinking it unwise to tempt yourself with more than a glimpse of what you cannot have?"

"Aye, what of it?" Rath's face stung. Could he be blushing for the first time in twenty-eight years?

"I dare not tempt myself with any more time here." The wistful look on Maura's face made Rath ache. "Otherwise, I may never be able to make myself leave."

But she *was* leaving a place of serenity she clearly craved, to venture into unknown danger on a quest of which she must have doubts. Perhaps the blood of that Velorken fellow ran in her veins, if such a man had ever truly lived. For she had all his resolve and courage.

More perhaps, for he had been a powerful lord, and she scarcely more than a girl. She had no rock-cleaving sword, only the snippets of plant and animal matter in her sash. No steed who could outrun the wind, only a sturdy mare, twice stolen, which would soon be of little use. No keen-sensed hound or hawk to guide her, only …

Was *he* meant to be what the hawk and hound had been to Lord Velorken? The notion of being used by some great invisible power in which he did not believe gave Rath a cold, clammy feeling. Yet something about the image of the hawk drew him. Proud, predatory bird, fierce and solitary.

"Besides." Maura pulled a rueful face. "We must reach Everwood by Solsticetide. You know the way. Can we afford to linger here if we are to reach the Hitherland in time?"

Rath did the reckoning in his head. Part of him wanted to lie and claim they had plenty of time. Urge her to do what part of her clearly longed to. Every additional hour they spent here would make it easier for him to dissuade her from her well-meant fool's errand.

"No." He forced the word through clenched teeth. "We had better make haste."

If she had the courage to undertake this task, he could not bring himself to undermine her. Instead he would see her through to the end, comfort her in her disappointment and hope she would turn to him afterward.

Climbing into the saddle, he hoisted Maura up behind him. Then, willing himself not to glance back, he pointed the mare southward and jogged the reins.

For a time they rode through the high country, both lost in their thoughts. More than ever, Rath was conscious of Maura seated behind him, clinging to his waist, sometimes resting her head against his back.

Ever since he had grown canny enough and powerful enough to attract followers, he had resented their intrusion on his solitude, their demands upon his skills and loyalty. With Maura it was different — perhaps because, in some odd way, she was his leader, not his follower. Yet he welcomed her reliance upon him.

He glanced back over his shoulder. "We have a few more long days' rides ahead of us. Would you care to tell me another one of your tales to pass the time?"

Her green eyes twinkled like starlight on a dewy leaf. "And give you a chance to laugh at my folly in believing such tales?"

The twinkle faded, replaced by a look of disappointment that made him cringe with shame. "I might laugh if the tale is amusing. Otherwise, no cheek, I promise."

"You mean it?"

"Upon my life." Rath nodded. "You see, I have traveled this country from Southmark to the Hitherland, but hearing your tale last night made me feel like I've been stumbling around half-blind all that time. Where did Bror's Bridge get its name? Who was the Oracle of Margyle?"

"Who *is* the Oracle of Margyle?" Maura corrected him. "As far as I know, she lives yet."

She paused for a moment, perhaps weighing his sincerity. "Would you like to hear about the Choice of Velorken's Children? It is not very amusing I'm afraid. It tells about how the Great Kin were sundered into Kin of Han and the Kin of Embri. If you do not know it, then you are more than *half* blind to what ails our land, now."

"It sounds like a gripping tale." Her words had set the back of Rath's neck prickling. "Let's hear it."

Maura's voice took on the compelling cadence unique to storytellers. "After Lord Velorken chased the Black Beast into the heavens, the Giver sought to reward his children with a wish. They could have knowledge of the special powers of things that grow upon the earth, or knowledge of the special powers of those things from deep within the earth."

Despite his resolve not to interrupt, Rath could not keep silent. "But they could not agree, could they?"

"No, they could not." Maura sounded grieved by the ancient breech. "Have you heard this story before?"

"Part of it, perhaps," Rath admitted. "Long ago, from Gan. After she died and I was left on my own, I tried to forget everything she had told me about the Elderways."

He'd had too many other things to occupy his mind, just to survive. Old, outlandish stories had felt like so much useless gear he must abandon to travel light. Now he wondered if he had maimed a part of himself by losing that connection to the past?

Maura picked up the thread of her story. "As you said, they could not agree. Han wished for mastery of metals and gems; Embri wished to be mistress of growing things. Some of their kin supported Han, others Embri, until it seemed they would wreak more destruction upon each other than the Black Beast had done. The Giver was grieved by their strife."

As Maura told the tale, Rath felt the miles and the hours slipping away. And a lost piece of himself restored.

During the next several days of hard riding, the land became more rugged with every passing mile. And Rath's hunger for Maura's stories seemed to grow with each fresh one she told him. She could feel something stirring and growing within him. It pleased her to be able to repay him in some small way for the great service he was doing her.

How many other of their country folk might harbor the same nameless craving to know of the past from whence they had come and the vast intricate tapestry of which they were a part?

On the fourth day, they stopped at a small trading post in a secluded valley. There, Rath bartered their horse for stout walking sticks and packs heavy with supplies for the next part of their journey.

While he haggled with the trader for a few more strips of smoked Southmark beef that looked like they should be worn rather than eaten, Maura slipped outside to feed the mare a carrot and say goodbye.

"You have borne us well for many miles." She stroked the horse's neck while it chewed on the carrot. "I hope you will find a better life here than the one you left behind in Aldwood."

The horse whinnied and shook its mane.

"Rath says we cannot take you with us, for the way is too rough and too barren for you to graze." Maura wished she knew beastspeech to reassure the creature. "And I would not wish to take you with us into Westborne for fear we might have to part with you there."

A few moments later, Rath emerged from the trading post looking well pleased with himself. "We have a few more hours of daylight and this time of day is best for traveling through the Waste. I reckon we should be on our way."

He helped Maura shoulder her pack. "Are you sure that is not too heavy I could take some more gear into mine."

"Never!" Maura strove to keep her breath from sounding labored. And they had not started walking yet! "If you stuff another pound of supplies into that pack, you will tumble backward and never be able to get up again. I can manage."

"You are certain?" Rath did not sound convinced. "Our packs will lighten as we go. Though not too quickly, I hope."

He turned to the horse and gave it an affectionate smack on the rump. "Farewell, old girl. Do not let Croll work you too hard. I told him he will answer to me one day if he does."

For what was left of that day, Maura missed the horse

dearly and often found herself wishing they had been able to ride it farther. She and Rath walked almost until sunset, by which time she could scarcely put one foot in front of the other. When she thought of how swiftly the horse could have brought them that same distance, she repented ever complaining of a sore backside.

With a groan she sank onto a large flat rock. "Can we spare a little of our lard supply for me to make a liniment?"

Rath shrugged out of his pack. "Is your back sore?"

Maura gave a weary nod. "I suppose a second warm spring would be too much to ask of the Giver?"

He helped her remove her pack. "If I had the power of your Giver, I would conjure you one on the spot." He gave a rueful shrug. "But I have not, and I do not know of any more around here. We will have to make do with liniment, I fear. I will gladly furnish the lard, if you can make enough for us both."

While Maura compounded the balm, Rath gathered sticks for a fire from some stunted bushes near their campsite.

"Why do you bother with a fire?" Maura glanced up from bruising a mixture of moonmallow and cheeseweed. "We ate well at the trading post. A drink and some dried fruit will do me for supper. This far south, it cannot get very cold at night."

"This is neither for heat nor for cooking." Rath laid a bed of kindling over which he arranged some midsized sticks. "Many wild creatures live here on the fringe of the Waste. Some have a taste for human flesh."

As if summoned by his warning, something howled off in the distance.

Maura glanced over her shoulder, half expecting to see a lank wolf or barren cat skulking behind a nearby bush. "As soon as I have made the balm, I will help you gather more wood."

"Do not fret." Rath struck his flint and soon had a small but steady blaze going. "We have enough to last until morning."

Maura set down the wooden bowl in which she had

compounded the liniment. The pungent scent of cheeseweed wafted on the still evening air. "I would like to be *certain* we have plenty."

She managed to gather a few good sized sticks before all the stooping and lifting became too much for her. Then she hobbled back to the fire like an old granddame with winterache.

"Could you boil some water for a tea, too?" she asked Rath.

"A good thought." He rummaged in his pack for the kettle. "While I am gone to fetch the water, you can undress."

"Undress?" The word came out of Maura in a high squeak. Then she realized what he'd meant. "Oh, for the liniment."

Rath shot her a grin that held something of his old impudence. "It will not do much good rubbed through your clothes, will it?"

"I ... suppose not."

Once he was out of sight, Maura puzzled a way to bare her back without baring a great deal more besides. Rath had made no secret that he found her desirable, yet he had behaved toward her in a most honorable way. She trusted he would not try to take by force what she could not give him freely.

But what if her resolve wavered and she surrendered to her desire for him? Rath did not believe in the Waiting King. He would have no reason to refuse anything she offered. Maura did not want to do anything to further tempt either of them.

When Rath returned, she was sitting near the fire, her shift pulled down around her hips, and her tunic modestly held in front of her. Her thick braid of hair hung down over her shoulder so as not to get in the way.

She half expected him to make some comment, but he did not.

Instead he rigged a frame of sticks to suspend the kettle above the fire. Then he picked up the bowl of liniment, sniffed it and made such a face that Maura burst into nervous laughter.

"It may not have a sweet perfume," she said, "but you will

not grudge the smell when you feel how it eases your back."

Rath gave the liniment a dubious look as he scooped a generous dollop onto his fingers. "One thing I will say for it. Lank wolves and barren cats would never want to eat creatures smeared with this stuff!"

While Maura laughed at the notion, he daubed the balm on her back. She flinched when the cool compound landed on her skin. Or perhaps it was the provocative touch of Rath's fingertips on her bare flesh?

Immediately the liniment began to work, sending delicious loosening, comforting warmth deep into her flesh.

"Down a bit farther if you please," she bid Rath, "then up between my shoulders and on my neck."

He did as she asked with a touch that felt strong and deft, yet deliberately gentle.

"How is that?" Rath asked.

Maura searched for a word to describe it. "B-better."

She had started to say *blissful*, then stopped herself.

"My turn, then."

She glanced over her shoulder to see Rath pulling off his vest and shirt. Her breath caught as she glimpsed the firm, lean perfection of his bare torso.

"A moment," she gasped, pulling her tunic over her head.

Then she turned and scooped up a dab of the pungent compound to smear over his back.

"Ah! You were right, lass." Rath chuckled. "This stuff feels so good, I do not care if it stinks clear to the Hitherland."

As good as it felt for her to touch him? Maura rubbed the liniment in deep, making the movement of her hands the kind of caress she would never be able to give him any other way.

"Where did you get this scar?" She ran her finger over a puckered seam below his ribs.

"Oh, that one. Escaping from a Hanish roundup of lads for the mines. Almost did me in, but I wouldn't let that slag spawn have the satisfaction."

"I'm sorry," Maura whispered.

"Sorry? Whatever for? It is long in the past and hardly your fault."

"Sorry for making you remember." The liniment was well worked in, now, but Maura could not bring herself to pull her hands away. "Sorry you've had such a hard life while I had such a sheltered one. Sorry I judged you ill for doing what you needed to do to survive that kind of life."

"No harm done." Without any warning, Rath rose and tossed another stick on the fire, though it was burning well.

He flexed his shoulders. "That is good stuff. I feel like I could walk another five miles." He grinned at Maura. "Well, perhaps not five. There, the water is boiling if you want to brew that tea of yours."

They took turns through the night, keeping watch and tending the fire. Rath gave Maura his dagger in case of attack.

Sometime in the thick darkness before dawn, Maura thought she heard the faint pad of paws and saw the menacing glow of the firelight reflected off watchful, hungry eyes. She fancied she heard something else, too, a soft distant chant of unintelligible words. Then the eyes disappeared and all was quiet.

She sat there admiring the flicker of firelight over Rath's features, as stark and rugged yet strangely beautiful as the wild land around them. Of its own accord, her hand stretched toward his stubbled cheek for a stolen caress.

Then the sound of deep, fierce growls flared from nearby. The sleek pelts of several large lean beasts gleamed in the firelight.

"Rath!" Maura's hand diverted from his face to his shoulder to shake him awake. "Lank wolves! They are at our packs!"

"Slag!" Rath grabbed his sword and leaped to his feet.

Roaring a rolling thunder of curses, he charged the clutch

of beasts. They scattered, but did not flee. Instead they drew back, circling with their teeth bared, threatening growls rumbling from deep in their throats.

Then, a large one, perhaps the pack leader, launched itself at Rath. His blade whipped through the air to meet it.

The big beast fled yelping in pain. But not before it knocked Rath's weapon from his hand. Another of the wolves lunged between Rath and the blade.

While Maura had been watching all this, her heart hammering in her chest, she had begun to fumble in her sash for her spider silk. Would the spell work on other creatures as well as it did on humans?

"Maura!" Rath cried. "Toss me my dagger!"

His dagger, of course! She was so unused to carrying a weapon, she had forgotten it. Now she hurled the weapon through the air, while silently begging the Giver to let it reach Rath, without taking his hand off when he tried to catch it.

The dagger hissed through the air. A shriek of vexation rose in Maura's throat when she saw it would fall wide.

It landed among a small clutch of wolves. One let out a yelp of pain and bolted off into the night. That left three — the one standing over Rath's sword, snarling, and two that had backed off a little from the packs when the dagger had landed in their midst.

Again Maura wondered if her spells would work on animals. If not, she had better have something else to fall back on.

But what? The wolves had both of Rath's weapons.

The beast standing guard over the sword bared its teeth and growled at her. Its haunches tensed, ready to spring. Maura took a step back, then jumped when her foot hit the fire.

The fire! With her free hand, she reached down and grabbed a burning stick by its end. Then she advanced on the lank wolf, chanting her binding spell.

Out of the corner of her eye, she saw Rath pull something

from one of the packs and swing it at the other two wolves, while bellowing a loud cry. The beasts let out a chorus of howls that sent chills down Maura's neck. Then they turned and ran.

The retreat of its pack mates distracted the last lank wolf for the vital instant Maura needed. She lunged forward, planting a wisp of cobweb on the beast's pelt as she spoke the last word on the incantation.

Perhaps she had blundered the words in her haste and panic. Perhaps she had not used enough spider silk for so large a creature. Or perhaps her spells only worked on humans.

Maura had no time to care about the reasons when the beast sprang toward her.

She thrust the stick from the fire in front of her, but it looked pitifully small to ward off a creature of that size. Besides, the flame had all but died out.

Maura braced to be knocked backward by the animal's charge. Instead she found herself flying sideways as Rath dove to knock her out of the beast's path.

The lank wolf hurdled past them, landing on the fire. Burning sticks flew everywhere as the creature followed the rest of its pack mates, yowling in pain.

Rath and Maura lay where they had sprawled, gasping for breath.

At last Rath hauled himself to his feet. "I doubt that lot will be back tonight. But in case something else decides to try its luck, I had better repair our poor fire."

Maura rose, too, though her knees felt like they were made of jelly. Staggering to where Rath's sword lay, she picked it up. "You had better keep this nearby, too, though that stick you took from your pack did well in a pinch."

Her gaze fixed on Rath as he rebuilt the fire. One tip of the "stick" flickered with an eerie flame of its own. "By the Giver, Rath, where did you get that thing?"

"This?" He glanced down. "Came in handy, didn't it? I —"

Before he got the words out, Maura knew. "You took it from that death-mage when you went looking for Gristel Maldwin?"

Rath nodded. "I picked up a few little keepsakes. Did I not mention it? I thought I had."

"I would have remembered if you'd told me you had that . . . that . . . abomination! Get rid of it at once!"

"No."

"Rath Talward, do you know what that thing is?"

"Stop shouting," said Rath. "I am not deaf. And I am not daft, either. Of course, I know what it is. A sight better that you do, I'll wager. I have been on the wrong side of one of these things. That scar you saw on my back was like a splinter in my finger compared to the pain I took from this."

"Then why in the Giver's name would you want to keep such a thing around you?"

Rath shrugged. "The same reason I *steal* anything, my lady." He seemed to relish reminding her he was an outlaw. "Because it might come in handy."

"This has." He gave the copper wand a little toss in the air and caught it again. "You said so yourself."

"I said that when I thought it was just a wooden staff."

"A wooden staff would not have sent a pair of lankwolves turning tail like that." He stared up at her and something harsh looked out of his eyes. "I mean to keep it, so save your breath arguing. I have a feeling we may need it again before we reach Everwood."

Maura quivered with indignation. Was it not bad enough the man did not believe in the Giver, the Elderways or the Waiting King? Did he have to embrace the evils of mortcraft, too?

Part of her wanted to march off to Westborne on her own. But she knew what madness that would be. Rath Talward had made her dependent upon him — curse his hide!

Her tardy sense of fairness protested. She had not put

up any great protest when he'd insisted on guiding her to Everwood.

"In that case …" She said the only thing she could say. "Make certain you keep that vile thing away from me!"

"Fair enough." Rath strode to where their packs rested and planted the copper wand between them with its fire gem pointing to the sky. "It can stand guard over our packs, since wild things seem not to like it any better than you do."

Maura grumbled her reply, but Rath hardly seemed to notice.

"Get some sleep if you can. I will finish this watch."

"What? Do you not trust me to keep watch while you sleep?"

"You need not be so prickly." Rath planted himself on a rock near the fire that gave him a good view. "You did well just now, waking me so quickly, then taking your part against those lank wolves. But I am used to going with less sleep than most folk. I know I will not be able to get any more rest, so it is foolish for both of us to stay awake."

Maura wanted to nurse her grudge for a while, but he made it so hard. "I doubt I could sleep, either, after all the excitement."

"There is still some water in the kettle." Rath pointed to it. "Put it back on to heat, then brew yourself a cup of that dreamweed tea. I reckon you will sleep sound until morning."

Why did he have to talk such good sense, the rogue?

As Maura put the kettle on and added more fuel to the fire, the lank wolves prowled the borders of her thoughts, stirring vivid, haunting images of what had happened such a short time ago. Her quarrel with Rath about the copper wand had distracted her. Now it all came back — the latest of too many brushes with danger she had suffered since her fateful birthday.

She began to tremble.

"Maura?" Rath stirred from his perch to kneel beside her. "What is it? Are you all right?"

She wrapped her arms around herself. "I will be."

"That is not what I asked." Before she could stop him, Rath gathered her close. "This has all gotten to be too much for a sheltered lass from Windleford, hasn't it?"

That was too close to her own thoughts for Maura to deny. She nodded.

Rath cupped the back of her head with his palm and urged her toward his broad shoulder. "I wish I could promise you it will get better."

Maura gritted her teeth. She would *not* weep.

"There is one thing I can promise you, though."

She trusted her voice just enough to ask, "What is that?"

A gust of his breath, half-sigh, half-chuckle, whispered through her hair. "I can promise that if the two of us stick together, we will best whatever other dangers we meet between here and Everwood. I almost pity the poor fools who try to stand in our way."

Maura chuckled at the thought of all the Han in Westborne trembling before their advance.

"Rath, will you promise me one other thing?"

"I reckon. Depends what it is."

She doubted he would agree, but she had to ask for it weighed on her mind. "If anything should ... happen to me between here and Everwood. If I should be ... killed ..."

His arms tightened around her. "That is *not* going to happen. I will not let it."

"But *if* it should," Maura persisted. "I want you to do the passing ritual for me."

"Maura, you know I do not believe in all that foolishness of the afterworld and dead folks talking to the living."

"It is not foolishness!" Maura pushed out of his embrace. "How would we have ever found the map to the Secret Glade if Gristel Maldwin had not heard Exilda speak to her? And do not try to persuade me she thought up that business about the pickles on her own. Who would think of such things at a time like that? It was *because* it sounded so queer that I knew it must be a true message from Exilda."

"Fortunate chance. Happens all the time." A shadow of doubt lurked in Rath's dark eyes.

About the passing ritual? Maura wondered. Or about his stubborn refusal to believe in anything he could not see, hear, smell, touch, taste or understand?

"You will not think so when you have a chance to experience it for yourself. I heard Langbard speak to me, that night he died. He told me things and showed me his memories, which then became a part of me, as if I had experienced them for myself."

"You were in a bad way, that night. Not that I blame you. But a mind that is wrought up plays tricks on a person."

"How is this for a trick?" She described the view of Tarsh from Bror's Bridge on a foggy day. The headland rearing up, dark in the mist. The peculiar keening screech of the dawngulls. The rolling drum of the waves as they scooped tiny pebbles off the shore and flung them farther up the strand.

For a moment Rath looked surprised — even haunted. Then his lip curled and he laughed. "I believe Langbard told you about it. But how am I to know it was in the few hours after he died and not some time in all the years before?"

Maura sprang to her feet. "You are to know it because I tell you it is true. If that is not good enough for you after all we have been through together, then I do not know why you have followed me the length of Embria!"

Rath looked like he might be asking himself the same thing.

"Please?" She had one last appeal to try. "The night Langbard was killed, you gave me time to observe the passing ritual with him, even though it might have put us in danger."

"We all do daft things now and again."

"You told me it did not matter whether *you* believed, so

long as I did." From that moment she had begun to fall . . . that is . . . to see him in a more favorable light.

Rath's features creased into the scowl of a man beaten with his own weapon. He heaved a put-upon sigh and asked in a sullen tone. "So what is there to this passing ritual, anyway? No dancing or any foolishness like that, I hope?"

"It is not difficult." Maura settled herself down beside him again. "You just sit with me. And you say a few words of *twara* — Old Embrian — as you anoint parts of my body with a little water. It will wash away the cares of the world and purify my thoughts, words and actions for the afterworld."

"Aye." He sounded leery. "Then what happens?"

"Then, you will hear me talking to you and you will see things in your mind that I have experienced." A strange peacefulness wrapped around Maura to think of sharing her memories with Rath. Achieving a kind of closeness that was forbidden them in this world. Bequeathing him memories of her happy, sheltered childhood with Langbard.

"And we will say goodbye . . ." Her voice trailed off in a whisper.

"We will not have to," said Rath, "because no harm is going to befall you."

"But —"

"But — just to humor you, mind — you can teach me this ritual of yours. It will pass the time while we walk."

"Thank you, Rath!" Maura started to throw her arms around him, then pulled back awkwardly at the last moment.

There had been too much touching between them tonight already. It only whet her appetite for more.

Chapter Three

R ATH HAD HOPED Maura's insistence on teaching him the passing ritual would ease once day returned and danger no longer stalked the boundary of their fire light.

But he was wrong.

"You put a drop of water on my brow," said Maura in a voice breathless from the weight of her pack. They had been walking for several hours, mostly uphill. "Then you say . . ."

"Do not say 'my,' " growled Rath. The weight on his back was not nearly as bothersome as the weight on his mind.

"Your pardon?"

"Do not say 'my' as if you expect to die soon." A cold, slimy force squeezed his entrails whenever she did, the way a lake viper wrapped around its prey. "It is bad luck."

"Rubbish." Maura rested for a moment, leaning on her staff. "It is just a way of talking, nothing more."

She did not look appealing in a womanly way, this morning. At least she should not to a man in his right senses. Her face was flushed, from exertion and the growing heat. She had dark hollows beneath her eyes from scant sleep the night before. Her lips were parched from the dryness, and the pack she carried gave her a misshapen look. Still, the thought of any harm coming to her made the marrow of his bones ache. He had never felt this way about a woman before and he hated how vulnerable it made him.

Perhaps that weakness showed somehow, for Maura relented, as if taking pity on him.

"Oh, very well, then. The *companion* puts a drop of water on the brow of the *sojourner* and says 'Wash the cares of this world from your thoughts and let them be made pure for a better life in the next.' Only it is said in *twara*, of course. '*Guldir quiri shin hon bith shin vethilu bithin anthi gridig aquis a bwitha muir ifnisive.*'"

"How am I supposed to remember all that mouthful, not to mention speak it without putting a kink in my tongue?"

Maura waved away his objections. "A body can remember most anything if they repeat it enough times. Come, it is not that hard and you are a clever fellow. Think of each word as a blow to the Han."

Rath liked the sound of that. This *twara* stuff was the tongue of his ancestors, the kin to whom this land had belonged when they had been proud, free folk. And it was not completely unknown to him. During his childhood, Ganny had used a number of Old Embrian words for things. He must try to recall them.

"*Guldir quiri … shin?*" He spoke the words to Maura, like an offering of sorts.

Her radiant smile rewarded him for his first tentative effort. "*Hon bith shin,*" she prompted him.

"*Guldir quiri shin hon bith shin … bathlu …?*" He wished he did not crave her approval so. It felt like weakness and she already rendered him weak in far too many ways.

"Very close!" Maura's eyes glowed with admiration. "The word is *vethilu*. It means thoughts, though an exact translation is 'the whisper of the bees in your hive.'"

Rath grinned. "That is how it feels sometimes. As though a whole crowd of bees were buzzing around inside your head."

"Making honey?" asked Maura.

Only when he thought about her. "What comes after *vethilu*?"

"*Bithin.*" Maura took no notice that he had ignored her question. "It means 'let it be so' or 'may it come to pass.'"

"Wait. I know that one. Ganny used to say it when she got

cross about something. '*Bithin ... rafail ...*'" Oh, what was the rest? "...'*thelwa shin!*'"

Maura laughed so hard, Rath was afraid she might tip over. "Well, what does it mean?"

She patted her chest until she caught her breath. "It means 'May the Beast eat you.'"

"The Beast?" Rath pointed to the sky.

Maura nodded. "Aye, *that* beast. Any other colorful sayings of Ganny's you remember?"

As it happened, there were. As they continued to make their way through the arid high country, Rath dredged those all-but-forgotten words from his memory, then laughed with Maura when she translated them. As they talked, the miles seemed to pass more quickly and he hardly noticed the weight of his pack.

Before midday, they found an overhang of rock that provided some shade to wait out the hottest hours.

"No need to build a fire now." Rath let his pack drop to the ground, then pulled out his drink skin. "At this time of day in the Waste, nothing stirs, so we are safe to sleep."

Maura leaned against the sheltering rock and slowly wilted to the ground. "I will not need any dreamweed tea to put me to sleep."

They chewed on their strips of spiced beef and ate some of the nuts and dried fruit they had got from the trading post. But they were careful not to drink too much, since there was no place handy to refill their drink skins.

While Maura settled herself in the shade of the rock, Rath climbed a nearby bluff to scout the terrain ahead of them. It looked as though they had reached the High Flat. For the next several days they could make better time.

He noted a spot or two of green on the pale brown landscape ahead, reckoning the distance and direction of each one. With luck, he and Maura might reach one of those before sunset.

Wiping the sweat from his brow, he stumbled back down to the shaded spot where he found Maura slumbering peacefully. Tired as he was, he sat for a time brooding over her — the soft delicacy of her features, the lush fullness of her lower lip, the vibrant glory of her hair. When he had first met her, she'd cast a spell upon his body. Since then, she had cast a much more potent spell upon . . . his heart? Did he still have one after all these years and the life he'd led?

It tormented him to be so close to her, yet not permitted to indulge the feelings she provoked in him. Yet that very boundary had freed him to know her as a person, not just a pretty object of desire. In that knowing, he had come to care for her in a way he had vowed never to care for anyone but himself.

If he continued like this, he asked himself as he curled a stray strand of her hair around his finger, might there come a time when he would care *more* for her life than for his own?

The notion baffled and chilled him.

Their journey through the Waste grew easier by the third day. The land was more level and their packs grew lighter as they consumed their supplies. Rath had marked a few watering places on their route where they had stopped for the night or their midday rest.

Though Maura still wished Rath would find a nice high cliff from which to drop that cursed copper wand, she had to admit it did a good job keeping wild animals at bay. She had seen a few flickers of eyes during her night watches, and once thought she heard a shrill growl that might have been a barren cat. But none of the creatures had ventured near enough to harm them.

"Now that I can recite the passing ritual in *twara*," said

Rath as they resumed the journey after their midday rest on the fourth day, "do you not think it is time you practiced your Comtung?"

"I know some." Maura wrinkled her nose. "Which is already more than I care to. Vile stuff!"

"I agree," said Rath. "But that *vile stuff* could be important for your survival once we reach Westborne. Many of the younger folk there do not speak Embrian at all."

"Not speak their own language — that is a shame!"

"So it is." Rath slammed his walking staff against the hard, parched ground as if he pictured a Hanish head beneath it. "Someday, perhaps, you can do something to remedy that. But not if your quest flounders because you could not make yourself understood."

Strange. He spoke as if he was beginning to believe she would one day rule Embria.

"Go on, then. What should I know?" She would rinse her mouth out well after their lesson.

"Simple things," said Rath. "Travelers' phrases. How to ask directions to where you are going. How to ask the price of goods. How to tell someone you are hurt and ask for help."

Maura hoped she would never need to use that last one. Rath was right, though. It would be just such times she would most need to make herself understood. Besides, if her lessons in Comtung passed the hours of their march as agreeably as Rath's lessons in *twara*, it would seem like no time until they reached Westborne.

"So," said Rath, "how would you ask what something costs?"

"*Referna ... takolt ... kotarst?*" Maura made a face as she spoke the words.

"*Refernug,*" Rath corrected her. "And I would say *pranat* rather that *takolt* ... unless you are buying something alive."

"A foul sounding language," grumbled Maura.

Rath shrugged. "Better than Hanish."

"That is not much of a boast."

"*Rosfin kempt!*"

"And what does that mean, pray?"

"It means impudent wench." Rath chuckled. "You had better learn more Comtung so you will know when you are being insulted."

"I expect I will know by the tone of voice, *lalump*. And to speak true, I would sooner not know when someone speaks ill to me."

"Now that is where we differ," said Rath. "I want to know exactly what someone is calling me. So, pray, what is a *lalump*? Ganny sometimes called me that when I was a wee fellow, but she never would say what it meant."

"There are more differences than that between us, Rath Talward." Maura felt the need to remind herself at every opportunity. "As for that word, it might mean 'scamp' or it might mean 'fondheart.'"

When he fixed her with a mock-scowl, she relented. "In truth, it is what someone calls a scamp they are fond of."

Rath was more than a "scamp," Maura reminded herself. She had seen the way he'd fought those wolves. He could be a dangerous man when he chose. There was a ruthlessness about him, but a kind of honor, too. The better she got to know him, the more clearly she saw what life had made of him — the bad and the good. Yet every mile they journeyed together, the bad seemed to fade and the good to strengthen.

He glanced back at her, a gleam in his eyes that warned her he meant to tease. Perhaps even in a flirtatious way. Though she knew she should not encourage it, the prospect set a gentle buzz going in her heart.

Before he could speak the words he intended, his gaze strayed to something beyond her and the muscles of his face tightened.

"Rath? What is it?" Maura spun about. From habit, her

hands moved toward the pockets of her sash.

They were near the crest of a very gentle incline, but the land behind them was so flat, she could see for miles.

Her alarm eased when she spotted nothing threatening. "Did you do that on purpose to throw a scare into me?"

"Come!" Rath clutched her arm in a grip that brooked no delay.

He pulled her the hundred yards or so to the crest of the rise, then dropped to the ground, hauling her down after him.

"What is all this about?" She wrenched her arm from his grip. "You'd better have a very good reason to —"

"Shush!" ordered Rath in a harsh whisper. "Look."

He craned his neck a little to see over the crest of the rise.

"I already looked. There was nothing."

"Well, look again."

Maura propped herself on her elbows and peered back the way they had come. "I still do not —"

Rath raised his hand and pointed. "Over that way."

Those three simple, quiet words made Maura's whole body pucker in gooseflesh. Looking where Rath had bid her, she could make out several small shapes that appeared to be moving in their direction.

"Slag!" Rath pounded the ground. "I should have been more watchful. Whoever they are, they've come down from the mountains. Nobody good ever comes down from the mountains."

He scuttled a ways back from the edge of the rise before standing up. "They probably spotted us hours ago. No help for it now. Come on."

Maura followed him in a hunched run. "Now that we are out of sight, can we not change course and try to cover our tracks?"

The strained squint of Rath's eyes eased a little and he flashed a fleeting rueful smile. "You have learned well, lass. I wish we could, but we are near Raynor's Rift and there is only one way across that will not take us many, many miles longer."

He began walking at a brisk trot. "By luck it is not far. If we can beat them to it, we should be able to put them off our trail on the other side."

Maura picked up her pace. "Let us waste no time then. The Comtung lessons can resume another day."

"Have you got anything in that sash to lend us speed?"

"I do!" She had forgotten about it until this moment. Now she praised the Giver for her faulty memory. "Hold a moment. It will be worth a short delay."

She turned her back to Rath. "Lift my pack and reach into the middle pocket halfway up."

The weight of her pack eased and through her clothes she felt Rath's fingers moving.

"A fine powder?" he asked. "With a waxy feel?"

"That is it! Powdered stag hoof. Get out as much as you can, then take off your boots and stockings."

"There," said Rath after a moment's digging with his fingers. "I think I have it all."

Maura dropped to the ground, fumbling with her laces then rolling off her stockings. She wrinkled her nose. They could use a good wash the next time she and Rath found water.

She turned to take her share of the stag hoof from Rath. He sat on the ground, struggling to untie his boot with one hand, while the other was cupped around the precious powder.

"Here, let me help." Clumsy with haste, she pried off Rath's boots and removed his stockings. "Why did you not tell me you have a blister on your heel? I will make you a salve for it tonight."

She held out her open palm, into which Rath shook half the translucent gray powder. Just then, a gust of wind whipped from out of nowhere, sending much of the powder swirling into the air before they could close their hands.

"Slag!" muttered Maura. "Quick, rub what is left onto the soles of your feet. It may still be enough. While you apply it, repeat after me, "*Rodiri … thisbrid … kerew ethro … bithin … en fwan … gen lorfin bryd.*"

Rath recited the incantation without a single mistake and with just the right lilt. "I know some of those words."

"I expect you do. You seem to have a gift for languages." Maura grabbed her stockings. "Now, let us get our boots back on and see if we can make better haste."

As soon as Rath was shod again, he leaped to his feet and held down a hand to hoist her up.

"That way." He pointed to a line of trees stretched across the horizon.

Keeping a firm grip on her hand, Rath set off toward the trees. Not too quickly, at first, but gradually increasing his pace.

"It is a good thing I forgot that stag-hoof until now," said Maura, her breath coming only a bit faster than usual, though she was running at a speed greater than she had ever run in her life. "When we needed it most."

"Are you not going to credit your Giver for that lapse of memory?" Rath shot her a teasing grin, but she sensed he was not completely in jest.

After that, they saved their breath and ran even faster. They would pay for it later, Maura knew. The muscles of the legs would cramp in painful spasms, just as back and arm muscles ached after bear essence wore off. She would worry about that later and tend them both with liniment and pain relieving tea. For now, they needed to put as much distance as possible between themselves and whoever was coming behind them.

The trees loomed up before them. Maura could see a gap in the greenery that looked like a path. They seemed to be headed for it.

She could feel the speed spell beginning to wane. Her heart pumped faster, her feet became harder to lift with every step.

Clinging tight to Rath's hand, she managed the final sprint into the wooded area.

Once in cover, they stopped, gasping for breath. Maura sank to the ground and pulled out her drink skin. The last watering hole they stopped at had been shallow and the water brackish. Now she quaffed it as though it was mulled peach cider.

Rath unstopped his drink skin, too, and took a quick swig. But he did not sit down. Instead, he staggered a few steps back to the edge of the trees.

"Can you … see them yet?" asked Maura.

"Not yet," Rath called back, his eyes still on the trail they had run. "That is a boon. We should have time to cross the Rift without them hot on our trail."

"Cross the Rift?" Why did those words give her a hollow feeling in the pit of her belly? "How do we do that?"

"Come." Rath strode past her. "I will show you."

She followed him along a well-trodden path.

After a few moments he came to an abrupt stop. "This is far enough."

Maura peered around him.

A few feet beyond where Rath stood, the earth plunged away in a sharp, sheer drop, the sight of which made Maura's whole body go rigid with terror. Between there and the far side of the rift sagged the feeblest excuse for a bridge Maura had ever seen — nothing but rope and boards.

The hollow in Maura's belly gaped to consume her whole body. She staggered a few steps backward from the precipice.

"Quite a sight, is it not?" Rath asked, over his shoulder.

When he received no reply, he turned. "Maura, what is the matter? Are you hurt?"

"The matter?" Maura asked in a tight, shrill voice. Then she broke into wild laughter. "I am not hurt. I am alive, and mean to stay that way."

"That is good." Rath nodded, but his brows knit in a look of puzzlement and concern. "So do I. Which means we had better waste no time crossing the bridge."

"Cross that?" Maura began to shake her head before Rath even finished speaking. "You must be mad!"

"I am not." He squatted on his haunches before her and took her hand. "I have crossed that bridge twice before and there is nothing to it. Just hold onto the side ropes, keep a steady pace and do not look down. Before you know it, you will be on the other side."

"Easily said!" Every time Maura thought of that sheer drop, she felt as if she were already falling. "A puff of wind, a rotten board and we could plunge to our —"

Speaking of wind, Maura felt as if the wind had been knocked out of her. She gasped for breath harder than she had done when they were running. If she had known what they were running toward, she might have turned and gone in the opposite direction.

"I know it is rather high," said Rath, "but —"

"Rather high?" Maura grabbed the breast of his cloak and pulled him toward her. "Until today, I have never been higher than the top of Hoghill. You could put twenty Hoghills in that ... that ..."

"Rift."

"Rift indeed! It is deeper than the Black Beast's maw, and just as deadly."

"That may be." Rath removed his cloak from her frenzied grasp. "But we have to get across, so we might as well do it and do it quick."

When she opened her mouth to tell him how impossible that was, Rath charged ahead with his words just as he was apt to do with his actions. "If you think that bridge is dangerous now, imagine a bunch of Han chasing you across it."

"How can you be sure they are Han?" Maura demanded.

"They may not even have come this way."

"If they came from the mountains, they are Han." Rath spoke with the implacable authority of someone stating the most basic of proven facts. "And there is no other way to come but this."

"Are you certain? Could we not go …?" She pointed north.

Rath shook his head. "That would take us up into the South Crescent. Mountains where you would find drops like that every mile, and no bridge to take you across them, either."

"Then …?" Maura pointed south.

"Perhaps …" he began, sending Maura's hopes soaring. Then his tone turned harsh. "*If* we had triple the supplies and you did not need to reach Everwood until Harvestide. Is there any herb in your sash that will give you courage?"

Maura shook her head. "Langbard said there is no substitute for true courage."

How disappointed he would be in her if he could see her now.

Leaping to his feet, Rath reached down and grabbed Maura by the arm, hauling her up after him. "Enough of this foolishness! I will not let any harm come to you."

Perhaps she was being foolish. Maura stumbled to her feet. True the bridge was a great height, but other people had crossed it safely — Rath, twice.

"If only it was more substantial." Maura allowed Rath to pull her toward the bridge. "Why could they not have built it of stone, with high sides so a body would not have to see what they were crossing."

"This place does not get enough traffic to merit the work of a stone bridge." Rath did not pull so hard once he realized she meant to come. "Besides, I doubt it would last. The earth trembles around here sometimes and rock has no give to it. Rope can bend or stretch a long way before it breaks."

They had reached the bridge again. Rath thrust Maura in

front of him. "Hold onto the ropes. Keep your eyes on the far side, and we will be across before you know it."

Her heart beat so fast and so hard, Maura feared it would crack her ribs. Forcing her gaze to the opposite side of the rift, she groped for the hand ropes and clung to them. Then she stepped out onto the fragile span over the abyss.

It swayed beneath her feet. Maura glanced down.

She had not begun to appreciate the rift's true depth. The steep rock sides plunged down and down in a bottomless drop.

"No!"

She spun about and plowed Rath down in her panic to get solid ground beneath her feet. "I ... cannot do it. I cannot! Let us hide until whoever is behind us passes, then turn around and go back to Southmark."

Rath picked himself up and turned to glare at her. "You agreed to come this way. The other way is even more dangerous, and will take too long."

"You did not tell me about ... that!" Maura's finger trembled as she pointed back toward the bridge.

"I never reckoned you would balk like this. I do not understand, Maura. You risked Hanish blades and the jaws of their hounds to save me. You trussed up a death-mage. You did your part to win our freedom from Vang. Yet you will not walk across a bridge?"

Everything he said was true. It made no more sense to her than it made to him. She had known fear before, but never this paralyzing terror that defied all reason.

"No." She backed farther away pulling a pinch of dreamweed from her sash. "I will not. Not that one. And if you try to force me again, I will cast a sleep spell on you!"

His features twisted in a look of shock and hurt. As if she had drawn a blade and thrust it into his chest. That look passed quickly, though. Something hard and fierce took its place.

"Stay then, coward! Liar!" Glaring at her, he stepped onto

the bridge and began to cross it walking backward.

"Coward I may be, Rath Talward, but I am no liar!"

"You are. A liar and a fraud, with all your empty talk about the Giver and the Waiting King and your quest! If you truly believed that pap you spew, you would trust your Giver to keep you safe from falling. There is no Giver. No afterworld. Just a hard, dirty life a body must wrest what they can from!"

"You are wrong!" Maura lurched to her feet. "The Giver created this world and breathed its spirit into every living thing."

"And stuck heroes up in the sky to chase monsters?" Rath's scorn stung like lye. "Rubbish! Stinking, daft rubbish!"

"No!" Maura barely noticed herself clutching the ropes and stepping onto the bridge again. Her gaze bored into Rath with such intensity, she had eyes for nothing else. "Do not say such things!"

"Stop me, then, *Destined Queen*!" His tone made a pitiful mockery of that title. "All your prattle about combing the kingdom for the Secret Glade. I see now you meant only the *safe* and *pleasant* parts of the kingdom."

"How dare you?" When she got her hands on him, he would regret his insulting tongue and his foul blasphemy!

"At least I do dare!" cried Rath, retreating faster. "I dare to live my life without the cripple's crutch of faith in some fraud of a Great Spirit! I dare to fight the Han every chance I get, instead of moping around waiting for some dead king to rise from his grave and do it for me!"

"Why you …!" Maura could not think of an insult rank enough as she charged after him. "I will make you sorry for every wicked word!"

"Why not let the Waiting King do it?" Rath beckoned, daring her to come at him. "Or pray the Giver to strike me down with its awesome power?"

He had stopped, now. His mouth stretched in a wide, triumphant grin.

"Take that back, you scoundrel!" Maura threw herself at him. "Believe or not as you will, but do not mock the Giver or the Waiting King! He is real — you will see!"

Rath latched onto her around the waist and plucked her off the ground.

"I will see, will I?" He spun her around, gasping out words between bouts of wild laughter. "When we get to the Secret Glade, you mean?"

"Yes, then you will see. Now put me down, before I ..."

He put her down, but he did not let her go. "Your pardon, Maura for saying those things. It was the only way I could think of getting you across that bridge without slinging you over my shoulder and carrying you. And that would have been far too dangerous for us both."

"Across the —?" Maura looked back.

Fortunately Rath was still holding her up, for her legs would not. Her head spun and her belly sluiced down into the toes of her boots. Her eyes stung with tears she refused to shed. Instead, she threw her arms around Rath's broad chest and held on tight as she joined in his laughter.

"You clever scoundrel! I cannot believe you taunted me across. Langbard was right about you!"

She tilted her head and looked into his eyes. Just as it had on the bridge, but for a far different reason, the rest of the world seemed to melt away, leaving only Rath — solid, forceful, full of life.

Slowly he bent forward, bringing his lips closer and closer to hers, and any reason to resist him had melted away with the rest of the world.

Then something hissed past them. Maura remembered having heard that sound before. But where?

Rath jerked his head up to look past her.

"Slag!" he growled, pushing her behind him. "We have company!"

Chapter Four

ANOTHER ARROW HISSED by.

"Get down!" Rath pushed Maura behind him. "Find a rock or a thick tree trunk to hide behind!"

He dropped down on one knee, well below the height the arrows were coming at, yet still able to see across the rift.

There were three, that he could see, on the other side of the bridge — two Hanish soldiers and a death-mage. If they were the same ones he had left alive back in Prum, he would never forgive himself.

Nor would he ever make that mistake again.

One of the soldiers was firing off arrows as fast as he could load his bow, not even making a pretense of aiming. He must be providing cover for one or both of the others to come across the bridge.

Maura tugged on Rath's cloak. "What are we waiting for? We must get away before they cross. This is my fault for balking so long on the other side."

"At least you came and they did not catch us on the other side or while we were crossing."

If either of them was to blame it was he. At first he had thought her fear of crossing the bridge foolish. Then he had realized it was like his fear of the mines — a suffocating terror beyond reason or control.

Once he'd understood, it amazed him that she had been able to break the grip of her fear and focus on something else to get her across the bridge.

As soon as she had crossed, he should have grabbed her hand and fled as though the Black Beast itself were howling at their heels. Not stood there like some love-struck boy clasping her in full view of the bridge, wasting precious time they needed to run or hide.

"Go!" he ordered Maura, his voice harsh with anger at himself. "Run. Get as far from here as you can. I will hold this lot for as long as I can."

"No!" cried Maura. Behind him, Rath could hear the faint rustle of her digging in the pockets of her sash. "We are stronger together than apart."

Rath could not deny that. It brought him a fleeting, but very sweet sense of satisfaction. Still, he could not take the chance of Maura falling into the clutches of the Han.

"I do not have time to argue with you, now." He wrestled off his pack and tossed it behind him. "Do as I say and get clear of here."

Rath drew his blade, though he did not need it ... yet.

Not only did Maura fail to flee as he'd bidden her, the fool wench crept forward until she crouched by his side. "Whatever happened to always looking out for yourself first?"

What *had* happened to it? Had he crossed the line, at last, past which he counted her life of greater value than his own?

Perhaps the Hanish archer thought he had scared them away. Or perhaps he had been trying to make them return fire, to see if they were armed with bows. Rath heard the fellow call out an order. Then the other soldier scuttled across the bridge, his shield raised before him.

"Can we cut the ropes?" asked Maura.

Rath shook his head. "If we try that, the bowman will skewer us for certain. If you will not leave, at least get out of sight."

He pulled her back behind a bush with thick foliage. "Is there anything you can do about those two on the other side?"

"I need to be closer to get the magic agent on them."

A daft notion blossomed in Rath's mind, when he most

needed to keep it free of distractions. What if an arrow could be fitted with a tiny cloth pouch containing one of Maura's *magic agents*? When the arrow hit, it would pierce the pouch and release the agent.

The idea had merit. Rath only hoped it was not destined to die with him. That Hanish soldier was almost across the bridge.

Rath steeled himself to fight when suddenly the strangest compulsion came over him. "Maura?"

"What?"

"If I am killed and you survive, will you perform the passing ritual on me?"

"If you wish, but —"

He knew what her hesitation meant. And he could not leave her without an explanation. If only he could find one to satisfy himself.

But there was no time left. The soldier had reached their side of the rift.

Turning toward her, he whispered, "Just in case."

And since his lips were passing anyway, he dropped a kiss on her ear.

For a moment, Maura sat stunned by Rath's request. The notion that he had made even such a tentative step toward belief made her want to laugh and cry at the same time. The possibility that she might have to speak the words of the passing ritual over his dead body filled her with the same helpless terror as when she'd glanced down from the bridge into Raynor's Rift.

Through the leaves of the bush, she could see the Hanish soldier peering around for an instant after he stepped off the bridge. Something caught his attention and drew him further into the trees.

While his foe was distracted, Rath leaped out from behind

the bush, his sword swinging. It struck the soldier's metal armor with a harsh clang.

Maura flinched. But as the two men continued to trade blade thrusts and parries, she could see the soldier's armor was only dented from Rath's blow.

A wail of dismay rose in her throat. With only his padded leather vest for armor, how could Rath prevail against the Han, encased in stout metal?

She must find some way to aid him.

The two men were joined so close in combat and moving so quickly, she dared not try to cast a spell upon the Han, in case it should strike Rath, instead. Neither could she risk distracting Rath when he most needed to keep his wits about him.

As she watched them trade and dodge blows, she realized Rath was not as much at a disadvantage as she had first believed. Without the weight and restriction of stiff armor, he was able to move more freely and quickly. Perhaps the best thing she could do for him just now would be to make certain he had only a single enemy to fight.

She crept around the other side of the bush to a spot where she could see the bridge. Though she knew she would not need to cross the rift again, Maura's insides still quivered and her head spun when she glimpsed its unforgiving depth. Then she saw something else that made a different kind of fear grip her.

The bowman was beginning to make his way across the bridge.

What could she do to stop him? She had no weapon, save her magic, and it would not work at this distance. She tried to dig up a rock to throw, but it was buried deeper than it looked and would not loosen. As she tried to think of something else, the Han drew closer.

Maura dug a generous pinch of madfern from her sash and stole as near to the bridge as she dared. In a whisper barely even audible to herself, she began to recite the incantation.

The bowman stepped from the bridge. But he did not glance down at Maura crouched in the underbrush.

Perhaps the narrowed vision of his helmet kept him from seeing her out of the corner of his eye. Or perhaps his thoughts were too tightly fixed on joining the fight, which Maura could hear continuing. The Han paused to grab his bow.

In that instant, Maura sprang up and hurled the madfern into his face. The Han threw down his weapon and staggered back with a startled cry. Maura hoped the madfern would make him see something that would frighten him into turning and running back across the bridge.

Instead he spun about, spread his arms like wings and leaped into the rift.

When Maura realized what the Han meant to do, she tried to grab hold of him and pull him back. She was only able to reach his long plume of hair, which slipped through her fingers as he fell. That was enough to send her sprawling to the ground at the very lip of the rift.

Too frozen with horror even to close her eyes, she watched him fall.

"Maura!"

The abrupt urgency of the nearby shout and the implacable grip of a hand around her ankle tore a scream from her throat. Yet even as she cried out, she recognized Rath's voice and his touch. Maura jammed her eyes shut to block out the shattering sight before her. She feared she would see it in her nightmares for a very long time to come.

Rath began to pull her back from the lip of the cliff, then suddenly he let her go. A hoarse howl broke from him.

Maura recognized the agony of that cry. She knew what had caused it.

Scuttling back from the edge of the cliff, she forced herself to open her eyes. It was as she had feared.

On the far side of Raynor's Rift, the death-mage had raised

his wand to point directly at Rath, who fell to his knees, spasms of pain gripping his body.

Though she knew little of how mortcraft worked, Maura feared its malevolent power. Would it be enough to get Rath out of the Xenoth's line of sight?

Scrambling to her feet, she clutched the end of his cloak and heaved with all her might. As he tumbled backward, his screaming stilled and his body went limp.

She bent over him, stroking his face and hair. "Rath, are you alive? Can you hear me?"

"Yes ... to ... both." The words rasped out hard.

"Thank the Giver!" Tears sprang to her eyes as she cradled his head in her arms.

"Later," growled Rath. "Is ... he ... coming?"

"Is who —? Oh!" Maura let him go, then crept to where she could see the bridge without being too visible from the other side ... or so she hoped.

"Yes. He is coming!"

Though clearly still in some residue of pain from the mortcraft attack, Rath tried to pull himself along the ground. "Wand." He forced the word through clenched teeth.

"No!" cried Maura. "We do not know how to use it, or what it will do."

Even if she did know, she was not certain she could bring herself to wield such a thing.

"Get it!" Rath kept crawling toward his pack, though every move was clearly a struggle.

"Very well, then." She could give it to him to hold, at least. Rath did not look capable of using any other weapon.

Maura ran the few steps to where Rath had dropped his pack, then fumbled it open to retrieve the wand. Meanwhile, her gaze fell to the body of the Han Rath had fought. Its head tilted at an unnatural angle and an appalling quantity of blood had seeped from a gash on its neck.

Maura's stomach heaved, but she managed to hold her gorge. The death-mage would not find her easy prey, huddled on the ground, vomiting.

Something else on the Han's corpse caught her eye.

First, she pulled the copper wand from Rath's pack. It felt hot in her hands, a heat she sensed could quickly travel to her heart, searing everything in its path.

"Here, take it!" Maura shoved the wand into Rath's hands, then hurried to the body of the dead Han. Gritting her teeth and willing her belly not to revolt, she pulled free the bow slung over his shoulder and plucked an arrow from his quiver.

She had never fired a bow before, but she had seen it done. Even if the arrow did not find its mark, it might be enough to make the death-mage think twice about crossing the bridge. Hopefully that would give Rath time to recover from the mort-craft attack so he could fire the bow himself.

When she reached a spot of cover near the bridgehead, Maura was relieved to discover the death-mage had gotten less than half way across. Still, her fingers fumbled notching the arrow. It took considerable force to pull back the bow string. Maura thanked the Giver for every heavy bucket of water she had hauled up from Langbard's well.

Now to aim. She had seen archers close one eye — but which one? Perhaps it did not matter. She could not hold the taut, quivering bow string any longer.

The arrow flew. Though it missed the death-mage by several feet, it caught his attention.

He raised his wand in Maura's direction.

She turned to run, but before she got a step, pain ripped through her. As bottomless as Raynor's Rift. Every bit as cruel. Every bit as terrifying. It was a pain of deep, searing cold. Jagged shards of ice driving into her flesh, but never bringing the blessed numbness of natural cold.

Maura heard herself scream, but it brought no release,

elicited no pity.

With the tiny morsel of herself not yet too overwhelmed with pain to think, she tried to move her twitching body closer to the edge of the cliff. The pain that waited her below could be no worse than this. It would be over quickly. Then all pain would stop.

"Maura!" Rath's voice came to her as if from a vast distance.

She clung to it. One flickering flame of warmth and comfort in a fierce blizzard of bone-gnawing cold.

"Take this!" When he thrust the copper wand into her hands, she realized she had dropped the bow. "Hang on to it!"

At once the pain eased to an almost bearable level. But something else took its place — a heavy, suffocating darkness that pressed down on her, stifling all good, all life from her body and her spirit.

Unless it lifted soon, she knew she would suffer something worse than death. She would be eaten by the Beast.

What had he done by giving her the copper wand to hold? Rath bent over Maura. The only thing he'd been able to think of to save them both from the death-mage.

It had saved him ... but had it doomed her?

Pain tore at his heart, not inflicted by any cursed gem, but every bit as intense as if it had been.

He unclenched her hands from around the cursed wand, then he pressed his fingers to her throat in search of a pulse.

There it was. Sluggish and erratic but holding on, bless her. He must find some way to revive her.

What was that tonic she had compounded in an effort to bring back Langbard? He did not recall the name of the herb she had used, if he'd ever known it.

But names did not matter. He remembered that night in

vivid detail, right down to the smells. He would find the right herb, if he had to sniff in every pocket of her sash.

But first he must heat some water.

The Hanish soldier had nicked Rath's arm, but the bleeding had almost stopped. His ribs hurt from a blow that his padded vest had deflected. And every muscle and joint in his body ached from the mortcraft attack.

Still he made haste to gather some twigs, rifle his pack for flint, kettle and water pouch. He did not have much water left, but perhaps that was just as well — a small amount would heat faster. Once he got a fire started under the kettle, he launched his search for the proper herb.

He cast his thoughts back to the night of the fire at Langbard's cottage. He remembered Maura bending over the old wizard's body, as he was doing now, with her. She had not shifted the sash around to dig something from one of the back pockets, he was certain of that. It made his job only half as difficult.

One by one, he began his search through the front pockets, now and then stopping to call Maura's name or give her face a fleeting caress. Some of the pockets were empty. Others held magical ingredients he had come to recognize — dreamweed, madfern, spider silk. From each of the others, Rath removed a tiny pinch and held it beneath his nose.

Was this it? Perhaps. He could not be sure.

Or this? No, definitely not. The scent was too acrid.

This? Yes! Without a doubt. This had been the ingredient of Maura's tonic — the one she had bid him chew to keep awake when he searched that house in Prum. With eager, trembling fingers, Rath extracted a larger amount and added it to the water in the kettle.

He probably did not have the herb in its proper measure, and he could not remember the words of the incantation Maura had used, but she had taught him enough Old Embrian, he hoped he could string together something acceptable . . . if the Giver would allow him a little leeway.

Rath shook his head hard. The Giver? Had that wand blast shaken his wits loose?

True, the vitcraft incantations were all phrased as petitions to the Giver. But that had no bearing on whether they worked, did it? For all it seemed so baffling, there appeared to be some rules to the practice of life magic. Perhaps one day folk would understand how it all worked and think their ancestors daft for believing some all-powerful spirit had cared what happened to the trifling creatures of this world.

Firmly reminding himself that speaking a spell did not concede the existence of the Giver, he poured the hot tonic into a mug. Then he lifted Maura's head and shoulders while he mangled a phrase of Old Embrian that he hoped would suffice to kindle the spell.

He held the mug to her lips, dribbling a few drops of the hot liquid into her half-open mouth.

Nothing happened.

Had he used the wrong herb, after all? Did spells only work if a body believed in the Giver?

Once again he felt for Maura's pulse. It seemed stronger.

Rath made up his mind he would not abandon hope until he had no choice. He coaxed another trickle of tonic between Maura's lips ... and another. Until the mug was almost empty.

At last Maura coughed and her eyelids flickered. "Rath? Are we safe? What happened?"

"We are safe enough for the moment." He choked the words out past an enormous lump in his throat. "If you stay quiet and drink up the rest of this, I will tell you what happened.

Maura gave a weary nod of agreement and took another sip from the mug he held to her lips. "The death-mage?"

"Quiet, I said. The death-mage will not trouble us any more. That copper wand did something to fight off the power of his. It was as though he had to struggle to control it. But I could see it was bad for you to hold the other one."

Maura moved her head in a barely perceptible nod.

Rath hoped he would never find out firsthand what she had suffered. "So while you were keeping him occupied, I grabbed my sword and cut the ropes on one side of the bridge."

"Clever," Maura whispered.

"Thank you for staying with me." Rath set the empty mug down. "I would be dead now, without you."

"I fear where I would be without you." Something dire haunted Maura's eyes, then it lifted a little. "Who brewed this tonic?"

"I did." It made him feel sheepish to admit it.

"But how —?" Every time she spoke, her voice sounded stronger. The color was returning to her face.

Rath shrugged. "I have picked up more from you than just what you've taught me."

A tender smile curved her lips. "So I see."

Just then something stirred in the underbrush nearby. Rath's heart lurched against his ribs. He could not fight again today.

Before he could do more than feel that alarm, a tree mouse scampered out from among the ferns and dead leaves to climb onto a nearby stump.

Rath's panic vented in a burst of hoarse laughter. "Thank you Master Tree Mouse for reminding me it is too dangerous for us to stay here."

Reluctantly he eased Maura to the ground. "Rest while I . . . make a few preparations. Then you feel strong enough to walk, we can go a little way off and make camp."

"What about you?" asked Maura. "Are you all right? Your shirt is torn — there is blood!"

"Not much." Rath glanced down at his wounded arm. "My ribs are sore. And my body feels like someone ripped it apart, then put it back together wrong. Do you have any herbs to cure that?"

"I reckon I can find something."

Rath checked the dead Han for any useful plunder before he disposed of the body. He would have liked to take the sword or the shield, but their distinctive designs would draw all the wrong sort of attention to him and Maura when they reached Westborne. He did take the Han's dagger, though, to replace the one he had lost to the lank wolves. The coins in a pocket of the soldier's belt would come in handy, too.

For the first time he could recall, Rath felt a tiny qualm about picking over a corpse. Then his usual good sense reasserted itself. This fellow would not need his dagger or his coins where he was headed, but they might be vital to Rath and Maura's survival in the days ahead.

Grabbing the corpse by its heels Rath dragged it toward the edge of the rift. When his aching muscles protested, he reminded himself it had to be done.

After a few steps, he halted for a rest. He glanced over to find Maura watching him.

"Do not look at me like that! What else am I to do with it? We cannot risk someone stumbling upon the corpse or they will soon be combing the forest for us."

"I do not blame you." Maura shook her head slowly, as if it were an effort. "Now that he is dead, what does it matter?"

"Now *that* is a sensible attitude." Rath tugged the corpse a little farther.

"They left us no choice, did they?"

"How's that?" Rath had pulled the Han's body as far as he dared. Now he got behind and rolled it the last few feet.

"The Han," said Maura. "They gave us no choice but to kill them."

Rath pondered her question briefly. "Not much of one. Kill them or let them kill us. I do not fancy the first, but it beats the second."

With that he gave the corpse a final shove, and over the edge it went. So steep were the cliff faces and so deep was the rift, that the corpse's fall made no more sound than the descent of a snowflake from a winter sky. It seemed strange.

Rath dragged himself back to where Maura lay by the small dying fire.

"Have we any more water?" she asked him.

"Whatever is in *your* drink skin. Why?"

Maura reached toward her sash. "Let us put some of it in the kettle and brew a tonic for you while there is still a little heat in these coals."

"We cannot spare the time." He tried not to sound as bone-tired and aching as he felt. "We need to get away from here."

The look she leveled at him refused to make light of his injuries. "Just put the water in the kettle, Rath. We will get away from here a good deal faster if you do not swoon on your feet. While it heats I will take a look at that 'scratch' on your arm. I reckon by that you mean it is not cut *all* the way to the bone."

With a sigh of surrender, Rath reached for the kettle. "You sound right overbearing for a lass who hardly had a pulse a little while ago."

"Proof of how well the tonic is working on me." Into the palm of her hand, Maura sprinkled the herbs she meant to use. "Think how much better it will work on you when I say the right words ... or rather, teach you how to say them."

Rath poured some water in the kettle and set it on the coals to warm. Maura dumped her palmful of herbs in the water, then turned to examine his arm.

"You are lucky it was not any deeper, or it would have bled a good deal more." She pulled a couple of wilted leaves from her sash, popped them in her mouth and began to chew on them.

Rath made a face. "What are you doing?"

She spit the chewed leaves back into her hand. "I am sorry I do not have time to mix these into a proper poultice, but this will work in a pinch."

Then she smeared the warm, wet wad of chewed leaves over his wound and bound it with a small strip of linen. As she worked, Rath sensed something weighing on her mind.

"What is wrong?" he asked. "You have seen for yourself, my wound is not so bad."

"It is not that." Maura tested the water in the kettle, then set it back on the coals to heat longer. "I want to ask your pardon for chiding you so often about your use of arms."

She nodded toward the edge of the rift. "Even vitcraft can be used to kill."

Rath reached for her hand and gave it a reassuring squeeze. "I told you ... or perhaps you told me. The Han gave us no choice. If they had not attacked us, we would not have gone seeking to harm them."

"Perhaps not this time." Maura's gaze searched his looking for answers Rath did not have. "But when the Waiting King wakens, how are we to rid Embria of the Han without attacking them? I do not think I have the stomach for it. Langbard taught me to believe that the power of life and death belong to the Giver. Mortals who take that power into their own hands do so at grave peril to their spirits."

Rath reckoned a rough tally of the men he'd killed in his life. Never wantonly, never taking pleasure in it as the Han seemed to do. But when it had needed to be done, he had not hesitated. Nor would he again. Yet he yearned for the luxury of a little peace.

He shook his head. "I am not the Oracle of Margyle, lass, just a simple outlaw from the Hitherland. Something tells me those are questions a body has to find their own answers to. For now, put them aside and take some rest."

Pondering what lay between them and Everwood, he thought, *You will need all the rest you can get for the days ahead. We both will.*

Chapter Five

"SHH!" RATH WHISPERED in a tone of harsh urgency as he and Maura prepared to leave the fringe of forest on the western edge of Raynor's Rift. "Did you hear something?"

Maura froze, her heart racing and her senses alert, listening for trouble.

How tired she had grown of these constant threats of danger! The past two days she and Rath had spent resting and recovering their strength had given Maura a bittersweet illusion of peace. But it had proven all too fragile.

She so longed for her old quiet life keeping house for Langbard — gathering and preparing herbs, visiting with Sorsha, studying the Elderways. With one small addition.

Or rather, one *large* addition.

She glanced over at Rath, still tense and alert. Her gaze lingered fondly over his rugged features. Any slight sense of safety she still possessed resided in her nearness to him. She had seen the lengths to which he would go to keep her from harm. But why?

That was a question she dared not ponder too long or it would spawn a host of wistful regrets.

Rath let out his breath and the tight set of his shoulders relaxed a little. "I reckon it was nothing. I am jumping at shadows. The sooner we get on our way, the better. Before somebody comes looking to use that bridge. Then this place will be crawling with Han."

"I wish we could stay awhile longer." Maura ran her hand down the stippled bark of a nearby tree in a kind of caress. "Even with all the Comtung we have practiced, I do not feel ready for Westborne."

"It will not be as bad as you think." The slight furrow of Rath's brow belied his reassuring words. "There will be plenty of crowds to get lost in. Proper inns where we can eat and sleep."

"Han thick as fleas." Maura muttered as he helped her shoulder her pack.

Rath gave a grim nod. "It is not only the Han you need to be wary of. Watch out for the *zikary*, too. They are Embrians who work for the Han, even try to copy their looks and their ways. Bleach their hair!"

He spat.

Casting a pensive glance around, he beckoned Maura and they set off, taking care to stay far west of the path that led to the Rift Bridge.

They walked in silence for a while, then Rath spoke again. "Even among the ordinary folk, take care. Watch your tongue. Do nothing that will draw attention to us. The yoke of the Han has fallen heaviest on Westborne and for the longest time. Folk do what they must to survive. If that means passing information to the Xenoth in exchange for food or slag, so be it."

"Slag?" said Maura. "I have heard you use that word as a curse. What does it mean?"

Rath shook his head in a way that suggested impatience, and perhaps a scrap of envy. "Langbard did keep you well sheltered, didn't he? Slag is dust ... from the mines. A wiser man than me once said it numbs the pained heart but rots the spirit. Some folk are desperate enough to reckon that a fair exchange."

Maura's nose wrinkled, as if at a putrid smell. "What do people *do* with this mine dust?"

"The men in the mines have little choice but to breathe the foul stuff." Rath's voice sounded harsher than Maura had ever heard it. "I reckon the Han saw it made them more biddable, so they took to giving them more of it to sniff."

He mimed inhaling something off the back of his hand. "Then somebody got the clever notion of using slag to pay off Xenoth snitches. Then they started selling it to other folks."

"Is this slag really so terrible?" asked Maura. "If it makes people more biddable?" Vang Spear of Heaven and his outlaws could use a dose.

Rath shook his head. "It is not so terrible what the slag does to you when you take it. It's what it does to you when you *cannot get it*. The stuff makes a body its willing slave."

"Did you ever …?"

"Once. For a while." Rath looked off into the distance with a rueful frown. "It is one of the worst feelings in the world when you come off it. Like the pain you feel when you warm frozen toes too fast in the winter, only it is not your flesh, but your senses."

Just hearing about it made Maura flinch. How many Embrians had fallen under the thrall of this slow, pitiless poison? Defeating the Han might be the least of the challenges the Waiting King would face when he woke.

"Light is too bright," Rath murmured. "Colors pain your eyes and patterns make you dizzy. Everything looks all jumbled, somehow. Any tiny noise is like a hammer beating against your head. Every smell makes you want to retch. It feels like every inch of skin has been flayed off your body and you're raw."

An echo of that old torment throbbed in his voice.

Maura moved closer to him and slipped her hand into his. It would be little, if any, comfort. But she had nothing else to give. Nothing else she dared give, though she wanted desperately to soothe his distress.

"Newlyn Swinley, you remember him — from Hoghill back in Windleford? I think he must have gone through something like that when Sorsha found him."

"I reckoned he might have been in the mines." Rath gave Maura's hand a little squeeze. Perhaps her clumsy attempt at solace had not been too wide of the mark after all. "It would take quite a man to win his way free of that vile place."

He thought for a moment. "And quite a woman to help him break free of the slag."

Sorsha and Newlyn, remarkable? Maura had never thought of them that way. They had been her neighbors and friends, beloved but familiar. Now, Rath's comment made her appreciate them in a new way. And long with all her heart to see them again.

"Langbard helped them, too," she said, "once Sorsha convinced Newlyn to trust him."

She cast her memory back to that time, one of the few brief episodes of turmoil she had known in her quiet life. "There is a weed called freewort. It grows in the mountains. It helps a person resist the slag. Newlyn must have eaten some after he escaped the mines."

Hearing her own words, Maura gave a little start. "I did not know that."

"How could you not know?" Rath cast her a glance of puzzled amusement. "You just said it didn't you?"

"Yes. But I did not know it before that. It must be one of the memories Langbard shared with me during his passing ritual."

She braced herself for a scoffing reply from Rath, but none came. Could it be that a tiny seed of belief had begun to take root within him?

He was not daft enough to believe most of the things Maura had told him.

Rath stole a glance at her as they emerged from the forest and walked toward a small trading post very much like the one back in Southmark.

No, he did not believe. But more and more with each

passing day, he *wanted* to. The trouble was, a man could not will himself to believe in things like that. Either he accepted them or he could not. No amount of proof could convince him if he doubted. No amount of scoffing could budge his faith if he was lucky enough to believe.

Rath made a sweeping gesture with his hand. "Welcome to Westborne, Mistress Woodbury."

Downhill in the distance, stone fences and hedgerows crisscrossed the gently rolling farmland. A narrow road wound its way north while a river meandered westward to empty into the Sea of Twilight.

Maura stared down at the Great West Plain. "It does not look so dangerous from here."

Even though he knew better, Rath had to agree. From this distance, Westborne looked fertile and serene. Perhaps it had been that way once. Was it possible the slender young woman beside him had the power to make it that way again? Or was he straying into dangerous delusion?

When Rath recalled some of the improbable things he had seen her do over the past weeks, the notion of her being the Destined Queen did not seem quite so farfetched.

"Come." He nodded toward the trading post. "Let us see what we can squeeze out of Yorg for some gently used camping supplies. Yorg is the brother of Croll, the fellow we bought all this from. The Waskin brothers trade back and forth these same few packs and pots, rope and bedrolls to travelers crossing the Waste. Yorg has a weakness for a pretty face. Show him a smile and he'll likely give us a better price."

Between that and what he had taken off the body of the dead Hanish soldier, they might be able to pay their way at least to Deadwood. Rath would figure out some way to get more by then.

A voice rang out. "*Stev retla dar!*"

Rath froze. He reached for Maura's arm, but she had

already stopped. Their Comtung lessons practice must be working. Or perhaps she guessed Yorg's meaning from his tone.

From around the side of the small, tumbledown cabin of undressed timber, Yorg Waskin shuffled out with his bow drawn and aimed at Maura.

"Who be you and what be you wanting?" Yorg called, in Comtung.

"Travelers from Southmark," Rath called back, "who took a more mannerly leave of your brother Croll, several days ago." As he spoke, he subtly angled his body to deflect any arrow that might fly toward Maura.

"Is this the way you welcome customers?" He glanced around. "No wonder you are not doing very brisk business."

"Oh, customers!" Yorg lowered his bow. "Your pardons, goodfolk! Customers are getting scarcer all the time. Fewer folks crossing the Waste. But I am plagued with cursed *slaggies* coming to steal. I will soon have to sleep with a bow under my pillow. Come in and show me what you have to trade."

When he got a clearer view of Maura, the trader ran a hand over his sparse hair, while he greeted her with a wide smile that exposed a mouthful of broken, rotten and missing teeth.

"Pardon my rude welcome, Beauty." Yorg's eyes gleamed with leering eagerness that made Rath's fist itch. "If I had got a fair look at you first, I would have been more friendly."

Maura replied with a tight, guarded smile as she backed a step away from him.

"Very fine, indeed!" The trader's gaze slid over her.

"She yours, friend?" Yorg asked Rath. "Or did you bring her in for sale?"

Rath wrapped his arm around Maura's shoulder. "She *is* mine."

His heart seemed to swell in his chest as he spoke the words. "And she is *not* for sale at any price."

Yorg shrugged. "I cannot blame you. Pity, though. What a

price she would fetch in the flesh market at Venard!"

"Speaking of prices …" Rath battled the urge to throttle the lecherous trader. "What will you give us for our gear?"

Fortunately for Yorg Waskin's thick neck, a question about business diverted him from leering at Maura.

"Let us have a look at what you've got." He beckoned them into the trading post.

The place did not appear to have seen much business of late. Dust lay over a pile of bedrolls and several coils of rope. Cobwebs clung to a shelf lined with pots and kettles.

Rath wrinkled his nose at the smell of the place. He did not want to think about the food Yorg Waskin might be peddling.

In Comtung, he bid Maura to empty her pack onto the long narrow table that was the cleanest thing in Yorg's cabin.

"We will keep one of the packs," he told the trader.

In fact, he was tempted to hang onto all their gear. But from what he recalled of Westborne, there were few good spots for camping. Most of those were already occupied by the kind of folk he did not want Maura to meet. Besides, they could use the coin Yorg gave them to pay their way north.

The trader swept a calculating eye over their supplies. "Five silvers for the lot," he said at last. "Mind, I am being openhanded on account of your pretty lady."

Five silvers? That would not get them far.

"If that is openhanded, I would hate to see you in a stingy mood." Rath began stuffing supplies back into Maura's pack. "We traded your brother a good horse and saddle for all this and our food."

"I told you, business is bad." Yorg shook his head. "Croll and me have to make what we can on the few there are. Say, six silvers, then, but I cannot go higher."

"Sorry." Rath stuffed the kettle into his pack. "If we cannot get twenty silvers, they are worth more for us to keep."

"Twenty!" cried Yorg. "You jest! Are you sure you do not

want to sell the lady?"

Maura shot Rath a skittish glance.

He shook his head, to reassure her and to set Yorg Waskin straight. "Quite sure."

In his haste to refill his pack and take their leave, Rath shrugged his cloak back over his shoulder.

"Hold a moment!" cried Yorg, staring at Rath's belt. "Where did you come by those?"

Rath glanced down. The three flaxen plumes he'd cut from the Hanish soldiers back in Prum hung from his belt. What folly had made him keep them? They were dangerous little trophies to be carting around Westborne for some Han to glimpse.

At least he had not revealed the copper wand that hung from the other side of his belt. That he meant to retain, for it had proven its usefulness. From now on, it had better stay hidden.

"I reckon it would be better for you not to know that." Rath narrowed his eyes in a look he hoped would discourage any more questions.

He twitched his cloak back in place. "It might be better if you forget you saw anything."

"Fear you not." Yorg gave a broad wink. "No one will hear a word about it from me. But you had best think twice about toting those much farther. Somebody might spy them and get the wrong idea."

Yorg would never believe what had really happened. Looking back, Rath could scarcely believe it himself. "Do not fret about us. We can take care of ourselves."

"Of that, I have no doubt." Yorg rubbed his hands together. "But if you would like to rid yourselves of those dangerous trinkets and make a nice coin or two, they are worth a good deal more than that rubbish you carry for gear."

"What would you want with such things?"

"Not me, friend. The *zikary*. They will pay for anything that makes them look more like the masters they fawn over."

The notion appealed to Rath. Make some coin, and a good bit by the sound of it, selling plumes he'd stolen from the Han to those *zikary* scum.

But he feigned an appearance of barely roused interest. "I might want to get them off my hands for the right price."

"Five silvers each!" cried the trader, forgetting to curb his eagerness.

Rath thought for a moment, then shook his head. "If you will give me that for them, I can surely get a better price in the first town we come to."

"If the Han do not spot your *bounty* and carve you up first," warned Yorg. "Seven each."

"Twelve," Rath countered.

"Twelve?" The trader began to sputter all the reasons that would ruin him.

Rath caught Maura's eye and jerked his head toward the door. They shouldered their packs.

"Eight!" cried Yorg.

"Ten," said Rath as he and Maura walked toward the door.

"Done!"

Stifling a smile of satisfaction, Rath stopped.

"Oh, very well." He pulled the three long hanks of pale hair from this belt, each knotted at the end to hold them together. "I am sick of toting them, anyway."

He held out his hand. "Let me see that silver, first."

"You shall!" Yorg scurried off through a curtained doorway.

While the jingle of coins sounded from the room beyond, Maura fixed Rath with a look of mock-reproach. "There are more ways to steal than lifting purses, Rath Talward."

"You mean Yorg?" Rath pointed toward the curtained door. "He will charge the *zikary* twice what he gives us. If they are eager to pay it, that cannot be stealing, surely? Or are you feeling sorry for those poor Han, going around with their pretty hair lopped off?"

"Hardly." Maura plucked some bits of cobweb off the pile of pots and tucked it into her sash. "They were fortunate you did no worse to them."

Under his breath, Rath muttered. "Oh, I wanted to."

The curtain over the rear door fluttered as Yorg scurried back holding a little cloth pouch bulging with coins. He exchanged it for Rath's *merchandise* with an air of mistrust on both sides.

Once they had made their bargain, Yorg scrutinized the three hanks of hair while Rath counted out the silvers to make certain he had received the promised sum.

"A pleasure striking a bargain with you, Yorg." Rath tucked the coins into the pouch on his belt. Suddenly he felt far more hopeful about this last leg of their journey. "Any chance you might have a riding animal for sale?"

With a decent mount and coin left over to keep them in food and lodgings, they might make it to Everwood by Solsticetide with days to spare. Rath reminded himself, once again, that it did not matter *when* they reached Everwood, since the Waiting King would not be there.

Somehow, the need for haste continued to goad him.

Yorg shook his head. "You would not want it if I had."

"Indeed? Why is that?"

"The Han watch the roads, friend. They don't favor folks traveling as a rule. The ones as do, they keep a right close eye on."

"I did not like the sound of that," said Maura awhile later, as they trudged down the gentle slope away from the trading post. "How are we to get from here all the way to Everwood, with the Han watching travelers?"

"There must still be some folk moving from place to place."

Rath's gaze roved restlessly, alert for the slightest hint of danger. "Food has to move from the countryside into the cities at the very least. Besides, I am used to making my way around without drawing much notice."

When he was younger perhaps. Now, Maura could not imagine him easily blending into a crowd. It was not only his size and his rugged good looks, which appealed to her more with each passing day. That air of danger she had first sensed about him was as potent as ever, though she no longer feared it … at least not in the same way.

Something else made him stand out, too. A bearing of command she had first glimpsed back in Betchwood when he'd tried to rally his outlaw comrades.

"I still have some hundredflowers." Maura tried to muster her optimism. "And I will keep an eye out for more, though I do not know if they grow on this side of the mountains. One thing we must do is get rid of that copper wand while we have the chance."

She braced for another argument. "If the Han find that … *thing* on you, the two of us are as good as dead."

Rath stopped in midstride. "By Bror, you are right!"

"I am?" Maura stopped, too. She did not doubt she was right, but it surprised her to hear Rath admit it.

"Indeed." He reached around and hauled the copper wand from his belt.

Just looking at it cast a shadow over Maura's spirit. She recalled the suffocating darkness that had enveloped her when she'd wielded it. Thank the Giver, Rath was finally getting rid of it. If she had her way, they would have tossed it into Raynor's Rift.

Rath shrugged off his pack.

Perhaps he was trying to unhamper himself so he could hurl the wand a greater distance. Maura did not like the thought of someone stumbling upon it. She opened her mouth to suggest they dig a hole and bury the thing, instead.

But other words burst out when Rath unbuckled his pack and thrust the wand into it. "What are you doing?"

He glanced up. "Just what you suggested. Making sure the Han do not catch me with it. At least, not without a search."

"Are you daft?" If she could have brought herself to touch the copper wand again, Maura would have wrestled it from him. "Have you not seen how dangerous that thing is?"

"I have *felt* how dangerous it is!" Rath's jaw tightened and his hands worked with ferocious strength far beyond that required for closing up his pack. "I have felt what one can do in the hands of my enemies and I have seen how this one countered that attack. I would no more toss it away than I would throw down my blade before a fight."

"Beware, Rath Talward. That blade has two sharp edges. Do not be surprised if the Xenoth turn it back against you."

"I would rather chance that than go into combat unarmed." He shouldered his pack. The stern, resolute look on his face declared the matter closed.

A tense, angry silence crackled between them for the next few hours, as they picked their way down the wooded foothills to the plain. The prospect of making their way through hundreds of miles of that wide, flat expanse gave Maura a feeling of perilous exposure. It galled her to be so dependent upon a stubborn man who scorned everything she believed in.

And yet ... she could not deny they had managed to strike a balance between their many differences to forge a formidable partnership.

Daylight had begun to wane when they happened upon a small farm tucked in a shallow scrap of valley between two low ridges. A thin plume of smoke rose from the chimney of the small house. A few fowl scratched near the doorstep. From inside the house came the shrill wail of an infant. In a field nearby, a wiry man and a slender boy turned slats of mown hay with long wooden forks.

Though this place looked far poorer than the snug, modest prosperity of Hoghill Farm, the sight of it provoked a soft ache of longing in Maura. In another few weeks, Newlyn and Sorsha would be making hay. Where would she be by then?

The more she had seen on her journey, the stronger became her desire to summon the Waiting King, and the greater her realization of the vast challenge that lay before them. Would he even recognize the kingdom he had left so long ago?

"Hail, friends!" Rath called in Comtung. He stopped and held his empty hands out in front of him to demonstrate that he was unarmed.

Maura followed his lead.

The man in the field raised his hayfork in a threatening stance. He spoke to the boy, who scurried to the edge of the field and returned a moment later with a hand sickle. The man called out a wary challenge.

Rath replied with calming reassurance — something about them meaning no harm.

As the two men continued to talk back and forth in Comtung, the farmer appeared to be growing less guarded with every exchange. Rath had a way of winning people's trust, when he wanted to. After all they had been through together, Maura had to admit, such trust was far better deserved than she had once thought.

While Rath and the farmer spoke, the boy stared at the strangers with undisguised curiosity. Maura met his gaze and smiled at him. After a moment's hesitation, he smiled back — a wan, pinched smile that looked as though it did not get much use. A moment later, a woman emerged from the house with a fretful baby in her arms, while a young girl clung to her skirts. When Maura smiled at them, the woman's worried frown only deepened, and the little girl hid behind her mother.

"Rath?" Maura interrupted him. "Can you ask the woman

what ails the child? Perhaps I can help."

The woman started at her words. "You speak Embrian, still?"

Maura nodded. "It is almost the only thing I *can* speak."

She edged slowly toward the woman and her children, ready to stop if bidden. Behind her, she heard Rath and the farmer lapse into Embrian as well. Something about this hay crop and a journey north.

"We come from the far side of the mountains," she told the woman. "We are only passing through on our journey. We mean you no harm. If the little one is ill, I know some healing."

"You do?" The woman brushed back a few lank strands of hair that had fallen over her brow. "There have been no healers in these parts since Auntie Roon passed over. The Han say the strong will thrive and …"

Maura could not listen to the rest for fear she would say something dangerous. "We are not Han."

Surely that could not be taken for openly rebellious talk. Yet, in a way, that simple statement was revolutionary.

They were not Han. They could never be Han, and they should not try to be. They were different. With a different language and beliefs they must not abandon. Or they would be nothing.

The woman seemed to understand. The tension in her pale, haggard face eased. She held the baby out to Maura, a gesture of trust that touched Maura's heart. "He's a-wasting, poor mite. Food goes through him, but does him no good. I have lost three other babes to the wasting."

As Maura cradled the frail, starveling child, pity for its mother subdued a bubble of eagerness. "I have a tonic that will help, if you can boil me some water."

"That I can!" The woman headed for the house, almost tripping over her skirts in her haste. "Come and welcome. Pardon our rude greeting. Some travelers that come from out of the hills are not the kind we want to linger. While you are tending the little one, Velsa has the worms and Young Blen has a sore swelling on his neck."

"I will do what I can." Maura followed the woman into the house. Before they departed, she vowed she would leave this family in better health than she had found them. And she would teach the mother as many of the most common remedies as she could, with a promise to pass them on to her neighbors.

Perhaps the infant sensed Maura's intention to help, for it quieted in her arms. With a gentle touch of her finger, she caressed its tiny cheek.

Behind her, Rath called, "Do you mind if we stay here a few days? Blen says if we help him bring in his hay crop, we can ride with him all the way to Venard when he takes it to market. He says he would be glad of my help to guard it."

"I would not mind at all." Maura turned back toward him, the sick baby cradled in her arms. "It sounds as though we can all do each other a good turn."

Even from a distance, she could not mistake the softening of his features as he gazed at the child. "A lucky chance we happened on this place."

A breeze stirred the cooling embers of her faith and purpose. A ride for them both in the kind of vehicle that would never rouse Hanish suspicions?

"This is not chance, Rath. Nor is it luck."

Once again, it seemed the Giver had smiled on them.

Chapter Six

RATH BIT BACK a grin as Blen Maynold's well-laden hay wagon trundled along the high road to Venard. They had passed several toll posts already. At each one, Hanish officers had waved them through with scarcely a glance.

He knew Maura considered this a boon from the Giver. Much as he wanted to scoff, the solution was so elegantly tailored to their need, Rath was tempted to credit something other than chance.

Glancing around to make certain there was no one within earshot, he leaned back toward the towering load of hay. "How are you faring, Maura? Can you breathe in there?"

He did not envy her, having to sit on the wagon pallet, covered with hay. But there had been no help for it. The driver's bench had only room for two, and Blen claimed it would look odd for a woman to be seen travelling with them. Apart from the discomfort of her hiding place, Rath was not sorry to have Maura out of sight for their journey.

Since their brush with the Han at Raynor's Rift and the past several days helping out on Blen and Tesha's small farm, her well-being had come to occupy more and more of his thoughts. Even in sleep, he could not escape. She ran through his nightmares pursued by lecherous Han and murderous Xenoth, and he was always powerless to protect her.

Three nights ago, he had stirred from one such evil dream to find her lying nearby, safely caressed by moonlight, wrapped in the relaxed, innocent beauty of sleep. Overpowered by relief, he had lain awake keeping watch over her. His arms had tingled with a phantom pain he had heard men suffered after losing a limb.

Now, the hay rustled behind him, and Maura's voice seemed to drift from out of nowhere. "It is hot, and the straw makes my neck itch, but I can breathe well enough."

"We shall have to stop soon." Blen looked around as if reckoning how far they'd come and how much farther they must go.

"Old Patchel needs to graze and drink." He nodded toward the big, raw-boned gelding that pulled the wagon. "I'll keep an eye for a quiet spot where you can safely slip out and cool yourself, mistress."

Rath thanked the farmer. "How many more days before we reach Venard?"

He and Maura meant to part company with Blen before he entered the city to peddle his hay crop. Would they be lucky or blessed enough to find another ride to bear them farther north?

"No more than three, I should say." Blen directed a grim stare at a bank of clouds gathering on the western horizon. "If the weather holds."

The two men fell to talking about the weather and about Blen's struggle to make his small farm support his family and the high taxes levied by the Han.

"If it wasn't for the hay crop, I do not know how we'd manage." Blen's shoulders seemed to sag under a huge, invisible weight. "Ours and our neighbors ripens sooner than any in Westborne and it fetches a good price in Venard since there is so little grazing land around the city. I do not suppose you would come back south with me, afterwards? Last year, my supplies from the market in Venard got pilfered on my way home. It has been a hungry winter. No wonder the wee ones are all ailing."

"I wish we could." Rath meant it.

He had worked hard during their short stay on Blen's farm. Though he had told himself it was only a fair exchange for the favor of a ride north, the sense that he was helping Blen, Tesha and their children brought him a glow of pride and satisfaction. It had warmed him further to watch Maura work her healing magic on the children. There had been more to it than herb teas and pungent balms. Her smile, her laughter and her stories had kindled the beginnings of a sunny cheer in the children that seemed fitting somehow. Whenever Rath had caught a glimpse of her gently tending Blen and Tesha's baby, a spasm of renegade tenderness had taken him by the throat.

With all his heart, he wished the two of them could return south with Blen and forget all about the Waiting King.

"We are ... expected," he added by way of explanation, "up north, in a fortnight."

That reminder of how swiftly his time was running out gouged a deep pit inside Rath. Strange, that he found it so hard to believe in the Waiting King who would free Embria from Hanish tyranny. But the Waiting King who would claim Maura and take her away from him loomed all too real.

Suddenly a small crowd of ragged children burst from the bushes beside the road. Rath recognized their kind. After Ganny's death, he had run with a similar gang of young beggars and petty thieves.

A pair of Hanish soldiers came chasing after the children.

Blen's old gelding gave a shrill, frightened whinny and reared. One of the soldiers, who just missed being struck by a great flailing hoof, bellowed a foul curse in his own tongue. Rath was glad Maura would not understand it.

"What was all that commotion?" she demanded in an urgent whisper.

"Just a couple of Han after some young scoundrels," muttered Rath. "We will be past them soon."

The hay rustled. "What can we do to help them?"

"Nothing." Much as he admired her for wanting to help, Rath bristled with impatience. "Young whelps like those are cunning enough to take care of themselves. The ones unwitting enough to get caught …"

" '*None should mourn the weak who perish?*' " Maura quoted from the hated Hanish maxim.

"That was not what I meant." Perhaps it had been … a little. "We cannot afford to attract notice from the Han. And we owe it to Blen's family not to draw notice to him, either."

"I suppose …" Maura did not sound convinced.

"That sort spend half their lives getting chased by the Han. They are plenty clever at dodging and hiding. Do not fret yourself about them." The whole thing stirred up memories Rath thought he had successfully purged.

He wanted to swat Blen's old horse on the rump to make it move faster. He wanted to flee the harsh memories those children provoked as fast as they fled from the Han.

The hay rustled again.

"Maura, what are you doing? Don't be daft now!"

"It was not me," she insisted.

A moment later, a squeak of dismayed surprise sounded from the back of the wagon.

Before Rath or Blen could ask what was going on, Maura spoke again. "It seems we have an extra passenger."

Her words were followed by a boy's voice, pleading softly, but desperately, in Comtung.

"Let me stay here, just a little while, worthy one! I hurt my foot on a sharp stone and cannot run fast. If I do not hide here, the Han will take me." That was what Rath thought he heard in the desperate gabble.

When Maura did not answer right away, the boy added, "If you make me leave and the Han catch me, I will tell them you are hiding here."

"Why you young…" Rath growled under his breath, quelling the traitorous notion that, under these circumstances, he might have made the same threat when he was the boy's age.

He twisted around in his seat, ready to thrust his hand into the pile of hay in search of a scrawny neck to throttle.

Maura's voice stopped him. Though they had mostly spoken Embrian with Blen and Tesha, she must have picked up more Comtung, perhaps from the children.

"I will heed a plea faster than a threat, boy." A little garbled with a heavy Norest accent, but understandable. Then her voice softened. "When we stop, I will tend to your foot."

"Blen?" Rath nodded toward the pile of hay behind them. "Will it be all right? Just until we stop to water the horse?"

The farmer's sharp features clenched in a worried frown as he pondered Rath's request. Clearly the young scoundrel's *threat* carried more weight with him than any plea.

"I ... reckon he can stay," Blen said at last in a grudging tone. "Only keep him quiet. And if you are found out, I will swear I do not know either of you ... not that it will help me much."

"You heed that, you little musk-pig," Rath growled in Comtung at the unseen beggar boy. "If any harm comes to the lady on your account, I will make you sorry the Han did not get you!"

Even though no one could see her, Maura rolled her eyes and shook her head. Rath's excessive protectiveness could be almost as vexing as it was ... touching.

How she wished she *could* touch him. Just lean her head against his shoulder for a moment, or slip her hand into his. She did not mind the minor discomforts of hiding in the hay for this part of their journey, but she did miss the chance to keep company with Rath — now that their time together was running out.

She wanted to know even more about him than she had

already learned. Since that was impossible at the moment, perhaps she could do the next best thing, by learning about the boy who reminded her so much of Rath as he had been when they first met.

"Are you hungry?" she whispered in Comtung.

"I guess." Hay rustled as the boy crawled toward the back of the wagon. "Why? You got food?"

"A little." Maura groped in the hay beside her for her pack. "A roll and a bit of cheese. Would you like some?"

"How much?"

"Not a lot." Maura's hand closed over the food. "But you are welcome to it."

"Not how much food." The boy spoke in a scornful murmur. "How much do you want for it?"

"Your pardon." Maura chuckled. "My Comtung is poor."

"What did you speak before?" asked the boy, his tone suddenly wary, "Hanish?"

Maura smothered a hoot of laughter. How long had it been since she'd laughed? "Not Hanish. Embrian. The true language of our people."

At least it had been before the Han had stolen it from so many.

"Never heard of it."

"I ask no payment for the food," she told him. Then remembering how Rath had once been suspicious of aid freely given, she added, "But to help me practice my Comtung."

After a moment's hesitation, the boy asked, "Are you *twarith*?"

"*Twarith*?" Maura knew what it meant, but hearing that word on the lips of a child who knew no Embrian took her aback.

"That is what they call themselves," said the boy. "They speak a queer tongue. They tell queer stories. They give folks things and help folks."

He sounded as though he found their generosity as unfathomable as their language and their stories.

"I reckon I am *twarith*." The word meant "believer" and she had believed enough to journey clear across the kingdom. "But I belong to no group. I would like to meet these other *twarith*. Where can I find them?"

"Give me the food and I will tell you."

"Here." Maura thrust the roll and the cheese into the hay and felt them snatched from her hands. "I give it whether you tell me or not."

"Good." The boy spoke while he chewed. "Because I don't know."

"Mind your mouth, whelp!" snapped Rath, whom Maura had forgotten must be listening. "The lady is treating you better than you deserve."

Twarith. Maura savored the name and the idea while she listened to the boy eat with muted gusto. So there were Embrians here in the most oppressed province of the kingdom, keeping alive the old language and following the precepts of the Giver?

She wished she had time to find them and talk with them. Give them hope that the Waiting King would soon come to their aid and reward them for their faithfulness during these dark days.

"Have you a name, boy?" she asked, when he had finished eating.

"Snake," he declared in a defiant tone, as if daring her to question or ridicule it.

In her mind, Maura heard an echo of Rath's words from many weeks ago. *No one gave it to me. Like everything else I have ever wanted in life, I took it.*

"Snakes are quick and cunning," said Maura. "Sometimes dangerous."

The boy made vague noises of agreement.

"I know a story about a very cunning snake. The Three-headed Serpent of White Rock. Would you like to hear it?"

"I guess." The boy made an effort to sound indifferent, but Maura heard an edge of hunger in his voice. Hunger of the spirit that could only be sated with the stories, songs and beliefs of which he had been starved.

"Once," Maura began, "in the shadow of White Rock, there hatched a tiny snake with three heads."

"Keep the story for later," Rath called back. "We are coming to a village. I do not want anyone to hear you and get suspicious."

"Is this village your home?" Maura asked the boy. "Would you like us to let you off here?"

"Got no home. We move about."

With that young Snake fell silent, robbing Maura of any distraction from the sounds that had become distressingly familiar to her on their journey north. Ailing infants crying. Women scolding older children in shrill voices of hostile desperation. Hanish soldiers bellowing orders and harassing folks. The sounds of blows and cries of pain. Now and then the flat, listless voice of a slaggie seeking a temporary escape from it all at a perilous cost.

Part of her wanted to cover her ears and block it out, too. But another part insisted she must hear the sounds and see the sights of Hanish oppression, to fuel her resolve. That did not make it easier to sit and listen, unable to help.

Gradually a quieter sound joined the others. It took Maura a moment to realize the boy had fallen asleep, lapsing into a soft snore.

She had done something to help, after all. Befriending a single boy might not seem like much, but it was a place to start.

The noises of the village began to fade until Maura could only hear the subtle, soothing music of the countryside — birds twittering, the drone of bees, and the whisper of wind through the leaves. It comforted and encouraged her to be reminded there were some things even the mighty empire of Dun Derhan could not subdue.

After a short while, the hay wagon slowed and veered off the road. Maura heard the nearby gurgle of flowing water as the rhythmic clop of the horse's hooves slowed and the wagon rolled to a stop. Next came the familiar sounds of Blen and Rath climbing down from their seat.

"There is no one about," said Rath. "You can come out ... both of you."

Maura wriggled out of the piled hay, careful not to knock too much of Blen's precious cargo onto the ground.

"There is only me." She pulled back the hood that protected her hair from chaff, relishing the cool tickle of the breeze on her flushed face. "The boy fell asleep."

She looked from Rath to Blen. "Can we not leave him and fetch him along with us a little farther? The more distance he puts between himself and the Han who were chasing him, the better for us all, don't you think?"

Rath scowled. "I would sooner you slipped the young rascal a little dreamweed and we leave him here. That way if he takes it into his ungrateful young head to tell someone about us, we will be long gone."

"Do you believe he truly meant that threat?" Maura strode toward the narrow brook that beckoned her with its promise of refreshment. "The child was using the only weapon he could command to sway us. Would you have done any different at his age?"

Rath ignored her question.

"Snake," he grunted as he stooped to refill his water pouch. "An apt name for a young viper. Mark me, you let him close he will poison us all."

"Please, Blen?" Maura turned to the farmer. "This boy can be no older than yours. I doubt he is running from the Han for amusement's sake."

"Aye, well . . ." Blen knelt by the edge of the brook and splashed water in his face. "I reckon it will not hurt for us to fetch him a bit farther. He cannot cause a commotion if he is asleep, can he?"

"Thank you." Maura rewarded the farmer with her warmest smile. "You honor the Giver with your kindness."

Rath and the farmer exchanged a look.

"The lad had better mind his tongue and his thieving fingers, though." Blen insisted in a gruff tone. "Or I will bounce his backside out in the dirt and let the Han have him."

"I will vouch for the boy," Maura promised. "And keep a sharp eye on him. I know the two of you think I must be daft to give him a chance, but I am not blind to what he is.

She fixed her gaze on Rath. "Perhaps he is not to be trusted, but how will anyone know unless someone dares to try?"

How reluctant she had been to give Rath Talward a chance. But circumstances had forced her to rely on him, and he had never let her down.

If only she could convince him to give others the same chance Langbard had given him.

Give to others as you have been given. Maura could not count how often Langbard repeated the Third Precept to her over the years. At the time, she had thought he meant the giving of material things.

Now, when she had almost nothing but the clothes on her body and the herbs in her sash, she glimpsed the need in her poor, broken land. She had plenty to give . . . from her heart, if she could find the courage to do it.

Did she think him too dense to understand what she meant? Rath wondered as he helped Blen unharness old Patchel for the night.

Langbard had trusted him at a time when even he had doubted his trustworthiness. Maura had overcome her well-warranted suspicion to have faith in him. Perhaps he owed it to them both to place a little of that trust in others. One day, he might overcome his natural wariness enough to do it.

But not if it threatened to put Maura in more danger than she was already. Each night he lay down to sleep caring more for her than he had just that morning. Looking back, he saw it had been going on almost from the first.

Every day he glimpsed some new petal of her beauty opening for him. The way she looked when she glanced up to find him watching her. The practical grace of her hands as she performed some task for his comfort. The stubborn set of her lips that made him long to kiss them into cooperation.

Though he had to admit such a kiss might win her *his* surrender, instead.

Most of his life he had thought of nothing beyond his next meal, his next theft, his next fight. Until he'd met Maura, survival and freedom had been enough for him. He had never allowed himself to slow down long enough for the emptiness of such a life to catch up with him.

Now that he had let someone else matter to him, he could see what a hollow shell his old life had been. Would it become that way again if some harm befell Maura? Rath feared so with a jagged-bottomed depth of dread he had never felt before.

For a man with certain skills, it was a good deal easier to keep himself from harm than to protect someone else. Especially someone who did not look out for her own safety as much as she ought to.

An expectant silence wrenched him out of his brooding. "Your pardon, Blen. Did you say something?"

"Just that I would fetch you and Maura back some supper from the inn once I have eaten."

"I hope for all our sakes the food is better here than the place we stayed last night." Rath fished a silver from his money pouch and tossed it to the farmer.

Blen tried to give it back. "Put that away. You will need it soon enough. Besides, who ever heard of a man's hireling paying him?"

"Keep it," Rath insisted. "We would have spent more to come this far on our own. And drawn all kinds of unwanted notice from the Han, I daresay."

It gave him a sense of sly satisfaction every time they rode under the noses of a Hanish patrol or got waved through a toll gate. Neither surprised him, though. A number of well-laden wagons like Blen's were making their way to Venard on this road. Most had a hired guard along to help the farmer protect his harvest.

Blen and Rath fit in well, and the Hanish garrisons along their route had enough to keep them busy without delaying the routine spring shipment of hay to Venard. Rath could not have ordered a swifter, more secret means of smuggling Maura north.

"Since you put it that way ..." Blen gave him a parting salute that looked almost jaunty. "I will not be long, I promise."

Rath led Patchel to the troth in the inn's courtyard for a good long drink, then brought him back to hitch beside the hay wagon. While Blen spent the night in the inn, his "hired guard" would keep watch over the horse and hay. Maura would probably insist on taking a turn during the darkest hours so he could catch some sleep.

Glancing around the courtyard to make sure there was no one within earshot, Rath whispered, "It looks safe for you to come out, now."

When he got no reply he tried again. "Maura? Are you awake?"

He thought he heard a faint rustle in the hay.

"Maura?" He jammed his arm into the pile all the way up to his shoulder. "Are you all right?"

His hammering heart slowed a little when his hand closed over her arm. "Your pardon! I did not mean to wake you. I only worried that ..."

Wait! That sleeve did not feel like Maura's wool tunic, nor her linen undergown.

Rath hauled on the limb he was holding, dragging out a squirming boy by what turned out to be the left leg.

He was a rangy, underfed youth, like too many Rath had seen during their long ride through the heart of Westborne. The lad was missing the little finger off his left hand and under a coating of chaff, his face was streaked with black.

That puzzled Rath for a moment until he realized the lad had tried to darken his hair with something, soot perhaps, which had run when he sweat.

"Oh, it's only you," muttered Rath in Comtung. He had all but forgotten about the boy.

"Let me go!" Snake writhed like his namesake. "I wasn't doing nothing! Just staying out of sight like the lady bid me."

Rath let go of the boy's leg, then before he could run off, grabbed him again by the breast of his coat, a bulky man's garment with the sleeves crudely hacked to half their original length.

"Where is the lady?" Rath gave the boy a shake for good measure. He knew from his own youth that Snake had been up to no good. "If you have harmed her ..."

The boy abruptly stopped squirming.

"Do I look daft?" He fixed Rath with an indignant glare that appeared ridiculous coming from such a tattered scarecrow. "Why would I harm the only one who's done me a good turn in as long as I can reckon?"

Those words struck Rath a stinging blow such as the boy could never have landed with his hands. That still did not mean he trusted young Snake. Rath had known too many like him — been too much like him, once.

"Where is she, then?" he growled.

The boy shrugged his bony shoulders and almost got a cuff on the head for it. "Right after we stopped, she heard somebody crying. She went off to look. Told me to stay here. That's all I know."

Rath cursed. Then he took a risk he might not have taken if he'd had longer to think about it.

"I am going to find her," he told the boy. "Stay here and keep watch on the horse and wagon. Yell at the top of your lungs if there is any trouble and I will come in a hurry."

The boy nodded.

At least Rath thought so. He was too busy worrying about Maura and wondering where she had gone. Someone crying usually meant trouble. The kind a body should stay away from — not go in search of.

Slag! If he had to surrender his heart to a woman, why could he not have picked one with a healthy sense of self-preservation?

Because, he decided as he made a circuit of the courtyard, checking for hidden nooks, listening for the sound of Maura's voice. That was one of the things he … loved about her. Might as well use the word, at least in the privacy of his thoughts. Calling it something else did not lessen its hold on him.

That was one of the things he *loved* about Maura. Her vast desire to help people, especially people no one else would see any benefit in helping. Because there was no benefit to helping outcasts … like him.

Or maybe there was, to her. A benefit as intangible as her Giver. And perhaps as powerful, if it existed and had done everything she claimed.

Where was she?

He wanted to bellow her name as loud as his voice could ring. But he dared not draw that kind of attention to himself, or to her.

When he finally caught the soft murmur of her voice, the

intensity of his relief made him light-headed. He followed that sound toward a narrow opening between the main part of the inn and a side wing. Suddenly a door opened in front of him and a pair of Hanish soldiers strode out.

By good fortune, they were headed in the other direction.

Rath scrambled for cover behind a two-wheeled dairy cart abandoned in a corner of the courtyard. When his foot landed on something yielding and a bit slippery, he glanced down to find several nuggets of horse dung around his right foot, and one under it. He swallowed a curse.

The soldiers walked past the narrow alcove from whence Rath had heard Maura's voice. Then, a few steps beyond it, one stopped and doubled back.

After a quick glance, he called to the other fellow and the two of them slipped into the alley. The swagger of their steps and the rough heartiness of their voices alarmed Rath.

Do not move! he ordered himself. *Keep your wits, for you will need them and so will she.*

Perhaps he had misheard and Maura was not there at all. If she was there, she might be able to get herself out without any interference from him. She had done it before, after all. No sense doing something rash that might draw too much unwelcome attention to their presence unless he had to.

The next few moments stretched on and on with every part of Rath clenched so tight he feared something would snap.

Then he heard sounds of a struggle and a cry he *knew* was Maura's. Before he could stir, she appeared, her arms pinned behind her by one of the Han. A slender trickle of blood seeped from the corner of her mouth.

Her gaze searched desperately around the courtyard. For him, no doubt. But whether to beg his help or warn him away, Rath could not tell.

Not that it mattered. For there was only one thing he could do now.

Chapter Seven

MAURA CURSED HER own foolishness and lack of caution. She had not even noticed the Han until they were upon her.

The sound of brokenhearted weeping had lured her from Blen's hay wagon into a tight little alley beside the inn's kitchen. There she had found a girl a year or two younger than herself, eating scraps begged from the innkeeper's wife.

With her improved command of Comtung, Maura soon learned that Angareth had run away from a pleasure house in Venard that served Hanish soldiers and government officials.

"They're only supposed to mate with their own kind, so they do not foul their superior race with half-castes." The girl passed a hand over her slightly swollen middle in a protective caress. "If one of the bed girls has a baby, the bawdwife does away with it soon as it is born. Sometimes sooner."

The thought made Maura's gorge rise and her heart clench. "I do not care so much what happens to me, now." Angareth scrubbed at her eyes with the wide sleeve of her tunic. "If only my baby can have a chance."

She glanced up at Maura. "Do you think I am foolish to care for it when it is not even born yet?"

When Maura began to shake her head, the girl added with anguished defiance, "Or wicked to love it even if it has Hanish blood?"

"No!" Maura reached out to stroke the girl's cheek, but Angareth flinched back. "Loving is never wicked."

Something about the girl stirred a memory within her, but Maura had no time just then to dwell on it. "Where are you bound, Angareth? How can I help you?"

The girl named a place that meant nothing to Maura. "It is a town west of here. I have family there. I only hope they will not turn me out for shame when they find out about the baby."

"Surely they will not." Maura wished she could sprout wings and fly to the Secret Glade. For the sake of girls like Angareth and boys like Snake. For Blen and Tesha and their children. And thousands more in need of deliverance. "I would let you come with me and my friends, but we are bound by a different road. Would a coin or two help speed your journey?"

Hearing the firm tread of a man, she knew Rath must have come looking for her. She wondered how she would persuade him to part with a silver or two to help this girl. He would put up an argument, no doubt, but she could not resent it. She recalled his words from the previous night when he had caught her making a poultice for a beggarman suffering a mild case of flesh rot.

"You can protect yourself from the Han if need be, lass. You are quick and clever and strong." His praise had surprised and touched her all the more because she had expected a scolding.

"If I can protect myself from the Han so well," she'd teased, "why did you come with me?"

He'd shaken his head and caressed her face with a gaze as fond as it was exasperated. "I came to protect you from yourself. I know you want to help folks and I admire you for it. But if you keep this up we will soon not have a coin between us and I will be on my way to the mines while they drag you off to a ... some place just as bad. You do not have the power to help everyone who needs it, but this Waiting King of yours will. The best thing you can do for all these folks is to reach him as quick as you can. That means staying hidden and not giving away all your herbs and all our coins."

"What if there is no king waiting for me in the Secret Glade, as you believe?" She had challenged him, hoping he might recant his doubts.

Her question had made him think, at least.

As he turned away, shaking his head, she'd heard him sigh. "If there is no Waiting King, then none of this matters."

Now, she turned to cast him a pleading gaze. She would ask five silvers for the girl, then let him bargain her down to two. In exchange for which, she would agree not to go away from the wagon again without his leave.

Angareth drew back with a high, frightened whimper.

"Do not be afraid," Maura reached for the girl's hand. "This is a friend of mine, he means you no harm."

Instead of Rath's resonant, mellow voice that made even Comtung sound tolerable, another voice rang out, loud and harsh. "What friend, wench? No friend of mine."

Before Maura could reach into her sash, the Han grabbed her and pinned her arms. Another one squeezed past them to seize Angareth.

"So which is the runaway the innkeeper reported?" the Han holding Angareth asked.

"I care not." The Han against whom Maura was struggling fetched her a clout on the side of the face that made the outlaw Turgen's blow seem like a love tap.

Maura cried out.

"They both look serviceable enough for a pleasure house." The Han shoved Maura back out of the alley. "Let's go."

What now? Maura forced herself to breathe more slowly — to watch what was going on around her and to wait for an opportunity. True, she had fallen into the clutches of the Han. But she had fought them before and won. She knew they were not invincible.

As they emerged back into the courtyard, Maura's gaze flew to Blen's hay wagon. Though she saw no sign of Rath, she did catch a glimpse of two dirty bare feet disappearing into the hay pile. Hopefully Snake would have the sense to stay there until the danger had passed ... if it passed.

What took place next happened so fast that it startled Maura quite as much as it did the Han.

Something hurtled through the air. Then the Han who held her cried out and pulled her arms so hard she feared he would wrench them from her shoulders. The other Han bellowed a curse, too, as the reek of horse dung assaulted Maura's nose.

Rath. She knew it must be him even before she heard him shout some Hanish words. They must have been a taunt or a gross insult, judging from the reactions of the two soldiers.

The next thing she knew, she was flung to the hard-packed dirt of the courtyard. Angareth fell on top of her, for which Maura was glad ... once she recaptured the breath Angareth knocked out of her.

While she lay there gasping for air, she heard the rapid thunder of hard-shod boots against the ground and the furious cries of the Han moving away from her.

"Angareth," she gasped when she had breath enough, "are you ... all right? The baby?"

"You have come to worse hurt than me." The girl rolled off Maura and tried to help her sit up. "What happened?"

Maura shook her head as she pulled herself up. It would take her too long to explain.

She needed to go to Rath's aid — the fool. It had been one thing to create such a diversion out in open country, from a good safe distance, with a horse hidden nearby to make a quick escape. In the close confines of the inn courtyard, in the middle of Westborne, it was dangerous folly.

Something tugged at her elbow.

"Come lady." The boy, Snake hovered over her. "You must get away ... now. Follow me!"

"No!" Maura staggered to her feet. "We must help Rath."

People were emerging from various doorways that opened onto the courtyard, where Rath was leading the two soldiers a chase.

Snake clamped his bony fingers around her wrist with surprising strength. "Come with me! I know this town. There is a place you can hide until night falls."

"Take Angareth." Maura tried to pull her arm away. "Rath needs me!"

The boy clung to her with stubborn insistence. "He does not need you caught by the Han, too. That is what will happen if you do not come with me now!"

A grudging part of her acknowledged the boy was probably right. His warning sounded like something Rath might tell her if he were able.

Perhaps Snake sensed he was winning her over. "Wait and see what happens. He may escape the Han on his own. Or if he is caught, you will have a better chance of rescuing him once all the fuss dies down."

"Please," begged Angareth, "let us get away from here before more soldiers come!"

The girl sounded ready to shatter from fright and the strain of her ordeal. Rath, on the other hand, had proven well capable of looking after himself. He had staged this diversion so she could get away. He would not be pleased if she refused to take it.

"Very well, then. Lead us to this hiding place of yours, Snake."

When the boy let go of her arm, Maura fished in the pockets of her sash for pinch of madfern and a few strands of spider silk. She meant to be prepared in case anyone tried to get in their way.

If only she'd been prepared when the Han had come down that alley, rather than taken unawares, Rath would not be fleeing for his life now.

Good! The Han were chasing him — both of them. Rath had hoped to draw off one, at least, so Maura could take care of the other. Two in pursuit of him alone was better still.

Well … perhaps not.

The Han appeared to know what was what and where was where in this village. He did not.

He heard them bellowing for reinforcements to join the chase. He had no one to help him — unless he counted Maura and Blen, whom he did not want to get involved.

His years as an outlaw had taught him to be fast on his feet and to think fast in a tight spot. This was one of the tightest he'd ever landed in.

He leaped over a fence, ducked under a line of drying clothes, climbed a rough stone wall, then twisted his ankle when he jumped down the other side.

If only he could find a spot to hide until nightfall.

Spotting a fowl coop set a little off the ground to discourage predators, he dove underneath it.

The stench of droppings made him gag, but he would have stayed there had he not heard a woman shriek, "There he is, under the coop! Get him!"

Rath rolled out, scrambled to his feet again and headed off in a direction from which he heard no Hanish voices.

He ducked into an alley, shinnied up a drain pipe and ran across the ridge pole of a roof.

An arrow whizzed in front of him. A step faster and he'd have been done for.

As it was, the shot startled him — checking his pace for an instant too long, making him lose his footing. He tumbled down the steep slope of the roof, arms flailing, hands groping for anything to stop his fall. But they found no hold.

He had only time for one thought as he plunged toward the ground. It was more of an appeal, really, in case there was a Giver and it could hear his thoughts.

"Let me land hard enough to kill me."
Any other outcome could only be worse.

When the racket from the streets finally quieted, Maura feared the worst.

She and Angareth cowered in a hollow gouged into the embankment beneath a bridge. She had sent Snake to see what he could find out, and to fetch the packs from Blen's wagon. While she waited for him to return and for darkness to fall, she fought to keep her fears at bay.

"Is it dark enough to come out now?" asked Angareth.

"You may go if you like. I had better stay until the boy gets back." *If* the boy got back. "I wonder what can be taking him so long?"

Maura leaned out of the hollow to listen, but a sinister hush seemed to have fallen over the town. All she could hear was the gurgle of the river, the patter of rain and the distant regular tramp of feet that sounded like a night patrol.

Where was Snake? Why had he not returned? Had she been wrong to trust him?

Perhaps he had run off with their packs to sell what he could in a neighboring town.

No. She would not let herself think that. "I hope no harm has come to him."

Angareth began to weep again. Sorry as Maura felt for the girl, she could not stem a rising surge of impatience. As Rath had once told her, in times of crisis folks could not afford to indulge their feelings too much if they meant to survive.

"I am so sorry I brought this trouble on you and your friend," Angareth sobbed. "You are one of the few folk who have shown me any kindness. Then your friend risked his safety so we could escape. I fear it may have all been for nought."

"Take heart, now." Maura wrapped her arm around the girl's shoulder. "We both made a choice, my friend and I. You are not to blame for our decisions. But you can make certain we did not act in vain."

"How is that?"

"Do not give up. Do whatever you must to make your way home. Raise your child well and be ready to give a hand to someone else who might need it. 'Give to others as —'"

"Shh!" Angareth pressed her fingers to Maura's lips. "I think I hear something."

Once Angareth fell silent, Maura heard it, too. The soft furtive sounds of someone approaching. Thinking it might be Snake returned at last, Maura brushed Angareth's hand from her mouth to call out to him.

Then it occurred to her the muted scramble of footsteps might belong to a Hanish soldier trying to sneak up on them. She pulled a wisp of spider silk from her sash and waited, her heart beating a rapid tattoo against her ribs.

"Psst!" Snake called in a whisper. "Are you still here?"

Maura's pent up breath gusted out of her in a sigh of relief. She leaned out of the hollow. "We're here. Are you all right? What news?"

As the boy moved closer, Maura heard the soft scrape of a bulky object along the loose-packed earth of the embankment. He had the packs, bless him! One of them, at least.

"There!" The boy sank down on the lip of the hollow. "We are even now for your hiding and feeding me." His gruff tone rang with a contrary note of satisfaction.

"I told you," Maura reminded him. "Our help was freely —"

Before she could finish, Snake interrupted her. "Do you not want to hear about your man?"

Her man? Those words sent a sweet ripple through Maura that was far too beguiling. Rath Talward was not hers. Nor could he ever be. But until that moment, she had never admitted to herself how much she wished he could.

"You saw him? He is alive? Why did you not bring him?"

"Hush!" snapped the boy. "Do you want every Han in this miserable village to hear you?"

Maura clenched her lips tight. She had not realized how loud she'd spoken. "Please," she whispered. "Tell me."

"He is not dead," said Snake, "and that is a bit of luck, for he fell off a roof."

"Can I go to him?" Maura's mind churned with balms and tonics she would need to prepare.

"Are you daft?" asked the boy. "The Han have him, of course, and you want to stay clear of them. I overheard two of the soldiers talking. They plan on sending him to the mines tomorrow, with their regular batch of prisoners."

A horrible sensation seized hold of Maura, like the one that had gripped her when she'd first looked over the edge of Raynor's Rift. She'd been horrified when Rath told her of the mines — the brutality, the danger, the slag poisoning a man's senses and his spirit. She had heard the dread and despair in his voice. He had been there once, or come near to it. Or perhaps someone dear to him had.

"The poor man," Angareth whispered in a tone she might have used if the boy had reported Rath dead.

Snake gave an indifferent grunt of agreement. "He was not the pleasantest fellow, but he led the Han a fine chase, I hear. The whole town is buzzing about it."

"I told that farmer fellow to get out of town before the Han start asking questions," he added. "And I fetched your packs. They were heavy to carry. Got any more food in 'em?"

A bewildered numbness eased the first sharp wrench of fear and grief that had torn Maura's heart. "I gave you all I had, but there might still be something in Rath's pack."

She groped in the darkness at the two packs, recognizing Rath's by its shape and the faint scent of him that clung to it. She reached in and hauled out a hard sausage and some bread. A shiver ran through her when the backs of her knuckles brushed against the copper wand.

An idea began to take root in her mind.

Breaking the bread and sausage in two, she gave half to each of the others. "I am sorry I have no more to offer you."

"Where will you go?" asked Snake, while chewing a large bite of food. "Now that *he's* gone?"

"He is not *gone!*" Maura clung to that feeble crumb of comfort.

"He might as well be. And it will not be safe for you or the other lady to linger in this town after sunrise. Once I eat, I am off."

"Where will *you* go?" Maura turned the question back on him.

"Away from here."

"I will not need both of these packs." Maura pushed hers toward him. "I can give you one to use or to sell as you wish."

"For what?"

"For helping Angareth, here, get back to her village. She needs the aid of someone like you, who knows his way about and how to survive."

When the boy did not reply right away, Maura fumbled in the darkness for his hand. "Will you ... please?"

He only let her hold it a moment before he pulled away. "I reckon so."

"Good." Maura wondered how she could feel such a weight of responsibility for two people she had barely met. "Now, I need one last favor from you before we part. Not because you owe me anything. You have already more than paid any debt between us. And not because I can barter for it, because I have nothing left that I dare give away."

"What?" Snake sounded altogether suspicious of such a one-sided exchange.

"Earlier you said you do not know where to find the *twarith*." Though torn about what she must do next, Maura knew she would need help. "Please think. Is there anywhere I might go to look for them?"

"Sorry," said Snake. "You get to hear about them from folk. Or one of them turns up out of nowhere, then disappears just as quick."

Maura swallowed her disappointment. Once she made her choice, she would have to operate alone. The prospect daunted her but she would not let it stop her. She had come too far and learned too much for that.

Angareth tugged at her sleeve.

"Your pardon," said Maura. "I know you must want to get on your way while the darkness lasts."

"I do," said the girl, "but it is not that. I know where you might find the people you seek. At least, I think I do."

"Truly?" Maura caught the girl's hand in a tight squeeze. "Where? How?"

"In the next village north. I was looking for something to eat and an old woman told me I might get help at a tavern called 'The Hawk and Hound.' When I found the place, I saw some Hanish soldiers coming and going, so I kept away."

That did sound suspicious, even to Maura.

But Snake piped up, "I hear the *twarith* like to work right under the noses of the Han, but I never knew what that meant."

"It makes a kind of sense, I suppose." Maura pulled Rath's pack toward her. "I reckon I must go and see for myself."

If nothing else it would put her some distance closer to Everwood. And the walk would give her time to decide what she must do.

Follow the dictates of duty and destiny? Or heed the pleading of her heart?

The pain brought him back to consciousness. Rath cursed his ill luck for being alive now that he had lost his freedom.

And yet, a small but stubborn part of him clung to life. For he now cared for something more than his own life or even his freedom. Not just Maura as a woman, but also as a token of something greater.

The pain struck him again. On the other cheek this time, accompanied by a jingling sound. At least it was ordinary pain, not mortcraft. Rath wondered how long his luck would hold.

"What is a dung-throwing hired guard doing with so much silver in his pouch?" someone asked.

Rath coaxed his eyes open a slit to find himself tied to a chair in a bare room, facing a dark-masked Xenoth who swung his well-laden coin pouch with lazy menace. Staring at it, Rath regretted every silver he had kept Maura from giving away. If he'd shared her generosity instead of guarding against it, those coins would have done some good, rather than making the pouch heavier to strike him.

Though he knew it would invite another blow, at the very least, Rath could not resist shrugging his shoulders and giving an impudent answer to the death-mage's question. "Perhaps I am very good at what I do."

To his surprise, the Xenoth let out a raspy laugh at his show of audacity. "An Embrian with some spirit — what a novelty. I am also very good at what I do."

The coin pouch flew upward, catching Rath under the chin in a blow that jerked his head back and made him bite his tongue.

"Enough jesting," his inquisitor snapped. "Where did you get the silver?"

Rath spat a mouthful of blood onto the floor. "Stole it."

"That is better." The Xenoth tossed the bag of coins into the corner as if it had served his purpose and no longer interested him. "Who did you steal it from?"

"A trader." That was almost true.

"Where did you come from?"

"The Hitherland."

The death-mage's parched lips curved in chilling mockery of a smile. "What a pity you had not stayed there."

A man in his right wits should be terrified at this moment. Paralyzed, soiling-his-breeches terrified. Rath was not.

Perhaps unmasking that death-mage back in Prum and seeing the frailty that lay beneath the menacing image had robbed the Xenoth of their power over his fears. Or perhaps that fall from the roof had knocked all sense out of him.

"I will make you a bargain." Rath coaxed the words around his swollen, throbbing tongue. "I will go back where I came from if you go back where you came from and take your whole slagging race with you."

The Xenoth whipped out his wand. It was wrought of a rare green metal known as *strup*. In its tip glittered a venomous green poison-gem.

Now, fear snaked through Rath's marrow. He had heard what poison-gems did to a body — the excruciating corruption that swelled and twisted limbs, making the victim retch blood while his flesh broke out in festering sores.

"Nefarion!" A voice rang out from behind Rath.

Though it was scratchy and strident, Rath thought it as sweet as bird song, for it delayed his coming torment.

The death-mage glanced away from Rath. He switched from Comtung to Hanish. "What are you doing here, Varoque?"

"I have come to fetch more workers for the mines," announced the other man — another death-mage, Rath assumed. Ordinary Han did not speak to the Xenoth in that contemptuous tone. "They are dying off faster than we can replace them up there. Our production is falling and the Lord Governor is not pleased."

Though Rath grieved the dead miners, he was glad they

were finally free of the mines and the slag. He even admired them for dying at a rate to cause trouble for the Han. Closing his eyes, he struggled to keep his features slack, so the Xenoth would not guess he understood them.

"Climbed a little too high, have you, Varoque?" asked Neferion, his tone as venomous as his wand. "It is a steep fall from where you perch, and there is always someone looking to give you a little nudge over the edge."

"Are you too comfortable here, fool? Torturing petty miscreants to keep your powers from failing?" Even in a foreign language, Rath understood that threat.

"Perhaps you would like to be sent on a mission over the mountains? The Lord Governor thinks we have not kept a careful enough eye on those barbarians."

"You would not dare give me such an opportunity to prove my worth."

"A chance to be broken or stripped, you mean. Mordake shattered his power on some old fool of a sorcerer. Vulmar has disappeared along with two of his men. And Nithard did what honor required after he was stripped of his mask and wand."

That piece of information intrigued Rath and made him struggle to conceal a flicker a pride. Did he understand right? If someone took a death-mage's wand and mask, then the mage was obliged by some twisted code of honor to do away with himself?

He must find a way to live long enough that he could relay this news to someone capable of using it to advantage.

The first name that leapt to mind was the Waiting King.

Chapter Eight

BY THE TIME she found her way to "The Hawk and Hound," Maura was reeling from fatigue

She had hoped to reach the tavern before too many customers arrived, especially Hanish ones. Unfortunately she had lost her way for a time in the dark after parting with Snake and Angareth. It had not helped that she'd been too preoccupied with the struggle inside herself to keep her wits about her.

Part of her insisted she must leave Rath Talward to look after himself while she made haste to Everwood. The ivory maps sewn into the hem of her tunic seemed to grow heavier with every step, reminding her of the responsibility with which she had been entrusted. She must not put the quest at risk to gratify her own selfish desires. Even if he did not believe in the Waiting King, Rath would not want her putting herself in danger on his account.

She did not *need* him to reach the Secret Glade. Every challenge overcome since leaving Windleford had helped convince her she was more capable than she had ever imagined. Once she woke the Waiting King, she could beg him to deliver Rath from the mines — the first and only favor she would ever ask of her lord.

Despite all those excellent arguments, she could not bring herself to abandon Rath without at least trying.

That was what had brought her here, to a village whose name she did not know and a tavern rumored to host some people who might help her.

Under her breath, she murmured a plea to the Giver, an old one Langbard had taught her many years ago. "Light my path. Guide my steps. Throw the mantle of your protection around me."

With that, she hurried across the street and pushed open the tavern door. For a moment she stood just over the threshold, letting her eyes grow accustomed to the dimness inside. The smells of hearty food and strong ale washed over her along with the sound of music from a flute and drum all but drowned out by a few loud voices.

When her vision brightened she saw the place boasted a dozen tables, less than half of which were presently occupied. Some Embrian villagers sat at those nearest her, while most of the noise came from a far corner table where three Hanish soldiers sat, quaffing the contents of oversized ale mugs.

Even though she was mostly screened from their view by the other patrons, and two of the soldiers had their backs to her, she still felt horribly exposed and vulnerable. Flitting from shadow to shadow, she made her way to the bar where a short woman was filling mugs from an ale keg.

"Pardon me," said Maura in Comtung.

The woman moved closer and turned an ear toward Maura. "Speak up lass, or I'll never hear you over all the tunes and talk!"

Maura sucked in a deep breath then blurted out the words she'd been practicing. *"Ban henwa chan Anreg, reg fi dimroth."*

In Old Embrian, it meant, "In the name of the Giver, let me have water." An innocent enough request to make in a tavern. Except that *dimroth*, the *twara* word for "water" sounded a great deal like *limroth*, the word for "help." To anyone who did not speak Old Embrian, it would mean nothing.

The last words were just leaving her lips when the music suddenly stopped, and most of the talk lulled at the same moment. Her strange speech seemed to hover in the silence, calling everyone's attention.

All that kept Maura from fleeing was her certainty that the Hanish soldiers would be after her in no time. So she waited, scarcely breathing, groping for the small amount of madfern she had left, hoping it would be enough if they approached her.

Behind the bar, the woman dispensing ale seemed unaware that the mug in her hand was full and overflowing. When she finally noticed, she set the mug down and bustled out from behind the bar, laughing. "This way, lass. The kitchen is this way."

Over her shoulder she called in Comtung to no one in particular, "Up-North girl looking for work. How queer they talk! I could hardly understand a word."

The music started up again, louder than before. When Maura heard no obvious sounds of pursuit, she started to breathe again.

The woman propelled her down a narrow galley way talking loudly in Comtung about food preparation and waiting on tables. Abruptly, she pushed Maura into a shallow alcove that held shelves of crockery.

Switching to Embrian, she demanded in a vexed whisper, "Were you not told to come around back?"

Maura shook her head, chiding her dangerous lapse in not thinking of that herself.

The woman reached past her and gave the left-hand wall of the alcove a solid shove. The whole wall swung out like a door leading to an even narrower passageway.

"What happened to your face?" whispered the woman. "Is your man a slaggie? We see a lot of that."

"No!" Maura's hand flew to her bruised cheek. She remembered how anxious Rath had been that folks not believe he would harm her. "A soldier did this."

"Well, mind your step," the woman warned once the door had closed behind them, plunging the passage into darkness. "Or you will have more bruises to match that one. There's stairs coming. Just feel your way down."

Fearing she might tumble and break her neck, Maura

groped her way down the tight, winding stairwell. Until about halfway, when some feeble light from below made it possible to see where she was going.

A few steps later, she emerged into a large, low ceilinged room lit by a few candles. A woman and two small children were sleeping on a pile of straw in one corner. In another corner stood a small work bench around which hung bunches of dried herbs. An old man working at the bench turned toward Maura and the barwife, beckoning.

"You go talk to Calvance," whispered the woman. "I'd best get back up to keep the ale flowing."

She glanced at the old man. "Can you give me a bit of muddlewort to make our customers forget they saw this lass come in?"

Clavance plucked a linen pouch from the bench and tossed it to her. "That is our last until the new crop blossoms. Make it go as far as you can."

He turned back to Maura. "Now my dear, how can I help you?" The words had barely left his mouth before he flinched at the sight of her face. "Foolish of me to ask. I could try to apply a poultice but ..."

"... they are hard to bind on to the face. I know." Maura shrugged off her pack and sank onto a stool near the workbench. "It is not for healing that I have come. Are you the ones folk call the *twarith*?"

Not that she had any doubt.

"Folks call us many things." Clavance passed a hand over the bald crown of his head in a gesture than reminded Maura of Langbard. "Fools, busybodies, dreamers ... even sorcerers. We prefer to call ourselves *twarith*."

He regarded her with a cautious, probing stare. "Do you know what that means?"

Maura nodded and smiled. She had never realized how comforting it could be to have contact with someone who believed as she did.

"*Sholia ban Anreg marboeth.*" She chanted the familiar words of the First Precept. *Trust in the Giver's Providence.*

The man's gray brows shot up. He peered closer at Maura's sash. "Who *are* you, daughter?"

His hushed tone betokened fear ... or awe.

"A traveler," she replied, "with far still to go and much to do. One who needs your help."

Clavance nodded. "Rest here and eat, then. You look weary. I will call a gathering for tonight."

Where was Maura, now? Rath wondered as the cart carrying a new shipment of miners lurched up a winding trail into the Blood Moon Mountains.

The Great Plain of Westborne spread out below. With his gaze, Rath traced a route northward, willing Maura to follow it.

The man to his left stirred and yawned. "Didn't we get lucky," he muttered quietly so the Hanish guards would not overhear. "A ride all the way to the top. Before, they always marched prisoners up. Lots died on the way, I hear."

Was it luck? Rath wondered. Or an opportunity from the Giver? Would it hurt him to pretend so, at least?

He leaned toward the man who had spoken and whispered just loud enough for a few others nearby to hear. "They are losing men faster than they can replace. They need to look after us better if they want to get their stinking ore out."

A low buzz rippled through the cart as that news passed from man to man. Vacant eyes flickered with life, or the possibility of it. Limbs slack with despair, moved and straightened.

Those subtle signs gave Rath enough encouragement to add, "No group of prisoners coming to these mines ever had a better chance of getting out of them alive than we do."

"Alive?" An older man gave a hollow, barky laugh, then covered it with a cough. "What kind of *life* is that? Slaves to the slag?"

"Where would we go if we did escape?" muttered another. "The Xenoth would only find us and fetch us back."

"Or worse," grunted a third fellow.

Rath could feel the slow suffocation of despair settling over them again. "What if I told you the days of the death-mages in this kingdom are numbered and fast running out?"

"I would bid you spin a story that's easier to swallow," the older man grumbled.

But the younger fellow sitting beside Rath asked, "What makes you say so? You seem to know a good deal."

"I know the Waiting King is coming."

Several of the other prisoners broke into hoarse laughter.

A whip cracked above their heads and one of the Hanish guards bellowed, "Quiet, lowlings! See how much you laugh in the bowels of the mountain!"

For a time they fell silent, as ordered. Then the young fellow beside Rath whispered, "The death mage must have made your brain rot with that cursed wand of his. The Waiting King is a tale for children and daft folk."

"So I thought," said Rath. "But I have seen the Destined Queen with my own eyes."

A vivid image of Maura rose in his mind. Of that first day in the Betchwood when she had turned him invisible. Of the way she had subdued that houseful of Han in Prum and how she had found the map. Of their battle with the lank wolves and how she had braved her fear to cross Raynor's Rift in defense of her beliefs. He remembered the stories she had told him, the spells she had taught him and the healing she had worked on him.

"I tell you —" his voice pulsed with conviction "— the lady is on her way to the Secret Glade at this very moment."

He braced himself for the other men to laugh again, but they did not. They stared at him, their eyes and their features betraying the inner battle waged within each man — between doubt and faith, despair and hope.

Perhaps he had no right to speak with such fervor when he still had not vanquished all his own doubts. But this was the only means he had left to serve Maura. He would not let some quibble about belief hold him back.

He watched as the others mulled over his claims. Their scowls and furrowed brows bespoke their disbelief. Yet hope quickened in the depths of their eyes in spite of their efforts to quench it. No matter what they might try to tell themselves to the contrary, they *wanted* something to believe in.

As he had, without ever realizing it ... until now.

"Destined Queen!" the older man muttered in a tone of scorn. "Waiting King! What if that hogswill is all true? By the time they could do us any good, none of us will care about anything beyond our next sniff of slag."

Rath wished he could deny it, but he could not. They would soon arrive at the mines to have their necks branded and their first sniff of slag forced upon them. After that, no force would be necessary. Unless Maura found some magical means to fly, she would have at least a week's hard traveling ahead of her to reach the Secret Glade. Then ...

Then, nothing, perhaps.

His gaze strayed back toward the plain, then fell on a straggly cluster of weeds that had taken stubborn root in the thin, rocky mountain soil at the edge of the road. The sight of that plant kindled a memory.

"Maur — er ... the Destined Queen told me of a mountain plant that helps a body resist the slag."

In furtive whispers, he shared the description of freewort that Maura had given him. On the slim chance it might help, he lifted a silent plea to the Giver to let them find some.

"If we can find this plant, and if it does what I claim, will that be proof enough for you? Will you follow me and rise up like men instead of cowering like slaves?"

Though he'd delivered it in a whisper, Rath still thought it a stirring speech. From the time he'd reached manhood, he had rued his dubious gift for attracting followers. Now, he hoped he had not lost the knack just when he needed it most.

But he had, it seemed. For none of the other men spoke, or would look him in the eye.

Well, he would rebel against the Han, even if he had to act alone, with no hope of success. After all ...

"What have we got to lose?" muttered the older man with a shrug. "If it all comes to naught, at least we are out of our torment that much sooner."

That should have been a discouraging thought. But Rath found it strangely liberating. The other prisoners appeared to share that feeling. A faint murmur circulated among them. Not zealous or exultant in tone, but grimly defiant and resolved.

He held out his hand, palm up to the older man. Unless he was sorely mistaken, this fellow had the makings of a fine second in command. "Rath Talward of Nonce. Some call me Wolf."

"Hail, Wolf." The man placed his hand on top of Rath's. "They call me Anulf. If we can find this weed of yours and it does all you claim, then count me with you."

Before Rath's grin could spread too broad, Anulf warned him, "Mind, though — *if* can sometimes be a big word."

"You mean to go where and do what?" The tallest of the men gathered around Maura in the cellar of "The Hawk and Hound" shook his head as if to correct his faulty hearing. "Lady, you must know that is madness! No Embrian goes up into the

Blood Moon Mountains of his own accord."

Maura had hoped the support of the *twarith* would shore up her resolve and perhaps show her the Giver's will. Strangely, their opposition had tempered her determination and made her believe that small, stubborn whisper in her heart might speak for the Giver.

"This Embrian will go of *her* own accord," she declared. "With or without your aid, though I would welcome it."

A pretty young woman with large, soulful eyes spoke up. "I admire your courage, mistress, but what you ask has never been the way of the *twarith*. We offer help — food, shelter, healing, hiding to those in need. Thus we live our belief in the Giver's precepts and strive to pass them on to others along with the material gifts we provide in the Giver's name."

Maura made the gesture of respect. "I honor your faithfulness to the Giver in these dark times. Others might have been tempted to doubt in the existence of a generous creating spirit. Or been moved to hoard what little they received for the benefit of themselves and their own."

Though the woman acknowledged Maura's praise, her fine mouth was set in unmistakable opposition. "Already the Han persecute us for what we do, though not as hard as they might. We have heard of Hanish women in Venard secretly appealing to the *twarith* for healing of their children. Our quiet, steadfast example may win them over one day."

"True, Delith. Very true." Several folk standing near the young woman murmured their support.

Delith lifted her hand to signify that she was not finished speaking. "The Han tolerate us because we engage in no open rebellion against them. If we take part in what you propose, they will make it their business to crush us. Then what will happen to the innocent victims of their tyranny?"

Not long ago, Maura would have been swayed by Delith's eloquent sincerity. After all she had experienced and with

Rath's life at stake, she must not lose faith in her destiny, now.

"If the Han are driven from our borders, there will be no more tyranny. The *twarith* will be at liberty to continue your work. Though, with the Giver's blessing, there may be less need ... or perhaps different ones."

"Who said anything about driving out the Han?" the tall man asked.

"I say it," replied Maura. "The Waiting King will wait no longer. The day of his return is at hand, and when he rises, Embria must rise with him. To do otherwise would be to spurn a most generous gift."

"The Waiting King?" cried the tall man. "And who are you? His herald?"

"In a way, perhaps." Maura quailed before the disbelief she saw in all their eyes. Was this some sort of punishment for her own early doubts?

"You must follow the voice of the Giver as you hear it," she turned away from them with a sigh. "And so must I."

"Wait, mistress." For the first time since the other *twarith* had gathered to hear her plea, the wizard Clavance spoke. "I am old, and perhaps would be more bother than help to you in such an enterprise. But I knew the Blood Moon Mountains before the Han ever began their cursed delving. If a guide will be of use to you, I will come."

For a moment, Maura did not trust herself to speak, or to turn and face him. One of the heaviest burdens of this destiny was the knowledge of how grave a price good folks had paid to aid her, and how many more might before she was done.

Rath Talward had never thought the day would come when he'd be grateful for slag.

But as he lay on the hard floor of the Beastmount Mine's

third level, his voice all but drowned out by the heavy snoring of true slag-slaves, he savored the way the black dust blunted his fear and tempered any rash impulses that might have doomed him and his comrades.

It had been a welcome surprise to discover how heavily the Han relied on slag to maintain control over their prisoners. The number of miners each guard had to watch was absurd, and those working below the first level were not well-armed.

Rath had passed five of the longest days of his life in the Beastmount Mine. Five days of grinding toil, vile food, stale air, suffocating darkness and fights between irritable prisoners hungry for their next sniff.

They had also been busy days of gathering information, laying plans and a growing bond with his fellow rebels. Privately Rath wondered how much of their resistance to the slag came from chewing on freewort leaves and flowers. And how much from having a little hope and purpose.

The time had now come when any more knowledge they could gather about the operation of the mine would not be worth the delay it cost them. The longer they stayed, the deeper into the mine they would be transferred and the more likely something might go wrong to trap them here forever. Besides all that, their precious supply of freewort was dwindling fast.

As the footsteps of the guard faded into the distance, Rath flexed his aching muscles. "It looks like our time is at hand, lads. Does everyone remember his part?"

One by one, the men around him stirred from their feigned sleep and muttered their instructions. By the time they all finished, his whole body was itching for action. So were theirs, it seemed, for they sprang to their feet, some quivering in their eagerness, others taut as drawn bowstrings ready to fire.

"Hold a moment." Rath motioned them toward him in the close dimness. A bewildering impulse had seized him and he could not deny it.

"Come." He thrust out his hand. "Everybody in. Before we start, let us ask the Giver's favor on what we are about to do."

He expected at least one of them to scoff ... maybe more. Instead, they rallied to him readily, with an air of reverence that defied this unholiest of places.

He managed to string together a few words of Old Embrian, though he probably mangled them beyond the understanding of anyone *but* the Giver. Still, he fancied he could hear Maura whispering those words in his ear. They lit a blaze of confidence deep inside him. Rath sensed it in the others as well. It was as if the act of praying alone went some way toward answering their prayer.

Off in the distance, the guard's footsteps began to draw closer again.

"To your places, everyone!" Rath whispered. "And wait for the right moment."

He settled down on the floor near Anulf and commenced a pretended snore, all the while listening for the guard.

At just the right moment, Anulf began to twitch and gasp and make the queerest noises Rath had ever heard. If he had not known better, Rath would have been convinced the man was truly in the grip of a palsy fit.

Anulf did not have to keep up his performance long. The guard's footsteps quickened.

"What is all this?" he demanded.

The rest of the men continued their feigned slumber. Anulf continued his feigned fit.

"You!" The Han bent down to give Anulf a shake.

At that instant, Rath and four others leapt to their feet and grabbed him. Odger, a former blacksmith with massive hands, clapped one over the guard's mouth. Theto, a nimble-fingered young pickpocket from Ulwin, deftly removed the pouch of slag from the guard's belt, opened it and held it to the Han's nose.

In a very short time, his struggling ceased and they were able to gag him and strip off his armor.

"Goar!" a voice called in Hanish. "Any trouble down there?"

Now came the moment Rath had been preparing for. He had been listening to the night guard, Goar, particularly when the fellow spoke in his native tongue to the other guards.

He called back in Hanish, using his best imitation of Goar's voice, "Just one of these cursed lowlings having a fit."

"Kick him hard in the head," the other guard advised. "That will quiet him quick enough."

Rath dredged up a rumble of malicious laughter, knowing how soon the other guard would join his comrade.

As the one closest in size to Goar, Rath donned the Han's armor as quickly as the others stripped it off. Once he was ready, he called for help. Soon both guards lay bound, gagged and slagged, while two of the rebels were armed.

Before long, they were in full control of level three. Now came the next big challenge. Each level of the mine was connected to the ones above and below by long rope ladders that were only lowered when someone needed to descend a level, then immediately raised again. If necessary, the Han could cut access to the upper levels, starving out any rebellion brewing below.

Was that what had happened recently to create the current shortage of miners? Rath wondered as he and his men approached the passage between levels two and three. Well, the Han had not reckoned on a group of prisoners resistant to the slag, with a leader who could speak passable Hanish.

One of his team had spied out the procedure for getting the ladder lowered.

Now Rath called up, "Some trouble on level six. They're sending a messenger up to report to the Leader."

"Always level six, isn't it?" grumbled the man above as he lowered the ladder. "What do they expect, the guards get almost as big a dose of slag as the prisoners. Hope I never get booted down that deep."

By the time the ladder guard had finished his litany of complaints, Rath had subdued him, and the team of Embrian imposters in Hanish armor had clambered up to the next level.

With their disguises, they secured level two even more quickly than they had level three.

"Now ..." Rath struggled to curb a sense of elation that no amount of slag could subdue, "it is time for us to split up. Anulf, you take your men and go after the lower levels. Rouse as many of the prisoners as you can and send them up. I want them boiling up to the surface just about the time their night dose wears off."

"I will see you up above, Wolf." Anulf clasped his hand. "And if I do not make it, I will go to the Giver happy to have been part of this."

"Do not talk so daft, man!" Rath growled. "Of course I will see you up above. I am counting on you."

An unfamiliar sensation twisted deep in his gut as he watched Anulf's men depart and turned back to the ones he would lead. Never again would he be able to lose followers without it cutting him to the bone.

He forced his mind back to their mission. "Keep your wits about you, everyone, and nobody get cocky. The Han did not overrun our kingdom because they are cowardly or stupid."

Perhaps not. But they had become as dependent on the slag, in their own way, as the miners had. Tonight they would pay the price for it.

Rath knew the conquest of level one would come at greater risk than those on two and three. Since the upper level housed newer prisoners, not yet fully subdued by the slag, the guards were more numerous and vigilant.

All went according to plan, until one guard they approached noticed the lack of plumes on their helmets. He called out an alarm before the blacksmith snapped his neck. Other guards came running and Rath's men were forced to fight with unfamiliar weapons in a dim confined space.

When the pickpocket, Theto, took a bad wound to his arm, Rath feared the tide of their small battle might turn against them. But he had not reckoned on the level one prisoners.

Roused from sleep by the noise, not yet fuddled by slag, a few of them recognized what was happening. Unarmed, they threw themselves upon the Hanish guards.

"Wolf!" One of Anulf's men staggered up to Rath panting. "Have you secured the last ladder yet? The prisoners from the lower levels are pouring up. There will be no holding them if they get this far."

Rath cursed. "Pull up the ladder between here and level two until I send word." He turned to his own men. "Hunwald, find something to bind Theto's arm. Strang, stop any prisoners from the lower levels who reach here until you hear me call. Then relay my signal and let them come."

He motioned to the blacksmith and two others who had given good account of themselves with their weapons. "Odger, Tobryn, Wake, you are with me."

They rushed to the ladder passage where Rath called up the lie that had gotten them up two levels so far.

"Level six?" called down the young Han in charge of the surface ladder. "What kind of trouble? I was told to let no one up until the change of guard at daybreak."

"Daybreak?" Rath bellowed. If they did not get up that ladder soon, all could be lost. "I will break your head when I get up there, you unlicked whelp! And put you on report to the Leader for letting the situation down here get out of hand!"

"Very well, then," replied the young Han in a sullen tone as the ladder unfurled. "But you will take responsibility if there is trouble. What did you say your name was again?"

"I did not say." Rath pushed the young guard through the

hole to the first level.

Below he heard Tobryn calling to the others that the way to the surface was clear.

"Best take off these Hanish helmets, lads," he advised his men as they climbed to the surface. "So our own folk do not turn on us."

He knew once the prisoners came pouring up, it would only be a matter of time before an alarm was raised and they found themselves under fierce attack. "Remember, we hold the head of this ladder until the last Embrian climbs out of that cursed pit. After that, where each of you go and what you do is up to you. But you will go with my thanks and blessing."

He pulled the Hanish helmet off his head and threw it as far as it would fly. Seldom had he felt a more welcome sensation than the cool breeze of a mountain daybreak blowing through his hair. He did not have long to savor it.

Chapter Nine

THE FIRST WAVE of miners came scrambling out of the mountain, like ants from a colony under attack. Most of them were black as ants and some were armed with stingers in the shape of Hanish blades taken from the guards below.

Their escape did not go unnoticed for long. A small party of day guards ran toward the mine head with blades drawn. Between Rath, his crew and the emerging prisoners, the Han did not last long. But two managed to escape the rout and dash back to the barracks.

An alarm bell rang from the barracks tower, loud and wild. Soon after, Hanish soldiers poured from the barracks faster than miners were climbing from the pit head.

As the first wave broke upon them, Rath threw himself into the fray with all his strength, speed and cunning. It felt as if his whole life, he had been a weapon in the hands of some greater power, being perfectly crafted and honed for this fight.

"Wolf!"

Rath was able to turn in the direction of the voice, for one of the prisoners had dealt a mortal blow from behind to the Han who had attacked him.

"Anulf!" he cried. "You made it! Well done!"

"You have not done so badly, yourself." Anulf hefted his stolen blade and glanced around the pit head, as if looking for a Han to use it on, but finding none readily available. "I would say Beastmount Mine will be ours before the sun is fully risen."

Then, above the cries of battle, a shrill, eerie wail rose.

"Slag!" Anulf spat on the ground. "It is one of those cursed death-mages."

Rath knew what he must do, though his courage faltered at the thought. "He has a fearful weapon in that wand, but he is only one man for all that. While I draw his spell, you must take some of our lads and go for his back."

"Are you sure, Wolf? I have taken a lick from one of those cursed things, and I would not willingly put myself in the path of one again."

"I am not *willing*, but it must be done and I cannot ask another man to do it." The screaming stopped as abruptly as it had begun. Perhaps the Xenoth was looking for a worthier victim. "Once he goes for me, strike hard and fast. I may not be able to stand it long."

With that, both men set off — Anulf readily, Rath forcing himself each step. Was he mad — to put himself in front of a wand-wielding death-mage, knowing what awaited him? He had better not think about it too much, or he might turn and run.

The Xenoth was all that stood in their way, now, Rath told himself. Once Anulf and his men brought the death-mage down, any other resistance was sure to collapse.

So he strode through the fray determined to appear braver and more confident than he felt. The fighting seemed to part before him until he caught the Xenoth's attention.

"Death-mage!" he bellowed, followed by a Hanish insult.

This was getting to be a habit with him — making himself a target for the Han. Only this time he would not run away and lead them a chase, with at least a hope of escape.

The Xenoth raised his wand.

Rath tried to brace himself for what would come. But that was impossible.

Still he locked his lips together, a mute challenge to the Xenoth to make him cry out. Then the pain hit him.

It was a different kind of pain than he had suffered before — a lethal brew of fear and all a man's worst nightmares. He saw Maura violated and murdered before his eyes, one hand reached out to him, her gaze imploring. But he could not go to her aid.

One tiny, detached part of his mind tried to reassure him it was only a wicked illusion, but his heart could not believe that. With each beat, it ached to bursting.

He was vaguely aware of Anulf and the others fighting the Han who guarded the death-mage's back. This would soon be over — it must, before it shattered his mind and heart, making him crave the slag as his only remedy.

Then a cry went up from the Han, making the death-mage ease his grip on Rath for an instant. But it brought Rath no relief.

He saw a second Xenoth surging up the mountain to join the first. At his back marched a troop of Hanish reinforcements to crush the revolt.

The sight robbed Rath of all hope. For he could not deny *it* was real.

The frantic ringing of a bell and the distant tumult of battle roused Maura from a restless doze.

Was she too late?

After laying their plans, gathering supplies and recruiting helpers, she and some of the *twarith* had started up the mountain the previous day. Maura could hardly wait to tear off the black robe she had been wearing since then.

Though it had never belonged to a real death-mage, there was still something oppressive about the hastily sewn disguise. As though it might transform her from the outside in. Or perhaps that was the insidious effect of the copper wand. Either way, she longed to rid herself of both, once and for all.

As soon as she had liberated Rath from the mine.

Her small troop was ready. On the way up the mountain,

they had ambushed enough Hanish checkpoint guards to provide everyone with armor, however ill-fitting. More than once she had jolted out of a moment's abstraction to feel a fleeting twist of terror at the sight of herself surrounded by Han.

Some of the *twarith* were willing to fight the Han with their own weapons. Others, Maura had taught the binding spell. Their meeting cellar beneath "The Hawk and Hound" had provided a well-stocked arsenal of spider silk. Clavance and two others skilled in the healing arts had come prepared with herbs and linen to tend any wounded.

Within a short distance of the mine, they had stopped to eat and rest before the attack they had planned to make once all the day guards went down to relieve the night guards. Then there would be the fewest Han above ground for her party to subdue. That information had come second hand from an escaped miner the *twarith* had given aid a few months before. It made a kind of sense, and it was all they had. Maura hoped it was still correct.

The noise from up the mountain did not sound promising. But the Giver had brought them this far. They could not turn back now.

In case any of her followers was even considering it, Maura urged them on. "Come! The miners may have risen up. They will need our help. Fly to their aid!"

She could not have spoken any words better calculated to rouse and inspire the *twarith*. For years they had labored in secret opposition to the Han. Now was their opportunity for a bold act of defiance in aid of their most oppressed countrymen.

Maura barely had time to pull the despised black hood over her head and grab the copper wand, before the rush of *twarith* carried her the final short distance up the mountain.

All was chaos around the mine head.

Miners fought Hanish guards with no weapons but their fists and feet. The sight brought Maura a surge of hope.

But what was this? Some Han fighting their own comrades with blades? The situation puzzled her for a moment, until she realized many of the men in Hanish armor wore no helms. Nor did they have the long flowing plumes of flaxen hair.

She turned to her comrades, half-laughing in a frenzy of relief. "Take off your helmets and keep a sharp eye who you attack! Some of those men in Hanish armor are Embrians!"

A cry went up from the *twarith*, as they came to understand what was happening. Casting their helmets aside, they threw themselves into the fray.

"You had best take off your disguise, too, Mistress," Clavance called to Maura. "Else someone may strike you down for a death-mage!"

"With pleasure!" She all but ripped the hood from her head and tore the robe in her haste to remove it.

She was about to hurl the copper wand away, too, when her gaze flew to the other black robed figure among the combatants, and his wand of *eisendark*.

Clearly he had it pointed at someone. But where were the screams?

Then she saw him. A tall figure in Hanish armor, a few day's growth of beard stubbling his lean cheeks. Tawny hair streaked with dark mine dust, desperately needed another good washing. No sound escaped him, but the taut twist of his limbs and features betrayed mute torment.

Maura ran toward him. Blades clashed above her head. A hand snaked out to grab her ankle, but she kicked free of it.

The last time she had thrust this wand between a death-mage and his prey, she had not known what she was doing nor had she guessed what might happen. This time, she knew.

She would have given almost anything to avoid doing it, but there was one thing … or rather one person, she could not abandon to the cruelest of mortcraft. No matter what it cost her.

She stepped between Rath and his tormentor.

For a delirious instant, a rush of power and mastery swept through her. Some seductive intuition whispered that she could be mistress of this potent dark force if only she had the courage and the will to dare it. It reminded her of all the evil the Han had committed against her people, urging her to take vengeance.

With such power at her disposal, what would she need with the Waiting King? She could be a warrior queen in her own right, second to no man, free to take a consort of her own choosing.

How that notion tempted her!

She glanced back at Rath to discover he had fallen, spent from his ordeal. His gaze sought hers, surely to urge that she claim the power offered her.

Instead he stared at her with aversion, as though she had suddenly grown repulsive to behold. Her grip on the power wavered, as did its grip upon her. Then it reasserted itself.

Never mind about the man, it urged her. If she wanted him, she would have the power to make him love her.

"No!" She wrenched her gaze away from Rath to face the death-mage once more.

Is it you who put such thoughts in my head to beguile me?

Better than that. I slither through your mind, collecting your deepest desires, then I offer them to you. You can have that same skill and more if you will only take it. Be warned, though. Either you master this power and make it your own or it will master you.

Suffocating darkness loomed over her, a warning of what she risked by defying him. Then as her desires lured her and her fears pushed her, she heard her own voice asking Langbard, "Why me? I am nobody special. I have no wish to be queen."

She'd had no such wish then, nor did she now. Perhaps that was what made her special and fitted her for this destiny.

Only if I try to master this dark force will it truly master me … as it has mastered you.

Though she held onto the wand with all her strength, it felt as though she had let go the leash of a huge, ravenous beast.

Which now turned to consume her.

Maura had rescued him from the death-mage's torment only to thrust him into worse. Where the Xenoth had taunted him with visions of Maura despoiled in body, Rath now saw the danger that she would be violated in spirit.

Never had she looked more beautiful or more regal, poised upon the field of battle, in a duel of wills with the death-mage. But she looked nothing like the woman he had come to love. There was something vain and cruel in her eyes that mocked him and his presumptuous feelings for her. If that was to be the price for saving him, he would rather perish.

Sensing her struggle to resist, he tried to call out to her, but he could not make his voice heard above the tumult of the fighting. He tried to rise and go to her, but his limbs were still half-numb.

This was one battle she would have to fight *for* herself and *by* herself. The only thing he could do was believe in her as he had never been able to believe in anyone or anything else. He must trust that her strength and goodness would prevail.

As he watched, Maura's body tensed and she twitched a little from side to side as if pulled in two different directions by powerful forces. Then, the wand in her hand burst apart with a violent crash, like a tall tree struck by lightning. Maura swayed and crumpled to the ground.

At the same instant, the death-mage's wand shattered, too. Rath scarcely noticed.

From somewhere, he dredged up the strength to drag himself toward Maura. Picking up the blade that had fallen from his hand when the death-mage attacked, he prepared to defend her with what was left of his life.

When someone rushed toward him, he swung the blade with more strength than he'd thought he possessed. Fortunately Anulf had quick reflexes.

"Steady on, Wolf." He dodged Rath's blow. "It's only me."

"Sorry." Rath let his arm fall.

Anulf knelt beside them. "We got him — the Xenoth." He made an oddly gentle gesture toward Maura. "Thanks to the lady."

He gazed at Maura's face. "That's her, isn't it? The Destined Queen."

Rath nodded. "She should not have come here."

"Aye, that's true enough. Nor should you have, the shape you're in." Anulf spared a swift glance at the battle raging around them. "I reckon we'll win the day now that the Xenoth is down. But there's bound to be some fierce fighting for a bit. We need to get the two of you away from here."

"We need to get farther than you think." Rath pulled a morsel of dried quickfoil from Maura's sash and cradled it on his tongue until his strength started to return.

He staggered to his feet. "Help me lift her."

Together, they carried Maura behind a clutch of small sheds. As they laid her down, a bearded old man in Hanish armor came puffing after them. "Who are you and what are you doing with the lady?"

Rath cast a withering glance at the Hanish blade in the old fellow's hand. "Put that down, before you do yourself harm. I am the reason the lady came to this benighted place. We only moved her away from the fighting so I might tend her."

"Have you skill in healing?" The old man handed his blade to Anulf with a grimace that showed he was glad to be rid of it.

"Only what I learned from her," Rath admitted. "If you can serve her better, then do, I beg you."

"I will do what I can." The old man knelt beside Maura and

bent his ear to her lips. "Could one of you fetch me water?"

Rath caught Anulf's eye and nodded. Anulf hurried away toward the barracks.

"Hot if you can get it!" The old man called after him.

Then he glanced up at Rath, hovering over him. "Clavance of Vaust at your service ... and hers."

"Rath Talward." Rath picked up one of Maura's hands and chafed the limp flesh. "This happened to her once before, though not so bad. I was able to bring her around with a quick-foil tonic."

Clavance nodded.

"She has a lot of herbs and things in her sash." Rath pointed toward the pocket that now contained only a tiny amount of quickfoil.

The grave, worried set of the old man's features made him add. "You will be able to help her, won't you?"

"So I hope." Clavance blew out a sigh. "Her strength is ebbing fast."

Rath seized the old man's arm. "She cannot die! She has something important she must do."

Something far more important than coming here to fetch him.

"I know." Clavance began drawing pinches of herbs from Maura's sash. "Long ago, I was a pupil of her guardian, Langbard. Did you know him?"

Rath nodded. "Only a short while."

"Solsticetide will soon be upon us. Do you have far to go?"

"Everwood, up in the Hitherland."

"I know the place." Clavance's wrinkled features settled into even deeper furrows of worry. "If I could heal her completely at this very moment I fear you would still be hard pressed to reach there in time."

"Reach where?" asked Anulf, who had returned with a steaming kettle and a mug.

Rath hesitated for a moment. But what was the good of secrecy, now, among friends of proven loyalty? "Everwood. We must get there by Solsticetide."

They *must* get there by Solsticetide. The intense urgency that pulsed within him convinced Rath that he believed the whole preposterous story, whether he wanted to or not.

Clavance sprinkled the herbs in the mug, then poured hot water over them. "Even if you had fast horses, none of the roads in this part of the mountains lead north."

Anulf nodded toward the sound of the fighting. "After this, the Han will even be turning their court boys out of Venard to watch the roads."

Rath lifted Maura's shoulders so Clavance could dribble the hot tonic into her mouth.

"Perhaps ..." Anulf mused. "No. It would be folly!"

"What?" demanded Rath. "Tell me."

Even if Anulf's suggestion was daft, it might distract him from his fear for Maura.

"None of the roads go north," said Anulf, "but the river does."

"The river?"

"Aye. It is how the Han get their cursed ore down to the plain — in barges. If you rode one of those down, and could get ashore before it reached the off-loading ports near the mouth of the river ..."

"If you can make it that far," said Clavance, "I can give you names of some *twarith* in downriver towns who would help you on your way from there."

"How can we?" Rath passed his hand over Maura's hair. "With her still like this?"

For all the tonic Clavance had given her, she showed no sign of reviving.

"There is nothing more I can do for her here," the old man said, "than you could do on your ride down the river. Perhaps getting away from here and closer to the Secret Glade might help her. Her wounds are not of the body, but of the spirit."

Rath knew that well enough. And he knew what Clavance said might well be true. Yet something held him back.

When he had been captured and brought to the mines, he'd made a kind of peace with losing Maura. Now that he truly believed she would find the Waiting King in Everwood, could he bear to lose her again of his own free will?

Suddenly, a tumult of barking and baying rang out above the noises of battle.

Slag!" Anulf spat. "They have loosed the hounds!"

Rath lurched to his feet. "Show me the way to the barges."

She had lost. She had failed.

The sense of that loss haunted Maura in the dark, desolate void into which she had fallen. The weight of her failure threatened to crush her spirit.

Was she dead? If she was, then neither Rath nor any of the *twarith* had survived to launch her into the afterworld with the ritual of passing. She would be forever lost.

Some intuition told her if she surrendered to the darkness she would find a kind of peace in oblivion. It was bound to come sooner or later. To struggle would only prolong her suffering.

No one could help her now.

Perhaps that was the very reason she *needed* to fight.

From the beginning she had felt unequal to her fate. Always in need of help — from Langbard, from the *twarith* and always from Rath. But she had helped him and others, too.

She had stood alone against the grim power and temptation of the Xenoth, and she had prevailed. She would not give up now. She would keep fighting — until she found her way back to herself once again, or until her strength failed at last.

She marshalled her weapons for the battle. The wisdom Langbard had bequeathed to her. The sacrifice of Exilda. Memories of all the people who were relying on her. Tender thoughts of Rath and all he meant to her. If she gave up now, he might lose his budding faith.

She thought of the Waiting King, too. Not as some mythical, heroic figure of legend, but as a real person, like herself. Perhaps he had been caught in a dark void like this for a thousand years. Perhaps if she could find her own way out, she would be able to help him find his way, when the time came.

As Maura armed her spirit with all of these, the weight that pressed down on her began to lighten. And the darkness around her began to shimmer. From an enormous distance, she heard the rush of flowing water and the beguiling whisper of a voice.

Though she could not make out the words, she followed it.

The roar of the river assaulted Rath's ears from every direction — ahead, behind, from both sides and beneath. Even above, when the bow of the ore barge plunged into a wave, sending a great spray of cold water splashing over him and Maura. He tried to shield her from it as best he could, though part of him hoped a good dousing might jolt her awake.

He gasped and sputtered and shivered in his sodden garments, half wishing he'd kept the Hanish armor on. But Maura did not flinch, nor did her eyelids so much as flicker.

Empty of its usual heavy cargo, the barge rode high in the river's swift feral current.

"You should open your eyes a moment, Maura," he urged her. "The trees on the shore are rushing by so fast, they fair set me dizzy."

When not sputtering from a wave of spray, Rath had been talking to her like that ever since Anulf had set them adrift. He doubted she could hear him, but on the slender chance that she could, he kept talking. Besides, it distracted him a little from his heaving stomach and his stark terror.

"There is another stream flowing into this one, Maura. I suppose there must be another mine up near its headwaters. When you find the Waiting King, I hope that will be one of his first tasks — to liberate all the mines. Then I expect you will find a way to wean those poor creatures from the slag. A proper team the two of you will make. Him to battle the Han and you to heal all the harm they have done to folks."

The barge lurched again, sending another wave of spray over them. With the cuff of his sleeve, Rath wiped the drops of water that clung to Maura's face like tears.

He shook his head and forced a laugh that sounded more like a sob. "There. You will be happy, now. My hair is getting washed again. I am glad to have that cursed mine dust out of it. A pity I did not have some of those sweet-smelling herbs you forced upon me when you barbered me back in Windleford. Remember?"

Perhaps she did not. No matter. He recollected it well enough for both of them. And afterward, that bantering walk into the village when he had threatened to kiss her.

He kissed her now, upon the forehead, with all the tenderness he had come to feel for her since then. "Come back, Maura. Please. Embria needs you. *I* need you ... even if you can never be mine."

The barge hurtled on down the mountain, the way events had driven him and Maura these past weeks, at breathtaking speed over abrupt, stunning drops and through treacherous rapids. But Maura lay cradled in his arms — cold, silent and still. If she *could* come back to him, he believed with all his heart that she would.

He had only one hope of getting her back, though he shrank from asking.

"Giver ..."

Rath phrased his appeal in Embrian, for he feared he could not find the right words in his limited *twara*. Surely a spirit wise and powerful enough to create the whole universe would understand his ordinary speech just as well.

"... likely I have no right to ask such a boon, since I have come to you so late. I have done plenty of deeds in my life that go against those Precepts of yours. I wish I could undo them, but I cannot."

All at once, in the roar of the water, he sensed the power of the Giver. In the cool caress of the breeze, he felt its mercy. He had the attention of the force that quickened all living things. It made him feel small, trifling, yet in some strange way, he felt important, too. As if he and what he wanted *mattered*.

"Anyway ... it is not for myself I am asking ... at least ... only in part. I mean ... Maura *is* the Destined Queen, and a fine choice if you ask me. How can she fulfil this quest of yours if she cannot walk or speak? You have gotten us out of some tight spots in the past. Surely you would not let us falter, now, when we are so close?"

The river continued to roar and the breeze to blow, but Rath could not hear the Giver's answer in either. Perhaps he had not made himself plain enough?

"I know I have not believed in you before, but I do, now. I am grateful for what you have given me. I swear, from now on, I will try to give as I have been given. And I will trust in your Providence. Only, please, please rescue her spirit from wherever it is trapped."

After one final jarring lurch, the barge settled into deeper, slower-moving water.

Rath held his breath, waiting for Maura to open her eyes or even for her heartbeat to rally. But nothing changed. She lay there in his embrace, her beauty taunting him with its empty perfection.

Chapter Ten

THE DEPTH OF his disappointment surprised Rath. He had been so ready to trust in a power greater than himself. Then the strangest thought blossomed within him and he had the baffling sensation of entertaining an idea that had come from outside his own mind.

Look for my power within yourself, Elzaban.

Rath made a wry face at the thought of his preposterous birth name. How much ridicule and how many beatings had he taken as a boy before he'd had the sense to call himself something less high-flown?

He did not have much time to ponder those bitter memories. Ahead on the river, one of the small Hanish vessels that towed ore barges hove in view.

Slag! He had not realized the barge-tows plied their work this far from the mouth of the river.

Rath had no time to plan, barely any to think. If he did not act quickly, the current would carry the barge to the waiting ship where he and Maura would be captured.

He had no intention of letting himself fall into Hanish hands again. Nor Maura, either, even if she was beyond their power to harm.

The temporary strength he had gained from that tiny scrap of quickfoil was rapidly wearing off. With as great an effort of will as he had ever mustered, he lifted Maura up to the rim of the barge. Then, twining his arm through her sash to lash them together, he dove into the river with her in his arms.

The water closed over them in a cold, primal embrace that entreated Rath to yield. If he had been alone, he might have.

But for Maura's sake, he struggled up, until his head breached the surface of the water. He had only strength to lift her head free, too, and let the current bear them where it would.

Suddenly ahead of them loomed the remains of a tall tree that had fallen into the river. Some of its roots still anchored the trunk to the shore.

Catching hold of an outthrust branch, Rath slowly inched toward shore, towing Maura into the shallows. There, he collapsed into the warm mud until he revived enough to haul Maura into the cover of a small thicket near the river's edge.

He pressed his fingers to her throat, searching for a pulse, however faint. He lowered his ear to her lips, scarcely daring to breathe, himself, as he listened for hers.

Maura showed no signs to life.

Magic had not worked. Prayer had not worked. There was only one thing left to do.

Wringing a few drops of water from his sodden garments, he moistened her brow with them.

"*Guldir quiri shin … hon bith shin …*" He spoke in a hoarse, hesitant murmur. "*Vethilu bithin anthi gridig aquis … a bwitha muir ifnisive.*"

Wash the cares of this world from your thoughts and let them be made pure for a better life in the next.

It tore at his heart to do this, but he had made Maura a promise. And she had promised he would hear her voice and share her memories.

He needed that.

Their last parting had been too abrupt, and their reunion had been no more than an exchange of gazes in the midst of a battle. If she was on her way to the afterworld, there would be no harm in revealing how much he cared for her.

He trickled a few drops of water on her lips, then on the palms of her hands, reciting the ritual words in a broken voice. Then he bent his head over her and opened his spirit.

Maura, where are you? You told me I would hear you.

No reply came. Not even within his thoughts.

Had he been right, after all? Was there no Giver? No afterworld? Nothing but this one, too brief life in which folk had to look out for themselves first and last?

Once he had been afraid to believe otherwise. Now ...?

A stubborn little seed of faith had taken root within him, and it refused to die no matter how many disappointments might wither it.

Rath?

It was no more than a distant whisper. But it filled him with a sense of wonder, hope and grace.

Their bodies did not move — hers there on the ground, his hovering over her. But in a baffling way Rath could not describe, their spirits sought each other and came together in a haunting embrace of selves. Closer and closer, until suddenly ... they were one.

He saw her past, through her eyes, and he felt her do the same through his. He saw himself through her eyes and tasted her love for him — with all his senses as well as some sweet, mysterious knowing that went beyond the limited scope of sense. It did not feel like she was dying, but rather like he was being reborn.

Take me with you! his spirit pleaded. *I cannot bear for this to end.*

Nor I.

All at once, they knew they had a choice. He could go with her, to be one in the afterworld together. Or she could return with him to a life where destiny would part them.

There was no need for words. No way to hide their true feelings from one another. Together they felt the pull of two much-desired futures that would be forever contrary.

When at last the decision blossomed, it bore no blight of discord. And their shared wistfulness for what might have been only shaded its color to a softer, more delicate hue.

Rath opened his eyes. Maura opened hers.

The ache and loneliness of separation from her trembled on his lips in a mute cry. But when their gazes met, he knew that in some baffling way a part of each of them would always remain with the other.

"There it is," said Rath, the barest trace of a sigh shadowing his words. "Everwood."

He and Maura stood on a low bluff looking down toward the mysterious northern forest. Each of them held the reins of a horse who cropped the new summer's sweet green grass as if this were any ordinary day and this ride any ordinary ride.

After rising from the dark innards of the Beast, the colors of the world looked sharper and brighter to Maura. The varied greens of the grass and trees, the vibrant yellows and purples of wildflowers, the deep abiding blue of the Hitherland sky.

Now she stared at the sky where a silvery-white phantom of the rising full moon shimmered in waning daylight. "I suppose we had better get moving so we will have light to see the symbols on that tiny map of Exilda's."

Reluctance tugged at the hem of her gown.

She and Rath had risked their freedom and their lives for this quest. Now they risked their hearts and their future happiness, as well. Part of her wanted to fly toward her destiny on swift hooves, so it would be over and done with no risk of her recanting at the last moment. Another part wanted to delay it for as long as possible — eking out every second between now and then in Rath's company, with the love they had acknowledged for one another wrapping around them.

"I have studied that map enough, I could find my way blind-folded." Rath reached for her hand. "Still, in case there are any Han coming after us, perhaps we had better be on our way."

Maura knew how doubtful *that* was.

When they had sought aid from some *twarith* in northern Westborne, word had already begun to spread of the successful revolt in the Beastmount mine. Once or twice, during their ride into the Hitherland, they had glimpsed other riders in the distance, all rushing south at great speed, with no heed to spare for a pair of wary travelers.

Maura made no move to remount, no move to release Rath's hand. There was something she needed to know and this might be her last quiet moment to ask.

"What will you do … after …? Where will you go?"

He lifted her hand and laid it to rest over his heart. "I will go … where you bid me. I will do *anything* in your service. The King may be your husband, and I swear I will never do anything to sully that. I only beg leave to be your champion."

His words brought tears to her eyes, hard as she fought to hold them back. After what she and Rath had shared, he would not need to see those tears fall to know they were locked inside her and to understand their source as well as she did.

"Will that not be unbearable for you? For both of us? To be always near but never near enough?"

Rath shook his head. "We have been as near as a man and woman can be. I trust that somehow, someday we will be, again. Until then, let me at least serve you and protect you. Let us work together with the King to free and heal this land of ours."

He made it sound easier than Maura knew it would be. Likely he knew it, too. Which of them would it be harder for?

Her? To wed another man, share his throne, bear his heirs? Wanting to be a faithful and dutiful wife, but forever torn?

Or Rath, to watch all that and ache?

He was right about one thing, though. They must not dwell on what might have been, but concentrate on what *could be*. This quest that had brought them together was only the beginning. They owed it to themselves, to each other and to a great many other people to see it through to its end.

"You have proven yourself a worthy champion, Rath Talward." She lifted the hand he had placed over his heart to rest against his cheek. "Even a queen could ask for no better."

"Then you accept my pledge of service?"

"With all my heart."

As if pulled by some invisible force, half against their will, he bent toward her and she raised her face to meet him. They sealed their pledge with a chaste, wistful kiss that neither dared to hold longer or take deeper, for fear they would never be able to stop.

Then they mounted their horses and rode toward Everwood as the full moon of Solsticetide grew brighter and brighter in the darkening sky.

"What shall we do with the horses?" asked Maura, when they reached the edge of the forest.

Rath lifted her down, then handed her the reins of her mount. "Bring them this way. Unless Everwood has changed a good deal, there should be a small glade not far in where we can leave them until we return."

Their return — of course, Maura mused as she followed Rath through a narrow gap between the trees. Though she knew better, what they were about to do still felt like an end of something. It was hard to imagine what would happen after she had wakened the Waiting King.

No doubt Rath was right. They would need the horses, later.

"Not changed a whit," said Rath as they entered the glade. He sounded pleased and a little surprised. "Good grazing, a bit of a brook over there, out of sight of any chance passerby. A body would think it had been put here on purpose, just for us and this day."

"Perhaps it was," Maura whispered to herself as the flesh

on the back of her neck bunched.

There was something silent and watchful about this forest, as if every tree stood guard. No wonder the folk in neighboring villages had been frightened of the place and warned their children to avoid it.

While Rath turned the horses loose to graze, Maura picked a few interesting leaves and flowerets that caught her eye.

"Old habits die hard," she explained when he shot her a puzzled look. "This would be a fascinating spot for gathering. I wonder if anyone knows what some of these plants are called, or what they can do?"

Rath shrugged. "Some of the old folk in the villages around here might. Ganny's friends, if they are still around."

Maura looked around. "Which way do we head, then?"

"We follow the brook for a while." Rath pointed toward it as he pulled Exilda's ivory map from his pouch. Until we come to a large rock. There we should find a path."

"Lead on." An anxious eagerness had begun to brew deep in Maura's belly.

Now that she had Rath had made their choice and sealed their pledge, her feeling of reluctance was waning.

They had done it. Trekked through almost every province of Embria to find the map, then followed it to the Secret Glade. When she thought of all the perils they had faced and challenges they had overcome along the way, the difficult, dangerous task of reclaiming their kingdom from the Han no longer seemed quite so daunting.

And what would he be like — the king who had slumbered so long, who would now be her husband and her lord? Though her heart belonged to Rath, she hoped and believed the Waiting King would be someone she could honor and admire.

Just as Rath had said, the brook eventually wound its way to a large moss-covered boulder, behind which they found a path that looked well-trodden, though Maura doubted many folk had ever ventured this deep into Everwood.

The path led Rath and Maura deeper still, to a giant hitherpine.

"My word!" Maura stared in amazement. "That trunk is so thick a body could take a chunk and carve a cottage the size of Langbard's out of it. Which way, now?"

"A moment." Rath handed her the little map, then pulled a small torch from his belt and set it alight with his flint. "There. I wanted to get that done while I still have light enough to see what I'm doing."

He pointed to another tall tree in the distance. "According to the map, there are six of these. We should be able to see the next one clearly from the last."

And so it proved.

As they rested a moment at the base of the fifth tree and took their bearings, Maura stared up at the night sky, where thousands of glittering stars paid homage to their monarch, the full moon. "After all we came through to reach Everwood, this seems almost too easy."

"I have been thinking the same thing," murmured Rath. "I never did trust anything that came without a struggle."

The torchlight flickered over his face, giving it the impudent look Maura remembered so well from their early days together. "Perhaps the Giver decided we deserve a little ease at last."

"Perhaps so." Maura rose. "We had better not take too much ease, though, if we want to reach the Secret Glade while the moon is still high."

They picked their way through the forest to the last of the large trees.

"Next …" Rath peered at the map by the light of his torch. "We must find … a waterfall, I think."

"Hush," whispered Maura, "I hear one over that way."

They followed the sound until they came to a narrow

cascade, tumbling from a high ridge, its waters sparkling in the moonlight. Rath found a set of stairs carved into the rocks on one side, which he and Maura climbed.

"The Secret Glade is very near here." Again Rath consulted the map, then held his torch aloft. "Do you see anything that might point us the way?"

Maura saw *something*, though when she tried to warn Rath, the words stuck in her throat. Finally, she got his attention by plucking his sleeve.

"What is …?" Rath turned to look. "Oh, slag!"

There, one good leap away stood the largest tawny wolf Maura had ever seen. If it had not been so deadly, she might have admired its wild majesty.

"Hold this." Rath thrust the torch into her hands. Dropping the ivory map into his belt pouch, he slowly drew the Hanish blade he had stolen in the mines.

The fierce weapon looked feeble against such a beast, especially if it was not alone. Maura knew tawny wolves always traveled in packs.

"Back away, slowly," said Rath. "Keep the torch in front of you. If he goes for me, run."

But the creature showed no sign of going for either of them. It did not growl or bare its teeth. It stood watching them, then turned and walked a few steps, before stopping to glance back.

"Rath, I think it wants us to follow."

"Inviting us back to its den for dinner, you mean."

"It does not look very hungry to me." Maura took a few tentative steps in the direction of the great beast.

Once again, the wolf began to walk ahead, then turned to see if they were following.

"Just so you know," said Rath as he hurried to catch up with Maura. "I do not like this. Unless it leads us to the Secret Glade soon, I …"

Maura never did find out what Rath meant to do, for as

he spoke, they stepped through a gap between two slender whitebark trees and found themselves in a place of moonlit enchantment.

It was not large, but ringed with whitebarks at regular intervals, like so many elegant columns. Rich grass covered the ground, groomed to the ideal height for a luxurious carpet. Not a single fallen leaf marred its perfection.

Before Maura could notice more, the tawny wolf raised its muzzle to the night sky and let out a loud, resonant howl that sounded almost like a trumpet. Then it slipped away so quickly and so silently, it seemed to vanish before their eyes.

"So here we are at last," Rath whispered, sheathing his blade. "But where is the Waiting King?"

"Why he must be ..."

Maura held the torch aloft. She had been so absorbed by the mystical beauty of the place, she had not realized what was missing. *Who* was missing.

She had expected some finely carved resting place, with the Waiting King sleeping upon it, still wrapped in the thousand-year-old spell of his beloved.

But there was no sign of him.

As he stared around the deserted glade, Rath felt like someone had chopped his legs off at the knees. He could only begin to imagine how Maura must feel.

Putting his arm around her shoulders to steady her, he took the torch from her hand.

She shook her head, as if in a daze. "I do not understand. Were you right all along? Is the Waiting King nothing more than a story? After all we went through. All the trouble we stirred up. All the false hope we gave folk. How can it be?"

"Do not lose heart now." Rath could scarcely believe those

words were coming out of his mouth. Could his fledgling faith continue to soar when reason and hard evidence would cut off its wings. "This is the Secret Glade. If ever there was a place full to the brim with enchantment, this is. The map led us here. You *are* the Destined Queen. I know it surer than I have ever known anything . . . except perhaps that . . . I love you."

This was what he had envisioned, back when they set out into the Waste. That Maura would face bitter disappointment at the end of her quest, and he would be here to console her and make her his own.

Now, in spite of what it meant for him, he *wanted* the Waiting King to be here. He wanted Maura's destiny fulfilled.

"But, look." She made an empty, hopeless gesture. "There is no King here for me to waken."

"Perhaps he will not appear until the moon hits just the right spot in the sky," Rath suggested. "Or perhaps there is a magical trumpet or a gong you must sound to summon him."

Maura nodded slowly. "Perhaps."

"What is that, over there?" Rath lifted the torch and nudged Maura toward the center of the glade. "Perhaps it will give us a clue. And do not forget what you told me."

"I have told you a good many things." A ring of confidence returned to Maura's voice. "Some of them pure foolishness. Which one do you mean?"

"This was not foolishness." Rath assured her. "You told me tales may be fancies of things that never happened but they may still hold great truths. Perhaps the tale of the Waiting King is one such."

"I suppose it might be." Maura strode toward something sticking out of the ground, like a tall tree stump. "But how are we to puzzle out the riddle?"

Rath stared at what looked like a giant's goblet. It appeared to have been carved from a good-sized tree, the roots of which still held it in place. From the base, a slender stem rose, with a wide bowl perched on top of it.

"What can it be, do you suppose?"

Maura inspected it closely. "I cannot guess. None of Langbard's stories of the Waiting King ever mentioned anything like this."

She knelt before it, peering at the base. Then she beckoned Rath to lower the torch. "There is an inscription carved here."

She groaned.

"What?" asked Rath, anxious for her.

"It is in *twara*, which I can speak a good deal better than I can read."

She murmured to herself for a bit in a questioning tone.

"Well?" Rath prompted her when he could stand the waiting no longer.

"I believe it says, 'Gaze ye here by the summer moon's light, behold the King who has been woken, and meet your doom.'"

"Slag!"

"Aye." Maura gave a soft chuckle that held no merriment. "Slag."

She rose. "I suppose there must be some enchanted potion in the font. Langbard told me the Oracle of Margyle sometimes looks into the future that way."

"Put out the torch, if you please." She bent to gaze into the font. "The instructions say to look by the moon's light."

"No!" Rath pulled her back. "I do not like that 'meet your doom' business. Let me look first. Then, if no harm comes to me, you may look to your heart's content."

"Rath, this is my quest . . . my destiny. There may be something here to be seen that only I can see."

"So there may." As Rath looked around for a way to douse the torch, it went out on its own. "Or there may be danger. When the Waiting King is woken, he will need you. I offered myself as your champion and you accepted. Let me do my duty."

"Very well." Maura did not sound pleased with the idea.

She reached for his hand and clung to it with all her strength. "Look, then."

Rath bent over the bowl. For a moment he saw nothing but darkness. Then his eyes became accustomed to the absence of the torchlight. Or perhaps the solstice moon waxed brighter.

And he beheld something that puzzled and amazed him.

"Rath." Maura tugged on his hand. "Are you all right? Do you see anything?"

"I see … something," he murmured, "but I do not know what it means."

"Let me look."

She gazed into face the font's shimmering water, to see her reflection beside his. The light of the solstice moon sparkled on their brows like a pair of luminous crowns.

A faint gasp escaped Maura as she understood what the Giver was telling them. Then one tiny circular ripple disturbed the still water in the font, followed by another and another as her tears fell.

"Do you see what this means?" she whispered.

Rath shook his head.

"The water shows us the King who has been woken." She turned and slipped her arms around his neck. "You, Rath Talward."

"Elzaban."

"What?"

"Elzaban," he repeated in a daze. "That *was* my name, once. I took so much grief for it from the other boys in the village, that after Ganny died, I took a new one, less apt to get me picked on."

"You never told me."

"I never thought to." He sank to the grass, taking her with

him. "It has been years since I thought of myself by that name. Until the Giver called me by it when I begged for your deliverance, in the barge."

"When I saw your reflection in the water crowned with stars, I *knew* what it must mean. It was as if Langbard and my mother, and all my forebearers back to Abrielle, herself, were telling me. I need no more proof from the Giver. But if I did, that would convince me beyond any doubt."

She hesitated for a moment, trying to take it all in. "There is one thing that puzzles me, though. I was told I must *waken* the Waiting King. I did not wake you"

"You did." He pulled her closer into his embrace, and she feared her heart would burst to contain the joy that swelled within it. "You woke me in a hundred ways. I was sleepwalking through life, caring for nothing beyond my own survival, believing in nothing beyond my next meal. Blind and deaf to everything it means to be Embrian.

"You woke my heart." He planted a tender kiss upon her palm, then rested it against his chest. "You woke my spirit and my honor."

Hearing him speak of it, Maura knew it was true.

"I find it hard to believe I might be king." Rath stroked her hair. "But if I *can be*, it is because of you."

"What will we do now?" Gazing around the moonlit glade, Maura wished they had the luxury to make it their palace and shut out the troubles of the world. But to do that would be to betray their quest and their shared destiny.

"I do not know." Rath shook his head. "For the sake of our people, I wish the Waiting King *had* been a great, magical hero, reborn. I cannot think where we will begin."

He lifted her thick braid and untied the ribbon that bound it, while he dropped a soft but provocative kiss on her nape. "But let those worries wait for morning. Perhaps it will bring us some of the answers we seek. For the rest of this night, let us think of only one thing."

"And what might that be, your Majesty?" asked Maura, as if she could not guess.

Rath fanned her unbound hair over her shoulders like a regal veil. Then, with the crook of his finger, he turned her face toward his. "Only that I am King of your heart."

His lips whispered over hers, no longer a threat to her destiny, but the perfect fulfilment of it. "And you are Queen of mine."

The Solstice moon shimmered over them like a fond benediction from the Giver — a blessing on their union and their mission. It cleansed any tiny lingering uncertainty in Maura's heart, filling her with the precious gifts of peace, joy, hope and love.

With a sigh of magical fulfilment, she murmured, "Our time has come."

Chapter Eleven

S TIRRING IN HER sleep, Maura Woodbury felt the strong arms of her beloved around her. Snuggling deeper into his embrace, she had never felt happier ... or more frightened.

Her movement startled Rath Talward awake, his lean body gripped with taut wariness. His right hand groped for a weapon. When it found only Maura's soft flesh, the tension bled out of him and he pressed his lips to her forehead.

"Can this be real?" he whispered, tightening his hold on her. "Or did I dream it all?"

Maura gave a husky chuckle. "This place does seem too wonderful to be true, doesn't it?"

For some hours they had slept on the grass in the Secret Glade. Over the tops of the trees, the rising sun now kissed the first blush of dawn into the eastern face of the sky. The luminous midsummer moon was fading, having revealed a sweet and terrible marvel.

"For most of my life I've slept on the ground." Rath stretched and yawned. "But it never felt like this before."

Maura nodded, her tumble of auburn curls rubbing against his shoulder in a caress. Since beginning the quest that had led them here, she too had passed many a restless night on the cold, hard ground. The thick grass beneath them now felt more comfortable than any proper bed she'd ever slept in. The soft, warm earth yielded to the shape of their bodies, cradling them in perfect repose.

Not even the faintest chill of night had nipped them while they slept. Instead, the darkness had wrapped around them, warm yet weightless. No queen and king could have asked for a more luxurious resting place.

That thought sent a muted shiver up Maura's back, making the fine hairs on her nape prickle. Many weeks ago, she had set out on her quest to find and waken the Waiting King — a legendary warrior destined to liberate her people and be her husband. The murder of her wizard guardian had forced her to rely on Rath for protection.

At first she had been as suspicious of the ruthless outlaw as he was of her modest magical powers. But each day of their journey, each new challenge or peril overcome, had forged a stronger bond of trust and respect between them ... along with other forbidden feelings.

"Are you cold, dearest?" Rath pressed his cheek to the crown of Maura's head and passed his large, warm hand down her arm. "Shall I pull my cloak over us?"

Maura shook her head, wishing it had been nothing more than a cool breeze that made her shiver. "Just hold me closer."

They had entered the Secret Glade at sunset, resolved to rouse the Waiting King, even though it would doom their unspoken love. Instead, the kind moon had revealed that Rath *was* the Waiting King, whose true nobility Maura had wakened during their journey. In a daze of delight, they had clung to one another, exchanging all the embraces and endearments they not permitted themselves until then.

Now she wondered if part of their eagerness had been an effort to forestall a host of troubling questions about their future. It had worked and worked well. As doubts threatened to ambush her again, Maura sought assurance and happiness in the one place she knew she would always find it.

Yet even such a delightful distraction as Rath's caresses could not prevent he mind from wandering into places that quickly grew dark. She could not stifle an anxious sigh.

"I do not know," Rath murmured his answer to the question she had dreaded asking aloud —*"What do we do now?"*

She had come to love him with all her heart and she could not have asked for a more precious gift than this sign that destiny had meant them for one another. Yet for all he had proven himself clever and brave and resourceful … even grudgingly compassionate, Rath Talward was not the superhuman warrior she had expected the Waiting King to be. He had no powerful magical weapons with which to fight the cruel Hanish conquerors who had long occupied their country. No enchanted army to oust their enemies from the shores of Embria.

"Where do we even begin?" Maura murmured, scarcely aware she was giving voice to her thoughts. "You liberated one of those horrible mines, which was an amazing feat for a single man and his prisoner comrades. But to free the whole kingdom …"

"We had help, don't forget." Gratitude for that aid and admiration for her courage warmed Rath's words. Then his arms tightened around her once again, and his voice took on a harsh edge. "And you barely escaped with your life."

How Maura wished she *could* forget. Forget the seductive poison with which the death-mage had enticed her. Forget the suffocating darkness into which she'd descended after defying him. One victory had not tempered her fear of the Xenoth and their death magic.

With gentle restraint, Rath disengaged himself from her embrace and sat up. He nodded toward the giant wooden font that stood in the middle of the glade. "Are you certain of what you thought you saw in there last night?"

"As certain as I have been about anything in this whole baffling business." With his arms no longer about her, Maura felt chilled for the first time since she'd woken. "And yet, now that I think back on last night, it *all* seems like a dream."

"Perhaps that's what it was," Rath reached for her hand, "a dream, a trick of the moonlight."

How much easier her life would be if she could believe that!

"I am no king." Rath shook his head. "Though I once bore his high-flown name, I did not reign over Embria a thousand years ago. I did not lie in an enchanted sleep after I took my death blow. I did not do any of the brave deeds you told me of King Elzaban. I am only an ignorant outlaw who has done a great many things he is not proud of to keep himself alive."

When he tried to let go of Maura's hand, she clung to it. "You have also done a great many things you should be proud of to keep others alive or help them in some way."

"And thought myself a daft fool for doing them." Rath's full brows creased into a scowl that could not conceal the flicker of satisfaction in his deep-set, dark eyes. "I cannot pretend it comes natural to me looking out for other folks."

"No one could have done better looking out for *me* these past weeks." Maura's gaze ranged over his rugged features as she relished the freedom to indulge in such loving looks.

Rath's mock scowl deepened, but the twinkle in his eyes glinted brighter. "You did not make it easy — always trying to help everyone who crossed your path, no matter how much trouble it might land you in."

He brushed his knuckles against her chin. "I would defend you to my last drop of blood. But to look out for the welfare of a whole kingdom, and one in such deep trouble, it is beyond me."

Scooping up his vest of black padded leather from the grass, Rath pulled it on.

"I know how you feel," Maura murmured.

When he cast a dubious glance her way, she insisted, "I do! The day Langbard told me it was my destiny to seek out the Waiting King, I could not believe it — did not want to believe it. How could a simple country girl who'd never stepped five miles from home search the breadth of the kingdom to find … a legend?"

As Rath secured his cloak around his broad shoulders he pulled a wry face, perhaps at the thought of himself as a legend.

"I did it, just the same." With a sweeping motion of her arm, Maura indicated the whole enchanted glade, ringed with slender white-bark trees, straight and regular as the columns of any palace. "I reached here in time for the full moon of Solsticetide, in spite of a good many obstacles."

"Obstacles?" Rath gave a snort of laughter as he shoved his feet into his boots. "I would call Vang Spear of Heaven, the lankwolves of the Waste, Raynor's Rift and all the rest more than *obstacles*."

Thinking back on those dangers made Maura shudder. She pulled on her cloak, but it could not warm her against the chill of fear. "Whatever you call them, if I'd had any notion such perils awaited me on my quest I would have hidden under my bed and never come out again. But I have learned to trust in the Giver's providence. And I have come to believe in my destiny."

"I don't want a destiny!" Rath growled. "Not this one at any rate!"

Maura shrank back from his hostile tone. It seemed like a long time since Rath had spoken to her that way. Back then, she'd scarcely cared, for she had feared him almost as much as any of the unknown dangers she'd faced.

As quickly as he'd lashed out, Rath repented and gathered her into his arms, "Your pardon! I am not angry with you, I swear. Last night, I was the happiest fellow in the world to find that I need not yield you to another man. I could think of nothing beyond that. This morning ..."

"I know." Maura passed her hand over his shaggy mane of tawny brown hair in a reassuring caress, as she might have done to a troubled child.

This morning Rath had woken to discover the vast bride price he must pay to claim her. Did he regret joining her on this quest? She could hardly blame him if he did.

"Poor lass!" Rath clasped Maura in his arms, still not trusting his right to do it. "You left behind everything you ever knew or cared for to travel all this way, facing dangers that would make a hardened outlaw flinch. All to find the mighty hero who would deliver your people. Look what you found, instead."

She had found *him* — a man who, until a few days ago, had despised the whole legend of the Waiting King. A man who'd just begun to have faith in the Giver. A man who had only lately come to care for anyone or anything beyond his own survival. She must wonder if Fate had played some kind of cruel trick on her. If only he could be certain she had given him her heart because of who he was . . . not what he was destined to become.

"Look what I found!" Maura tilted her head to gaze at him with her luminous green eyes and perhaps to invite his kiss. "That the man I have come to love and admire was meant to be my partner in the greatest adventure of Embrian history."

The fond tone of her voice and the hopeful springtime glow in her eyes might convince Rath, if he let them. But the life he'd led had cultivated a bone-deep wariness of anything that seemed too good — like the possibility of happiness with Maura. With a great effort, he willed himself to put those doubts aside, and kiss her the way he'd so often longed to during their journey.

A few moments later, the flutter of wings and an insistent squawk stirred them from their embrace.

Rath glanced back to see a large brown and white bird perched on the lip of the carved wooden font, into which he and Maura had gazed last night.

"Go find your own nest mate, noisy one!" he called. "Leave us to kiss in peace."

But when his lips sought Maura's again, she squirmed out of his embrace and moved toward the font. "This is a messenger bird. It looks just like the one that brought Langbard word it was time for me to begin my quest."

"What word?" Rath hung back as she approached the bird with steady, deliberate steps so as not to frighten it. "From where?"

"The Vestan Islands, Langbard said." Maura brought her hand to rest upon the bird's back in a touch that might have been meant to reassure it, or to grab the creature if it tried to fly away. "He told me scholars there had studied the writings of the Elderways and reckoned the time was right."

The bird seemed accustomed to being handled by people, for it made no effort to fly away. Not even when Maura peeled a strip of parchment from around its leg.

Rath's curiosity battled his apprehension and won … but just barely. He moved toward Maura, peering over her shoulder. "What does this message say?"

She unrolled the slender strip of parchment. An anxious frown creased her features as she deciphered the words written there. "It says, 'Come at once.'"

"Come?" Rath stared hard at the message, as if willing the strange letters to have some meaning different than the one Maura had gleaned. "Come where? And how?"

"To the Vestan Islands, I suppose. And there's more. It says, 'Captain Gull of Duskport will convey you.'"

"Duskport." Rath seized on the only part of the strange message he understood. "I've been there. It's a fishing town on the Dusk Coast, a rough place."

Perhaps satisfied that it had fulfilled its task, the bird gave another raucous cry. Then it launched itself from the lip of the font, wings moving in strong, rapid strokes to bear it skyward. As Rath and Maura watched, it circled the glade then headed off in the opposite direction from the rising sun.

Maura glanced down at the message again then lifted her gaze to meet Rath's with a look of apology. "I suppose this answers our question, doesn't it?"

"What question?" he demanded, his tone gruffer than he

meant it to sound.

"The one you read in my thoughts when we woke," Maura replied with greater patience than he deserved. "The one about what we should do next."

"Oh, that." It was a question Rath had been eager to delay answering for as long as possible. "I reckon so. Does the message say anything else? Anything to prove it was meant for you and me?"

Maura shook her head. "Who else could it be meant for?"

"How should I know?" Rath half wished some hunter's arrow had struck down that cursed bird before it reached them. "Not a fancy scholar of the Elderways, am I — living free and easy on their safe, island paradise?"

The few tales he'd heard of the Vestan Islands had long made him burn with resentment. Why had *they* never come to Embria's aid during the long, bleak years the mainland had suffered under Hanish tyranny?

"Rath . . ."

"Does it not gall you that they summon us like this?" His features clenched in a scowl that would have intimidated braver folk than Maura. "Taking for granted you'll have reached here and done what needed doing — as if it was some dance through a garden, rather than a near-impossible trek that might have killed you a dozen times over?"

"I'm sure they did not mean it to sound that way," she entreated him with a soft, green gaze that might have moved the heart of a death mage . . . if such creatures had hearts.

There'd been times Rath wished he had no heart. The cursed thing was a weakness he could ill afford.

"I know it sounded rather . . . curt." Maura held out the strip of parchment to him. "There is hardly room to write a long, courteous letter on something small enough to wrap around a bird's leg."

Rath gave a grunt of grudging agreement. Much as he

loved Maura, he hated it when she was right.

"I doubt the Vestan wizards take it for granted I have accomplished my task," she continued. "This message is a sign of their faith that I would prevail. Now they will be waiting and watching for us to come, perhaps fearing we will not."

Rath pointed skyward to where the messenger bird had disappeared from sight. "When that fellow returns with his leg band removed, it should give them reason to hope."

"True." Maura reached for his hand with the air of a weary laborer once again shouldering a burden from which she had hoped to rest. "All the more reason we must not tarry."

"Why should we not?" Rath demanded. "You were all but dead a few days ago, and I am not long out of the mines. Who has the right to deny us a little well-earned rest and a chance for some quiet time together? Embria has waited countless years for its Waiting King. Can it not wait another day or two?"

An even more defiant notion followed on the heels of that one. "Why must we do this at all, Maura? Any half-wit would know better than to think the two of us can liberate an entire kingdom. If those oracles and wizards on the Islands have done nothing about it in all these years, who are they to lay an impossible burden upon *our* shoulders. Slag them all, I say!"

When he would not let her lead him away quietly to do the wizards' bidding, like some tame dog, Maura headed off on her own. "You do not mean that."

"I do mean it." Rath had little choice but to follow her. "What makes you think I don't?"

Maura whirled about to face him. That soft green gaze had turned as hard and fierce as glittering poison gems. Rath had not seen that look since that day he'd taunted her into crossing Raynor's Rift. He had missed it — daft as that seemed.

"Where is the man who brought me to this glade last night?" She peered around Rath, pretending to look for someone else. "The man who offered himself as my champion? The man who promised to go wherever I bid him and do anything in my service?"

Rath growled. The only thing he hated worse than Maura being right was when she managed to turn his own words back against him. "That was different!"

"How? Was your pledge of homage just empty talk?" Beneath the scornful challenge of her questions, Rath heard a bitter edge of disappointment.

"I did mean it — every word!" Could he put into words all that had changed between then and now, in a way that would make sense to himself, let alone her? "Like you, I expected to find some powerful warrior king of legend. I would gladly have served him, and you, playing my small part in his certain victory over the Han."

A sigh welled up from the depths of his belly. "But there is no magical warrior king. There is only me and you. Whether something went amiss, or this whole Waiting King business is only an ancient jest, there is no way I can do what people expect of King Elzaban."

The sharp angle of Maura's brows slackened and a flicker of doubt muted the righteous anger of her gaze. Perhaps she was remembering the dread of certain failure with which she'd first faced her own impossible quest.

Rath had done enough dirty fighting in his life to know that he must strike hard while her resolve was weakened. "What good will our deaths do anyone? A failed uprising will only make the Han clamp down harder on the people of Embria and serve to discourage more able rebels who might come after us."

Maura caught her full lower lip between her teeth. A troubled look crept into her eyes, like an ominous shadow. Rath knew how she would shrink from the prospect of bringing harm to others. Part of him felt ashamed to exploit such a noble vulnerability, but he told himself it was for her own good.

If it were only *his* life at stake, he might have risked it. But he had felt the helpless, gnawing torment of seeing Maura in peril. It weakened him in a way he could not abide. Let the rest of Embria perish — he must keep her safe at any cost.

"We will do more good by going back to Windleford once all this fuss has settled down." His tone mellowed as he spoke of his modest dreams. "We can rebuild Langbard's cottage, make a peaceful living and raise a family in the Elderways."

That kind of life would be enough of a challenge for a man who'd lived as he had, but Rath felt confident he could succeed, with Maura's love and support to anchor him.

A smile tugged at the corner of his mouth as he pictured the two of them sitting at a cozy supper table surrounded by several ruddy-haired, merry-eyed younglings.

He could tell Maura was imagining it, too, for a brooding look softened her features. Her arms angled, as if cradling a phantom child. He prepared to take her in his arms again and kiss away any dangerous ideas of Vestan wizards and Waiting Kings.

But before he could enfold her, a tremor vibrated through Maura's slender body. Her eyes misted with tears, even as they flashed with indignant fury.

"Damn you, Rath Talward!" she cried, shattering his fragile fancy of a safe, peaceful future. "Damn you!"

Then she turned and fled from the pristine enchantment of the Secret Glade into the tangled peril of the ancient forest that surrounded it.

There was nothing Rath could do but mutter a curse ... and go after her.

As she fled toward the soothing sound of the waterfall they had passed the previous night on their search for the Secret Glade, Maura heard the pounding of Rath's footfall behind her.

Contrary urges battled within her. A powerful one tempted her back to the beguiling haven of his arms and his dreams for their future. Another, less strong but all the more desperate, made her run from him as if a pack of Hanish hounds were baying for her blood.

"Maura, stop!" he gasped, catching her by the full sleeve of her tunic. "How can we ... decide anything ... if you will not ... stay and listen to me?"

"I don't dare listen!" She twisted the cloth out of his grip and ran on.

It would be as foolhardy as stopping to face a Hanish warrior in armed combat. Rath had shown he was armed with potent weapons of persuasion — weapons she had forged for him.

"I mean you no harm!" His breathless words held a plaintive plea. One she was powerless to ignore.

She stumbled to a halt, wilting onto a fallen tree trunk. "That is what makes you so ... dangerous."

"Me, dangerous to you?" Rath dropped to the ground at her feet, his chest heaving beneath his padded leather vest. "What daft talk is that?"

He reached for her hand, raising it to graze the backs of her fingers against his stubbled cheek. "I want nothing more in the world than to keep you safe."

She had no doubt of that. He had proven it again and again on their journey. Should she not feel the same way about him?

"You are dangerous," she repeated, "because you tempt me worse than that Xenoth with his nightmare wand."

During the few days they'd spent recovering their strength for the last leg of their journey, she and Rath had avoided speaking of their terrifying battles with the death mage.

"He made the mistake of offering me the last thing in the world I desire — power. But you lure me with visions of something I want with all my heart — peace."

Rath clasped her hand tighter. "If it is what you want, why should you not have it, love? After all you have done and all you have risked, you deserve every scrap of peace and happiness I can wrest from life for you!"

"But don't you see, Rath, my task is only half done. What does anything I have ventured thus far matter if I cannot persuade the Waiting King to fight for the freedom of his people? I want what you offer me, so badly my bones ache for it and my heart feels like it will tear itself in two. But I know it is an illusion."

"You doubt I could protect you and provide for you?"

Maura shook her head. "I believe you could give me everything you promise. But how could I breathe fresh air and savor the sunshine on my face when I know there are men forced to labor in the stifling darkness of the mines, breathing that foul slag? How could I watch my children play in the yard or eat their supper, knowing hordes of young beggars run the countryside one step ahead of the Hanish soldiers, with no one to care for them?"

Rath flinched from the harsh truth — something Maura had never seen him do before. "You are a dreamer if you think all Embria's problems will be solved by ousting the Han from our shores!"

"Dreamer? Is that another way of saying *fool*?" Perhaps she was both, for believing she would find a long-dead hero sleeping in this forest, waiting to be wakened by her.

"No!" Rath dragged a hand down his face. "I told you of my dreams. They may not be as grand and noble as yours, but they are good and they are *possible*."

His arguments were sensible, sincere … and too convincing by half! Part of her wanted to forget about the mine slaves, the bedgirls and slaggies and think only of herself and her beloved. But another part clung to the beliefs in which her wise guardian Langbard had raised her. Somehow, it felt as if she was fighting for her very soul ... and for Rath's.

"Can you be so certain my dreams are not?" Her voice fell to a whisper. "That night at the inn in Prum, when I first told you of my quest to find the Secret Glade and the Waiting King, you thought *that* would be impossible. Yet here we are."

Rath made a sudden movement toward her, his mouth open, as if pouncing to contradict her. But the words seemed to stick in his throat. He looked around at the swaths of lacy fern, the ancient, towering trees and the misty beauty of the waterfall, as if seeing it all for the first time.

"Yet here we are," he murmured.

"How many times did my quest appear doomed only to be saved at the last moment? Little by little I began to believe this was my destiny." She held out her hand to him. "*Our* destiny. If we have faith in it, I trust that whatever we risk to fulfil it may be difficult, but not impossible. I must answer this summons. Will you go with me?"

Rath stared at her hand for a long, anxious moment. What would she do, Maura wondered, if he refused? Did she truly have the resolve to go on without him?

At last a sigh shuddered through his powerful frame and he reached for her hand with a shrug of surrender. "Stubborn wench. If I could not let you go back in Prum, do you reckon I can now?"

The force of her relief sapped every ounce of strength from Maura's body. She pitched toward Rath, throwing her arms around his neck. "It will be well, *aira*." She used the ancient Embrian word for *dearest* or *beloved*. "I know it will! Think how much we dreaded coming here last night and the parting it would mean for us. Instead, the Giver blessed our union."

At length Rath drew back. "If the Giver had offered me a choice last night, between following the Waiting King to certain victory with you lost to me as his queen, or risking defeat with you by my side — this would have been my choice. Do not expect me always to behave in noble ways, just because you saw a crown of stars on my head. I am still an outlaw at heart, whose first instinct is to save his own hide and fill his own belly."

She would hear no ill of him, not even from his own lips. "Even when you were an outlaw, there was more of a king in your heart than you ever guessed, Rath Talward. The first time I saw you, you were rallying others to escape a Hanish ambush. If they had trusted in you and held together, instead of scattering…"

Rath leaped to his feet, brushing away some bits of bracken that clung to his breeches. "Let's go, before my doubts get the better of me. Perhaps if we travel fast enough, we may outrun them."

Before he had a change of heart — or she did — Maura rose and took his arm to begin their new journey. She only hoped they were not rushing into an ambush of Fate.

Chapter Twelve

A S RATH AND Maura picked their way down the narrow stone step beside the waterfall, he struggled to suppress the memory her words had stirred. Against his will, he recalled that day in Betchwood when he had failed to keep his outlaw band together, long enough to gain the relative safety of the forest.

He told himself he had done all he could. Those men had each thought and acted for themselves. When a few had taken fright and bolted, splintering the strength of their cluster, it had doomed the rest. That was why he preferred to act alone. He could always count on himself.

But one man alone could not hope to defeat the Hanish army that occupied Embria, any more than a single drop of rain could quench a wildfire.

Spying a hollowed stone filled with water at the base of the rock staircase, he asked Maura, "May we stop long enough for a drink, at least?"

She nodded, then stooped and gathered the clear water into her cupped palms. "A wise outlaw once taught me I should always eat, drink and rest when I have the chance. Otherwise I might find myself hungry, thirsty and tired at a time when I dare not stop."

In spite of all the worries that weighed on him, Rath could feel an impudent grin tug at his lips. "If you want good advice about staying alive, ask an outlaw."

A musical chuckle bubbled from the depths of Maura's throat, in perfect harmony with the splash of the waterfall. "So I shall, outlaw."

As she sipped the water from her hands, Rath bent to drink.

He had never tasted anything like this! If Maura's life-magic had a flavor, it would taste just so — clean and wholesome, with a wild, vital tang that quenched more than thirst. For a moment at least, it seemed to ease his foreboding and self-doubt, nourishing fragile seedlings of hope and confidence.

"This is better than ale!" He drank until he could hold no more, then he filled his drink skin and bid Maura do likewise.

Then he jerked his thumb toward the waterfall and the pool at its base. "Do we have time for a wash up before we head off to Duskport?"

"The message said, 'Come at once,' " Maura reminded him with an air of apology. "Besides, I fear the longer we stay here, the harder it will be to make ourselves go. Who knows but we may already have been here longer than we think. Did you not tell me the local folk claim time runs slow in Everwood, and what feels like only a few hours may be months or years in the outside world?"

"I did." Rath forced himself to turn his back on the inviting pool and walk in the direction of a giant hitherpine some distance away. "I always thought such tales were only fanciful nonsense. Now that I have been here, I am not so sure."

"A pity it could not have been the other way around." Maura hurried to catch up with him. "Then we might have dallied here a long while with only an hour or two passing in the outside world."

"That would have been fine indeed." Rath reached for her hand.

Together, they followed the trail of six tall hitherpines until it brought them to the path they had travelled the night before. Now and then, Maura paused long enough to gather a sample of flowers or leaves from some unusual plant they passed.

"Perhaps one of the Vestan wizards can tell me what

magical or healing properties these may possess." She tucked a cluster of tiny, red, bell-shaped flowers into one of the many pockets in the sash she wore over her tunic.

Rath also wondered what those innocent-looking little blossoms might do — make his mouth lock shut or knock him into a dead swoon? Since meeting Maura, he had learned the difference between the gentle vitcraft she practiced using plant and animal matter, and the lethal mortcraft wielded by the Xenoth with their wands of metal and gemstones. Though he had come to respect the capricious power of her life-magic, he still had trouble trusting it.

When he spotted a familiar-looking boulder, draped with moss, Rath beckoned Maura off the path, though part of him wondered where it might lead them if they continued to follow it.

"Where next?" she asked.

"A brook, wasn't it?" Rath glanced around, his ears pricked for the sound of flowing water. "Why don't you check the map to make certain."

"I thought you had it."

Rath shook his head. The last time he recalled seeing it was the previous night, after they'd climbed the rock stair beside the waterfall. The appearance of the massive goldenwolf who'd led them the final leg of their journey had driven all thought of the map from his mind.

Maura patted the pouches of her sash then checked the hidden pocket in the hem of her skirt. "We must have left it behind in the Secret Glade."

Rath shrugged. "That might be for the best. I believe either of us could remember how to find the place again in need. But I would not want that map falling into the wrong hands."

Not that the Han would find anything of value there. But the thought of them invading Embria's last sanctum set his blood afire and made his sword hand itch.

"True enough," said Maura. "And you were right about the brook. I hear it over that way."

The brook led them back to a small glade just inside the bounds of Everwood, where they had left their horses the previous evening. So much had changed since then, it seemed much longer to Rath since he and Maura had entered the ancient forest.

"Our mounts are still here." He gave his an affectionate pat on the rump. "And their manes are no grayer than when we left them. I take that as a good sign Everwood has not bewitched our time here."

"Unless the horses were caught in the spell, too." Maura chuckled to show she was only joking then quickly turned serious again. "I *hope* our time is not out of joint. I would not want the friends who helped us get here to have waited in vain for our return."

Rath nodded, remembering the men he had led in the miners' revolt, the struggling farmer's family from the south and the beggar boy who had reminded him of his younger self. What would they think if they knew he was the Waiting King?

With his mind less than half on his task, he retrieved some food from their saddle pouches. "I reckon we have enough to get us as far as Duskport, if we are careful. I only hope this Captain Gull will not want big pay for taking us to the Islands."

He had heard of smugglers who kept open tenuous ties with the tiny part of Embria that remained free — whispered tales of the lavish ransom they charged to ferry human cargo. Many of whom were rumored never to reach the destination for which they'd paid so dearly. Rath did not fancy putting his and Maura's fate into the hands of such men.

They wasted no time eating their bread and cheese in thoughtful silence. Now that Maura had persuaded Rath to accept his destiny, she did not want to linger in Everwood for fear he might change his mind ... or she might. After washing their breakfast down with swigs of delicious water from the falls, Rath helped Maura onto her mount and they set off for the coast.

Nothing about the countryside beyond the borders of Everwood gave a clue as to how much time had passed in the rest of the world while they had sojourned in the enchanted forest. It was clearly still midsummer, though of the same year Maura could not tell. Yet some vague stirring in her heart told her this was their own time.

Whenever she glanced at Rath, he appeared to be lost in thought. Though she knew two horses would bear them more swiftly and easily than one, she found herself yearning to ride pillion behind him, as she had through the Long Vale — telling him legends from Embria's past, sometimes falling asleep with her hands clasped tight to his belt and her head resting against his back.

The sun was high in the sky by the time they reached a narrow river.

"If we follow this, it will lead us to Duskport." Rath slowed his mount. "Let us stop for a while to rest the horses."

When he helped her dismount, Maura pressed herself close against him as she slid off the horse's back. And even when she had firm ground beneath her feet, she did not loosen her arms from around his neck. Rath accepted the invitation of her lips as she raised her face to his, but he broke from their kiss far too quickly to suit her.

"This is not Everwood." His answer to her unspoken question trailed off in a tone of regret. "We cannot afford to be caught off guard by the Han or whoever else might be lurking."

Maura did her best to hide her disappointment. After all, this protective vigilance of Rath's was a practical token of his love for her.

"May I hold your hand, at least?" She tried to tease a smile out of him. "And stand close to you? Or will that interfere with your efforts to keep watch?"

The tense furrow of his brow eased. He raised his hand then let the back of it slide down over her hair. "Both will distract me worse than I can afford, but I will do my best to bear it."

Maura laughed. "You favor me with your tolerance."

"So I do." Rath feigned a stern look, but the flesh of one cheek twitched from the effort to maintain it. "Do not impose upon it more than you can help."

"How far is Duskport from here?" Maura wedged herself into the cleft under Rath's arm so he had no choice but to drape it around her shoulder.

He stared off downriver. "It has been a long while since I last made this journey. After Ganny died, I was fool enough to fancy I might make an honest living crewing on a fishing boat."

"And?" Maura scarcely needed to ask. If he had succeeded in finding honest work after the death of his foster mother all those years ago, she would never have encountered him that day in Betchwood fleeing a Hanish ambush with his outlaw band.

Rath's lips curled in a sneer at his childish folly. "I was lucky to escape the place with my throat and a few other parts of me unslashed. I know the Han spread many false rumors to frighten ordinary folk of wizards, outlaws and smugglers, but I believe the one about Duskport fishermen using human flesh for bait. I swore I would never go back again."

Maura shuddered. It was no use saying she wished Rath had told her all this before she'd urged him to take her to Duskport. She would not have let it stand in her way … at least she *should* not.

"Then again," murmured Rath, tilting his head to rest against hers, "I've done a good many things I never thought I'd do before I met you, enchantress. Are you sure you haven't bewitched me?"

"If I had, it would only be a fair exchange for you stealing my heart, outlaw! Now, are you going to tell me how far it is to Duskport? A day's ride? A week?"

"If we can keep up the speed we made this morning, we should reach the coast in two or three days."

As it turned out, their ride to Duskport took every hour of three days, because Rath refused to risk the least chance of them meeting up with Hanish patrols in open country.

"How can your hundredflower spell make us blend in with the crowd when there is not another Embrian around for miles?" he demanded, leading her in a wide loop to avoid a ford he guessed might be guarded.

They passed a few scattered farms and two small villages, both of which Rath insisted upon giving a wide berth. "It is warm enough to sleep out of doors and we have supplies to last us until we reach the coast. I'd rather not draw any more attention to ourselves than we must. Besides, if anybody nasty comes following our trail, I'd just as soon the folk around here have nothing to tell them."

Was that all? Maura wondered. Or did Rath not want anyone else guessing who they might be and raising hopes he feared he could not fulfil?

"Well, there it is," he said at last as they crested a bit of rising ground.

"There is what?" Maura peered down the far slope toward a thick bank of dark fog. If she squinted hard enough, she fancied she could make out a cluster of rooftops rising from the mist.

"Duskport." Rath pointed in the direction of her rooftops. "The rest of the year, it is a good deal warmer than most towns this far north. But in summer, that gray fish soup of a fog rolls in. Haven't you heard the saying 'Better a winter in Bagno than a summer in Duskport'?"

"Cold, is it?"

"Aye." Rath gave his horse a little nudge forward, and they headed down into the fog. "The kind that settles right into your bones after a while. The smugglers and cutpurses like it well enough, for it hides their crimes ... or hides *them* if they get caught. Whatever you do, stick close to me and pull a scrap of something from that sash of yours to have handy in case of trouble."

Swallowing a lump that rose in her throat, Maura edged her horse as close to Rath's as she dared without risk of their hooves getting tangled and pitching both riders to the ground. After weighing the merits of a few defensive magical items she carried in her sash, she extracted a generous pinch of madfern and cradled it in her clenched fist.

Bless the *twarith* of Westborne who had refilled the empty pockets of her sash! A pity they'd had no cuddybird feathers. Where she and Rath were headed, it might be very useful to be able to disappear at the first sign of trouble. As it was, they'd have to make do with confusing any enemies they encountered. Fortunately, it was a good strong spell if the madfern was fresh — capable of befuddling quite a large crowd.

Once they reached the edge of town, Rath signalled Maura to slide down from their saddles and lead the horses. "We'll draw less notice that way. Besides, most of the streets are narrow and crooked — easier to get about on foot."

They met only one Hanish patrol — three soldiers and a hound, whose gazes roved warily as if expecting an ambush at any moment from any direction. For all their heightened caution, the soldiers took no notice of Rath and Maura thanks to the hundredflower spell she had cast on them both before they entered town. The hound seemed aware of them, though, straining in their direction on the end of its short chain, a menacing growl rumbling in its throat.

Once the patrol passed without challenging them, Maura breathed easier — though not for long. She and Rath spent the next little while approaching some of Duskport's less threatening citizens. To each, Maura murmured a phrase in Old Embrian that followers of the Giver might understand and respond to.

But the people she spoke to only gave her puzzled, frightened looks before hurrying on their way.

"There's no help for it," Rath muttered at last. "We'll have to leave the horses at the stable we passed on the way into town. It looked halfway respectable — like they might not sell the beasts off to somebody else before we're all the way out the door."

So they tracked back to the stable, almost getting lost in the cold fog. When they asked to leave the horses with him, the proprietor gave them a suspicious look.

Suspicion changed to something else when Rath asked him, "Is there an eating and drinking place handy where the fisherfolk gather?" He lowered his voice and glanced behind him. "One where the patrols don't visit too often?"

The stable owner looked around, too, before answering. "You mean *The Monkey*, down on Wharf Row? You'll find plenty of sea-goers there. Though you might soon wish you hadn't, if you take my meaning."

Maura knew better than the man might suppose. She pictured a sea-going band of outlaws rather like the ones who had held her captive in Aldwood. Why would the Vestan wizards instruct her to seek out a man of that sort?

"*The Monkey* it is." Rath grabbed Maura by the wrist and pulled her out into the thick, chilly fog that smelled of rotten fish.

He led her through a maze of narrow, fog-shrouded lanes and alleys. The only way she could tell they were getting closer to the water was that the fog became even thicker and the smell of fish more rank, until it nearly gagged her. When she struggled to fix her attention on something besides her writhing belly, Maura realized she could hear the rhythmic slap of waves against wood.

"This looks like the place." Rath pointed up at a hanging sign, barely visible in the fog. It bore the crude likeness of a Tolinese monkey.

From within the building came sounds of raucous laughter, angry shouts and the high-pitched tinkle of breaking glass.

As Rath pushed the door open and tugged Maura into the place after him, she heard him mutter, "May the Giver watch over us ... if it can see through this fog."

The common room of *The Monkey* reminded Maura a little of the tavern in Westborne were she'd gone seeking help from the secret followers of the Giver who called themselves *twarith*. But only a little.

The smell of strong spirits overpowered the ever-present stench of rotting fish, but that came as no comfort to her suffering stomach. Somewhere on the other side of the crowded, noisy room, someone was torturing wheezy music out of an instrument Maura had never heard before. Most of the patrons huddled on low wooden benches that ran along either side of three long, narrow tables. They guzzled some drink from earthenware mugs and either argued or laughed loudly with their neighbors.

It eased Maura's fears just a little when she realized the customer were not speaking in Comtung, the language her people used to communicate with their Hanish conquerors. Instead they spoke native Embrian, though with a strange accent unlike any she'd heard before.

The noise did not quiet as Rath threaded his way through the crowd, towing Maura behind him. No one turned to look at them. Even the people they brushed against as they made their way toward the bar seemed to stare through them. Yet the flesh between Maura's shoulder blades prickled, as if sensing many curious, hostile gazes aimed at her back.

When he reached the bar, Rath spent a while trying in vain to catch the eye of a short man dispensing drinks behind it. Reaching the end of his limited patience, he lunged forward, grabbing the man by the front of his shirt and lifting him off the floor until they were nose to nose.

Having succeeded in gaining the fellow's attention, Rath spoke in a quiet, mannerly voice quite at odds with both his actions and their surroundings. "I'd like to see a Captain Gull, if you please."

Maura braced for the surrounding hubbub to fall into an expectant hush, as everyone's attention fixed on her and Rath. The prickling sensation between her shoulder blades intensified, but the noise continued as loud as ever.

The barkeep did not answer, though his face grew redder and redder. His gaze skittered to a large man standing beside Rath, whose shaved scalp bore a tattoo that looked like a map.

The big man leaned toward Rath and spoke in a friendly tone that surprised Maura. "You fancy seeing Gull, do you, inlander? I can take you to him."

"When?" Rath eased his grip on the barkeep's shirt, lowering him back onto his feet.

The man with the tattooed head shrugged. "As soon as you like, inlander. Now?"

"Now." Rath let go of the barkeep.

"Follow me, then," said the man, his tone still affable.

A month or two ago, his obliging manner would have eased Maura's apprehension. Since then, a little of Rath's wariness had rubbed off on her.

The big fellow turned and began to make his way through the crowd, which parted to let him pass. With Rath and Maura following close on his heels, he strode toward the opposite end of the room. As they approached, Maura could see that a shadowed corner was in fact a shallow alcove. Their guide pulled back a bit of curtain to reveal a door, which he opened and entered.

Maura clutched Rath's hand tighter when he drew her toward the doorway and the dark passage beyond. He glanced at her, brows raised, as if to ask what other choice they had.

"At least we knew there *is* a Captain Gull." He gave her hand a reassuring squeeze. "You haven't lost faith in that destiny of yours already, have you?"

"*Our* destiny," Maura corrected him, trying to sound more confident than she felt. How could she expect Rath to place his fledgling trust in that baffling power when her own doubts were all too evident? "Lead on."

She reached back to shut the door behind her — no easy task with the madfern still clutched tight in her fist. A glance back showed that it was not necessary. Several more people crowded into the narrow passage after them, their sinister-looking forms lit from behind by the flickering candles in the tavern.

Rath's grip on her hand betrayed the tension that clenched the rest of his body as he led her into the darkness. They seemed to shuffle along the dim, narrow passage for a long time. It twisted several times confusing Maura as to the direction they were headed. Would they emerge somewhere behind the tavern ... or down the street from it?

Suddenly a light appeared ahead of them and the passage opened into a room. Rath lurched forward, stumbling on something. An instant later, a raised doorsill caught Maura's foot and made her stumble too. As she squinted against the light, she felt Rath's hand wrenched out of hers.

Before she could open her other hand to release a cloud of powered madfern into the air, Rath cried, "No!"

"In case you haven't noticed, inlander," their tattooed guide chuckled. "You aren't in any position to be giving orders."

Maura knew Rath had been speaking to her — not that it mattered. For at the same instant, someone grabbed her hands and pulled them tight behind her back. She concentrated on keeping her fist clenched around the powdered madfern until she could get a better opportunity to use it.

"Well, well, what have we here?" asked a voice.

Maura glanced up at the speaker as he rose from a chair and turned to look them over. He was a small, slender man, a bit less than her own height, which was tall for a woman. The man wore tight black breeches and leather boots that reached halfway up his thighs. His shirt, the color of dark blood, billowed in loose folds over his arms and upper body, while a long strip of the same cloth had been wound around his head. It covered all his hair except for a long, black plume that stuck out of an opening in the top — a mockery of the way Hanish soldiers pulled their pale hair through the tops of their helmets.

For a moment Maura thought he had a fur collar draped around his shoulders. Then the "collar" raised its head, stared at her and hissed. She flinched from the creature, a long-legged hillcat with sleek brown fur.

"Mind your manners, Abri." The man raised his hand to caress the beast.

He wore snug-fitted leather gloves with holes through which his bare thumb and fingers poked. Only three fingers, though. The smallest on each hand was missing.

"This inlander strolled into *The Monkey*," the tattooed man announced, "with a wench twice too pretty for the likes of him. Said he wanted to see Captain Gull."

"Indeed?" The little man sauntered toward Maura.

When he lifted his hand, she flinched, but he only tilted her chin with the gentle pressure of his fingers to turn her head to one side.

"Tell me, inlander, was that all you wanted — to *see* me?" He let go of Maura, stepped back and struck a pose. "Now you have seen me."

He glanced toward the tattooed man. In as mannerly a voice as he might have used to bid them be escorted away, he ordered, "Kill them."

"We wanted more than to see you!" Rath cast Maura a sidelong glance that she sensed meant, *"Get ready!"*

She flashed him one back that she hoped he would understand to mean, *"This is not going to work."*

Oh, she could mutter the spell under her breath and drop the madfern. Perhaps even kick it up into the air. But in this small, crowded room, there was a good chance she and Rath would become as befuddled as everyone else. Or the others might do them some harm while in the grip of their confusion.

"We were told you could take us to the Vestan Islands," said Rath. "Can you? Will you? It is vital we reach there!"

Captain Gull looked from Rath to Maura and back again. All the while he petted the cat draped around his neck. "You must know it is death for any Embrian to sail more than five miles from the mainland. My friends and I are but humble fisherfolk."

Maura could not bite back a retort. "You do not look like any fisherman I ever heard of!"

"Ha!" Captain Gull let out a laugh that seemed far too deep and loud for his slender frame.

"A bold wench!" He remarked to the cat. "I like that."

The cat looked over at Maura and hissed again.

"Mmm, I reckon you're right, Abri." Gull shook his head, a look of deep regret shadowing his fine features. "These two must be Hanish spies."

He glanced toward the large tattooed man and amended his previous order. "Kill them slowly."

Chapter Thirteen

As Rath listened to Captain Gull order their deaths in such an offhand tone, he sensed the strange little man was more truly dangerous than the outlaw Vang Spear of Heaven, with all his bluster.

He should never have brought Maura here, Rath chided himself. He should have left her somewhere safe while he'd come in search of the smuggler. In truth, the notion had crossed his mind, but he'd worried what harm she might come to if he was not there to keep her safe. Instead, he'd hauled her into danger from which he would be hard-pressed to protect her.

If she could give him the slightest edge by casting her spell, he would try to fight their way out of here ... though he didn't fancy his chances.

"Kill us if you must and if you can!" He hurled the challenge at Captain Gull. "But do not let it be because you believe us Hanish spies!"

Though it made him feel unbearably vulnerable, he bent forward, baring the back of his neck for them to see. The flesh still felt tender where the Han had branded him, almost a fortnight ago.

Rath heard Maura suck in her breath through clenched teeth. He had not told her about the brand, though he knew she could have compounded a salve to soothe and heal it. Once or twice, when she'd thrown her arms around his neck too eagerly, he'd had to bite back a grunt of pain.

"Well!" Captain Gull sounded shaken out of his amused indifference. "I have never seen one of those marks on a living man, inlander. How did you come by it?"

"The usual way." Rath straightened up and shot a look around at Gull and his men. "It is the first thing they do to you when you're sent into the mines . . . after a whiff of slag to dull the pain and sap the fight out of you."

"How do you come to be here, then?" Gull's dark eyes narrowed. "No man has ever escaped the mines . . . unless he made a bargain to spy for the Han in exchange for his freedom."

"You disappoint me, Gull." Rath hoped the insult would not cost him his head.

"Do I?" Gull sounded intrigued rather than enraged. "How so?"

"I took you for a man who makes it his business to know what's what in the world. There have been escapes from the mines, though not many and not much talked of. The Han try to keep word from spreading, in case it should inspire more miners to try. And the men who escape are not eager to call attention to themselves by bragging."

The hillcat rubbed its head against Gull's cheek. He reached up to pet it, but his gaze never left Rath's. "Do not flatter yourself that I let you see all I may or may not know."

Perhaps the time had come for Rath to try a little flattery. "It does not take a clever man to guess that the first must far outweigh the last, Captain."

Gull chuckled. "Believe it, inlander. A man like me does not survive in this town unless he is well armed with the right knowledge."

"Then you must have heard rumors of a revolt at the Beastmount Mine. A successful revolt."

"Amazing if it is true."

"It is true." Rath could not keep a ring of triumph from his voice. "And it was amazing."

Feeling the hold on his arms loosen, he tugged them free, but made no rash move to draw his weapons. "I led those men and now the lass and I have been summoned to the Vestan

Islands. If you cannot take us, let us go so we may seek passage elsewhere."

Gull took some time to reach his decision... or to announce it, at least. While everyone stood waiting, he sauntered around the room, petting the cat and feeding it small scraps of what looked like raw fish from a heaping platter on the table.

At last, when Rath had prepared himself for another casual death order, Gull looked up at him and Maura as if wondering what they were still doing there. "Lucky for you the summer Ore Fleet has already sailed with its cargo of metal back to Dun Derhan. Otherwise nothing could persuade me to venture those waters."

He directed his next words at the tattooed fellow standing behind Rath. "Don't just stand there, Nax, find our guests food and a place to sleep."

"You will accept my hospitality, I hope?" he asked Rath and Maura. "We will need to be on our way very early tomorrow."

Before Rath could reply, Maura spoke up, "You honor us with your kindness, Captain. May the Giver's favor fall upon you."

Gull accepted her blessing with a wry smirk and an exaggerated bow.

Rath guessed the man did not risk his life keeping open links between the Embrian mainland and the Islands out of duty to the Giver. Likewise, his offer of food and shelter was an act of caution, not kindness. If they were spies, Gull would not give them a chance to steal away and tell the local garrison about the forbidden voyage he had agreed to make.

Rath suspected Maura knew it too. But since they had no money and knew no one in Duskport, even a smuggler's hospitality beat sleeping out in the fog. Perhaps destiny was taking care of them after all.

The man called Nax led them through a maze of narrow hallways and up two flights of stairs to a snug, windowless room. The latter did not sit well with Rath, who preferred open spaces and always liked to have an avenue of escape. But he hid his misgivings from Maura, who seemed pleased enough with Captain Gull's "hospitality."

"Luxury!" She threw herself down onto the thick straw mattress in one corner of the room. She sniffed. "The straw's clean too, strewn with honeygrass and pestweed."

Rath forced a smile and nodded. The most comfortable cage in the world was still a cage.

"There's plenty of room for us both." She patted the mattress.

"A good thing," he teased. "I would feel bad making you sleep on bare floor."

The door opened and Nax entered bearing a well-laden tray. "I hope you're hungry. There's plenty here."

Maura scrambled up from the mattress. "This looks like a feast for twice our number! Give Captain Gull our thanks for his generosity."

"Very good, mistress." The large, menacing smuggler sounded so meek, Rath could scarcely keep from chuckling. "If there's anything more you need — anything at all — just give a call."

That cordial invitation did not reassure Rath. It only confirmed his certainty that one of Gull's men would be standing guard outside the door.

Nax set the tray down on a low table in the opposite corner of the room from the mattress. Once he had gone, Maura pounced on the food.

"Hold a moment!" Rath grabbed her hand on its way to her mouth bearing a biscuit of some kind. "How do you know that's not poisoned?"

"Don't be daft." Maura jerked her hand free and took a bite before he could stop her. "If Captain Gull decided to have us killed, he had no need to go to all this bother. He could just have let his first order stand."

"Or his second," Rath muttered. How could she talk about threats of cold murder as if they were trifles?

"Just so." Maura swallowed her first bite and took another. "It would make no sense for him to pretend he was going to take us to the Vestan Islands, then waste perfectly good food by using it to poison us."

She stared at her left hand, which was still clenched in a tight fist. "I had better wash off this madfern, though, or I could do myself worse harm than our host means us."

Her tone reminded Rath of the gentle scoldings he used to get from Ganny when he was a young fellow. Maura was probably right. Somehow, when it came to her safety, caution got the better of his good sense.

He picked up a fried patty of some kind and gave it a suspicious sniff. "Smells all right."

Maura shook her head and chuckled as she washed her hands in a small basin beside the bed. "I'm certain this food is no more poisoned than the barleymush I fed you the night I brought you to Langbard's cottage."

How foolish it seemed, looking back, for him to have suspected her and her kindly wizard guardian of treachery.

"That was different," Rath growled, taking a nibble of the patty, which turned out to be a toothsome mixture of fish and vegetables. "I had no good reason to mistrust you, except that the Han had made me suspicious of all magic users. Placing your trust in a fellow like Gull is a quick way to get yourself killed. You mark me."

He'd only meant to take the one tiny bite then wait to see if it made him ill. Now Rath looked down at his hand to find he'd wolfed the whole patty.

"I mark you very well." Maura stole up behind him and wrapped her arms around his waist, pressing her cheek to his back. "I did not trust you, in the beginning, any more than you trusted me, remember? I was certain you would murder

Langbard and me in our sleep on the road to Prum. As it turned out, I could not have been more wrong. So if I have become less wary of dangerous-looking men, you have only yourself to blame."

Bad enough she was right. Did she have to remind him he was the rogue who'd taught her this dangerous lack of caution?

He echoed what he had said to her after she'd tricked him into eating that barleymush. "Oh well, if the food is poisoned and the room a trap, we are done for anyway. Might as well die with a full belly and a decent sleep."

A loud banging jolted Maura from the warm haven of sleep in Rath's arms to the baffling fright of impenetrable darkness and hard limbs thrashing around her.

Then a blessed sliver of light appeared and a deep, hoarse voice called, "Time to rise! Sea-going folk cannot afford to loll in bed till all hours, like inlanders."

Rath's thrashing stilled. He must have remembered where they were, as Maura had.

Someone — Nax by the sound of his voice — thrust a lit candle into the room and set it down on the table.

"Take these." He tossed a soft, bulky bundle onto the mattress. "And make ready to go as quick as you can."

Despite the need for haste, Rath gathered Maura into a swift embrace. "I didn't do you any harm just now, did I?"

When she assured him she had only been frightened by their abrupt summons in the darkness, Rath cursed. "I hate not knowing where I am when I waken. It does not happen to me often, but when it does, it gives me a wicked fright and makes me lash out at whoever is nearest at hand."

He pressed a kiss on her brow, "I entreat your pardon."

"It is yours, now and ever." She clung to him an instant

longer then turned to peel open the bundle.

"A change of clothes for us." Rath grabbed a shirt that appeared to be his size and pulled it on. "So we do not look quite so much like inlanders."

Maura picked up the smaller of two pair of breeches. "And I do not look so much like a woman. How do you put these on?"

With Rath's help, she dressed in boy's garments then hid her braided hair beneath a cloth cap. Not knowing if they would be given any breakfast, they ate some of the food left over from the previous night.

"At least now we can be certain it is not poisoned," Maura teased Rath as he gobbled up several cold fish patties.

He replied with a menacing growl that only made Maura laugh. Then he lifted the candle and looked her over with a critical stare. "If we meet up with anyone who might cause trouble, keep behind me. You won't fool anybody who looks too close."

He began to gather their clothes into a bundle, when another knock sounded on the door and Nax pushed it open without waiting for an invitation. "You ready?"

"We are." Rath tucked their bundle of clothes under his arm and bid Maura bring the candle.

"Hold on." Nax pointed toward Rath's scabbard. "You'll have to leave that behind and the clothes too."

As the first sounds of protest left Rath's mouth, the man nodded toward Maura's sash. "And that. Off with 'em."

"Damned if I will go unarmed!" cried Rath.

Maura dug a pinch of spider silk from its pouch. She had been stripped of her sash once by an enemy, and she had no intention of being rendered so vulnerable again.

"Captain Gull don't care whether you're armed," said Nax, "so long as the weapon's not metal or you will damn us all!"

The way the two men glared at each other, Maura feared they would soon trade blows unless someone stopped them.

Fighting her ingrained instinct to flee or hide from conflict, she pushed herself into the middle of their quarrel. "Metal will damn you all? What does that mean? My companion's blades have been tempered of mortcraft, I promise you."

"Your pardon, mistress." Nax shook his head. "But tempered is not good enough." He glared at Rath over Maura's shoulder.

"Not good enough for what?" she persisted. "Forgive our ignorance — we are inlanders, as you know."

He should know, for he had reminded them of it often enough in a tone that proclaimed his contempt. Did all coast folk in Embria look down on inlanders? Maura wondered. The way people from the Hitherland considered all Dusk Coasters smugglers and pirates? And folk in Norest poked fun at Tarshites for their rustic speech and manners? Before Embrians could hope to throw off the yoke of the Han, they would need to forget such prejudices and come together.

"You do not know?" A look of doubt softened Nax's fierce countenance. Had he thought Rath opposed his order out of arrogance or stubbornness?

Maura shook her head.

"It's the Islands, see?" Nax explained. "Do you not know why the Han haven't overrun them along with the rest of the kingdom?"

"I have heard the waters are treacherous," said Maura, "and the Han are not the best of sailors."

"The Islands have nothing the Han want," snapped Rath. "If they were riddled with metal and gems like the Blood Moon Mountains, they would have fallen to the Han long ago."

Maura stabbed backward with her elbow and made forceful contact with some part of Rath. She loved the man to the depths of her heart, but that did not mean he had lost his power to try her patience.

She directed an apologetic smile at the fierce-looking smuggler in front of her. "Is there more keeping the Han from the Islands than those things?"

"Aye. The waters around the Islands have a powerful warding spell upon them. They sense the presence of metal, and when any comes too near, they swallow it up. After losing a few ships, the Han had sense enough to give the Islands a wide berth."

"Of course," Maura whispered, wondering why the idea had never occurred to her before.

"Then how are we to reach the Islands without being swallowed up by the sea?" asked Rath. "Does Captain Gull have a ship that is held together with string?"

Maura turned to skewer him with a look. This sort of bravado had worked last night to win the smugglers' cooperation. Now a little courtesy would take them farther.

Suddenly, from behind her, she heard Captain Gull's voice. "You may soon see how my ship is held together, inlander, if you have wit enough to leave behind your blades and other metal. If you will, then come. You have wasted too much time in talk."

Spinning around to face him, Maura saw no sign of the colorful character who had ordered their deaths last night. Instead, only a gray-bearded old man stood beside Nax, clad in tattered garments that looked to have been woven with a waterproofing spell. Her heart went out to him, for his back was pitifully bent with a cruel hump deforming one shoulder.

As she watched, the hump seemed to swell and ripple. Maura's gorge rose.

Then Rath let out a burst of scornful laughter. "That disguise won't fool anyone, Gull, unless you keep that cat of yours from moving about."

Maura chided herself for not seeing through the ruse.

The smuggler performed a mocking bow. "Do not fret, inlander. The wharf guards are so used to seeing me shuffle past, they would not notice if Abri turned tumbles under my coat. I'm more uneasy about sneaking your wench past them. It'll take more than a pair of breeches to make her look like a proper boy."

He flashed her a smile that might have been meant to look admiring. His false beard and several blackened teeth quite spoiled the effect.

Rath brought his hands to rest on Maura's shoulders. "I've already told her to stay behind me."

"Do not fret about me!" Though Maura knew he only meant to watch out for her, sometimes Rath's intense protectiveness vexed her. "If I dose myself with enough hundredflower, the wharf guards will pay me no more attention than the garrison at Windleford used to."

"Hundredflower?" murmured Gull. "You're an enchantress?"

Maura nodded and patted her sash. "Which is why I cannot surrender this. You have my word it contains no metal. But now that we understand about the warding spells around the Islands, my companion will gladly surrender his weapons."

"Not *gladly*," Rath muttered under his breath.

But Maura heard him ungird his scabbard and hurl it onto the mattress. Then he stabbed his knife deep into the wood of the doorjamb. It occurred to her how defenseless he must feel surrendering his weapons.

"You *will* be glad," she assured him, "when we do not drown in the Sea of Twilight."

"Come, inlanders —" Captain Gull started down the hall "— or we will never get to sea this morning!"

Maura grabbed Rath's hand and followed. A quiver of excitement gripped her belly. To think she would soon be sailing upon the great ocean!

Once the small fishing boat pushed away from the wharf, Rath felt as though he could breathe properly again, without iron bands of dread tightening around his chest. Passing under the scrutiny of the Hanish wharf guards without even the tiniest knife to protect himself and Maura was one of the hardest tests of nerves he'd ever undergone.

For a moment, he'd glimpsed a flicker of heightened interest in the eyes of one of the guards, perhaps seeing through Maura's hundredflower spell to pick out a pair of unfamiliar faces among the regulars. When the guard approached, Rath had tensed, preparing for the worst.

But before the Han could challenge him, a scuffle had broken out in another part of the wharf, distracting the guard long enough for Rath and Maura to slip past and board a boat with Gull, Nax and another man.

"Stay to the back," Gull muttered. "Make like you're tending to the nets. Keep your heads down until we're out of sight of the shore."

He climbed up into the prow of the boat and detached the loop of rope that held it to the wharf pilings. Nax and the other fellow had taken their places on a wide bench in the middle of the craft and commenced to wield a pair of broad oars in strong, rhythmic strokes.

"Where are we bound for?" asked Rath as they drifted out into the foggy darkness, the lights of the wharf growing dim behind them. Off in the mist, he could hear the dip and splash of other oars, and above them, the screech of seafowl.

"We aren't rowing all the way to the Vestan Islands in this, are we?"

Though he had heard plenty of tales about the Islands, he did not have a clear idea how far off the western coast of Embria they lay.

"Inlanders!" Gull let out a hoot of mocking laughter as he peeled off his false beard of brushed fleece. "This poor little dory would not last more than a mile or two off the coast, which is why the Han will not let us fish in anything bigger."

He did not offer any further explanation, but continued to remove his disguise.

Rath glanced sidelong at Maura. Did she guess whatever Gull was not telling them?

She only shrugged and murmured, "We will find out soon enough, I suppose."

True, but Rath did not like surprises. What would *he* do in Gull's place, to get around the Hanish edicts that bound sea-goers so tight to the coast?

By the time he had come up with a couple of possibilities, the fog did not seem quite as thick as when they'd pulled away from the wharf. Behind them, dawn had begun to light the sky for another day.

"Ease off, lads," Gull ordered his oarsmen, peering into the mist. "We're getting close."

True to his word, a large, dark shape reared up out of the fog before them. Someone called out a challenge, to which Gull bellowed back an answer, neither of which Rath understood. They sounded a bit like the Old Embrian language, *twara*, of which Maura had taught him a few words.

Now he understood what was happening and reckoned himself a fool for not guessing earlier. "They must keep a sea ship anchored in some hidden cove," he whispered to Maura, "then they sail the little fishing boats out to meet it."

Gull made a sound between a chuckle and grunt. "You're clever enough . . . for an inlander. The Han still haven't figured it out after all these years. Mind you, we keep the local garrison busy enough that the officers aren't eager to stay on the Dusk Coast a day longer than they have to. Before they guess our little scheme, they're back to Venard or over the mountains where the locals don't give quite so much trouble."

Perhaps Maura resented the smuggler's tone of contempt

for the region that had been her home. Rath heard a sharp edge to her tone when she asked Gull, "Do the wharf guards not get suspicious when the small boats don't come back at night?"

Someone on the deck of the ship tossed down a rope, which Gull caught and tethered to their boat. "Never fear, wench, we make certain the same number return at night as sail in the morn and with a good catch, too. That's all the Han care about. They never notice if each boat is missing a man or two."

Grudging admiration for the smugglers of Duskport began to grow in Rath. He knew the penalties for their trade were as gruesome as those for attempting to escape the mines.

A rope ladder rolled down the hull of the ship. Gull scrambled up it with the hillcat still clinging around his neck. Motioning for Rath and Maura to follow, he called. "Welcome aboard the *Phantom*, inlanders — the most elusive vessel in the whole Sea of Twilight!"

Rath scrambled up the ladder behind Maura and climbed onto the deck. There he found Captain Gull with his arm wrapped around her waist and his hip pressed tight against hers. With the speed of events since they had wakened, Rath hadn't had enough time or light to fully appreciate the tantalizing way those breeches and that shirt clung to the sweet, womanly curves of Maura's body.

Gull glanced up at Rath with an impudent grin. "The wench is a mite unsteady on her feet. Common for inlanders."

"I'll take her, then." Rath struggled to hide his jealous temper. It would only amuse Gull and vex Maura. "You must have plenty of tasks to oversee before we sail."

"True, alas." The smuggler lifted Maura's hand and pressed a slow, provocative kiss upon it. "Otherwise I would be tempted to linger here all day with such comely company."

The hillcat on Gull's shoulder gave a hiss that Rath was tempted to echo. When the creature swiped its paw toward Maura, she drew back and he was able to pull her into his arms without too obvious a tug-of-war.

"Mind your ship, Gull," he growled, "and I'll mind my wife."

Gull's dark brows shot up as he mouthed the word *wife*. Then he strode away calling orders about hauling anchor, hoisting sails and other sea-going cant that meant nothing to Rath.

He eased Maura out of the way as Gull's crew swarmed over the deck of the *Phantom* and up the rigging of the large, three-cornered sails. Meanwhile, the small fleet of fishing boats that had borne them from shore dispersed. A stray breeze caught the sails and the ship began to move.

"Did you mean what you said to Gull?" asked Maura. "Or were you just trying to make him leave me alone?"

That sounded like a worthwhile reason for saying ... whatever it was he'd said.

"You don't even remember, do you?" She shook her head. "I suppose that answers my question."

"You mean about being my wife?" A flash of heat kindled in Rath's cheeks. "Your pardon if I got ahead of myself, but you are ... at least you're meant to be. You will, won't you?"

She had to, didn't she, if he was the Waiting King and she the Destined Queen? That was the one part of all this that made the rest almost bearable.

"Of course I will." Maura leaned into his embrace. "Once we reach the Islands, I think we should have a proper wedding with one of the wizards to bless our union. Perhaps even the Oracle of Margyle."

At that moment, the *Phantom* broke through the last tatters of fog. It surged out into a vivid, sparkling world of blue, white and gold. The majesty of it took Rath's breath for a moment.

No wonder Captain Gull and the others risked their lives to ply this trade. Rath sensed it was not only for riches, but for the tang of adventure they smelled on the sea air. He could almost feel it stirring *his* blood.

He closed his eyes and inhaled deep, invigorating breaths.

Awhile later, a young crewman approached them. "Captain says he'll show you around the ship if you care to see."

Rath was more than eager. The only watercraft he'd ever used were small rafts like the one he and Maura had used to cross the Windle. He wanted to know where and how the *Phantom* had been built, how Gull and his crew navigated the vast, open stretches of water and made the vessel take them where they wanted to go.

"Shall we?" he asked Maura. She didn't look quite as anxious as he for a tour of the vessel. In fact, she looked pale and a little ... green.

But she nodded, just the same. "Perhaps it will help me keep my mind off my belly. It feels like everything inside me is sloshing around and trying to get back out."

"Don't fret," said the young crewman who'd been sent to fetch them. "I had that when I first sailed. It comes back now and then when the sea is rough. Here." He rummaged in his trouser pocket and pulled out a tight-packed little brick a disgusting greenish-brown in color.

Rath made a face when he caught a whiff of it, for it stank of salt and fish. "What is that?"

"Dried sea grass," said the lad. "Once you get used to the flavor, it's a treat to chew. Calms a sick belly better than anything else I've ever tried."

"Thank you." Maura took it from him and broke off a small pinch. Then with a dubious look, she shoved it between her back teeth and began to chew.

She grimaced at the taste but did not spit it out or hang over the deck railing retching up her breakfast. After a few moments, she even managed a wan smile. "Perhaps this stuff is like cheeseweed — the smell is a sign of its potency. I believe I feel a little better already."

She kept up a valiant appearance of interest while Captain Gull showed them over his ship.

Rath did not need to pretend. "Amazing that you were able to build a craft this size without any metal at all!"

Gull shrugged. "The sea is not kind to iron. Wooden pegs swell in the wet and hold better than nails that will rust away. The *Phantom* was built in a shipyard on Galene. Some of their trees produce wood that is almost as hard as metal. And some bits have been treated with strengthening spells."

He ran his hand down the middle mast in a proud caress such as a father might bestow on a beloved child he was praising.

"Why do your sails run the length of the ship and not its width?" asked Rath. "Would they not catch the wind better that way?"

Gull grinned. "When the wind is blowing in your favor, that is true, inlander. The Han rig their sails as you describe. That is why their fleet must sail only at certain times of the year. Like now, to take advantage of the Midsummer Blast."

"Midsummer ...?

"... Blast." Gull shook his head. "You are sadly ignorant of the sea. The Blast is a fast, cool wind that whips down the coast this time of year. The Han ride it with their big waddling tubs full of ore. Slow as oxen, they are, and just as stubborn to steer. But the wind is more fickle than a beautiful woman with many suitors. When we set our sails, we become masters of the wind, not slaves to it. If the wind blew against them, we could dance rings around anything in the Hanish fleet!"

Picturing it made Rath grin. "That sounds like fine sport! Do you often harry them?"

"Do I look like a fool, inlander?" Gull held up his hands and wriggled his eight fingers. "I am fond of the ones of these I have left and mean to keep them. My handsome head, too, for that matter and a few other bits I will not mention in the presence of your queasy lady."

"But if you could dance rings around them?"

"Around the galleys, aye. But the Han are no fools — they do not send their precious ore back to their homeland unprotected. The fleet is escorted by fighting ships that would soon crush a greater threat than my pretty *Phantom*. They're sleek and narrow, fast as demons when the wind is behind them. And if they catch a wooden craft like this one, they have a sharp iron prow that could slice through our hull like a blade through pudding."

The smuggler's warning put Rath in mind of the hounds the Han used to terrorize the people of Embria — fast, sharp and vicious.

By the time Gull finished showing Rath and Maura around the vessel, the wind had risen and the clouds had massed on the eastern horizon, dark and threatening.

Gull sniffed the air. "Smells like a storm. Most often they come out of the west, but now and then the Blast will send one down the coast. It will get us to the Vestan Islands all the faster. I only hope it does not push us up the tail of the Ore Fleet."

Before Rath could reply, Maura spoke. "Did you not say the Han sail faster when the wind is behind them? The storm should push them farther ahead of us."

"Aye, wench!" Gull gave her a hearty slap on the back. "So you did mind what I was saying. We'll make a sea-goer of you yet!"

Maura shook her head, chewing the seagrass harder as she clutched the little block of it in her hand. "I think not."

The storm broke just as night began to fall. Rath took Maura below, where they huddled in dark, mute misery on a narrow shelf that folded down from the inside of the hull.

Time slowed to a crawl, until it seemed that day would never come again, and they would be trapped forever in the bowels of the pitching ship, deafened by the howl of the wind and the crash of the waves. The *Phantom's* hull shuddered with every flex of the sea's formidable strength. Soon Rath lost count of how many times they slipped between the jaws of death, only to slide out again before its sharp teeth gnashed. Each time left his heart pounding fit to burst, his belly churning, and a fine dew of sweat prickling on his brow.

The weight of his own helplessness and uselessness ground down his courage. If only there had been something he could *do*! He heard the muted thunder of footfall on the deck above his head with longing. Even if it had meant treading closer to the slippery edge of disaster, at least being up there with duties to perform would have given him some tiny illusion of control.

The knowledge that he would be worse than useless up on deck kept him below. And the conviction that Maura needed him.

"There, there, *aira*." He held her head as her belly gave another violent heave and she spewed what little she'd eaten into the hold of the *Phantom*. "You'll feel better once you get it all out."

He didn't have enough experience of the sea to be certain of that. But right now, he'd say any daft thing if it might ease her. He wished their places could have been reversed. He would rather endure this himself than watch her suffer. No doubt she'd have tended him better, all deft and gentle and reassuring — unlike his rough, awkward efforts on her behalf.

She subsided against him, gasping for breath. "I'm sorry, Rath ... should have listened to you and gone home to Windleford. What good will we do anybody ... dying out here on the ocean?"

"Hush, now. We're not going to die!" Had he ever spoke words he believed less? "Mind what you told me about believing in our destiny? Why, you *were* dead, or near as. Yet you came back to me."

Somehow, his faltering effort to convince Maura began to have a true effect upon him — as if someone had thrown him a rope to cling to in this storm-tossed night. He did not know where the other end might be anchored. But as the night wore on, a feeling of certainty grew in him that it must be somewhere firm and true.

At last Maura fell into an exhausted doze, a blessing for which Rath muttered a garbled but grateful word of thanks that somehow lulled him to sleep when the storm was at its worst.

He woke some time later, astonished to find Maura and himself alive. For a while he sat holding her, savoring the simple luxuries of quiet and calm, and the soft light of dawn streaming through the open hatch. A powerful sense of belief took hold of him, as it had in the mines and on midsummer night in the Secret Glade. Though he knew it would not last, he welcomed it just the same.

A while later, Maura stirred, stretched and opened her eyes. "It's so quiet," she whispered. "Are we in the afterworld?"

Rath chuckled and dropped a kiss on the crown of her head. "Your ears might make you think so, *aira*, but your eyes and nose will soon tell you the truth."

He grimaced at the reek of bile that had been spewed in the hold last night — not all hers by any means. "Shall we go up on deck and get a breath of fresh air?"

She gave a weary nod then leaned against him as he helped her aloft. There they found the crew making repairs to the ship and going about their other duties in a mute daze. Most looked as if they had not yet recovered their wits from a hard blow to the head.

Only Gull had a relaxed, well-rested appearance, though Rath doubted he had left the deck all night. His clothes and his hair still looked a bit damp, though the cat lolling around his neck seemed dry enough. Rath wondered how it had weathered the storm.

Gull perched on a raised platform near the front of the ship that was girded by a waist-high railing. He scanned the horizon through a long tube that might have been carved from very pale wood, or perhaps ivory. Rath guessed what he was looking for.

"Any sign of the Ore Fleet?" he called to the captain.

"Not a glimpse, inlander." Gull lowered the tube from his eye and leaned back against the platform railing. "I reckon it is too much to hope that the storm might have blown them east into the warding waters around the Vestan Islands. They were likely long past the Islands before it hit."

Maura sighed. "I wish *we'd* reached the Islands before it hit."

"We have a saying where I come from, wench." Gull climbed down the short ladder from his perch with a jaunty step. " 'The worst wind is better than none at all.' This one blew us toward our destination all the faster. By my reckoning, we might make Margyle before nightfall."

"The sooner the better," Maura muttered under her breath.

After the tempest of the night, the day passed quietly. Late in the morning, Rath and Maura watched in fascination as a herd of sea beasts called *nieda* swam past the ship, lunging up into the air with surprising grace for their size. Now and then two of the larger ones would butt each other with their great, curled horns that put Rath in mind of Hitherland wild goats.

Through the warm hours after midday, Rath and Maura curled up in a quiet, shaded corner of the deck and let the motion of the ship and the soothing music of the waves lull them to sleep.

Later, the sound of a voice calling down from high on one of the masts startled Rath awake. Though he didn't understand the words, the tone warned him it was not good news. The sudden, urgent rush of the crew confirmed it.

Maura stirred too, as several men ran by in different directions. "I wonder what's wrong."

Rath had a good guess, but he did not want to alarm her.

Then the young crewman who had given Maura the sea-grass dashed up to them. "Captain says you're to go below and stay out of the way. We've spotted ships coming up fast behind us — the Ore Fleet, Captain says."

The boy spat on the deck. "Slag the scum! If they catch up, grab something heavy and jump overboard with it. I'd rather be food for the fish than let the Han get hold of me!"

Rath could not concur with the lad's dire advice, he realized as he hoisted Maura up from the deck. More than once, when faced with the choice between death and capture, he had not hesitated to choose death. Now, when he looked within himself and found a fragile bud of belief taking root, he knew death was no longer an honorable choice for him.

Chapter Fourteen

WOULD IT NEVER end? Maura wondered as Rath helped her up from the deck. Would the two of them never know more than a stolen moment's peace before they were plunged once again into turmoil and peril?

Her belly no longer pitched and heaved as it had last night. Instead, a deep hollow seemed to gape inside her as she stared at the ominous dark shapes growing larger behind them. It was not as though she'd never faced the Han before. She had been running from them, hiding from them, and fighting them in one way or another ever since that fateful day the messenger bird arrived for Langbard. Yet none of those encounters had shaken her in quite the way this one did.

Out on this vast water with nothing between the sea and the sky, there was no place to hide — nowhere to run. And the number of enemies was far greater than the few she and Rath had so far confronted on their travels. Only at the Beastmount Mine had they encountered anything like this. Then, they'd had time to plan surprise attacks.

This time, the surprise was on them.

Around her and Rath, the crew scrambled, adjusting sails and performing other tasks, the purposes of which she did not understand. The air seethed with an undercurrent of alarm, ready to erupt into outright panic at any moment. It felt contagious and Maura feared she might be the first to catch it.

"Come." Rath tugged on her arm. "Let's get you somewhere safe. Then I will see if I can do anything to help."

Maura braced her feet on the wooden decking. "You heard the boy. If the Han capture this ship, nowhere will be safe. I would rather stay with you and do what I can to make sure that does not happen."

For a moment, Rath looked ready to argue.

She did not give him the chance. "We must trust in the Giver and in our destiny. They have never let us down yet, no matter how bleak things looked. I cannot believe they led us all the way to the Secret Glade only to abandon us so soon."

Her words worked — on herself at least. A strange, potent energy swelled to fill the void of doubt within her. All the challenges she and Rath had overcome to get here flooded through her memory, magnifying that power. Looking back, it almost seemed those obstacles had been contrived to increase in difficulty and risk. Each time testing them harder, calling forth greater wit, strength, courage and faith. Preparing them to meet the next trial — to seize the next opportunity.

As she spoke, Maura could see every blow of Rath's inner battle between doubt and trust reflected on his rugged features. Hard as all this had been for him to accept, he had never let her down, either. Nor did he, now.

He nodded toward the stern of the ship. "Let's go talk to Gull. Find out what he means to do and what part we can take. The Giver knows, we've had plenty of practice fighting the Han."

Hand in hand, they moved toward the rear of the vessel, trying to stay out of the way of crewmen rushing here and there. They found Captain Gull standing on a raised section of the deck peering through the strange instrument Maura had seen him use earlier.

Langbard had told her about such devices. The far end of the tube was enchanted with flesh from the eye of a great northawk preserved in a thin coating of clear sap from the giant hitherpine. It allow the person who looked through it to see as far, and as well, as one of those keen-eyed birds perched atop that tallest of trees.

First Gull peered behind to the east then to the west. "Slagging scum!" he muttered, just loud enough for Maura to hear. "They should have sailed a week ago, rot 'em!"

Maura and Rath exchanged a look. Had the sailing of the Ore Fleet been delayed by the miners' rebellion?

"East south east!" cried Gull. "Can you get me no more speed?"

From high in the rigging a crewman called down, "Not with these sails and this wind, Captain! Do you reckon it'll be enough to let us slip through their noose?"

Gull laughed. "The Han have been trying to get a noose around my neck for a while now and never succeeded. They will have no better luck today!"

Again Maura met Rath's gaze. Did Gull's crew recognize a desperate boast when they heard it?

"How close are the Han?" asked Rath. "And what 'noose' you are trying to dodge?"

"What are you doing here?" Gull lowered the seeing tube and stared at them, a look of puzzlement and annoyance wrinkling his brow. "Did I not order the pair of you belowdecks?"

He sounded much more vexed than when he'd ordered their deaths, yet Maura did not find herself intimidated. "Answer Rath's question! Our lives are as much at risk as any on board. Perhaps more. We have a right to know what is going on!"

"Very well, wench. I will tell you what is going on." Gull pointed off to the east with one hand and to the west with the spy tube. "A line of Hanish fighter ships from either side of the ore convoy is moving up like a pair of pincers. Damned if I know how they signaled one another to spring this trap, nor do I care. Unless we can break through one way or the other, they will catch us between them and crack us like a roasted bristlenut."

His gaze flickered in a strange manner as he spoke. Maura

wondered if it was a sign of the fear he dared not show his crew.

Rath glanced toward the setting sun. "Did you not say we might make the Islands before nightfall? Can we outrun the Han long enough to reach the enchanted coastal waters you told us about? The ones that can sense metal and sink Hanish ships."

Gull shook his head. "To repeat my crewman — not with these sails and this wind. I don't suppose your pretty enchantress could make the wind change course for us?"

"I wish I could." As Maura reached toward her sash, rough hands seized her from behind and she heard Rath cry out.

Too late, she realised Gull's skittery eye movements had been wordless orders to his crew.

"What treachery is this?" She put up a token struggle and shot Captain Gull an indignant glare. "Our enemy is out there! We have done nothing but offer you our help against them!"

Glancing at the cat draped around his shoulders, the smuggler addressed his next words to it. "Ah, but is our enemy *only* out there? I wonder. Or was I right about this pair in the first place — figuring them for Hanish spies? Perhaps we had better toss them overboard."

"Gull," Rath growled, "you do not have time for this. If we were spies, we would have jumped into the sea already. I am not a strong swimmer, but I could stay afloat long enough for one of those ore tubs to retrieve me, rather than stay here to be cut to pieces by their warships!"

An instant of silence greeted his words, as if Gull and his men were trying to work out whether they might be true. In that instant, an idea blossomed in Maura's mind. Seizing the chance to be heard, she blurted it out before she could question her own ignorance of seafaring or reject the notion as madly dangerous.

"Turn on the Han!" she cried. "You said they are too fast for you with the wind behind them, but the *Phantom* is nimble and can sail against the wind. Prove it!"

Time seemed to slow as Gull stepped toward her, his mouth opening. Maura thanked the Giver there were no metal weapons aboard the *Phantom*. If Gull had held a sword, she feared he would have run her through for daring to tell him what to do with his ship.

The words that came out of the captain's mouth were the last she expected. "You heard the wench! Turn and dart in among the galleys. That should take the Han by surprise!"

The crew leaped into action and slowly the *Phantom* swung about to meet the Ore Fleet head-on.

"Captain," called the man holding Maura, "does that mean we can let go of these two?"

Gull looked from Maura to Rath and back again. Then he nodded. "But keep a close watch and seize them again if they make any move to jump overboard. I swear if this goes awry, I will kill them with my own hands."

Rath shook off the hold of the two large crewmen it had taken to restrain him then gathered Maura into the shelter of his embrace.

"A bold plan, love!" He chuckled. "Ordered like a true —"

"I know," muttered Maura. That jest had no power to amuse or soothe her now. "Like a true outlaw."

"No." Rath shook his head then lifted her hand to his lips. "I was going to say, ordered like a true *queen*."

It *was* a bold plan. Rath pressed his lips to Maura's hand, in admiration and homage. But would it work?

The *Phantom* was only one ship and small compared to the monstrous vessels bearing down on them. Her crew was not even armed to repel boarders. It was one thing for Gull to boast of sailing circles around the Hanish ore galleys. If the

Phantom got caught in a squeeze between two of those big iron hulls, the wooden ship would be smashed to splinters.

"Oh, Rath —" Maura gripped his fingers so tight that he almost cried out "— what have I done?"

"Only what you needed to do and what you bid me do." For her sake, Rath cast all his doubts adrift. "Trusted in the Giver and in our destiny."

"But what if . . ."

Rath knew what she was feeling — the weight of leadership pressing down upon her. The fear that a bad decision of hers might harm more than just herself. He had no advice to give her for he had never learned how to overcome that feeling. The best he'd ever been able to do was ignore it until the crisis passed.

He pressed his forefinger to her lips. "We have no time for what-ifs now. Besides, the plan may have been yours but the decision was Gull's. I do not suppose he is a man to heed bad advice when it comes to his ship and crew. He must believe this is our best chance."

Or perhaps he had decided, since there was no hope of escape, he would rather die in some grand, hopeless attack on the Ore Fleet. Rath remembered the day he had turned to face a whole host of Hanish warriors, and how astonished he'd been when they had all run past him. He also remembered a fight with the Han at Raynor's Rift and an idea he'd feared he would not live to try.

But he *had* lived and here was his chance to give it a go.

"Have you any madfern left in your sash?" he asked Maura.

She looked puzzled by his question. "Two or three pockets full. Why?"

"Come!" He tugged her toward Captain Gull. "Perhaps there is something we can do to help, after all."

Action was the best antidote he had ever found to the paralysing venom of doubt and fear.

"Are you daft?" demanded Gull when Rath asked if there

were any bows aboard the ship. He pointed toward the front-most of the ore galleys, now close enough for their bulk to strike cold terror into the stoutest heart. "Do you reckon those hulks will feel a few pinpricks?"

Either their crews had not seen the small wooden ship turn to charge them, or they could not believe their eyes. Rath was eager to foster that disbelief. In as few words as possible, he explained his plan to sow confusion with Maura's madfern.

"Very well," snapped Gull between issuing other orders, "we have bows, but I am not fool enough to place one in your hands."

He called four of his men bidding them to arm themselves and take their orders from Rath ... provided those orders did not endanger his ship.

As the men rushed off to find their bows, Rath turned to Maura. "Have you any more of that linen for binding wounds?"

She had listened to what he'd told Gull, so she did not ask why he needed it. Instead, she lifted the flap of a large pocket at the base of her sash and pulled out a roll of the bleached cloth. She handed it to Rath, who began tearing the linen into small scraps. When he gave these back to her, she placed a large pinch of madfern into each one, then tied it closed with a bit of thread pulled from the torn edge of the binding cloth.

"This may not work, you know," she muttered as she knotted the last fragment of thread.

"We will never know unless we try." In truth, Rath did not care a great deal whether his plan worked. As long as it gave him and Maura something to think about besides the danger into which they were sailing and over which they had not the least control.

The *Phantom* slipped between two of the ore galleys as Rath fitted the first of the madfern bundles onto a wooden arrowhead.

The archer grimaced. "It won't fly well with that thing on

the tip. An arrowhead must be sharp to cut the air."

"Do your best." Rath pointed toward the mast of the nearest Hanish ship. "It does not have far to travel. Loft it as high as you can and try to hit something so the arrowhead will burst the pouch."

"Aye." The young archer did not sound very confident. He fired off the arrow, while Maura chanted the madfern spell.

Rath wished he could borrow that seeing tube of Gull's to watch the arrow's flight and be certain it hit. Since he doubted Gull would lend it and since everything was moving so swiftly around them, he murmured a plea for the Giver's help, instead. Then he bid the other archers to fire as the *Phantom* threaded its way among the ore galleys. Maura's madfern supply was soon exhausted, with no effect that Rath could tell.

Then one of the archers nudged him, "Look back there!"

Rath surged up on his toes and craned his neck. At first he could see nothing remarkable. Then he noticed that one of the ore galleys they had passed was drifting toward the one nearest it. The other ship did not make any effort to avoid being hit. Closer and closer the two vessels drew with lumbering grace until they slammed together in a thunderous shriek of metal.

The deck of the *Phantom* erupted in cheers. A dozen hands appeared out of nowhere to thump Rath on the back. The crewmen suddenly looked at Maura with the respect she deserved.

"Well done, inlanders!" Captain Gull cried.

Rath caught Maura by the hand and the two of them exchanged a questioning look. Had those little packets of madfern caused the ore galleys to collide?

Perhaps they would never know, but for now Rath was more than willing to take the credit. A new energy seemed to sweep over the deck of the *Phantom*, as if the wind had suddenly begun to blow in a more favorable direction.

"Look sharp, men!" shouted Gull as the galleys on either side of them edged closer together. "Don't get cocky!"

From high in the rigging, a scream pierced the air and a crewmen plunged to the deck below, knocking down one of his mates who had been standing near the mast.

"Hanish archers!" someone called. "Firing from the galley!"

Rath pulled Maura down as an arrow whistled over their heads, ripping through one of the *Phantom's* sails.

She shook off his protective grasp and began crawling across the deck toward the tangle of twitching limbs. "I must see if I can help those poor men!"

The four bowmen on the *Phantom* returned fire and Rath had the grim satisfaction of seeing a Hanish archer plunge from his ship into the sea.

Maura quickly checked the injured men lying on the deck. "They're both still alive." She unwadded more linen from her sash to staunch the bleeding of the man who'd been hit by the arrow. "It is in his shoulder and may have hit bone. I won't be able to push the barb through the way Langbard did for you ... even if I knew how."

Both men had been knocked senseless. Now the fellow who had been struck by the falling body began to waken, moaning.

"We must get them below decks," said Rath, "where you can tend them properly."

And where she would be in a little less danger ... for now.

The rest of the crew were occupied, returning bow fire and navigating the *Phantom* through the perilously narrow strip of water between ore galleys.

Rath reached for the arrow shaft sticking out of the wounded man's shoulder. Grasping it near the base where it stuck out of the flesh, he snapped off the rest of the shaft, thankful the injured man could not feel what he was doing.

"So it will not catch on anything when we move him," Rath explained to Maura as he hoisted the injured man under his arms. "Can you get his feet?"

The words had barely left his lips before Maura lifted the fellow's ankles. Fortunately, he was not too heavy and the hatch that led down to the ship's hold was not far off.

"Set him ... right here," Maura gasped when they had wrestled the unconscious man down the ladder, "so I will have ... some light coming through the hatch ... to see what I'm doing."

Rath did as she bid him, laying the injured man out to one side of the ladder. "You stay here and see to his wound, I'll go back for the other fellow."

"Are you sure you can manage on your own?" Maura rummaged in the pockets of her sash for healing herbs.

"If I can't, I will fetch you to help me," Rath lied. He would find some way to get the man down here without summoning Maura from the relative safety of the hold.

As he squeezed past her to reach the ladder, his hands closed over her shoulders in a swift caress.

She reached up to cover his hands with hers, making him linger for a moment, which he was glad to do. "The other man may have broken bones. Check if any of his limbs are twisted at odd angles. If one is, tie it to a piece of wood or anything you can find to keep the break from shifting worse."

"Aye, *aira*." He dropped a fleeting kiss on her neck before heading off. "I may not have your gentle touch, but I will do my best for him."

"Water," he heard her mutter as he climbed back up to the deck. "A whole sea out there, but not a drop where I need it."

"There's a barrel over in that corner." Rath pointed. "If it is empty, I will find you water as soon as I get back."

He had just crawled out of the hold when he met two crewmen carrying their injured comrade toward the hatch. The fellow was conscious now, his features twisted in pain.

Rath caught the injured man's eye. "The lady will soon set you to rights, friend. She has healed me of a good many wounds and always left me better than I was before."

He made a hasty circuit of the deck, looking for more wounded he could send down to Maura, but found none.

When he asked Gull, the captain shook his head and answered in a tone of grim pride, "The Han are better swordsmen than archers. They got one lucky shot. We hit four times that many. You know, inlander, I am beginning to think we might get out of this alive after all."

Gull pulled hard on the rudder and the *Phantom* veered to squeeze between another pair of ore galleys.

How many did that make? Rath had lost count. He wondered that there was any ore left in the Blood Moon Mountains, with this much hacked out and shipped away every year since the Han had conquered Embria. How many men had sweat, bled and retched away their lives to fill this fleet with its vile cargo year after year?

Impotent fury seethed within him. His fist ached for a weapon powerful enough to channel and purge it, but even the Han did not possess one that destructive.

A harsh chuckle from Gull roused Rath from his fruitless rage. "Do my eyes deceive me, or is that open sea beyond those cursed tubs?"

Rath peered ahead, his rage ebbing for a moment. "I am only an inlander, so you might not want to take my word for it. But that looks a good deal like open sea to me."

Something about the tone of Gull's laughter told Rath it was partly directed at himself. "I *will* take your word for it. And I reckon I had better find something else to call you ... friend."

"I like the sound of that."

Gull thought for a moment then he grinned. "So do I. And to think this was all the idea of a pretty wench. If you ever tire of her ...?"

"The lady will tire of me long before I tire of her." Though Rath meant the words only in jest, somehow they turned back to sting him hard and deep.

He did not have time to fret about it, though, for just then the *Phantom* broke through the final row of ore galleys.

"Slag!" muttered Gull. "Nothing's ever that easy, is it?"

Rath glanced up to see one last Hanish cutter sailing toward them.

"We didn't come through all that to let them get us now!" Gull snagged Rath's arm and hauled him toward the tiller. "Hold on to this and keep it pulled as far that way as you can until I tell you different. Aye?"

"Aye!" Rath struggled to hold the tiller that had seemed to take no effort at all from Gull.

Meanwhile, the captain strode the length of his ship, calling out orders for setting the sails. From what little Rath had learned about wind and sails, he reckoned Gull was putting the *Phantom* on a course that would force the Hanish ship to veer out of the wind. But would it lose speed quickly enough to keep it from ramming the smaller vessel?

Rath guessed it would be a near thing one way or the other. With each passing moment, as he strained to hold the rudder firm, his fear grew that they would not make it. He glanced toward the hatch, willing Maura to climb up looking for something she might need to tend the injured men.

With danger so near at hand, he wanted her close so he could be certain she was all right. And so he could do whatever he must to protect her, if it came to that.

He did not dare leave the post Gull had assigned him, or he would have gone to her at once. Instead, he made frantic plans how he would reach her and what he would do if the Han boarded Gull's ship, or if the cutter's sharp prow caught it broadside.

As the latter seemed more and more likely, Rath braced for the crash. Then suddenly, the Hanish cutter veered back to its original course and the *Phantom* slid past.

Rath sagged under the warm weight of his relief — so

much that he almost lost his grip on the tiller. What had made the Han flinch at that last instant? Surely they did not fear a collision with Gull's little *Phantom*.

Could this be the working of his and Maura's destiny?

Gull soon appeared to give Rath a few answers. He fairly danced over the deck in his excitement. "Look, man, look! Slag the tiller — let it go and look!"

He pointed past the Hanish cutter to the bulk of the Ore Fleet in the distance. Though the sun had dipped near the western horizon, it was still possible to make out what was happening to the Hanish ships. Galleys and cutters alike, they floundered as if each were caught in its own private squall. The wind blew no harder than it had all day, yet some invisible tempest churned up giant breakers that tossed the huge, heavy-laden vessels about like wood chips.

Only the ship that had been chasing the *Phantom* seemed not to be ensnared . . . yet. Seeing the rest of the fleet in trouble must have made its crew veer away so suddenly. Now they furled sails and slowed.

"I have heard of the warding waters." Gull shook his head in wonder. "But never thought to see them at work with my own eyes." He pointed toward the cutter. "The Han cannot decide whether to go to the aid of the others or hang back so they will not be caught in whatever this is."

Whatever this is. Those words set a chill gnawing deep in Rath's bones — his old wariness of magic. During his travels with Maura that fear had eased as he'd come to understand how she channeled the special power of living things for modest feats of healing and defense. But he'd never seen Maura unleash anything like this. Rath hoped he never would.

Gull appeared to have no such reservations. "The whole Ore Fleet! And to think my little *Phantom* lured them into it. Why this will be talked and sung of on the Dusk Coast for a hundred years!"

Rath did not point out that last night's storm had likely played a part as well. No harm in letting Gull savor his triumph. If the Han had not been so distracted by the Embrian vessel sailing in their midst, they might have noticed the first of their own ships running into trouble while they still had time to avoid it themselves. The little madfern missiles might have played a part, too.

One by one the sea began to swallow the floundering Hanish vessels. What would the loss of the Ore Fleet mean for the Han and for Embria? Rath wondered. A growing shortage of weapons for the garrisons, perhaps? A whisper of crippling uncertainty among the Han that rust was beginning to erode the iron grip in which they had long held his country?

"What will we do now?" he asked Gull.

The captain chuckled and took the tiller from Rath. "Quit gloating, I reckon, and head for harbor."

He called out to his crew, "Trim those sails one last time, lads, then we'll sleep and feast tonight in Margyle!"

The crew seemed to fancy that idea, for they scrambled to obey Gull's orders. Soon the *Phantom* sailed west in a wide arc that kept plenty of distance between it and the ravenous stretch of water that had engulfed the Ore Fleet.

Rath headed off to find Maura. She might need his help tending those wounded men. He was also anxious to tell her what he had just witnessed and what he thought it might mean.

He found her holding a mug to the lips of the man who'd been struck down by his fallen comrade. She had strapped his right arm close to his body with long strips of linen and bound his left leg to what looked like the handle of a mop.

She glanced up when she heard Rath on the ladder, smiling when she saw it was him. "I hope all that cheering means we are out of danger at last."

Rath nodded as he sank down beside her. "Gull says we'll sleep and feast on Margyle tonight."

He did not tell her about their close brush with the Hanish cutter. He would save that for later, when they had firm, dry ground beneath their feet and deadly warding waters between them and any Han who might wish them harm.

"You should have seen what happened to the Ore Fleet." He began to describe it. "For once, they met a force even more merciless than themselves, rot them!"

The man with the arrow in his shoulder stirred and moaned, though his eyes did not open.

Maura cast an anxious glance his way. "I hope the poor fellow will not waken until we've reached Margyle. They must have more skilled healers than I who can remove that barbed arrowhead from his flesh."

"Arrowhead?" The thought paralysed Rath for an instant.

The unconscious crewman had a chunk of metal in his flesh. Metal, like the kind that had made the warding waters devour the Hanish Ore Fleet.

"Gull!" He leaped to his feet and surged up the ladder toward the deck. "Turn back! Arrows! Metal! The warding waters!"

Rath hurled himself up through the open hatch and staggered toward the tiller. The moment he saw Gull's face, he could tell the captain had understood his garbled warning.

But when a huge wave rose out of nowhere to slam across the *Phantom's* bow, he also knew his warning had come too late.

Chapter Fifteen

RATH'S CRY OF alarm and his hurried footfall on the ladder made fear tighten around Maura's throat. For a moment, though, she did not understand what had driven him toward the deck shouting at the top of his voice.

Then she heard the crash of a great wave and the *Phantom* reeled like a fighter struck hard on the head. The sudden pitch of the ship flung her sideways on top of the unconscious man. She just managed to keep from hitting the poor fellow's shoulder and driving the arrowhead deeper into his flesh.

The arrowhead! Rath's words echoed in her mind and finally made sense. Could one tiny shard of metal truly be to blame for the tempest now tearing at the *Phantom*?

The injured man moved and groaned when Maura landed on top of him. "What happened? Where am I?"

She pulled herself off him, but kept low, with her arms splayed out to brace her against the next roll of the ship. "You're in the hold. A Hanish archer from one of the ore galleys shot you down from the rigging."

The other injured man spoke up, his voice a bit slurred from the pain-easing brew Maura had given him. "You might be dead, now, if I hadn't broken your fall. Say, lady, why is the ship rocking? Are the Han ramming us?"

The *Phantom* gave another great heave ... and so did Maura's belly. She rummaged in her sash for the rest of the sea grass, popped a piece in her mouth and began chewing furiously. She'd be no good to anyone huddled in a corner retching her guts out.

"It isn't the Han." Maura mumbled the words around a

mouthful of sea grass.

"No." Rath's voice rang out from above. "It's that arrow."

He climbed back down the ladder, stopping halfway and clinging to it when another huge wave lashed the ship, sending a shower of spray through the hatch. "There are more stuck into the masts and the deck. Gull has his crew scouring the ship for them now."

He jumped down the last few rungs, landing on his hands and knees near Maura. "Can you get this one out?"

"I told you, I don't —"

Before she could finish, Rath leaned close and whispered, "If we cannot get it off the ship any other way, Gull will have this poor fellow thrown overboard!"

She had to try, then. She could not let a man drown because he'd had the bad fortune to be shot by a Hanish arrow. Whatever she might do to prevent it, she would have to work quickly. The ship could not take much more of this violent buffeting and still remain afloat.

If only she had not woken the poor fellow by falling on him! Anything she did to dislodge that arrowhead was sure to cause him terrible pain. Maura shrank from that.

"What can I do?" she asked Rath in an urgent whisper. "I have nothing sharp I can … cut it out with. Remember what Langbard said about Hanish arrows, how the barbs catch in the flesh if you try to pull them out."

"Push it through, then, like Langbard did for me!"

"I don't know how!"

She heard voices overhead. Gull must be sending someone to fetch the wounded man.

"You may know more than you think." Rath clutched her hand. "Did Langbard share any of that skill with you in the passing ritual?"

As she chided herself for not thinking of it, Maura marveled that Rath had. The passing ritual was the first stage of a journey between this life and the afterworld. When the spirit of a living person accompanied a dying one, a sharing of memories took place, so that part of the dying person would live on.

Maura's passing ritual with her wizard guardian had been too brief, rushed by the threat of lurking danger. But since then, she'd discovered unexpected memories of Langbard's among her own, stirred by a chance word or experience. She had never yet tried calling upon a memory she could not be certain was even there.

She heard someone scrambling down the ladder.

"Hold them back," she begged Rath. "Do not let them take him until —"

"Do it!" cried Rath. "I know you can."

If only she could have half the confidence in herself that Rath had in her. Maura crawled over to the wounded man who was moaning in pain. She wished she had time to brew him a draft ease it, but that would have to wait. Another shower of cold, briny spray crashed into the hold. The boards of the hull groaned under the beating they were taking.

"Lie still," she bid the wounded man. "Take a deep breath and hold it."

She groped for the stub of the arrow shaft sticking out of his shoulder, hoping that action would unearth the memory of what she must do next. She pictured the upstairs chamber of Langbard's cottage with Rath lying on the bed, a Hanish arrow imbedded in his arm. She pictured Langbard perched on the side of the bed, preparing to expel the arrow.

Then, suddenly, she *was* Langbard, seeing the whole scene through his eyes. Knowing what he ... what she must do.

Spikeroot — that was what she needed! But did she have any left in her sash? Not knowing its use, she had once thought of emptying that pocket to store something more needful.

The dark, wet, pitching hold of the ship seemed to recede around her. Maura heard Rath's voice as if from a long distance, first pleading, then challenging. "I will not let you disturb the lady at her work. Gull can have my head for it, if he wants."

"The fish will have all our heads and the rest of our flesh too," the crewman shouted, "if we do not throw that cursed arrow into the sea one way or the other!"

"They want to throw me overboard!" The wounded man thrashed about, then howled in pain as he jerked the stub of the arrow shaft in Maura's grip. "Don't let them take me!"

"Be still!" she ordered him, startled to hear the words came out in *that tone* — the one Langbard had only used on rare occasions to compel instant obedience.

When the man froze, she turned to the one who was trying to push past Rath. "Stay back!"

The sounds of a struggle between the two men ceased.

A heady sense of power pulsed through her. Might the warding waters heed her if she ordered them to calm? Maura decided to save that as a last resort.

Her fingers fumbled in her sash pocket. The spike-root — she had not thrown it away after all! Perhaps Langbard's slumbering memory had roused just enough to prevent her.

Pulling out as much of the powdered root as she could hold, she held her palm to catch a few drops of water spilling through the hatch. The seawater bound with the spikeroot powder to make a thick paste that Maura packed around the wound.

Then the words of the incantation whispered through her mind. Maura spat out the sea grass and began to chant them, hoping she could hold her gorge long enough to recite the whole spell.

The nub of the arrow shaft began to vibrate beneath her fingers and the wounded man screamed in torment until all Maura wanted to do was jam her fingers in her ears and flee from the awful sound. She stumbled over some of the words.

Then she felt Rath hovering behind her. "Don't stop now!"

He wrapped one arm around her then reached with his other hand to grip the arrow shaft. What was he doing?

Maura chanted the spell louder, trying to drown out the man's screams. The arrow shaft vibrated harder and harder until she feared it would shatter.

Then something taut snapped.

The screams choked off and the butt of the arrow shaft thrust through flesh and bone to gouge into the floorboards of the hold beneath. Maura slumped forward, gasping for breath as if she had just run many miles or hefted a weight far beyond her strength.

Rolling the injured man out of the way, Rath pried the arrowhead from the wet wood. Then he lunged up, twisting around to shove it into the hands of the waiting crewman. "There — go! Get rid of it!"

The man clambered up the ladder as huge waves pounded the *Phantom* from every direction at once. The ship's hull quivered like the arrow shaft had. Then the unbearable tension broke with a shudder that sounded like the ocean had heaved a great sigh. A breathless, exhausted calm settled over everything.

"Well done, *aira*!" Rath spun Maura around into a swift, hard embrace, with a kiss to match.

She yielded for a sweet, delirious moment, then pushed him away with pretended annoyance. "Enough of that! Let me tend this poor man's wound while he still has a drop of blood left in him. What a mercy he swooned when the pain became too great. I'm not sure I could have kept up much longer if he hadn't."

Pulling another strip of linen from her sash, she wet it with the seawater now dripping more slowly through the hold. Then she sprinkled the damp cloth with candleflax to staunch the bleeding. While she was busy with that, Rath moved the man with broken bones to a drier part of the hold and fetched him a blanket.

"What were you doing," asked Maura "when you put your arm around me and grabbed hold of the arrow shaft?"

Rath chuckled. "I remembered some wise words an old wizard once told me."

"Langbard said many wise things. Which one do you mean?"

Why was she blinking back tears after all this time and everything that had happened? Was it the strange sinking of spirits that often came after danger had passed? Or was it the fleeting but intense connection she had felt with her beloved guardian while she'd worked his spell?

Whatever provoked such intense feelings Rath seemed to sense and understand them. He made his way back to her and dropped to his haunches, raising his hand to rub up and down against her arm.

"I did not get to hear many of Langbard's wise sayings in the little time I knew him. But I do recall him saying, 'Spells are all very well, but sometimes there is no substitute for a swift application of physical force.'" He imitated Langbard's husky, resonant voice so well it made Maura laugh and sob at the same time.

Rath brought his hand higher, to rest against her cheek. "I reckoned your spell could use some physical force to help it along. It seemed to work."

Maura nodded. Then a stray breeze found its way down the hatch to whisper over her damp clothes, making her shiver. "Not a moment too soon."

"I wonder." Rath fetched a coarse-woven blanket and wrapped it around her shoulders. "If we had needed another moment, something tells me the Giver would have found it for us."

Beneath his wry tone, Maura heard a note of belief, tentative but sincere. Not a high-flown, zealous faith fired by witnessing marvels and doing great deeds, but a sturdy, workaday belief that grew slowly over time. One that would warm a body against the cold of despair and wear well through the years.

"Just think —" she caught his hand and gripped it tight "— if one tiny ship can bring about the destruction of the Ore Fleet, there may be hope for us to liberate Embria, after all."

Rath drew in a deep, slow breath. "Don't get ahead of yourself, love. The *Phantom* did not sink those Hanish ships — it was the warding waters."

"Perhaps we will find some other great power to turn to our advantage." At the moment, nothing seemed beyond their reach.

Though the hold had grown too dark to see more than shadows, she could make out Rath shaking his head. "I don't know, *aira*. Great powers can be dangerous things."

Then, more to himself than to her, he murmured, "And not only to the folks they are used *against*, either."

Just then, one of the crew called down through the hatch. "Come on up on deck, inlanders! The captain wants you."

"Tell your captain he can wait," Maura called back, "until I have these men properly tended."

Rath smiled to himself, wondering how many of the fierce men on this ship would have the courage to delay carrying out one of Captain Gull's orders.

He tugged on her sleeve. "Listen." From both wounded men came the soft, regular breathing of sleep. "You cannot do much for them now that a good rest will not do better."

"True." Maura's hand fumbled out of the darkness to find his. "I will need light to set those bones and clean that arrow wound properly. No doubt there are healers on the Islands with greater skill than I who can set them both to rights."

Rath hoisted her to her feet. "There may be healers better equipped than you, *aira*, with gardens of rare herbs and such. But I would defy any of them to do half what you have done with only that sash and whatever you could gather along the way to fill its pockets."

Maura gave a weary chuckle. "Langbard often used to say, 'Necessity is a harsh teacher, but a thorough one.' I confess I never understood what he meant until I began my journey."

She held tight to Rath's arm as they groped toward the ladder, in a way that told him she depended upon him to support and guide her. His heart ached the way his belly had after those few times in his life when he'd eaten more than his fill. Now his love for Maura felt like more than his heart could comfortably contain.

"There is more to it than that," he said as she started up the ladder. "All the skill and supplies in the world are nothing without the will to help folks. I have never known anyone with as great a measure of that as you have."

Maura scrambled up onto the deck then turned to offer Rath a hand. "Perhaps you should have looked longer in the waters of the Secret Glade. Then you would have seen someone with vast reserves of that will."

Perhaps, Rath admitted to himself, but did he have the courage to tap it? Like every other power, it had its perils.

Several small lanterns hung from the lower masts, shedding a shadowy light over the deck.

Captain Gull stepped out of a patch of shadow and performed a deep bow before Rath and Maura. "I have never met a pair of inlanders so handy to have about when there's trouble. My thanks to you for saving my ship. I am in your debt."

Rath returned the bow with self-conscious awkwardness, though he could not decide how to reply. His past had taught him more about trading threats and insults than accepting courtesy.

Instead, he glanced out into the night where clusters of distant lights flickered. "Will we put in to harbor tonight?"

Gull shook his head. "We'll drop anchor here and wait for the dawn tide. Though if you are anxious to reach shore,

I can let you have one of the small boats and a couple of my men to row you in."

"Should we?" Rath whispered to Maura.

He had no wish to hasten their arrival on the Islands. For all its dangers and hardships, this short voyage had been like a welcome return to his old life. To these men he was no Waiting King with a heavy mantle of impossible expectations, just another inlander who had managed to earn their grudging respect. All that would change once he and Maura set foot on the island.

But he knew she must long for the safety and assurance of firm earth beneath her.

Perhaps Maura sensed how he felt, or perhaps she felt something like it herself. "The sea is calm here. Another night aboard ship will do us no harm. Besides, I want to be near at hand in case those wounded men wake and need tending."

"As you will, then." Gull sounded pleased with their decision. "I reckon a little festivity is in order, to celebrate our daring victory over the Hanish Ore Fleet. Will you join us?"

This time Rath did not hesitate. "With pleasure!"

"You heard the man." Gull snapped his fingers. "What are we waiting for?"

All at once the night air bubbled with the rollicking, infectious music of wooden pipes and hand drums. Rath found himself seated on a sack full of something soft, with Maura nestled on his lap. This was definitely better than whatever reception might await them on the Islands!

When someone thrust a tall jug into Rath's hand, he took a long swig that made his eyes water.

"What is that?" he gasped when the liquid had burned its way down his throat, numbing as it went. He was no stranger to strong drink ... at least he hadn't thought so. But this ...!

"Your first taste of *sythria*?" Gull took the jug from Rath's hand and guzzled the fiery brew without betraying the least distress. "You must have sea-going blood in you. Most inland-ers spew their first drink back up and scream for water."

So that was *sythria*. Rath had heard of the stuff and assumed its reputation exaggerated. Now he knew better. His belly felt as if it was full of flaming oil.

Maura grabbed the jug out of Gull's hand and sniffed its fumes. "The stuff doesn't smell that bad. What is it made of?"

Before Rath could stop her, she tipped the jug back and drained it. After what he and Gull had drunk, there could not have been much left. Still, Rath expected her to choke and gag or belch a cloud of steam.

But she only fanned her mouth. "That *is* strong! Remind me not to it drink so fast next time."

"I will try," said Rath, though he wondered if he would remember.

From that single drink, he already felt dizzy and a good deal more carefree than he had in a long time. Perhaps he could stomach another sip of *sythria*, now that the first one had numbed his throat. For some reason that notion made him laugh like a fool. But foolishness felt strangely pleasant. The look on Gull's face as he stared at Maura made Rath laugh, too.

"Your pardon, mistress." Gull blinked his eyes as if trying to decide whether they still worked properly. "I have never before known a women ask for a second drink of *sythria* after she has had her first."

Maura sniffed the mouth of the jug again and shrugged. "I've tasted worse. My guardian was the most terrible cook in Norest . . . perhaps in the whole of Embria. What did you say this was made of?"

"Pardon, mistress, in my amazement, I did not answer your question. *Sythria* is distilled from the rind of sythfruit that grows on the Islands. Folk here brew a very fine wine from the fruit itself, but Duskporters like a drink that has a bit more . . . brawn to it. Cheap, too, for sythfruit rind is bitter and would only be thrown away. We put it to much more worthwhile use."

The hillcat around Gull's neck rose and stretched. For the first time Rath had seen, it bounded off its master's back into a shadowed part of the deck.

"Abri must be hungry." Gull seized another jug from a passing crewman and took a long drink from it. "Rats beware!"

He rose from his perch on a small keg and made a sweeping, rather unsteady, bow before Maura. "Will you do me the honor of a dance, mistress? I dared not ask you while Abri had her claws in me. Jealous creature — she would never have permitted it."

Maura made no move to accept his invitation. "I fear it would be less an honor than a torture for your toes, Captain. I have never danced with a partner."

"Never danced?" Gull staggered back. Either he was pretending to be shocked by Maura's words, or those two long, fast drinks from the *sythria* jug were having an effect on him.

It must have been the first, for he recovered quite nimbly to swoop forward and grab Maura by the hand. Before she or Rath could protest, Gull pulled her to her feet and thrust another jug at Rath to keep him company in her absence.

"That is a grave misfortune we must put right at once." Gull tucked one hand around Maura's waist, while the other, outstretched, gripped hers. In that hold, he galloped her several times around a small circle of deck where none of the crew was sitting.

At first Maura squealed with a mixture of excitement and dismay as Gull whirled her around. Those squeals soon gave way to breathless laughter and her stiff, reluctant posture relaxed. By their last circuit, she appeared to be leading Gull a merry dance.

Rath took several slow drinks from the jug in his hand. In between them, he sat scowling while the *sythria* kindled a blaze in his belly.

Gull? Hmmph! The man's name should be *Gall*, for he had plenty of it. More than enough to suit Rath.

What did the scoundrel think he was playing at, plying Maura with strong drink, then dragging her out of her husband's arms for a wild jaunt around the deck? Did he not have the sense to know that she would draw the lecherous gaze of every man on board, the way her feminine curves filled out that boy's shirt and breeches? Or did he not care?

Rath tipped the *sythria* jug again. He was beginning to enjoy its burnt, musky taste. Curses — the jug was empty!

He lurched to his feet only to find them as contrary as a mismatched team of balky horses. Each wanted to go its own way and neither would move in the direction he wanted them to go. Rath was not about to be thwarted by parts of his own body. So he started forward, letting each leg do what it wanted while he concentrated on keeping his balance.

He had managed to stagger a few steps when a clever idea occurred to him. If he waited at the edge of the ring of crewmen, Gull and Maura's spinning dance would bring them right to him. He congratulated himself on getting stopped without pitching face-first onto the deck.

When Gull and Maura pranced past, Rath stopped them with a heavy hand on Gull's shoulder. "I reckon you've done enough dancing for one night, friend ... with my wife at least."

Gull winked at Maura and laughed. "Fie, he's almost as bad as Abri! We should have sent him off with her to hunt rats."

"Sit down, Rath." Maura lifted his hand off Gull's shoulder. "Before you fall down. Don't spoil the celebration."

Her gently chiding tone did nothing to soothe Rath's temper. Besides, his mind was so fixed on Gull's last words that he scarcely heeded what she said.

"Hunt rats, you say?" He grabbed Gull by his long plume of dark hair and wrenched him high on his toes. "I won' need to go far to find a rat, will I?"

"Leave off, you daft inlander!" cried Gull. "No man lays hands upon me aboard *my* ship!"

Suddenly, Gull heaved his feet from the deck, making Rath bear his full weight with one arm. Before Rath could let go of him or lose his balance and toppled forward, Gull swung by his hair, driving his feet hard into Rath's belly.

The air whooshed out of him as pain exploded within. He collapsed onto the deck, writhing and gasping for air that would not come fast enough. But pain and even air meant little to Rath Talward when his fighting blood was roused. Gull had roused it to a blazing pitch — first with his insults and now with this attack.

"Let that be a lesson to you, inlander." Gull pulled himself up from the deck where Rath had dropped him. "Most men I'd have killed for what you just did, but ..."

Did Gull reckon he meant to lie there and swallow such humiliation? Ha!

Rath swung his arm in a wide swath and caught Gull by the ankle, jerking him off his feet. Before he went down, Gull kicked Rath in the face with his free foot. Rath flinched, blood spewing from his throbbing nose.

The little demon could fight better with his feet than most men twice his size could with their fists! A distant, detached part of Rath's mind acknowledged it even as he kept hold of Gull's foot and landed a good hard blow to some part of the smuggler's compact body.

For a few moments, the two men rolled around the deck, thrashing away at each other with feet, fists, knees and elbows.

"Stop this at once!" Maura cried out in a tone of ringing rage. "Both of you!"

To his credit, Rath did hesitate for an instant. But Gull took advantage of that hesitation to drive his sharp little knee hard into Rath's groin. Rath let out a savage bellow of pain but managed to get his hands around Gull's slender throat and squeeze with all his strength.

Just as he was savoring the bulge of Gull's eyes, a familiar but detested sensation stole through his flesh, making his hands fall slack and freeze motionless along with the rest of his body. The same must have happened to Gull, for he did not take advantage of Rath's paralysis to land another unsporting blow.

Instead, he channeled his hostility into a black glare. "What have you done to me, inlander? I will not stand for this, curse you!"

"You have no choice but to stand for it," Rath growled. "Or lie down for it. And it is none of my doing." He tried to turn his head to glare at Maura, but his neck refused to move any more than the rest of him. "It is *hers*. Curse those fool cobwebs!"

"Hers?" Gull's gaze shifted sidelong, but he had no better luck making his head turn than Rath had. "You mean ..."

At some point during their brawl, the music had stopped, but Rath only noticed the silence now. He expected Maura's voice to fill it, with a firm rebuke to him and Gull.

Instead, a male voice sliced through the silence, speaking Embrian, but with a distinctive *twaran* lilt. "What is the meaning of this, Gull? You fouled our warding waters beyond further use by leading the whole Hanish Ore Fleet into them. Now you anchor offshore, engaging in all manner of violence and debauchery."

Something about the fellow's tone made Rath forget his good-natured tiff with Gull. Perhaps it was his outlaw nature to resent any figure of authority. Or perhaps the *sythria* made him spoil for a fresh fight.

Into the cowed hush that followed the man's words, Rath muttered, loud enough for all to hear, "You ought to try a little debauchery now and then. It might be just the thing to loosen those tight bowels of yours."

The silence that greeted *his* words put Rath in mind of a very thin-shelled egg teetering on the edge of a high wall. Even the waves seemed to stop their quiet lapping against the hull of the ship to listen. In that brittle stillness, the soft, deliberate approach of a pair of leather-soled boots sounded louder than the earlier thunder of the hand drums.

It occurred to Rath, not for the first time that taunting a mobile opponent while he lay helpless was a stupid thing to do. He could not help himself, though.

The slender leather toe of a boot hooked under his chin, turning Rath's head as he was unable to do for himself. A good-sized foot poised above his throat. Long ago he had learned to hide fear, and he flattered himself that he'd become skilled at it. But it never got easier.

He stared up at a man who appeared very tall and lean ... at least from his angle. Clad in tight leggings and a long pale brown tunic, the man had piercing dark eyes and features so straight and perfectly proportioned Rath's fist ached to knock something askew. Or at the very least, to muss the fellow's close-cropped dark hair from its unnatural tidiness.

"And who are you," asked the owner of the boot, "to fling insults about without having either the courage or manners to rise and say them to my face?"

"I'm the Waiting King," Rath growled as if it was only a contemptuous jest meant to shock the other man. He would have had a harder time uttering the words as if he meant them. "Who are you?"

"Don't mind him, Lord Idrygon!" cried Gull. "You can't hold an inlander responsible for the blather he spews after his first bellyful of *sythria.*"

Lord Idrygon? Well, well. Lord of what? Rath wondered. He tried to stifle a traitorous notion that Lord Idrygon looked the way he'd once pictured the Waiting King.

Rath shifted his gaze to Maura. When she finally stopped gaping at Idrygon long enough to spare him a glance, he mouthed the word *"please."*

She made a face, as if she had bitten into something sour. Then her lips began to move in a silent incantation and soon Rath was able to make his fingers wiggle.

In the meantime, Lord Idrygon had withdrawn the toe of his boot, letting Rath's head fall slack again. "A man who cannot curb his tongue when he drinks too much should not drink at all."

His hand now free to move, Rath seized Idrygon's foot before it reached the deck. He held it an inch or two in the air, enough to keep the other man off balance. Except that Idrygon seemed more poised and steady standing on one foot than most men looked on two.

Since the move was clearly not achieving its purpose, Rath let go of Idrygon's foot and staggered upright, hauling Gull along with him. He swiped his shirtsleeve across his lower face to wipe away some of the blood dripping from his nose.

"I'll make you a bargain, *my lord.* If you curb your tongue, I will try to curb mine." Rath jerked his head in the direction of the warding waters. "If you had asked before casting blame, we could have told you Gull did not *lead* the Ore Fleet here. A storm blew them nearer your coast than they usually come. We are guilty of nothing more than some damn fine sailing to wriggle out of their clutches."

"I saw what happened." Idrygon's well-shaped mouth compressed into a thin, rigid line. "If this ship had not distracted the Han, they might have seen how close they'd strayed to our coast and made some effort to avoid the warding waters. Gull should know better than to come here so near the time when the Ore Fleet sails."

With all the anticipation he would have felt pulling a bowstring to return enemy fire, Rath drew breath to reply.

Before he could summon the right words, Maura appeared at his side, looking pale and agitated. "Are you saying you did not summon us with that messenger bird? But Langbard told me the first one came from here. And the second message said Captain Gull would bring us."

"Messenger birds?" murmured Idrygon in a flat, dazed-sounding voice. His haughty features twisted in a grimace of disbelief as he looked from Maura with her boy's clothes and wild hair to Rath, all beaten and bloody. "But that cannot be."

Much as he relished making this arrogant lordling squirm, Rath also wished it *could not be* — that somehow this was all a huge mistake.

"We send those fool birds out all the time." Idrygon's contemptuous tone left no doubt what he thought of the practice. "No one has ever answered their summons."

Maura's shoulders slumped and Rath sensed what she must be thinking — that Langbard's death and all their struggles had been for nothing.

He wrapped his arm around her and gave a heartening squeeze. He might not be very promising king material, but he wasn't a man to give up without trying either.

Leaning toward Lord Idrygon, he flashed his most impudent outlaw grin and announced. "Someone has now."

Chapter Sixteen

WHAT DID LORD Idrygon mean about sending messenger birds *all the time*? The fiery *sythria* seethed in Maura's belly until she feared she might make a complete fool of herself by retching on the Vestan lord's elegantly shod feet.

She'd assumed that she and Rath would be expected and welcomed here — find answers to all their doubts and questions. Now it appeared their arrival might pose far more questions than it answered.

When Rath wrapped his arm around her, Maura could not decide whether to savor his clumsy gesture of support or to turn and throttle him for making such an ass of himself! No wonder Lord Idrygon looked so dazed. Any high-flown fancy the poor man might have had about the Waiting King and Destined Queen must be dying a painful death indeed.

To give him credit, Lord Idrygon rallied his shaken composure quickly.

"Your pardon for beginning our acquaintance on an inhospitable note." He made a stiff bow to them. "These are ... surprising tidings indeed. I think you had better come ashore with me now. No doubt you will desire an audience with the Council of Sages as soon as one can be arranged."

Maura gave a tentative nod. She supposed they would. Was it the Council of Sages who had sent the messenger birds? Would they be able to answer *some* of her questions, at least?

"And you will surely wish to prepare yourselves for the audience," continued Lord Idrygon. "Rest, groom, tend your hurts. I offer you the hospitality of my house for your stay on Margyle."

On the still night air, Maura fancied she heard a hushed buzz spread among Gull's crew. The tone of that murmur told her Lord Idrygon's offer of hospitality must be a great honor.

But his mention of tending injuries reminded her she had other obligations. "Our thanks to you, sir. But two crewmen were wounded during our fight with the Han. They may need me in the night." She patted her sash. "I am a healer, though perhaps modest in skill compared to many on the Islands."

"The wounded men should be brought ashore now, as well," said Lord Idrygon almost before Maura finished speaking. The haste of his offer suggested eagerness, but the set of his well-bred features looked more as though he was compelled to swallow some foul tonic. "They will be taken to a place where they can receive the best possible care."

Put that way, Maura couldn't very well refuse the man's invitation, could she? She glanced at Rath, her brows raised.

He replied with a repentant shrug. His earlier belligerence seemed to have deserted him. "Go, stay, it's all the same to me. Whatever you think best, *aira*."

"I believe we should accept Lord Idrygon's generous invitation. He is right that we ought to make ourselves presentable before we meet with anyone else."

She did not want to risk making as unfavorable an impression on the Council of Sages as they had on Lord Idrygon. At least he appeared willing to give them a second chance. Others might be less forbearing.

"Very good." Lord Idrygon bowed again. This one looked less apt to crack his spine. "The wounded crewmen, we would find them below decks?"

When Maura nodded, he turned and gave some hushed but forceful orders to three men he had brought on board with him. All wore the same boots with slightly curled toes, tight-fitted leggings and high-collared tunics, though theirs were shorter than Idrygon's.

The instant he finished speaking, two of his men headed toward the hatch while Idrygon and the third man escorted Rath and Maura to a long slender boat moored beside the *Phantom*.

As they climbed down into the craft, Maura heard Idrygon call over his shoulder to Captain Gull, "Make sure you do not sail until we have had a chance to talk!"

Rath tried protest that none of this was Gull's fault, but Idrygon gave no sign he heard ... or cared.

They rowed ashore in silence. By the light of the waning midsummer moon, Maura could make out a large number of pale-colored buildings clustered on gently sloping hills that surrounded a small bay. A sense of safety and tranquility hung about the place. It seemed to open its arms and welcome her, perhaps recognizing how deeply she craved what it offered.

Langbard's cottage and Hoghill Farm had once seemed like peaceful havens to her. But even there, peril had always lurked. Kept at bay by Langbard's power, it had skulked in the shadows waiting for a moment of weakness or inattention to strike. Here, she sensed true peace, unlike any she had ever known.

At last the boat tied up to a small wharf. Idrygon disembarked with quick, lithe movements then turned and extended his hand to Maura. Once he had helped her ashore, he offered his hand to Rath, who ignored it, almost tipping the boat as he staggered onto the wharf.

A mild sea breeze wafted up from the bay, but it did not smell of brine and fish like the air in Duskport. Instead, the subtle mingling of flowers and herbs reminded Maura of her garden behind Langbard's cottage and the warm spring in the Blood Moon foothills where she and Rath had rested on their journey.

Idrygon froze for a moment, as if watching or listening for something. Then he strode off into the night calling softly, "This way."

Though Maura had no idea where they were going, it seemed Idrygon might be taking them by a roundabout, little-used route. Now and then he would stop for a moment and listen before going on. He acted as if he was smuggling something forbidden, and possibly dangerous, onto the island.

After walking uphill for a time, then doubling back, at last they reached a large house. Again Idrygon stopped, listened and peered into the darkness before pulling open a door of elegantly carved latticework and ushering them inside.

A single tiny lamp burned in a sconce beside the door. By its light, Maura could see they had entered an enclosed courtyard at the center of which a small fountain gurgled softly. A number of potted shrubs stood in clusters, giving the place the air of a forest glade transplanted indoors.

"It's beautiful!" she whispered. "I could sleep quite comfortably here."

She could sleep comfortably anywhere the ground was not rocking beneath her. Ever since they'd stepped off the boat, she had relished the firm foundation of solid earth under her feet.

"No need for that." Idrygon sounded mildly shocked at the idea of their spending the night in his courtyard.

His reaction made Maura grin to herself in the darkness. This would be a far more comfortable sleeping place than most of the ones she and Rath had shared on their journey.

"There is a guest chamber you may use." Idrygon took the lamp from the wall sconce and started toward a wide archway in the right hand wall of the courtyard.

After a few steps, he stopped so suddenly that Maura and Rath almost bumped into him. When she peered around their host, Maura could see a faint light coming toward them. It flickered and grew brighter, as someone approached, also bearing a lamp.

An instant later a man emerged through the archway. At first glance, he looked so much like Idrygon that Maura fancied he might be some enchanted reflection.

The other man startled at the sight of them. "You are late coming home!"

"And you are late going to bed, Delyon," replied Idrygon in a chiding tone. "What keeps you up?"

Delyon held out his right hand, which gripped a scroll. "Reading." He sounded almost guilty. "What else? Have you brought guests with you?"

He held up his lamp to get a better look, which gave Maura a better look at *him*. His clothing was almost identical to Idrygon's, but he had a rumpled air about him. He wore his hair a bit longer, and the way it curled around his face had a softening effect on his fine, regular features.

"I have brought guests." Idrygon took a step toward him, perhaps to block his view. "But the hour is late and introductions can wait until morning."

"I suppose they can." Delyon yawned, then headed across the courtyard, raising his scroll in a kind of salute. "Sleep well, guests. I look forward to meeting you tomorrow."

"My brother," said Idrygon. Then, as if to explain or apologize, he added, "Delyon is a scholar."

They passed through the archway and by several doors on either side of the wide, tiled gallery furnished with clusters of chairs and small tables.

Finally Idrygon stopped in front of one door and threw it open. "I hope this will serve you for tonight."

Behind her, Maura heard Rath give a snort of laughter. She knew what he was thinking. This spacious chamber would be easily the most luxurious place in which they'd ever spent the night ... apart from the Secret Glade, perhaps.

A wide, low bed thrust out from the opposite wall with a canopy of fine netting draped over it, suspended from a hook in the ceiling. A pair of chairs and a small table occupied one corner, in front of a shuttered window, while another corner held the most elaborate washstand Maura had ever seen. Finely woven rush matting covered the floor, from which rose a faint aroma of dried flowers.

"This will do very well, my lord." Maura tried not to laugh. "We thank you for your hospitality."

"It is an honor." He set the lamp down on the elaborate washstand. "I believe you should find everything here that you might require for the night. I would ask that you remain here in the morning until I come for you."

A simple enough request, but it made Maura uneasy somehow. Before Rath could take it into his head to protest, she answered, "If that is what you wish, you are our host."

"Very good." Idrygon stepped back out into the hallway and drew the door closed behind him. "Sleep well."

Maura turned to find Rath had pushed the netting aside and settled onto the bed.

"Ah! Hope this will serve, indeed! We could have brought back half of Gull's crew to sleep with us!" He winced as he raised his arms to tuck behind his head, but his features soon lapsed into a roguish grin. "I'm glad we didn't, though."

"You can stop looking at me that way, Rath Talward!" Maura investigated the washstand where she found a ewer of the most delicate glazed pottery filled with water, as well as a matching basin and some washing and drying clothes. "If you reckon I mean to let some battered brawler have his way with me, you had better think again."

"But Maura . . ."

"But what?" She filled the basin and carried it to the bed, some clothes spread over her arm. "Gull did not sully my honor this evening. He only showed me how to dance . . . which is a good deal more than I can say for you."

In a gentler tone she added, "Now peel that shirt off so I can see how badly you're bruised."

She set the basin on the floor beside the bed and wet one

of the cloths. As Rath struggled out of his shirt, she swiped at the dried blood all over his lower face. "You must remember you are not an outlaw anymore. You are a king. You cannot answer every imagined insult with your fists."

"We have had this talk before." Rath threw his shirt onto the floor, then clamped his hand around her wrist. "Besides, I thought you liked the outlaw."

He drew her toward him, as much with the shimmering heat of his gaze as with the tug of his hand.

Maura tried to hold on to her anger, but it slipped through her grasp like a rope greased by Rath's rough-edged charm and by the long-forbidden feelings she was now at liberty to indulge.

"Behave yourself, now!" She swooped to kiss a spot on his neck she knew was ticklish. "At least let me clean you up and apply a poultice where Gull kicked you — that'll teach you to pick on a man half your size!"

Removing her sash, she mixed a potent compound of laceweed, marshwort, moonmallow and winterwort, bound with a bit of water warmed over the lamp flame. Then she smeared it on Rath's belly and bound it with the last of her linen strips.

"This reminds me of the time you tended me after I fought Turgen." Rath chuckled. "When I squirmed under your touch, you worried that you were *hurting* me."

"Make fun of my innocence, will you?" Maura seized the water basin and pretended she meant to douse him.

"Have mercy, *aira*," he pleaded, laughing. "I am sorry I picked that fight with Gull. It was a daft thing to do. I should have known such a little fellow could never command the way he does without being able to fight like a demon. I swear I'll beg his pardon the next time I see him."

"I suppose . . ." Maura set the basin back on the washstand and dried her hands. "Will you promise to make better use of your wits after this before you let your fists fly?"

"I will!" He promised, opening his arms to her in an unmistakable invitation. "You have my word."

"The word of a king?" Maura inquired as strolled back toward the bed. "Or the word of an outlaw?"

"Why, the outlaw, of course." Rath grinned, his dark eyes twinkling with irresistible mischief. "He is the one who needs your help to mend all his wild ways."

Maura gave a deep, purring chuckle. "I am not sure I want *all* his wild ways mended."

Slipping into his arms, she whispered, "I will make you a bargain."

Rath clasped her to him. "Anything!"

"If you will promise to play the king in the council chamber," she vowed, "I will let you play the outlaw with me."

Play the king in the council chamber. Play the *king* in the council chamber. Rath repeated the words over and over in his mind like an incantation for one of Maura's spells. He feared it would take stronger magic than hers to turn him into a king.

Would the sages of the Vestan council think so, too? He could feel the weight of their curious, uneasy stares resting upon him while Lord Idrygon explained how the Hanish Ore Fleet had come to flounder in their warding waters.

After a miserable night's sleep, Rath had woken with a headache so fierce none of Maura's remedies could do more than blunt it. All their preparations for this appearance before the Council of Sages had not helped his head ... or his temper.

He craned his neck and twisted it, trying to relieve the pressure around his throat. Though Vestan tunics flared out below the waist, the chest and arms were close fitting, as was the high collar. The one Idrygon had lent Rath fit very snug on his muscular torso, and like a noose around his neck.

Maura caught his eye and flashed a reassuring smile. She looked every inch a queen in her loose, sleeveless gown of pale blue-green linen with slender filets of matching ribbon twined through her hair.

She'd admired *his* hair, too, after Idrygon's mother-in-law had washed it and cut it in the Vestan style. Rath had no illusions this short trim suited his shaggy mane the way it did Idrygon's straight hair or Delyon's crisp curls. But he'd stopped fretting about his hair when the forceful old lady had proceeded to shave him so close he feared she would scrape all the skin off his lower face.

No question — this being a king was an uncomfortable business. Rath wondered why a war-leader needed to look well-groomed any more than an outlaw did. But Idrygon had insisted with some confusing talk about council factions and support for an invasion. Though Rath had not warmed to his lordship since their first meeting, he knew enough to respect Idrygon as a man of ability, drive and vision. The kind of man who might be able to make the dream of a free Embria come true if he put his mind to it.

"To conclude —" Idrygon's words drew Rath's attention back to the council chamber "— we cannot hold Captain Gull and his men responsible for what happened when they acted on instructions from this council. How do we know the storm that blew the Ore Fleet toward our coast was not the Giver's will at work?"

Though Idrygon spoke in a tone of hushed reverence, Rath questioned whether the man felt any more true belief in the Giver than he'd once had.

"Your pardon." A voice of quiet authority drew all eyes to a tiny old woman sitting three places to the right of Idrygon. "I am not aware of any instructions from this council that might have summoned Captain Gull to our shores at such a hazardous time. I hope you have not taken it upon yourself to act in the council's name without our knowledge or consent, Idrygon."

Her cheeks were sunken, her dark hair heavily frosted with white and she looked as though a hard gust of wind might blow her off the island. But her penetrating gaze and regal bearing told Rath she was *not* someone a smart man would cross if he had a choice. He wondered if anyone else on the Vestan Islands dared address the forceful Lord Idrygon in that chiding tone.

"I protest, Madame Verise!" Idrygon looked so offended, Rath knew he must be guilty of whatever the old lady had hinted at. "My aim has always been to serve this council, the Vestan Islands and the kingdom of Embria."

This, Rath sensed, was altogether true.

Madame Verise must have known it, too, for she waved a withered hand. "Oh very well, then be plain, lad. What summons of ours brought that ship from the Dusk Coast? And while you are at it, who are these guests you have brought before the council?"

She did not sound as though Rath's sacrifices in the cause of good grooming had impressed her much.

"How clever of you to pose those two questions together, Madame." As Idrygon looked around at the council, he did not rub his hands with glee at the opening he'd been given. But Rath sensed he wanted to. "For they are inextricably bound."

Rath wondered if *inextricably* meant what he thought it did.

"The summons," said Idrygon, "is one we have sent out so often, in vain, that some here may have forgotten we do it. Others, including me, to my shame, may have come to believe it was all a fool's deed and that those messages would never be answered."

Fevered whispering broke out around the Great Circle. By watching who whispered to whom, Rath could guess which side they supported. Idrygon's talk of factions, which had only aggravated Rath's headache first thing this morning, suddenly began to make sense.

There seemed to be two generations of sages — elders like Madame Verise, roughly the age Langbard had been. They made up the majority of the council. Perhaps a third of the counsellors were closer to Rath's age, including Idrygon and his brother, Delyon.

According to Idrygon, many of the older generation had become content with their peaceful, prosperous life on the Islands and were in no hurry to go to the aid of their suffering countrymen on the mainland. When pressed for action by younger members of the council, they urged delay until the coming of the Waiting King and the Destined Queen.

Well, the Council of Sages was in for a surprise today!

As Maura listened to Lord Idrygon speak, she felt as if she were teetering on the edge of Raynor's Rift, with that terrifying chasm gaping before her.

"Every year, spring and midsummer, we send out those messenger birds." Lord Idrygon looked around the Great Circle, fixing each of the sages with his forceful gaze. " '*Her time has come.*' '*Come at once. Captain Gull of Duskport will convey you.*' Only the name of the captain has ever changed with the passing years. We have never known where these birds were bound, nor had any assurance they did not simply fly away to become food for hawks."

Maura's heart sank. She had thought herself special … chosen. Her fears had eased as her faith in their destiny had taken root. Now she wondered if that destiny had all been an illusion. As she remembered the disasters she and Rath had so narrowly escaped, all the times they had poised on the brink of death and worse, she grew dizzy and bilious with fear.

She could not sit still or remain silent a moment longer.

"I don't understand!" She leaped to her feet, not caring that she had interrupted Lord Idrygon and drawn stern glares from more wizards, healers and scholars of the Elderways than she'd ever imagined could exist. "The first messenger bird found its way to our little cottage in Norest a few months ago, on my eighteenth birthday. Langbard told me it had come from you. He told me you had studied the ancient writings and determined the time had come for me to begin my quest. Now are you saying it was all a mistake?"

If Lord Idrygon's words had shaken her world, Maura's outburst appeared to shake the Council of Sages even more. The great chamber buzzed like a wasp's nest under attack.

Maura braced for a stern rebuke from Lord Idrygon. After his first hostile exchange with Rath, the man had extended them every courtesy. But she suspected, if she turned quickly enough, she might catch him wrinkling up his well-bred nose at the smell of them. Now he stood silent and calm, at the center of the tempest she had created, looking strangely pleased with it.

Maura turned toward Rath. He replied with a look that told her destiny might let her down but he never would.

Before Maura could say anything to him, the tiny woman who had spoken so sharply to Idrygon appeared before her. "My dear, you mentioned Langbard a moment ago. My sister, Nalene, is his wife. Are you ... their daughter?"

The anxious glow in the woman's eyes made Maura wish she could say yes, for both their sakes. Growing up with only Langbard, she'd secretly yearned for parents, but never thought of a wider family ... aunts, uncles, cousins.

"Though I loved Langbard as dearly as any daughter, he was my guardian. My mother died when I was very young and she entrusted me to his care."

The woman's eager gaze faltered when Maura spoke of Langbard in the past.

"I call for silence!" Idrygon's tone of authority quelled the tumult of voices. "We all have questions that want answers, but we will never hear those answers if we do not listen."

The Council appeared to see the wisdom in that. Many who had risen sat down. Several who had moved from their accustomed places returned to their seats, including Madame Verise.

Once quiet and order had been restored to the chamber, a stout wizard with a wild shock of red hair cleared his throat loudly.

Idrygon motioned for him to rise. "You wish to speak, Trochard?"

"So I do. I believe there is one question most pressing on all our minds." He swung to fix a stern gaze upon Maura. "Young woman, do you mean to tell us *you* are — the Destined Queen?"

His tone of disbelief dismayed Maura. She'd expected it from Rath and people like Captain Gull. But the wizards of the Vestan Islands were the ones she believed had sent her on her quest. The ones who had summoned Rath and her once she'd completed it. If they did not believe …?

"*Am* I the Destined Queen?" She looked around at them. "I thought I was. I did what she … what *I* … was meant to do. Yet everything I have heard today makes me question if it can be true."

"By *what you were meant to do*," said Trochard, "I take it you mean finding the Waiting King?"

Before Maura could reply, Rath rose and stood beside her. "Why?" he challenged her inquisitor. "Is there some *other* quest the Destined Queen was supposed to undertake?"

"Please, Rath …" Maura begged him through clenched teeth. Had he so quickly forgotten his promise to play the king in council chambers?

Well-groomed and wearing the regal Vestan garb, which forced him to stand tall, he looked more like a king than she had ever imagined possible.

In a few blunt words, he told the Council of Sages how Maura had found and rescued him within hours of the messenger bird reaching Langbard's cottage. He went on to speak of Langbard's murder and their flight to Prum, where they had discovered Exilda, the guardian of the map, murdered also.

He cast a challenging glare around the Great Circle. "The Xenoth seem to place more faith in this legend than the lot of you."

Trochard's face flushed redder than his hair and others among the older sages betrayed similar signs of chagrin.

While they chewed on that tough crust, Rath went on to recount the rest of their adventures. As he spoke, Maura noticed how the older members of the council winced and paled at the dangers they had faced. Meanwhile, younger members like Idrygon hung on every word, an eager glow in their eyes. All looked equally perplexed when Rath told what he and Maura had discovered in the Secret Glade.

"So *you* are the Waiting King?" murmured Madame Verise. "How can that be? You did not lie sleeping in the Secret Glade for hundreds of years."

Rath shook his head then cast a sidelong glance at Maura. How could he explain what they had not fully fathomed?

Then Delyon rose from his seat. "I believe I can answer that, if I may speak."

"Go ahead." Rath tried not to let his relief show, but Maura sensed it as he sank into his chair beside her.

"As most of you know —" Delyon looked around the Great Circle "— I have worked for several years to decipher our oldest scrolls which are written in a language that predates *twara*. I believe that language may have been spoken by the Great Kin before the Sundering, which divided the Children of Embri from the Children of Han."

"Speculation!" muttered Trochard, loud enough for all to hear.

Delyon pretended not to. "My study of these works leads me to believe that Queen Abrielle used the Staff of Velorken to work her enchantment upon King Elzaban."

Trochard leaped to his feet. "We asked for answers, not star-tales, upstart cub! Everyone knows the Staff of Velorken was destroyed during the Sundering."

Delyon ignored him. "Abrielle was a powerful enchantress, wise beyond her years, having served as apprentice to the Oracle of Margyle. I believe she knew or discovered the where-abouts of the Staff of Velorken and used it to keep Elzaban's spirit alive in this world. When a young child or a pregnant woman entered Everwood, Elzaban's spirit might be reborn within that body, waiting to be fully woken by a future daughter of Abrielle."

A fresh buzz greeted Delyon's explanation. The tone of some comments sounded doubtful and hostile, but more sounded guardedly accepting.

Maura was not certain what to think. Did this mean there had been other men who'd lived and died, never knowing the spirit of the Waiting King slumbered within them? Other women, destined to call forth that fallow potential for great-ness, only to fail? The possibility chilled her.

"I smell a conspiracy!" Trochard pointed a blunt forefin-ger at Delyon. "This *research* of yours everyone thought so harmlessly foolish has been nothing but a ploy to justify your brother's machinations!"

"Enough, Trochard." Madame Verise fixed him with a reproachful stare as she rose from her seat. "We may question young Delyon's scholarship, but I am satisfied as to his integrity. And I can vouch that the man who raised this young woman..."

She glanced toward Maura. "Your pardon, my dear. I do not believe you were properly introduced to us."

"I am Maura." She rose and made a self-conscious bow to the Council. "Maura Woodbury, ward of the wiz —"

But she did not get to finish, for the Vestan Council of Sages suddenly erupted in a more fevered clamor than before.

Maura cast a questioning look at Rath. He only raised his brows and shrugged, clearly as puzzled as she. When she shifted her gaze to Idrygon, hoping for some explanation, he replied with an approving nod and a cold smile that did not dispel her confusion ... or her misgivings.

Chapter Seventeen

"I FINALLY HAVE Trochard where I want him!" Idrygon beamed at Rath and Maura as they ate their evening meal in the fountain courtyard of his villa. "Exposed to the Council for the carping old hypocrite he is."

"Explain this faction business to me again." Rath took another bite of a tasty dish of eggs, cheese and vegetables. Now that he had seen the Council is session and knew the names of some members, it all might make more sense to him.

"With pleasure, Highness." Idrygon raised his wine goblet in a salute that made Rath almost as ill at ease as Idrygon's use of the title. "It is quite simple. As you saw today, many among the Council are elders. Some made their home here before the Hanish Conquest, others fled here to escape it. The years since have been full of trouble and danger, but the elder sages provided prudent, cautious leadership that has served us well."

"But times have changed?" said Maura.

Idrygon looked surprised by her comment. His wife and mother-in-law were eating in silence, which Rath guessed was their custom when Idrygon started on this subject. Delyon had a scroll draped over his knees. Reading while he ate, he scarcely seemed to notice the conversation or the food that he popped into his mouth at regular intervals.

After an instant's hesitation, Idrygon recovered his composure and nodded to Maura. "True, Highness. Times *have* changed. In recent years, younger members have joined the Council. Members who grieved the oppression of our kin on the mainland and who believed we should take measures to aid them."

Rath raised his goblet in a salute to Idrygon. So there *had* been folk on the Islands who thought beyond their own peace and comfort to care what happened in the rest of the kingdom. That came as welcome news.

Idrygon shook his head. "I regret our efforts have been thwarted by Trochard and his followers, always protesting that we must take no action until the coming of the Waiting King."

Beneath the table, Rath clenched his fist. He'd once despised the whole notion of the Waiting King for just that reason — because his countrymen might linger idle and passive in their misery expecting to be delivered from the Han, rather than seizing the chance to rise up on their own behalf.

"To be fair," said Idrygon, "some of the elders, like Madame Verise, were sincere in their beliefs and would endorse necessary action if and when the Waiting King answered their summons. I suspected all along that the others had no true faith in ... you. All they wanted was to protect their own interests."

"It makes more sense now." Rath unfastened the top button of his tunic and leaned back in his chair. "Why that Trochard fellow and some of the others were so unwilling to believe Maura and I could be who we say we are."

"How dared he cast aspersions upon my brother's integrity as a scholar?" Idrygon glanced at Delyon for the first time since the meal had begun. "Brother! The king and queen of Embria are our guests. Can you show them the small courtesy of *not* reading at the table?"

"Your pardon!" Delyon hastily rolled up the scroll and dropped it beneath his seat. "When I read something that takes my interest, I become blind and deaf to everything around me."

Maura chuckled. "I take no offense, Delyon. In fact, it makes me feel quite at home. My guardian was the same. He did not even need a scroll to read — he could just as easily get lost in his own thoughts and never hear a word I said. You remind me of him."

For some reason that notion did not sit well with Rath. Perhaps because he could not read the simplest scroll in modern Embrian, let alone some ancient language. Even if he was able to help liberate the kingdom, how could a man with so little schooling and experience hope to rule it?

After a despairing look at his brother, Idrygon was quick to turn the discussion back to his favorite subject. "Speaking of your guardian, Highness, it is fortunate he was the brother-in-law of Madame Verise. She is well respected by all factions of the Council. If she endorses you, Trochard will have to go along, or risk being exposed for the cowardly fraud he is."

From what he'd seen of her during the Council meeting, Rath had formed a good opinion of Madame Verise. It was clear she held strong opinions from which she would not be easily swayed, but neither was her mind completely closed to new ideas. Rath could imagine Maura maturing into just such a wise old lady.

"It was canny of Madame Verise to suggest consulting the Oracle," said Idrygon. "Even Trochard will have to abide by *her* decision."

But so would Idrygon and his faction. Rath sensed a shadow of apprehension in their host.

Maura set down her goblet after a deep drink of *sythwine*. "Why did they all start talking so loudly after I told them my name?"

"Do you not know, Highness?" Whatever it was, the notion seemed to restore Idrygon's confidence. "The Woodburys of Galene are a family of noble lineage, descendants of Queen Abrielle. They have lived quietly since their patriarch Brandel died. He was a strong force on the council and much respected."

Maura lowered her gaze to her lap for a moment and Rath sensed her struggle for composure as she whispered, "Then I do have a family?"

That would mean a great deal to her, he knew. Enough,

perhaps, to keep her here on the Islands if the Oracle determined there had been some mistake and the Council ruled against aiding them? Or was that wickedly selfish of him to hope?

"Would you like to go to Galene and meet them?" asked Idrygon. "I am not certain what relation they might be to you, but their endorsement can only strengthen our position with the Council."

"I should like that very much," replied Maura. "Once I have met with the Oracle."

"Of course." Again Idrygon looked unsure. "The Oracle."

Rath had sensed a similar hesitation from several of the sages when the Oracle of Margyle had been mentioned. What lay behind *that*? he wondered.

Back on the mainland where life was a raw struggle for survival, he'd enjoyed a measure of confidence. Here on the Islands, Rath felt far out of his depth.

"Follow this lane. It will bring you to the dwelling of the Oracle." Delyon pointed to a gated trellis between two high banks of hedging. It was so overgrown with twilight vines that it almost blended into the shrubbery walls on either side.

"Are you not coming with me?" asked Maura. The prospect of meeting this mysterious woman whose memory reached deep into the past and who could also catch glimpses of the future intimidated her.

"I wish I could." Delyon sighed. "I have been trying to arrange a meeting with her for the longest time — to talk over my research and find out if I am on the right track. But the Oracle is getting more and more reclusive as time goes on, Madame Verise says. I wonder how the Council persuaded her to see you and His Highness?"

For a moment Maura wondered who Delyon was talking about. Then it dawned on her that he must mean Rath. She found it difficult to get used to everyone in Idrygon's household addressing them by title.

"I can wait for you here," Delyon offered, "if you think you will not be able to find your way back afterward. I wish I'd thought to bring a scroll with me to read."

"I will not keep you hanging about here when you have work to do." Maura pointed toward a lower hill. "Besides, I can see your house from here. I'll have no trouble finding my way back when the time comes."

This was not the mainland, after all, where a young woman had to be careful about walking alone. Perhaps one day that would change. And her dreaded meeting with the Oracle of Margyle might help pave the way.

That thought gave Maura courage to smile and nod when Delyon said, "You're sure?"

She did not wait to watch him go, but squared her shoulders and pushed open the vine-covered gate. Once through, she followed a path that wound through a bit of woodland until it opened near a cottage with white plaster walls, like those of Idrygon's elegant villa. Its thatched roof made the place look much more homey and inviting to Maura. Perhaps she did not need to be so anxious about meeting a woman who lived in a modest dwelling like this one.

"Hello." The sound of a child's voice startled Maura.

She spun around to see a young girl with a mane of wild dark curls picking mushrooms by the edge of the wood. The child looked no older than Noll Howen back in Windleford, perhaps ten or eleven years.

"H-hello." Maura pressed her hand to her chest to quiet her pounding heart. "Do you live here?"

A ward of the Oracle, perhaps, as she had been of Langbard.

"I do." The girl rose from the ground, dusting off her

skirts. "You've come from the mainland, haven't you ... Mistress Woodbury?"

"That's right." Maura wondered how the child knew her name. "To see the Oracle. I have heard people talk about her since I was your age and younger, but never thought I would meet her face-to-face. Is it true she is hundreds of years old?"

The child laughed so hard she practically doubled over. When she had finally mastered her mirth, she picked up her mushroom basket. "What queer ideas people get! Though I suppose it is not so far wrong."

The door of the cottage opened just then and a middle-aged woman bustled out carrying a bundle of washing.

"Is *she* the Oracle?" Maura whispered to the child. It was difficult to imagine such a famed personage stooping to a mundane chore like laundry. Then again, people might think the same of her and Rath — the Destined Queen compounding liniment and the Waiting King cutting hay on Blen Maynold's farm.

"No, silly!" The child began to laugh again as she shook her head. "*I* am."

Maura almost laughed at that jest until the woman with the laundry called, "Is that the guest you were expecting, mistress? If you want to bring her inside, I can fetch you some cakes and *lipma* cordial."

"Cakes!" squealed the Oracle like any other child her age at the prospect of a treat. "I should have guests more often!"

While Maura tried to recover from her shock, the servant woman shook her head. "Now, mistress, you know the council doesn't approve of you being bothered too often. Madame Verise said this lady is a special case."

"Your pardon, great Oracle!" Maura made a deep bow to the child. Her face felt as if she had a bad sunburn.

"It's all right." The child shrugged. "You gave me an excuse to laugh. I don't get those often enough lately."

In her large misty-gray eyes, Maura caught a glimpse of wisdom and sadness far beyond her years.

"Will you come in for cakes and a drink?" The Oracle nodded toward the cottage. "The cordial is from a batch the last oracle put down two summers ago. We had a fine harvest of *lipma* fruit that year."

"The … last oracle?" Maura followed the girl into a snug cottage, where she immediately felt at home. "Is a new one chosen when the old one dies?"

"Oh, no." The Oracle laid her mushroom basket on the table. "That wouldn't do at all. Then the memories would be lost."

The memories? Maura wanted to ask, but refrained lest the Oracle get tired of hearing herself repeated over and over.

Perhaps the young Oracle divined her question anyway, for she beckoned Maura through the cottage to a large open porch with a spectacular view down to the sea. "Come, sit down and I will tell you how it is."

Maura sank onto a cushioned chair that looked to be made of many slender branches woven together into a light but sturdy seat. She wondered what other astonishing revelations the Oracle had in store for her.

The child seated herself on the chair opposite Maura's. "Like every other oracle for hundreds of years, I was brought to this house when I was an infant to be raised by the last oracle."

"Do you ever see your other family?" Maura thought of the Woodburys of Galene whom she could hardly wait to meet.

"I have no other family. That's how the council knew I was the one. An orphaned girl child born at the right time."

Maura nodded. That made a kind of sense.

"Have you ever performed the passing ritual?" asked the Oracle.

"For my guardian, Langbard, this past spring."

"Langbard?" The Oracle's eyes took on a far-off look and

her innocent young lips curved in a not-so-innocent smile. "He was a fine-looking fellow. If we'd been twenty years younger…"

Realizing what she'd said, the Oracle hid her face in her hands. "Your pardon! Please do not think ill of me. That name brought back such vivid memories that, for a moment, I could feel the old oracle within me."

Maura wondered what *that* meant.

The child hastened to explain. "When an old oracle raises her successor, every day is like a prolonged passing ritual. There would never be time to share all the memories going back so many generations, otherwise. By the time the old oracle is ready to depart this world, the new one has received the accumulated wisdom and experience of all those who have gone before her."

"Amazing!" Maura whispered, not aware she'd spoken aloud.

"It can be." The Oracle sighed. "When all goes as it should."

The child's wistful words jolted Maura upright in her chair. "But your oracle died too soon, didn't she, before your training was completed?"

With a wary nod, the child drew her legs up onto the chair and hugged her bent knees. "Just a few months ago, she got very ill suddenly and the healers could do nothing to help. At the end I was with her all the time while she poured memories into my mind until I was afraid my head would burst."

Maura rose from her chair and knelt beside the child. "That must have been a sad and frightening time for you."

"It isn't fair!" The young Oracle struck the side of her chair with her fist. "This never happened to any of the others — why me? These are restless times. So many things will change. So many important decisions will need to be made. People will want my advice. But what can I tell them and how can they trust me? I am not ready, and so much wisdom gathered over the generations has been lost."

How long had the poor little creature been brooding about this? Maura wondered. Though she might be the custodian of memories stretching back hundreds of years, she was still only a child who had lost her beloved foster mother too soon. A child with no one to confide in but her servant and perhaps some council members who might not want to hear their Oracle voice such doubts about her abilities.

The child rested her forehead against her knees and her delicate frame shuddered with sobs.

"You're right." Maura wrapped her arms around the child. "It *isn't* fair. If it helps, I know a little of how you feel."

While the child wept, Maura told her about Langbard's surprising announcement on her birthday and of events that had overwhelmed her since then.

"So you see," she said at last when the child's sobs had quieted, "when I started out, I felt unready for such a huge task. I feared I would fail and let everyone down."

She lowered her voice to bestow a confidence. "I still feel that way sometimes. If I dwell on it too much, it can freeze me worse than a spidersilk spell."

The Oracle wiped her eyes with the hem of her gown and sniffled. "How do *you* keep yourself from thinking about it all the time?"

Maura pondered the question for a moment. "I remind myself to trust in the Giver's providence. I try to keep moving ahead and doing what I need to do. Each little bit of success I gain makes me feel more confident, even if it is only a few miles closer to where I'm going."

She ran her hand over the child's hair, wondering if anyone else dared to show the Oracle of Margyle a little affection. At that moment, a most comforting thought settled over her. "Do you suppose the Giver's will might work *better* through people like us, who aren't fully prepared for what we must do?"

The child gave a final sniff as she regarded Maura

thoughtfully. In her soft gray eyes glowed the accumulated wisdom of many generations — fragmented but still sound.

After a moment she nodded. "There would be more room for the Giver's power to work."

Just then the Oracle's servant bustled in. "The wash will dry in no time with that sun and the breeze. Here are the cakes I promised you."

She stopped in her tracks, staring at Maura and the child. "Is everything all right, pet? Is this too much for you? Should I send this lady away?"

"No, Orna!" The Oracle clasped Maura's hand. "We were having a fine talk. I hope she will come and visit me often while she is on the Islands."

"Orna?" Maura smiled at the woman as she returned to her chair. "That is a very familiar name to me. The mother of my dearest friend was named Orna. You remind me of her."

Clearly the woman was much more than a servant in the Oracle's household — a warm, protective caregiver who did not forget that this special, troubled little girl was a child first.

"Orna's a real common name over Norest way." The woman beamed at Maura, clearly reassured by her young charge's words. "My folks came to the Islands from there when the war started. Now I'll fetch that cordial."

"What does this *lipma* cordial taste like?" asked Maura. "Anything like *sythwine*?"

The child wrinkled her nose. "It will make your mouth pucker but it's very refreshing. Now tell me about this friend of yours from Norest. What kinds of things did the two of you do when you were my age?"

For the next little while they talked like any two new friends getting better acquainted. Orna's cakes proved delicious with their glaze of fruit and honey. At first Maura wasn't sure she liked the sour *lipma* cordial, but each time she took a sip, she found the flavor improved from the time before.

As the Oracle plied her with questions about her friend Sorsha and the town of Windleford where they'd grown up, Maura wondered if she felt embarrassed over betraying her uncertainty to a stranger she should have been trying to awe.

Gently she steered their talk back to the task they had been set. "Do you know why Madame Verise sent me here?"

The child drained her glass of cordial with an air of resignation that their pleasant social time had come to an end. "I am supposed to talk to you and to that man. Then I must tell the Council if you are truly the Destined Queen and the Waiting King."

Why had Idrygon's rivals on the council agreed to these interviews? Maura wondered. Did they hope the young Oracle would be too uncertain of her own judgment to give a decisive answer? If she endorsed Rath and Maura, would Trochard's faction try to discredit her because of her age and unfinished training?

Maura did not envy her young friend the task. "Are there any questions you need to ask me?"

The Oracle tapped her forefinger against her chin and her clear brow wrinkled with concentration. "You said Langbard was your guardian. Did he have any other children?"

"None." Maura plundered her memory for everything Langbard had told her on the fateful afternoon of her birthday. "He said the Oracle had told him he would be father to the Destined Queen."

"She did." The child squeezed her eyes shut. "I can picture it as clear as anything. I wish you could have seen the look on his face!"

"I can imagine it." Maura chuckled. Delyon would probably look the same — eyes wide with horror at the prospect of a destructive little creature getting muddy hands on one of his precious scrolls! "I wish the Oracle had told Langbard I might not be his daughter by blood. He went through a terrible time after his wife died without bearing a child."

"Poor man!" The girl winced as if she knew something of such pain. "The way oracles are fostered, we know it is love and care that make a family bond, not blood alone. She would never have thought to remark upon the difference."

Rising from her chair, the young Oracle approached Maura with a solemn gait and laid a hand on her head in the manner of a benediction. "You are Langbard's daughter and you come from the line of Abrielle. I may not be certain of many things, but I *know* you are the latest Destined Queen."

"Latest?" The word trickled down Maura's spine like a drop of water from a deep, cold well. "That is something *I* do not understand. The sages spoke of sending out messenger birds every year and of King Elzaban's spirit having dwelt in other men before Rath. Does that mean what I fear it might? Have there been other Destined Kings and Waiting Queens before us who failed?"

The young Oracle nodded with an air of regret. "Those were some of the most important memories Namma passed on to me. We spoke of it too, though I am not sure I understood it all. You see, before the Han came, there were troubled times, but not the very darkest hour. Some Destined Queens laughed off the whole notion of what they were meant to do. Others were too frightened to stir from their own doorsteps."

Maura could not condemn them. "I laughed at first. I was afraid. If Langbard had not offered to go with me, then Rath, I might still be hiding in Windleford hoping destiny would get tired of waiting for me and choose someone else."

She gazed up into the child's face, for the first time wishing she *had* found a wise old woman here to advise her. "That's what I cannot understand, though. If those others were truly destined, how could they fail? It took me such a long time to learn to trust in my destiny — now you're telling me it doesn't matter?"

Maura tried to blunt the sharp edge of frustration in her voice. It wasn't the child's fault, after all, or anyone else's. And she did not truly expect an answer that made sense. As Langbard had once said, *"Look around you, my dear, at all the marvels of the Giver's creation. How can simple creatures like us hope to fathom its plan or purpose?"*

Maura wished she could understood a little at least.

The Oracle held out her hand. "Will you come for a walk with me before you have to go?"

The burden of too much knowledge had left her eyes, and she looked like any child her age, eager to run and play. No doubt she was tired of all this grave talk and hearing words come out of her mouth that she did not fully understand.

"I would like that." Maura took the oracle's hand and rose from her chair with what she hoped was a convincing pose of enthusiasm.

Together, they left the porch and wandered out into the meadow that sloped down toward the sea. But the Oracle did not go that way. Instead, she led Maura toward a wooded hill.

She pointed toward the summit. "Up there is the most beautiful place of meditation in all the Islands. I go there often when I'm troubled. Everything seems clearer there, somehow. If there is any place in this world where you might find the answers to your questions, it will be there."

Answers — Maura could do with a few of those. The hill looked steep and quite thickly wooded, though a gap between the trees at the base of the hill might be the beginning of a footpath. "Very well. Let's go."

The child released her hand and ran ahead, calling, "I'll see you at the top!"

"Wait for me!" Maura did not relish the prospect of a race up the steep, wooded hill. Hiking up the hem of her gown, she ran after the child, who had already disappeared into the trees.

"Oh, these shoes!" Maura bit back a mild curse when the

curved toes almost made her trip. The stout walking boots Sorsha had given her when she left Windleford would have been much better for climbing this hill.

Darting through a gap in the trees, Maura saw that the path divided almost immediately. Which way was she to take?

She peered down each branch as far as she could see but both curved after a few yards and the Oracle was already out of sight.

"Hello!" Maura called. "Which way am I supposed to go?"

No answer came, but she heard laughter off in the distance. The right-hand path seemed to lead in that direction so Maura followed it, grumbling to herself about inconsiderate hostesses.

Before long, she was doing more than grumbling. The wooded path wound its way up the hill in a complicated maze, twisting, branching, turning back on itself, and sometimes coming to a dead end. Would she ever find her way to the top?

Maura considered turning back, or sitting down and staying put until the naughty little tease of a child came looking for her. She did stop for a short rest, but soon grew bored with waiting and started off again. If she'd been sure she could find her way back to the cottage, she might have given up. But by this time she had made too many turns and was hopelessly confused.

So she kept going, encouraged that she seemed to be climbing higher. The nearer she got to the top, the less space there would be for the path to branch. As long as she kept going she must reach the summit at last.

And, at last, she did. Footsore, out of breath and very much out of temper.

She found the Oracle sitting in something that looked like a little house without walls — stout beams holding aloft a roof. Only when she drew very close did Maura realize the beams were living trees, their branches concentrated at the top and turned inward to twine together, creating a roof shingled with broad leaves.

The structure stood in the middle of a meadow carpeted with wildflowers of the most vivid and varied colors Maura had ever seen. Springwater bubbled up from a tiny stone fountain beside the little house of trees. A soft breeze wafted and swirled about the summit of the hill, stirring the fresh, sweet perfume of the flowers.

By the time Maura reached the Oracle, most of her irritation had been soothed away by the peace and beauty around her. Understanding blossomed within her, as unexpected and breathtaking as this place.

"You meant to leave me behind, didn't you?" she asked the Oracle.

The child nodded gravely. "I'm sorry. I know it is bewildering and tiresome. This was one of the first lessons Namma taught me when I was old enough to understand."

She pointed to the fountain. "You must be thirsty. Have a drink. It will make the long climb seem worthwhile."

Maura stared around the summit glade. "It already does. But you're right, I am thirsty." With cupped hands, she lifted the water to her lips and drank until she could hold no more.

The Oracle had spoken true, for the water was so cool, fresh and sweet, it would have been worth the long, wearying climb all by itself.

"Namma told me this path through the woods is like our destiny," explained the oracle while Maura drank. "We cannot tell which way it may take us, and we may make many wrong turns."

Maura nodded. The frustration she'd felt while trying to grope her way to the top of the hill echoed some of the feelings she'd experienced during her quest to find the Waiting King.

"The path could not pick you up and bring you here against your will or with no effort on your part," the Oracle continued, "and you had many choices to make. Some of those would have led you away from the top of the hill, others were dead ends. If you had become too discouraged to continue, you never would have reached the top."

Once Maura finished drinking, the Oracle beckoned her to take a seat beneath the living canopy. "Did you notice that some of the trail doubled back on itself?"

Maura nodded.

"This path may confuse the person who climbs it for the first time." The Oracle patted Maura's hand. "But for those who keep trying, there are not as many wrong choices as may first appear."

But there *were* wrong choices and Maura could not abdicate her responsibility for them. The specter of failure returned to haunt her. Others before her had failed and she sensed that the closer she and Rath came to their goal, the greater their opportunities for disaster might be.

A dark whisper of temptation slithered through her thoughts as well. If she and Rath abandoned their destiny, another Waiting King and Destined Queen would come after them ... some day.

But in the meantime, how much darker could Embria's *darkest hour* get?

Chapter Eighteen

"WHAT DID THE Oracle tell *you*?" asked Maura the following evening while she and Rath prepared for dinner at Idrygon's villa.

Rath wondered if the evening meal was always such a formal occasion in Idrygon's household, or whether it was in honor of visiting royalty—uncrowned though they might be. "Well?" Maura prompted him. "Did she make you walk up that hill maze to teach you about destiny? Did she promise to tell the Council of Sages you are the *latest* Waiting King?"

When he did not answer right away, her gaze became more searching. "Did the Oracle look into your future?"

Oh, she had looked, all right. And what she'd seen had shaken Rath to the core. He tried to convince himself that, though she might hold the memories of countless generations, the present oracle was still only a child. One whose training had been cut short, at that. Perhaps she had taken the wrong meaning from whatever she'd glimpsed in his future.

For all his doubts and denials, he could not escape a chilling fear that the child *knew* what the coming years held for him. He wished she had kept that troublesome knowledge to herself, though, for he feared it could mean only one thing—that he would lose Maura.

Could the Giver be so cruel, to rob him of the happiness he'd so lately found? Rath tried to believe otherwise, but his faith was still new and untested. He had far more experience with the impersonal cruelty of whatever forces shaped the lives of folk like him.

Maura's voice broke in upon his brooding, like a ray of

sunlight penetrating some dark dungeon cell. "She did foretell your future, didn't she? Come, what did she predict? Something dire, I suspect, by that grim look on your face."

"I do not look grim!" he snapped, then repented his quick temper. "All right, perhaps I do. But it is not on account of that young seer."

Not for all the world would he burden Maura with the foreboding that weighed upon him. He could worry enough for both of them. "It's all the talk of an invasion and this business of playing off one council faction against another. Here I reckoned the Vestan Islands would be so peaceful, with folks all getting along and having not a care in the world!"

"I cannot say I like that much, myself." Maura laid down the ivory comb with which she had battled her unruly hair into temporary submission. "But is it so hard to understand? Trochard and his followers just want to look after their own interests . . . like a certain outlaw I once knew."

Rath grumbled something about how he'd been forthright in his selfishness, at least. Then he craned his neck. "Can you help me fasten this miserable collar button without throttling me? Thank the Giver that Idrygon plans to have his soldiers kitted out in gear that will let them move . . . and breathe."

"Whose soldiers?" Maura asked with a teasing lilt in her voice as she fastened the troublesome button. "You will be leading them — will that not make them *your* soldiers?"

Rath shook his head and dropped a kiss on the tip of her nose. "Idrygon has been planning all this for a great while. Gathering supplies, amassing weapons, training men. This army will be his to command, which is just the way I would have it. What do I know about leading any force bigger than the band of outlaws you first saw me with in Betchwood? Look what happened to them, poor devils."

"That was not your fault!" Maura reminded him.

Rath tried to pretend he believed her.

She quickly changed the subject. "I thought it strange at first that Idrygon should care so much what happens on the mainland."

So had Rath. He did not reckon Idrygon had planned and schemed so long to liberate the mainland out of the goodness of his heart. After watching their host the past few days, he'd concluded that the man was a born commander, a role with limited scope on these islands. Much as they delighted Rath and Maura with their beauty, peace and plenty, to a man of Idrygon's forceful personality, they must seem like a luxurious prison.

"You said *at first*." Rath wetted a comb and tried to tidy his hair. "What changed your mind?"

"Something Delyon told me." Maura dipped her fingers into a tiny crock of delicate pottery and drew out a drop or two of scented oil to anoint her neck and wrists. "He said their parents put him and his brother on the last Embrian ship to escape the mainland. The boys were raised here by their grandparents, who were both members of the council. Only many years later did they find out their parents had been killed by the Han."

Rath winced at Maura's account, though he'd heard plenty worse stories of things that had happened to Embrian children after the Hanish conquest. He'd lived worse, himself, come to that. Though Idrygon and Delyon had been orphaned, at least they'd gotten beyond the reach of the Han and into the care of folks with the means to look after them properly.

Would he have switched places with them, though, if he could have changed the past? He'd suffered his share of guilt after Ganny died. How much worse might it have gnawed at him if he'd ended up somewhere safe and prosperous? Might it have driven him to do whatever it took to oust the Han from Embria?

"I'll admit," he said, "I was wrong in thinking the island folk came to no harm on account of the Han. I reckon it's harder sometimes to know somebody else is being ill-used and not being able to aid them than it is to take the lumps yourself."

"You're a wise man, Rath Talward." Maura took his arm. "Now we had better get to dinner before Idrygon sends a search party after us. Delyon told me important guests will be dining with us tonight."

"Delyon tells you all sorts of interesting things, doesn't he?"

Maura seemed not to hear anything beneath Rath's bantering tone. "I have to get my news from someone and Idrygon's wife always looks so busy I'm afraid to stop her long enough to ask."

She lowered her voice as they stepped out in the wide, elegant gallery that ran between two sets of bedchambers. Rath could see people gathered talking in the courtyard. He recognized several council members.

As they walked toward the company, Maura leaned closer to him and whispered, "There is one drawback to relying on Delyon for information."

He cast her a sidelong smile, struck afresh by her delicate beauty. "And what might that be?"

Maura's lips twitched. "He doesn't seem to know what is going on half the time, himself."

A hoot of laughter stuck in Rath's throat when he saw the formidable Madame Verise bowing to them. Did that bode well?

Apparently so, for Idrygon appeared beside the old lady, looking more cheerful than Rath had ever seen him. He held a goblet in each hand, which he offered to Rath and Maura. "We have cause to celebrate, Highnesses! Madame Verise informs me that the Oracle has declared you are indeed the Waiting King and Destined Queen of Embria!"

So this dinner was a celebration. Rath glanced around

at the other guests. Unless he was hopelessly confused, they belonged to the group Idrygon hoped would support them against those who opposed going to war. If Idrygon's painstaking preparations were not to be in vain and if Rath was to get the help he needed to fulfil his destiny, these folks would need to be convinced that he was the king they had been waiting for.

The weight of responsibility pressed down on Rath's shoulders, like the heavy pack he'd carried into the Waste.

"The Giver does work in strange ways." Madame Verise looked him up and down, shaking her head. "To think, King Elzaban's spirit in the body of an outlaw."

Again the high, stiff collar of his Vestan tunic tightened around Rath's throat. He struggled to frame a reply that would not curdle on his tongue.

Then Maura spoke in a tone of quiet dignity befitting a queen. "Considering the present *law* of that land, Madame, do you not think better of His Highness for having been outside it than in?"

Rath bit back a grin, remembering how he'd flung those words at her soon after they'd met. That she had recalled them after all this time and summoned them up at a crucial moment to come to his defense sent a fresh surge of love for her flowing through his heart.

"Now, Highness …" Idrygon's dark eyes flashed. Clearly he did not want anything to threaten this vital alliance.

"No, Lord Idrygon." Madame Verise made a dismissive gesture with her delicate, withered hand. "Her Highness is right. Outlaws, smugglers and that ilk are the only ones who have kept a spirit of resistance alive in our poor captive land. Perhaps it *is* fitting that the spirit of King Elzaban should return to us in such a one."

She bowed to Rath with an air of sincere deference. "I beseech your pardon if I gave offense with my thoughtless remark, my lord. I fear we on the Islands have grown self-righteous in our good fortune. We forget how hard it may be to serve the Giver in harsher circumstances."

"I cannot claim I have always served —"

Before Rath could finish, Idrygon shot him a warning look and interrupted. "I am certain His Highness understands, Madame. Now, I see our meal is ready. Shall we be seated?"

He steered Rath toward the head of the long table, while his wife drew Maura to her place of honor at the other end. On their way, he muttered, "Take care what you say to Verise. Without her support, we are lost. Let me do the talking. I have learned how to handle her."

Rath nodded. He had never felt so out of place in his life — like a bird thrust underwater and expected to swim, or a fish tossed into the sky, to fly or perish trying. He wished they'd let Maura sit near him. He felt a little more confident with her by his side, knowing she had seen him at his worst, yet still recognized a spark of nobility within him.

A feast was served, fit for a king. But the king barely managed to eat a bite for fear he would commit some glaring lapse in table manners. He tried to follow what Madame Verise and Idrygon were talking about but they might have been speaking that ancient language from Delyon's scrolls for all he understood.

Finally he gave up and stared down the table to where Maura sat laughing and talking with the person seated to her right ... Delyon. So the fellow could make conversation when he didn't have his gaze fixed on some ancient scroll. Now he had his gaze fixed on Maura instead, which made Rath's pulse pound in his ears.

It was pounding so loud he did not notice Madame Verise rise from her seat until Idrygon gave his foot a nudge under the table.

The Councilwoman looked up and down the table, her gaze settling at last on their host. "I believe I speak for all your guests this evening, Lord Idrygon, when I say how overjoyed we are to welcome the king and queen for whom we have waited so long. I promise you our full support in the council for a campaign to liberate the mainland."

Idrygon rose and picked up his wine goblet. But before he could propose a toast to their alliance, Madame Verise continued, "We have only two conditions to make."

"May I ask what those might be?" Idrygon's fingers tightened around the stem of his goblet until Rath feared it would snap.

"Can you not guess?" A dry half-smile arched one corner of the old lady's tiny mouth. "A proper royal wedding for our king and queen, of course, and a grand coronation."

"Agreed!" cried Idrygon without bothering to consult Rath or Maura. "Now, a toast to our newfound monarchs. May their reign be long and victorious!"

As the company drank to them, Rath tried to look properly pleased and dignified. He liked the idea of having his union with Maura blessed, but he wasn't so sure about a *proper royal wedding*. The thought of a *grand coronation* made him itch all over.

A few days later Maura's palms grew suddenly clammy and her belly churned as the island of Galene filled more and more of the horizon, beckoning her to glimpse a missing part of her life.

She turned to Captain Gull. "How much longer until we get there? It was kind of you to bring me."

"Not long now." Gull stroked his cat's head. "And no thanks needed. This beats being moored off Margyle and told to sit tight, though not told what's going on. I don't suppose you could give me a hint what *is* going on — just between us?"

"I wish I could tell you everything I know." Maura gave

a rueful shake of her head. "But Lord Idrygon said I mustn't and ..."

"And," Gull finished her thought, "Lord Idrygon is not a man you want to get on the wrong side of. Ah well, I reckon I can content myself with being left in the dark awhile longer. Just answer me this, if you can — the council isn't going to hold it against me for luring the Ore Fleet into their waters, are they?"

"Of course not!" Maura wondered why a man who seemed to fear nothing else cared what the Council decided or what Idrygon decreed. "Rath explained to them about the storm and how you only brought us here because of a summons from them. They still aren't happy about it, mind you. Delyon told me having so many ships sunk there will make that part of the warding waters useless for a long time, and if the Han ever find out ..."

Was that another factor in deciding the Council to support an invasion? she wondered. Even Trochard and his supporters? With the security of the warding waters breached, they could no longer afford to tolerate a menacing Hanish presence so nearby.

"I see where that could be trouble sure enough." Gull made a face that soon twisted into a grin. "It was a fine sight, though, all those big ore-tubs being tossed about like the leaf-boats I used to sail in puddles when I was a lad."

"At least until the *Phantom* started getting tossed along with them!" Maura shuddered, remembering. It had only been a fortnight ago, yet it felt much longer.

She had quickly grown accustomed to island life. To eating hot meals at a proper table instead of snatching a quick bite from a pack. Sleeping on a real bed rather than taking turns with Rath keeping watch through the night. Clean clothes. Water to bathe. And the most precious luxury of all — freedom from lurking fear.

If only this were the end of their journey instead of a pleasant way station on a long, twisting, uphill road.

A short while later, the *Phantom* made harbor at a small port. Gull offered to accompany Maura in search of her relatives, but she declined with thanks. She wasn't quite sure what her mother's kin might make of the flamboyant smuggler. She wished Rath had been able to come with her, but he was busy with Idrygon studying old maps and discussing strategy for the coming invasion.

A few children gathered near the wharf to see what manner of visitor the ship had brought. They reminded Maura of the younglings back in Windleford. But these carefree boys and girls never had to worry about picking up a pain spike or running into a Hanish hound that had slipped its chain.

"Good day, mistress," said the oldest boy, nudged forward by his friends. "Are you looking for someone? We can show you the way."

"Why, thank you, young sir," said Maura. "I have come looking for the Woodbury family."

The children laughed until the boy shushed them. "Any special one, mistress? There's Woodburys aplenty on Galene." He motioned forward a small girl, her ruddy hair plaited in four long braids that looked to be the fashion here. "Jophie is a Woodbury. Quilla's ma was born a Woodbury and so was Gath's. Both my granddames were."

"Really?" Maura looked around at them, a smile stretching her lips wide, while a tear tingled in the corner of her eye. This was the first time she had met anyone with her kin-name. "No wonder you are all so handsome, then! My mother was Dareth Woodbury and I was told she came from Galene. Perhaps you could direct me to one of the elders of the family who might remember her."

The boy thought for a moment. "My house is near and my granddames are smart as anything. They tell me lots of stories about the old days. Likely they'd know about your mother if anybody would."

"Very well, then." Maura took two small girls by the hand. "Lead me to them, if you would be so kind."

The children conducted Maura down a narrow lane that wound through the village to a house that looked like Idrygon's, only less grand. Thick vines climbed over the stippled white walls, and a fragrance of wholesome sweetness from the tiny blue vine flowers perfumed the air.

"Granna Lib! Granna Jule!" The boy's voice rang through the center courtyard of the house. "Visitor to see you!"

"Visitor?" A tall, slender woman strode into the courtyard carrying a basket of flax tow in one hand and a distaff spindle in the other. "Who would be visiting at this hour?"

Another woman, grayer and a bit more stooped, followed the first. "What did the boy say, Lib?"

The woman with the spinning gear turned and shouted. "Visitor, Jule!"

"Oh. Who'd be calling at this hour?"

The two women peered at Maura.

She bowed. "Your pardon if I have called at a bad time. I have come from Margyle in hope of finding some of my kin. My name is Maura and my mother was Dareth Woodbury."

Lib's basket dropped to the tile floor of the courtyard with a soft thud, followed by the clatter of the falling spindle. She seemed not to notice as she stared at Maura. Her hand trembled as she raised it to her lips.

"What did the lass say?" demanded Jule.

"The girl claims —" Lib's voice cracked with emotion "— she's Dareth's daughter."

"Dareth?" Jule picked up the fallen spindle and basket. "Oh, that can't be. There must be some mistake."

"Look at her, though. The very image."

Jule stepped closer, her head cocked like a bird's, staring.

"So she is. But how can it be?"

Lib recovered her shattered composure. "Well, don't stand there like a stranger, my dear." She took Maura's arm. "Come in! I am your mother's aunt and Jule here is a cousin of ours."

"Run off and play," she called to the children. "All but you, Bran." She beckoned her grandson. "You were a good smart lad to bring the lady here. Now I want you to go around and fetch Auntie Zelle and Uncle Mayer ..." She rattled off a list of names so long it made Maura's head spin.

"Are those *all* my kin?" she asked when the boy had run off on his errand. After years of having no one but Langbard, and him no blood relation, the thought of such a large family overwhelmed her ... but in the most pleasant way.

"Oh my, no, dear." Lib chuckled. "That's not half of them! Only the ones nearest related that live handiest."

"Dareth's child?" Jule shook her head as Lib drew Maura toward some chairs clustered in a shaded corner of the courtyard. "Whoever would have thought it? What became of poor Dareth? The last we heard, she and Vaylen had been captured by the Han. Then never a word until now."

Maura took a seat between her kinswomen and told them everything she knew of her mother, which was pitifully little. She concluded with a question that left her breathless and a little dizzy. "Who was this Vaylen you spoke of? And how did my mother come to be on the mainland for the Han to capture?"

The two women looked at each other, as if silently arguing who should be the one to break the news.

Finally Lib spoke. "Vaylen was the son of the last Margrave of Tarsh. He led a rebellion against the Han. Oh, it must be all of twenty years ago. For a time Tarsh was free."

Tarsh, free? That came as surprising news to Maura.

"My brother, Brandel —" Lib's voice caught for a moment "— your grandfather, was fierce in his support of Vaylen. He said if Tarsh could hold on to the freedom it had won, then

Norest might rise up next, then Southmark or the Hitherland. He was forever urging the Council to send more aid to Tarsh, but many of the sages felt it would put the Islands in danger if the Han found out we were abetting the rebels."

No wonder Idrygon had spoken well of her grandfather, Maura thought. Brandel Woodbury sounded like a man very much after his heart. But how did her mother fit into all this?

Lib wasted no time coming to that. "After a great deal of secret communication with Tarsh, Brandel agreed to send one of his daughters to marry Vaylen. He thought if there was a Vestan-born descendant of Abrielle on the throne of Tarsh the Council might find a little more courage and generosity in its dealings with the rebels."

"So this Vaylen was my father? And you say both he and my mother were captured by the Han?"

The two old women gave weary nods, as though this grief were a weight they had carried on their hearts for many years.

"Libeth should have been the one to go." Maura's great-aunt sighed. "But she was a delicate creature, so Dareth offered to take her place. She had met Vaylen years before, when he'd come to the Islands as a guest of her father, and she thought well of him."

"I warned Brandel," Jule grumbled. "Told him he had no business sending his daughter off to marry a man she hardly knew. And into such danger."

"Hmmph!" Lib clearly did not hold with criticism of her brother. "What a waste you weren't apprenticed to the Oracle of Margyle! You know very well Dareth had her heart set on going."

"She'd have done *anything* to please her father," Jule muttered, just loud enough for Maura to hear.

For the first time Maura sensed a true connection with the mother she had never known. She'd felt the same way about Langbard. In fact, all that had kept her moving forward during those first difficult days of her quest had been the determination not to let him down.

"None of the Council knew," Lib continued, "but the ship that carried Dareth to Tarsh was loaded with weapons and supplies to aid the rebels …"

Her voice trailed off and her eyes took on a distant look, as if she were watching that ship from long ago sail away.

After a few moments, Maura's curiosity got the better of her. "Then what happened?"

"Oh!" Lib roused with a start from her pensive daze. "By and by the ship came back. So we knew Dareth had reached the mainland safely. After that we heard no more for the longest while. Then word came that Tarsh had been overrun by the Han. The Margrave had been killed and the Han had captured Vaylen and Dareth."

Even in the shade, the courtyard was warm. Yet a chill rippled through Maura.

"Brandel wouldn't believe they were dead." Jule shook her head. "He used to get that provoked when anybody spoke of them as if they were. And whenever a ship sailed into the harbor, he'd be the first one down to the wharf in case Dareth might be aboard."

"The old fool." Lib wiped her eyes with the back of her hand. "I wish he'd lived to see Dareth's daughter set foot on Galene."

Maura wished so too. There were many questions she would have liked to ask him.

A muted clamor of voices and footsteps approached.

Lib heaved a sigh and rose from her chair. "That'll be some of the rest of the family come to see you for themselves, my dear. I hope you don't mind my sending for them?"

Maura shook her head. "I have waited such a long time to meet all of you."

More and more Woodbury relatives poured into the little

house, until the courtyard could scarcely hold them. Maura's head began to spin from all the names and faces and convoluted connections.

"...this is Wildon Broadroot. His mother was a first cousin of your grandmother's. And here's Cousin Kedrith. She's one of the Westbay branch of the family ..."

Yet in each eager, smiling face, Maura caught a glimpse of something strangely familiar — a bit of her mother, or of herself, perhaps. As the hours passed, she listened to endless introductions, received bashful bows and vigorous embraces, and heard stories of Dareth Woodbury's younger years that brought her mother alive to her for the first time.

She remembered the night she and Rath had stopped in the foothills of the mountains and soaked their aching flesh in a warm spring pool. This gathering of her family was like a warm spring for her spirit — reviving and renewing her in places she had never realized were empty or weary.

Yet part of her remained detached from it all, mulling over the brave, tragic account of her parents. No wonder her mother had died of a broken heart that even Langbard could not heal, with all his skill and devotion. And what had become of her father? Had he been tortured to death by the Xenoth? Or sent to the mines where his spirit had perished before his body?

Though part of Maura wished she could stay on peaceful Galene forever, basking in the quiet joy of kinship, another part itched to get back to the mainland. Liberating Embria had become something more than her destiny. It was now a hallowed duty she owed her parents — to finish the task they had begun.

A task that had cost them everything.

Chapter Nineteen

"WHEN YOU FOUND your family, you didn't do it by half measures, did you, *aira*?" Rath wrapped his arms around Maura from behind, resting his chin on the crown of her head. "If we must have a big, fancy wedding and crowning ceremony, I reckon this is a good place for it."

They stood in the large courtyard of the house that had belonged to Maura's grandfather. The house in which her mother had been born. A festive celebration swirled around them as twilight dappled the vast western horizon. Merry music from string and wind instruments floated on the evening air along with the mouthwatering fragrances of fresh bread, roasted meat and fruit stewed in honey.

Maura's past two weeks on the island of Galene had been like a dream come true — going wherever she liked, whenever she wished without the smallest fear. A perfect blend of safety and freedom. She'd been rapturously welcomed by her kin, a precious boon indeed after growing up with no family and few friends. Only one thing had been missing to complete her happiness.

Then Rath had arrived from Margyle aboard the *Phantom*, along with the Oracle and the whole Council of Sages to take part in their wedding and crowning ceremonies.

Now Idrygon stood in one corner of the courtyard involved in a grave discussion with some of Maura's uncles and cousins. Madame Verise danced by in the arms of Captain Gull, looking as if she was enjoying herself immensely. Beyond the courtyard, the Oracle of Margyle was playing a hiding game with young Bran and some other Galeni children. Delyon perched on the edge of the fountain, poring over an old scroll from Brandel Woodbury's private library. Gull's hillcat sat on Delyon's lap, content to suffer the occasional absentminded scratch behind the ears.

Maura's happiness should have been complete. But the brooding distraction she had sensed in Rath before she'd left Margyle had not lifted, hard as he tried to hide it. Maura wished he would confide in her whatever was troubling him. Was she a fool if she could not figure it out for herself? Or did she guess the truth but not want to face it?

"Shall we steal away for a walk on the beach?" She reached down to twine her fingers through one of the hands Rath had clasped around her waist "We've hardly had a moment alone since you got here, and the shore is so beautiful."

For an instant, Rath seemed not to hear her. Then her words must have sunk in, for he squeezed her hand and he spoke with forced brightness. "That sounds like a fine idea. Let's go."

It took them a little while to wend their way through the crowd. Some of Maura's cousins who had not met Rath stopped them for introductions. They waved to the children who were running to hide from their new playmate.

"You had better find good cover," Rath teased them "if you hope to stay hidden from an oracle who can see the future."

"Why did you have to remind them she's the Oracle?" Maura chided him. "She is still only a child, after all — one who doesn't often get to enjoy games with others her age."

"You're right." Rath scowled and kicked the turf as they walked. "It just doesn't seem right — a child that age with a head full of memories she can't understand and a gift of foresight she can't make sense of."

"People might say the same of you and me. A king who has never commanded an army. A queen who has never set foot in a palace. We cannot help those limitations and we're trying our best in spite of them."

"So we are," muttered Rath as they picked their way down a steep slope to the shore. "I only hope our best will be good enough."

"It has been so far." Maura told him what she and the young Oracle had concluded, about how the Giver might work all the better through flawed instruments like them.

Rath mulled over her words as they pried off their shoes. "It would be comforting to believe that."

"Do you find it so hard to believe?" Maura tugged him toward the edge of the shore, where fine, wet sand welcomed their feet with its cool caress and white-foamed waves rolled in one upon the other in a ceaseless, soothing rhythm. "Here, of all places?"

Rath stared into the distant, broad horizon blushed with twilight into the vivid hues of the island flowers. Even its serenity and splendor could not ease the subtle tightness around his eyes.

"My mother stood here once," said Maura, "and looked out at a sunset like this one. It is the most vivid memory Langbard passed to me from her. When I first saw this place with my own eyes, it took my breath away. Not just because of its beauty, but because of the closeness I felt to her."

They ambled along the beach, the cool surf breaking over their feet, and the tangy ocean breeze whispering through their hair. Overhead, seafowl wheeled and glided, their haunting cries echoing through the gathering dusk. Her hand holding tight to his, Maura told Rath as much of her mother's story as she had learned from her kinfolk.

"Your mother was a brave lass," said Rath when she had finished. "Like her daughter. Your father sounds a noble fellow, too. It is a shame you never knew them, and that they gave their lives for nothing."

"But don't you see?" Maura turned toward him. "It wasn't

for nothing. If my mother had never gone to Tarsh and begotten me, then somehow escaped from the Han and found her way to Windleford, all those prophesies of the Destined Queen would never have come true. The ones about my being descended from Abrielle and raised by Langbard. If we succeed in liberating Embria, my parents will not have died in vain."

Her words did not dispel the cloud that hung over Rath.

"What is troubling you, *aira*?" She reached up to brush the backs of her fingers against his cheek. "And do not insult my wit by pretending nothing is."

"Taken lessons from your little friend, the Oracle, have you?" Though his voice sounded gruff, Rath leaned into her caress, nuzzling her hand with his cheek, which was shaved closer than she had ever felt it before. It seemed almost to belong to another man.

"You are not so hard to read," she teased him. "Like one of Delyon's ancient scrolls. You are more like a tavern sign, with the words writ large and plain, and a picture carved above them for good measure. Out with it, now. Perhaps it is not as bad as you think."

"All right, then." He inhaled a deep breath of the briny ocean air. "There is something I must know from you, and it *must* be the truth, mind."

"Rath Talward!" She jerked her hand back as if he had stung it. "Do you think I would lie to you?"

"To spare my feelings? Aye, you would. Or if you felt you had other good reason. Remember how you strung me along on our journey to Prum, with tales of an old aunt and an arranged match you had to make?"

"That was different!" Maura protested. "I hardly knew you back then. And it would have been dangerous to go about telling everyone I met that I was the Destined Queen. Now that we are to wed, you will have the truth from me, I promise."

A chill wave of worry broke over her, quenching her flash

of anger. What question could he mean to ask that he feared she might not answer truthfully?

"We are soon to be wed," Rath repeated. "And I need to know, are you wedding me because I am your heart's choice? Or is it like your mother, who went to her marriage for the sake of duty and destiny? You promised me the truth, remember."

Relief swamped Maura with such force she might have crumpled onto the sand if Rath had not caught her by the arms.

Instead, she collapsed against him, giving his broad chest a token swat. "You fretted yourself and me over *that*? Of course you are the choice of my heart! It almost tore me in two when I thought the Waiting King would come between us."

"But you chose him before you knew we were one and the same. I remember our journey to the Secret Glade and how you were prepared to sacrifice your happiness for the sake of your people. I cannot accept such a sacrifice from you, *aira*."

Maura raised her face to meet the challenge of his gaze. "*We* made that decision together, remember? I cannot swear how I might have chosen if you had set yourself to change my mind."

"Truly?"

Did he *want* to doubt her? Or was it just that doubt and distrust were still stronger in him than belief and hope.

"How can I convince you? Being your destined partner is the one part of my fate I can embrace with a joyful heart and no reservations. Have you forgotten our joining of spirits when you thought I was dead and performed the passing ritual? When you saw yourself through my eyes and tasted the flavor of my love for you?"

"Perhaps I had forgotten, a little." He canted his head and leaned toward her. "Looking back now, it all seems like a dream — too good to be true."

"Perhaps this will remind you." Maura slid her hand up his chest and around his neck, pulling him toward her.

Her lips met his, parting in welcome. He kissed her with

all the hoarded yearning of their journey, when it had seemed impossible that they would ever be together like this.

Even as she responded to his anxious ardor Maura could not help wondering if there was something more troubling him. Something he could not bring himself to share with her. Perhaps something he had not fully acknowledged to himself.

She pulled back from him just far enough to murmur, "What about you?"

"Me?" He lifted her off her feet and spun around until she squealed with laughter. "Can you suppose for a moment that I am not eager to wed you?"

"Not that," she said when he had finally set her back on her feet. "I practically dragged you out of Everwood. But I do not want you to accept the crown and all that goes with it only for my sake."

"Not such a bad reason, is it?"

Perhaps he had made himself dizzy spinning around. Now he clung to her for support, as she knew he would in the years to come. He was a strong, forceful man, but there were other kinds of strength and Maura sensed there might be times ahead when he would need to call upon hers.

"Not a bad reason, just not good enough. I want you to do this because it is the right thing to do. And because it is *your* destiny."

"Do not fret yourself." He leaned down and pressed a kiss to her brow, like a benediction. "I wasn't thinking right that morn in Everwood. The whole notion of being the Waiting King had thrown me off balance like that spinning did just now. And I had a good many wrong ideas I've since learned the truth of."

Maura listened for a false or forced note in his voice, but heard none.

Rath took her face in his hands and gazed deep into her eyes by the dying light of day. "Now that I have seen what life is like here on the Islands — what it *could* be like on the mainland — I cannot rest until I have done everything in my power to make it so."

"Spoken like a true king," Maura whispered.

"I still doubt we can oust the Han from Embria all by ourselves. Though, who knows … if the Giver wills it? But we will not be alone. Idrygon has been preparing for this day for years. Waiting and hoping that I would come to lead the force he has assembled."

His words stirred and reassured Maura. "You're convinced we can prevail now, aren't you?"

"I am." Rath looked so regal in his confidence she wished she had the crown in her hands to nestle on his windblown hair.

Then the banished shadow returned to darken his gaze. He gathered Maura close again, as if she were a frightened child in need of his comfort. Or perhaps the other way around.

"I am convinced we can prevail," he repeated in a harsh whisper. "But at what cost?"

At what cost? Those words haunted Rath's dreams on the night before his wedding and crowning ceremonies.

What Maura had told him about her parents did nothing to ease his dread. Quite the opposite. He might have reconciled himself to a heroic death like the kind her father had suffered. But to endure the loss of his beloved, as her mother had — the thought of it sapped his courage.

He rolled over in the narrow bed he'd been provided by one of Maura's relatives, cursing the custom that they must sleep apart during the days leading up to their wedding. He had not minded it so much while she'd been off to Galene visiting her kin. Now that they were on the same island again, he could scarcely bear to be parted from her.

If she'd been sharing his bed now, he could have held her close, soothed by the warmth of her body, the whisper of her breathing and the murmur of her heartbeat. He could have convinced himself to savor whatever time they had and trust to the Giver's providence that it would not be cut short.

No matter what the young Oracle prophesied.

Thinking back over his talk with Maura on the beach, he burned with shame for questioning *her* honesty when he had been hiding something from her. But he could not blight her happiness by telling her the truth. From now on, he must keep his worries better hidden from her — not writ large with pictures like a tavern sign!

"Highness!" Someone shook Rath's shoulder.

He came awake with a violent start, to find his hand around Delyon's neck.

"Your pardon!" He let go at once. "Don't ever wake me sudden like that."

"No harm done." Delyon's voice sounded hoarse as he rubbed his throat. "My brother sent me to fetch you. It will soon be dawn — time for the ceremony."

As Delyon set down the candle he was carrying on a small table beside the bed, Rath thanked the Giver that the young scholar hadn't dropped it on the bedclothes during their brief struggle.

"Your robes are all laid out over there." Delyon pointed to a low chest in the far corner. "You'd better hurry."

Rath scrambled out of bed. "I'll be right along."

As he headed for the door, Delyon paused and turned. "Highness?"

"Yes?" After two weeks in Idrygon's household, Rath was slowly getting used to answering to that title.

"I wish you every joy in your union, sire." Delyon bowed. "It will be an honor to witness the joining and crowning of the Waiting King and the Destined Queen."

"Um ... thank you." Rath knew he sounded gruff and awkward, but he couldn't help himself.

The young scholar was a decent enough fellow, but the two of them were as unalike as men could be. And given a choice between them, Rath had no illusions about who was the better man.

After Delyon left, Rath quickly slipped into his wedding robes, relieved to find they were a good deal looser than the tunics he worn on Margyle. Delyon had told him their brown color symbolized the fertile earth. When he emerged from his chamber into the courtyard, it was packed with men, talking quietly by candlelight.

Idrygon stepped forward with a woven circlet of leaves and placed it on Rath's head. "We had better get going to reach the wedding grove by dawn. I hope you slept well, Highness. This is going to be a grand day."

Rath nodded, stifling a yawn. This would be a grand day and he must do nothing to spoil it for Maura or these good folks. He tried to approach it as he might a coming battle — concentrating on the tasks at hand, while firmly locking away any distracting worries.

With his usual efficiency, Idrygon mustered all the men into a procession that headed off toward the wedding grove. As they walked, they sang a ritual chant in *twaran*, of which Rath could make out a few words. It did not matter, though, for he'd been told the bridegroom took no part in the singing. He brought up the rear of the procession, following the bobbing lights of many candles, through the predawn darkness.

Soon they reached the wedding grove, a cultivated ring of trees, shrubbery and flowers with four openings — one each for north, south, east and west. The bridegroom's procession entered through the eastern one into a large grassy circle that sloped to a low mound at the center. The men walked around the rim of the circle, moving westward, while Idrygon led Rath to the middle of the grass, where they waited.

The moment he stopped, Rath could hear a high, clear chorus of women's voices coming from the west. Soon the first women began to file into the grove through the western entrance, their chant weaving a haunting harmony with the men's voices. They walked around the circle in the opposite direction the men had, while Madame Verise and one of Maura's aunts led her toward Rath.

Maura wore a gown the color of spring leaves. Her ruddy curls hung loose over her shoulders and down her back, crowned with a wreath of flowers. By the flickering light of a hundred candles, and the first rays of dawn, she was a vision of near-unbearable beauty.

Suddenly the chanting stopped, and all the candles were blown out.

"Let us meditate with one pure will," said Madame Verise in a quiet but resonant voice. "And ask that the gracious spirit of the Giver may hover over this holy place and bless the union of this man and woman."

In the expectant silence that followed, Rath heard the distant pounding of the surf, the whisper of the breeze through the leaves and the first clear, sweet notes of birdsong to herald the rising sun. As he had on the swift, treacherous ride down that river from the mines, Rath felt a presence enfolding and uplifting him.

When at last Madame Verise began to pronounce the ritual of union, he was able to meet Maura's gaze with a warm, untroubled smile.

"Elzaban and Maura. As you embark upon a lifetime voyage across the uncharted ocean of the future, we gather today to witness your compact of union and to invoke the Giver's blessing upon you."

She nodded to Rath, who held his right hand out to Maura, palm up, and spoke the words he had worked hard to memorize. "Maura, I offer myself to you — all that I have and all that I am. I promise to protect you, defend you, support and cherish you as long as I live."

"Elzaban …" Maura stumbled a bit over the unfamiliar name and her voice sounded thick with unshed tears. "I accept you as my lifemate, with a joyous and thankful heart."

Her right hand was cold as she laid it palm down upon his.

Madame Verise led the guests in a chant, asking the Giver to bless Rath with the strength, wisdom, tenderness and patience to fulfil his vows.

Then Maura extended her left hand to Rath. "Elzaban, I offer myself to you — all that I have and all that I am. I promise to sustain you, heal you, support and cherish you as long as I live."

She had scarcely finished speaking when Rath laid his left hand upon hers. "Maura, I accept you as my lifemate, with a joyous and thankful heart."

This time the company chanted a blessing upon Maura, while Rath stared deep into her eyes and silently begged the Giver to endow his bride with an extra measure of patience. She would need it.

When the chant ended, Madame Verise nodded to Rath and Maura, who raised both pairs of clasped hands toward the sky — a symbol of growth.

"All here witness," proclaimed Madame Verise, "that Elzaban and Maura have freely pledged themselves to one another for life. May their union grow and flourish. And may it bear an abundance of sound, sweet fruit in the years to come."

Rath flinched at the mention of the fruits of their union, but quickly shoved that renegade worry into a deep, dark corner of his mind. By the time he and Maura had lowered their clasped hands and she could see his face clearly, Rath flattered himself that she glimpsed nothing but what he wanted her to see — his joy, his pride and his love.

With hands still clasped between them, he leaned forward and sealed their vows with a kiss.

The rings of men and women ranged around the edge of the grove broke as the guests surged toward Rath and Maura to offer their blessings. Those already wed hung back to let the younger folk reach the center of the circle first.

Untangling their hands, Maura lifted the circlet of flowers from her hair while Rath removed the garland of leaves from his. Then they threw the wedding wreaths into the air, where they broke apart, showering down on the approaching guests.

Young men lunged after the falling leaves, while the maidens each tried to catch a flower that meant they would one day find true love.

Rath laughed with a full heart as he watched the merry scramble. Just then, he wished everyone in the kingdom could know the surpassing happiness he had found with his destined bride.

Maura had only ever witnessed one other wedding — her friend Sorsha's. And it had been very different from this splendid ceremony. She and Langbard had gone with Sorsha and Newlyn to a tiny glade in Betchwood where the two had made their vows. All the while, they'd listened for any sound of a Hanish patrol or an outlaw band. Rather than tossing her bridal wreath in the air, Sorsha had carefully lifted it off her head and placed it on her friend's, saying she hoped the Giver would bless Maura with a fine husband someday. At the time, Maura had judged the chances of that very slight.

Her eyes misted with tears.

"What is it, love?" Rath stopped laughing at the antics of the young folks scrambling for groom's leaves and bridal blossoms. "Nothing wrong, is there?"

She shook her head. "I've never been happier. I only wish Sorsha could have been here today."

For all she was delighted to have been welcomed into the bosom of a large, loving family and to have her Woodbury kin witness her ritual of union, Sorsha was her oldest and dearest friend. A friend who was still in danger of having her family torn apart, if the Han should discover the secret of Newlyn's past. A friend who had to observe the rituals of the Elderways in secret.

"Maybe it's just as well she couldn't be here." Rath's voice lilted with teasing humor. "I'm not sure Sorsha would have approved you wedding a dangerous character like me. She wasn't too happy about you going off with me in the first place."

His jest lifted Maura's spirits as they received congratulations from all the company. "Sorsha would change her colors soon enough, I'm certain, once she got to know you. You and her Newlyn are a good deal alike."

Hand in hand, they led a merry procession that wound in and out through all the entrances to the grove. Finally they departed through the northern one, to signify that their union would endure through adversity. Remembering the hardships it had already withstood to reach this moment, Maura felt confident she and Rath could weather whatever storms the future might bring.

From the wedding grove, they walked back to her grandfather's villa. A bountiful feast awaited them there, with food spread on long tables from which everyone could help themselves. Before anyone else could eat, Maura and Rath peeled two hard-boiled eggs decorated with *twaran* letters and fed them to each other.

"Well, this is fitting!" Maura chuckled. "Do you remember the morning after we left Windleford, how you peeled those eggs Sorsha gave us?"

"I do." Rath's dark eyes twinkled with glee. "Though if I'd

known then what it meant, I might have thought twice."

Afterward, they helped each other to more of the food — strands of bread twisted into fanciful shapes, wedges of flavorful cheese and pieces of island fruit threaded on wooden skewers in colorful patterns. *Sythwine* and *lipma* cordial flowed freely along with other delicious drinks Maura had never tasted before.

After Rath and Maura had eaten their fill, Idrygon and Madame Verise summoned them away to change into their coronation robes for the ceremony that would take place at noon.

Madame Verise smiled through tears as she helped Maura into a gown the color of midsummer sunshine. "Bless the Giver that I should live to see the Destined Queen crowned. I only wish Nalene and Langbard could be here. They devoted their lives to making this happen. Though you are not their daughter by birth, your coronation still honors them and fulfills their hope."

Maura clasped the old woman in a gentle embrace, and in their shared tears, the spirits of Langbard and his wife seemed very near, bestowing their special blessing upon her.

"Enough now." Madame Verise at last thrust a handkerchief at Maura. "Dry your eyes, child. We cannot have the Destined Queen blubbering through her coronation."

The crowning ceremony took place in the same hallowed glade as their ritual of union, which was fitting, Maura thought. In a way, she and Rath were being united with their people into one very large family. Rath looked so regal in robes that seemed to have been woven from threads of the deep blue Vestan sky. Maura even found herself thinking of him as *Elzaban*.

Delyon read from a scroll that prophesied the coming of the Waiting King. The uncanny parallels between what had been foretold so long ago and the adventures she and Rath had shared to reach this moment gave Maura chills of wonder.

There were several chants by the assembled witnesses, calling down the Giver's blessing on the new king and queen. Rath spoke his vows, similar to the ones he had made Maura, to protect and defend his kingdom. Then it was her turn to promise she would sustain and nurture her people.

She and Rath knelt before the young Oracle of Margyle, who looked a little uncertain. Maura flashed the child a reassuring smile, to remind her that they were no better prepared for this than she. Yet the Giver was with them, and all would be well.

The child stood a little taller as she looked out at the assembled crowd. "I am perhaps the only one here with memories of other Embrian kings and queens crowned." Her high young voice rang with the accumulated wisdom of all her predecessors. "But never has an oracle placed the crowns of our realm on the heads of two worthier sovereigns."

She turned to Madame Verise and took from her a crown of ivory, carved to resemble the flower wreath Maura had worn in her hair that morning. Placing it on Maura's head, she said, "Wear this crown, Destined Queen, in token of the Giver's wisdom, courage and compassion. May your reign be long, peaceful and prosperous."

Then she took a larger crown from Idrygon, also of ivory and carved as a ring of leaves. So skillful had been the artistry of the carver that Maura almost fancied it had been fashioned from real leaves, bleached to the color of fresh cream.

"Wear this crown, Elzaban, Waiting King, in token of the Giver's wisdom, courage and compassion. May your reign be long, peaceful and prosperous."

Signaling the newly crowned monarchs to rise, the Oracle turned to those gathered and cried, "Embria waits no more!"

End of Book Two

Glossary

barleymush – a thick barley porridge eaten in the Northern provinces

Comtung – the lingua franca between Embrian and Hanish.

fenfolk – a legendary non-human race said to live deep in the marshlands.

greenfire – an enchantment that allows branches to give off a soft green light without burning.

Han – a race of humans from the south who have conquered Embria.

isendark – a very hard black metal

lalump – an Old Embrian endearment for a rogue of whom one is still fond.

lifebane – an effect of metal weapons that taints wounds from them unless washed away with water or bleeding.

lowling – term of contempt used by the Han for most Embrians.

mortcraft – also called death magic. The potent destructive power from beneath the earth that attaches to metal and gems.

pain spikes – look like ordinary nails, but tainted with mortcraft so that anyone touching them recieves an intense
burning sting.

slag – dust from the mines. Dulls the senses and makes the
user docile. Highly addictive.

Solsticetide – the first month of summer.

strup – a rare green metal.

twara – the Old Embrian language, now only used for cere-
monial purposes.

vitcraft – also called life magic. The gentle, fickle creative power
of living things, chiefly channelled through herbs,
wooden wands and the essence of animals.

Xenoth – also called deathmages. Powerful sorcerers of mortcraft. Serve as a secret police of the Hanish Empire.

zikary – Embrian collaborators with the Han

"The Magical and Healing Properties of Some Common Umbrian Plants"

from

A Shorter Vitacraft Compendium by Gelys Torkin

Candleflax – staunches bleeding of open wounds

Cheeseweed – soothes aching muscles

Dreamweed – induces sleep, slowly if imbibed in a tea, rapidly if inhaled

Fleawort – kills body vermin

Freshwort – helps resist the effects of slag

Honeygrass – makes hair shine

Hundredflower – helps a person blend in to their surroundings and escape notice

Icemint – mild stimulant

Laceweed – staunches internal bleeding

Madfern – causes temporary delusions

Marshwort – soothes pain of burns or wounds when applied as a poultice

Merthorn – speeds healing of burned flesh

Moonmallow – eases swelling

Muddlewort – blurs recent memories

Summerslip – causes mild numbing of senses and drowsiness

Queensbalm – combats mortcraft/short-term stimulant

Quickfoil – potent stimulant/restorative

Winterwort – heals bruises

Made in the USA
Monee, IL
02 September 2020